# A SECRET SKY
## CAN LOVE ALWAYS FIND A WAY?

### Jane M Cullen

SPELLBOUND BOOKS

## The Chanting Heart
## Don't Go Without Me

Dancing in ecstasy you go,
My soul of souls,
Don't go without me,
Laughing with your friends,
You enter the garden.
Don't go without me.

Don't let the sky turn without me,
Don't let the moon shine without me,
Don't let the Earth spin without me,
Don't let the days pass without me.

The two worlds are joyous because of you.
Don't stay in this world without me.
Don't go to the next world without me.

Some call you love,
I call you the King of Love.
You are beyond all imaginings,
Taking me places I can't even dream of.
O Ruler of my Heart, wherever you go,
Don't go without me.

Rumi

# Chapter One

*There is a path from me to you that I am constantly looking for.*
*Rumi*

Hold on! Hold on! I'm coming for you, Bear. I'll always come for you. I'll save you, Bear, I'll save you from yourself. Just hold on!

Don't you go without me!

Remember when we walked home from school, me balancing on every wall and swinging around lamp posts and you gazing at clouds and teaching me about Rumi? I climbed trees, scraped my knees and fell off my bike. You stood under those trees, dreaming of angels and the magical landscapes of Ireland, waiting to catch me if I fell. I won't climb anymore if you aren't there to catch me.

The black beast was at your door and there are cracks in my heart but I'm running hard and fast to you, hoping we can walk together towards the light.

Don't you go without me!

This world would not be my home without you. You said the stars were all asleep, the sky was falling in on you and the white horses were galloping away across the sand. We can jump on their backs and hold their shining manes. We'll catch the snowflakes, Bear. We will soar like kites towards a secret sky, you and I.

Remember what we promised? Let's fly towards a secret sky.

Bear, I'm going to sit beside you until you wake up. I won't let you go without me. I'll talk to you constantly until your eyes open. I can't stay here without you. You know that, so wake up, bloody well wake up. I'm lost in darkness. Wherever you are right now, they don't need you, but I do. Your mouth is tinged with blue. Your voice, like running molasses, is only in my head now. I'm being haunted by the thought that I might have lost you. I'm on my knees because you might never be you again.

Sitting by this hospital bed now, I can feel keenly the outer edges of my own existence moving further away with every breath you take because I can't see you there with your arms open wide. The lines of my life are becoming blurred as I stare at the jagged line of your heartbeat on the screen beside me.

I'm going to speak to you about everything because I know you can hear me and I won't stop until I've said it all. You used to say I was the strong one, strong and fierce and spirited. You said I was your Guardian Angel. That wasn't true. I was careering through life like a runaway stallion and struggling to make sense of all the hormonal mayhem in my brain. You were the steady one, an old soul who had been here before and instinctively knew so much more than I ever would. How did you know so much?

We were complete opposites in every way. I was a noisy, naturally athletic young girl who climbed trees, raced around on my roller skates and walked on her hands to impress you. I couldn't be bothered with studying. I just wanted to run hard and fast like a wild horse. I did cartwheels and handstands until my head was spinning.

September that year we met was exceptionally warm and the

early morning heat had left the dusty streets of south London in a golden, hazy glow. The only reason I remember any of that is because you described it all to me in detail. I learnt to see the unromantic, dense maze of littered streets where we lived through your poetic lens.

I had been sitting with some of the others on the school bench at the back of the playground when you wandered in. We were all clothed in bravado on that first day but you had an enviable relaxed confidence. Striking looking even then with your uniform perfectly pressed and your satchel slung carelessly but stylishly across your body. You stood out immediately. You were slim and tall for your years with shiny dark brown hair that reminded me of conkers. I felt sorry you had to walk in on your own, but years later you told me you weren't alone. You had many unseen friends beside you. I was always intrigued by that comment because I had left my imaginary friends behind in primary school.

When we were asked to stand up and say our names in class, you glanced over as I said my full name, Amy Lee. When it was your turn and you had announced your name was Bear, there was some shuffling of feet and some smothered giggling.

'Boy, that is your nickname, not your *real* name,' the teacher said with a hint of impatience. 'What is your *real* name?'

'My real name *is* Bear, sir, so it is, just as my parents wrote it on the form when I applied here.'

Those few words, said so boldly with a strong Irish accent, but with such softness and dignity too, had in that moment sealed my fate forever. But you hadn't noticed. I couldn't take my eyes off you. Considering where we are now, had destiny touched our heads lightly that day? Was I always meant to save you?

All day you had been so poised, even when between lessons everyone else threw rubbers at each other or flicked pens across the room. You were staring out of the window at the sky, as if in a trance. The other boys were rough and clumsy, but you were gentle and elegant. Where they were inarticulate and struggled to express themselves, you were eloquent and could quote Shakespeare and poetry as if you had written it yourself.

Just before lunch, when the bell sounded and the teacher strode out, I scrambled over a few of the desks and bags and crouched beside you. 'I'm Amy. Can we be friends?'

You looked at me with surprise, your eyes a hazel green and watchful, like the cat next door. 'You want to be my friend, Amy Lee?'

'Yeah, I love your name,' I'd said quietly and I had been astonished at your response.

'Bears look soft and tender hearted, but underneath they can be ferocious and unpredictable. But I'll be your friend if you want me to, so I will.'

'I wish I knew long words like that.'

'I like reading and you find long words in books, so you do.'

'I don't read books, I like being out in the street on my roller skates. Can you teach me long words?'

'Yes, if you like.'

I had perched on the edge of your desk kicking my legs and watched as you carefully wrote your full name, Bear Nathan Flynn on the exercise books we had been given. I thought you would say something else but you didn't. You were quiet and serene in the middle of a room full of noise and childish behaviour. 'Which bus are you getting home, Bear? I live in Church Street, near the end by the school. I went to that school.'

'I live in Church Street too. I think we live opposite you. I saw you with your daddy the other day. You had dungarees on and with your short hair I thought you were a boy. You were holding your daddy's hand and I thought it was grand, so I did.'

'We can go home together then. Why didn't you go to my school?'

'We were in Dublin. We've only just come over for my daddy's job.'

Another girl had then called my name. 'Amy, come and get lunch with me.'

You had gestured in her direction. 'I think she wants you to go with her.'

I hadn't wanted to get lunch with her, I wanted to stay with you, but you had already been pulled up roughly by your shirt by a boy with white-blonde hair and a mischievous face. You didn't seem to mind.

The boy had persisted. 'Come on, Yogi Bear, I'm starving.'

You gave me a faint smile. 'I'll wait for you at home time. I'll wait for you, Amy Lee.'

That afternoon we were taught maths by a teacher who I was pretty sure was a witch in her spare time. She had a hooked nose and black cape. She only needed to take a broomstick out of the cupboard for the picture to have been complete. I didn't understand any of it and felt out of my depth. I repeatedly glanced at you and you were listening intently and occasionally frowning. At one point I saw you look over at me with a reassuring smile. I felt, in that fleeting moment, that you had instinctively sensed my apprehension from the other side of the room. I'll never know how you did that, Bear.

Our school was a three-storey, Victorian building, old fashioned and forbidding and the teachers all looked pretty much the same. They would stride purposefully down the corridors with their intimidating, dark cloaks flying behind them and weird-looking head gear that resembled the head of a crow. I found it all quite strange and I longed to be outside in the fresh air charging about and climbing on whatever I could find. You seemed born for study and soaked it all up, quietly and reverently.

At half three I had looked for you in the corridor by the lockers and you were there, surrounded by other boys all larking about. You were joining in but in a gentler way, allowing the others to mess about with your hair. You did the same to them but without any kind of force. I could tell, by standing back and watching, that they were all as taken with you as I was. You were in the centre of an admiring circle and already I didn't want to share you. Your charisma, even as a child of eleven, was effortless.

I thought you would forget about getting the bus with me but you didn't and when the others had all shuffled off, you looked for me and beckoned. 'Are you ready, Amy Lee?'

We chatted all the way. On the bus you offered your seat to an elderly lady and nudged me to do the same for her husband. The bus stopped two streets away from where we lived and I balanced on walls and swung around the lamp posts without worrying about showing my knickers. You weren't looking at me anyway because you were gazing at the clouds and talking about how we couldn't see the Milky Way at night because of the lights in London.

'The Milky Way is miraculous, so it is and it's where the angels live.'

'I like eating them, they are delicious.'

'You're funny, Amy Lee, so you are.'

Do you remember I jumped off a wall in front of you, my hair flying in my face, and I moaned about school? 'I don't like maths, Bear, or any of it really. I don't understand fractions. I mean, what are they for?'

'I'll teach you, it isn't that hard to understand.'

'Will you? Will you really? I don't understand Shakespeare either. It's not even written in English, is it?'

'Sure it is, but it was written a long time ago.'

'It's boring, Bear.'

'No, Amy, it has beauty and melody running through it, so it has.'

'Mrs Miller said we're going to dissect a vegetable tomorrow. Why do we have to dissect a vegetable? That's not going to help us in life, is it? I bet my dad didn't dissect a vegetable at school.'

You laughed at me. You always seemed amused by what I said even when I thought I was being quite sensible. Often I didn't understand much of what *you* said, but you never made me feel stupid or daft.

'It's called biology and it's about plant structure. There is a reason for it.'

'How do you know all that? And what was that weird thing the biology teacher described?'

'It was an amoeba. It mates with itself.' When I had turned my nose up in distaste, you laughed and asked, 'Don't you think it's fascinating?'

'No, it's weird, I'll never concentrate. I only like P.E. I'm good at that.'

'I love English literature most. I'd like to be a writer one day.'

'Will you write about me?' You had your face towards the sun and didn't answer. 'Bear, will you write about me?'

'It's so hot for September, don't you think? We'll have a heat mist in the morning. I like heat mists, they make me think of webs and ghosts. I love the way they disappear right in front of your eyes. It reminds me of being on my granny's farm in Ireland, so it does. The heat mists there are like silk.'

I was attempting to shin up a lamppost right outside your house. I knew it was your house because there was an Irish flag in the window. Climbing had always been easy for me and I couldn't walk a hundred yards without trying to balance on a narrow wall or swing on the branch of a tree. 'Bear, can you help me with my homework? I'll never do it on my own. I'll do it on the bus in the morning if you don't help me.'

'I'll help you. Now come down from there, you'll be falling, so you will.'

'Do you promise?'

'I promise, Amy Lee.'

'You won't forget?'

'No, I won't forget. Now come down.'

'I won't fall,' I called, but as the words left my lips I did just that. I jumped up again and brushed the grit off my knees. 'It didn't hurt.'

'One day it might. Pride goes before a fall and we can't be having any pride, so my granny tells us all.' You touched my face gently with your finger. 'You have so many freckles. My granny says, if you have freckles you've been kissed by angels. I'll count your freckles one day. I think there are hundreds across your face.'

I laughed at you and felt a surge of embarrassment mixed with pleasure. 'I don't like them. My mum says I'll grow out of them. I'll meet you here tomorrow morning.'

You nodded, but by this time your mind was on picking up some walking boots on your doorstep and then you opened your front door and went inside. My parents quizzed me that evening, asking what I had learnt and who I had made friends with.

'Bear Flynn,' I told them proudly. 'My friend is called Bear Flynn. He's the cleverest boy in the class. He lives opposite.' My father smiled knowingly. 'What are you smiling at, Dad?'

'That's a bit of luck, darling. He can help you with your homework then. Mind you, he'll need the patience of a saint with you.'

'That's true enough.' My mother was peering through the hatch from the kitchen where she spent most of her time cooking, singing, laughing and burning just about everything. 'Does he realise what a scatterbrain you are, Amy? That's an unusual name to have, isn't it? No other friends, darling?'

'No.'

You waited patiently for me the next morning even though I was late. And you were right, there were strands of mist like silver threads hanging in the air. They almost moved in one great mass like calm water. It was caressing the pavement and the trees and you said it was wrapping its ghostly arms around us to keep us safe.

On the bus you told me you had three older brothers called Tommy, Daniel and Patrick and that Patrick was deaf and wore hearing aids so you had learnt sign language with him. The rest of your family hadn't bothered, you said. Kindness seemed to shine out from you in beams of light shooting out of the top of your head and at the end of your finger tips.

After school that second day you waited for me again. You didn't forget. You didn't prefer to walk with some of the boys you had befriended. When we arrived at your house again, I had been jumping over all the cracks in the pavement and pretending to be a gymnast while you had been reciting some lines you had read by an old poet with a weird name. You asked me to tell my mother that I was bringing in a friend for an hour to help me understand maths. You knocked on our door ten minutes later, in jeans and a black T shirt that accentuated the colour of your hazel eyes. You put your hand out and spoke politely to my mother.

'I'm very pleased to meet you, Mrs Lee.'

'Oh call me Lucy, love,' she replied with her usual joie de vivre, but you had shaken your head solemnly.

'No, I can't do that, it would be disrespectful. That's what my mammy says.'

'That's an Irish accent, isn't it?'

'Yes, Mrs Lee, I'm afraid it is. There isn't much I can do about it. I'm from just outside Dublin.'

'It's a lovely accent. Well, as you wish, love. Call me what you like, whatever you're most comfortable with. Amy, stop standing there like a tit in a trance. I've cleared the table for you both. It's very kind of you to help Amy with her maths, very kind indeed.'

My mother had then left us to it, singing loudly in the kitchen and swearing when she dropped anything. You commented that she was very pretty and that I looked like her. My two sisters were staring at you and overcome with shyness when you smiled at them and asked their names. I remember distinctly what it felt like as we had our heads together over the books and your leg touched mine under the table. You didn't seem to notice but I did and I wished our legs would touch every time you came to my house.

I repeatedly asked you what fractions were actually *for*. You just laughed and told me I was funny again. Eventually, after weeks of you helping me with infinite patience, I think I mastered them. We continued to do our homework together and often you would stay for tea and then we'd listen to music in my bedroom. Your mother would then send one of your older brothers to fetch you because your father would soon be home and she needed you there.

That first year flew by and through a glorious, golden-tinged autumn and a harsh start to winter we became inseparable. You were able to quote from so many different poems it made my head reel and I excelled at sport and not much else. We made other friends and you were increasingly popular because of your ability to get on with everyone. Our classmates swarmed around you and I would feel jealous, until you waited for me at the end of every day.

That first winter after we met, with soft, February snowflakes floating by the orange street light, I would go up to my bedroom just before nine. You had already turned your light on. We agreed to start waving to each other just before sleep. You never forgot until the black beast overcame you and neither did I. You taught me some sign language and it was the same every night.

*The breeze at dawn has secrets to tell, don't go back to sleep.*

It snowed heavily again in March that year and transformed the bleak, dreary, litter-strewn streets into a hushed white world of silence. Your brothers took you sledging in the local park. You were thrown headfirst into a pile of snow by them and your mammy was horrified, you said, because she thought it would dislodge your brain. I had never met the rest of your family and you spent every spare minute with mine. So much so that my parents called you their adopted son and my two sisters adored you. I often asked if I could come to your house but you would shake your head and frown.

'No, not quite yet, but one day, Amy Lee, one day you can.'

In the summer term I won the tennis cup but I longed to be clever, like you. I struggled with almost every subject, mainly due to not paying attention and I would complain to you constantly. You always answered with the same words.

'"Stop acting so small. You are the universe in ecstatic motion."'

'Is that by the same poet you're always quoting?'

'Yes, he's called Rumi, so he is.'

'How come he knew everything?'

'I don't know. I guess he was just very clever.'

'Like you, Bear,' I would say, 'just like you.'

Our school photograph taken at the end of that first year is still in my drawer with all the others. All the girls clamoured to sit next to you because, by this time, puberty was racing through our bodies and spilling over into our emotions like a powerful, gushing waterfall. There was so much squabbling and shoving, Mrs MacDonald lost her temper. I had sat quietly apart, watching from afar and feeling unnerved by your popularity and their burgeoning desires. The photograph was taken outside in the playground on a still, warm day. Mrs MacDonald was directing proceedings, pointing to each student and telling them exactly where they were to sit and not to answer back. I bided my time and waited to see where she told you to go.

'Bear Flynn, you sit here at the front on the end, away from some of these stupid girls. I don't know what you do to command such devotion, do you?'

'No, Mrs MacDonald, I surely don't.'

'Amy Lee, you stand behind him, just here. You seem to be the only one not making a fool of yourself.'

I hadn't had to make a fool of myself because although I often felt unwanted and sharp pains of jealousy, I knew you were *my* best friend and only mine and that later we'd be lying chastely side by side on my bed listening to music. I stood behind you that day and gazed at your thick, wavy hair growing longer at the back and curling over your shirt collar. I longed to touch it and I even put my hand out to do so, but I thought one of the others might see and I wouldn't have embarrassed you for the world.

Now when I look at that form photo, you shine so brightly and stand out like the sparkling Milky Way you were always talking about. Your half smile, your arms folded across your chest and your tie perfectly straight, so different from mine. Mine looked as if I had been pulled along the street by it. I am looking ridiculously happy to be inches away from you, knowing I would spend the whole of my education and my life inches away from you too.

Years later, when you had looked at that photo with adult eyes, you seemed wistful. 'Amy Lee, you were always my Guardian Angel, right behind me constantly, protecting me and fighting my corner.'

'Bear, it's always been the other way round.'

'It really hasn't,' you had replied.

At the end of that first school year together, we wandered home on the last day before the summer holidays. I had been ecstatic and feeling carefree at the thought of not having to sit in a stuffy classroom all day. There would be no learning unimportant facts and figures when I longed to be outside running and cycling and climbing trees. Long, lazy days with no homework, sleeping in and going to bed late were stretching ahead of us both. We could talk long into the night and you could sleep over in the spare room.

You were unusually quiet and my thoughts had turned to all the trees I had climbed so far that summer, making my way through their dense branches until I could see the whole world. Their earthy, woody smell always energised me. You stood below me, urging me to take care and telling me I would scratch my legs or fall and break an arm.

'If I fall you'll catch me, so keep looking. Look, I can swing from this branch to this one just holding on with one hand.'

'You be careful, Amy Lee. I don't want you to fall.'

'You'll catch me, Bear. You'll always catch me.'

'But what if I wasn't here? Just be careful now, please.'

My heart jumped into my throat and stuck there solidly. 'If you weren't here I wouldn't climb.' I'd stared down at you, wondering why on earth you had said that. You appeared so jittery that I asked, 'Did you hear me? I said I wouldn't climb without you standing underneath.'

'Do you promise?'

'Yes, I promise, but you *will* be here, so don't muck about.'

I gazed happily around me. The sky was a light blue with wispy, stringy clouds moving slowly across it and the streets dusty and grubby and littered with bright graffiti. The tiny, neat suburban front gardens, almost bare in winter months with only leggy, thorny roses growing, were alive with colourful summer flowers.

You had remained unusually quiet so I poked you gently with my elbow. 'Are you coming in for tea tonight? Mum says we're having fish and chips from up the road. I love their fish and chips, it's all crispy.'

'No, I have to go straight indoors today. Amy, I'm going away tomorrow, to my granny's house in Kerry, where we always go every holiday. We're all going, except my daddy. He never goes. He has to work. It's a beautiful place, so it is.'

I had just begun skipping with a pretend rope, like a boxer does in training. 'How long are you going for?'

Your face was unusually pale and drawn, as if someone had sucked all the blood out of you and you seemed unable to speak at first. I could feel tension flying off your body towards mine and was so fearful my joyful skipping stopped abruptly.

'The whole summer, I'm afraid. The whole six weeks.'

'How do you mean?'

'The whole six weeks holiday I'll be on my granny's farm, my brothers too and my mammy. My granny says we need roses in our cheeks and that London air is no good for us. She says it's suffocating, so she does. She's never been here, so I don't know how she knows that, but granny knows about everything. We leave at six in the morning to avoid traffic.'

'What will I do?' I said plaintively, selfish to the last.

'You'll be fine, so you will. It's only six weeks.' I felt my eyes sting as tears that felt like acid hit the back of them. 'Amy, don't you be crying now.'

'What will I do?' I said again, my voice breaking. 'Six weeks is ages.'

You looked uneasy, unsure of how to deal with me. 'I'll see you soon, yeah? I'll write to you. I'll tell you everything I'm doing. Watch every day for the postman. Don't climb trees without me, Amy Lee.'

I ran away from you. I just fled and left you there, childish sobs struggling up my throat. I didn't look back but I knew you were watching me until I put the key in my door. I flung myself onto the sofa. My sisters were already home and they both wanted to know what was wrong.

'Nothing,' I cried, gasping for air.

'Is Bear not coming to tea today?' Isabelle asked innocently.

'No!'

'Where's Bear, darling?' Our mother had her head in the serving hatch as usual and she was scrutinising my face. 'Amy, did you hear me?'

'He's at home.'

'That'll make a change for his mum, to have him home,' Ava added, without knowing how her words cut into me.

'Are you crying?' Isabelle said, frowning. I shook my head and wiped my hand across my eyes. 'You are! Don't tell fibs, Amy.'

'No, I'm not. Well, I was but I'm not now. Bear is going to Ireland tomorrow for the summer holidays so he won't be coming to tea for a long time.' There was silence and surreptitious glances between my mother and sisters. 'But I don't want to talk about it.'

'We won't mention him then,' Isabelle said succinctly.

There it was left and I went to my room to cry my eyes out. Six weeks without you, Bear. Six weeks without you. My heart was broken and I didn't know, until you told me years later, that yours had been too.

You wrote every day, every single day. You described roaming in the fields with your brothers, swimming in the sparkling rivers until your legs turned blue and wandering through the farm at night just looking at the stars. You wrote of open fields like a patchwork quilt, the sound of the owls and foxes at night and the early summer heat mists hiding the mountains. You said that the stars were your favourite though, because the sky was so black and vast without any light or tall buildings.

'You can see millions of them,' you had written. 'Millions of stars that fill the night sky and the fields are so quiet and still in the moonlight. I'd forgotten how quiet it is. The silence is startling when you've been in London all year. I can hear the snuffling of creatures in the undergrowth and foxes calling to each other and at dusk bats fly into the old barn. The air is so clear and fresh and smells sometimes of hay and sometimes of cows. The blackberries are early this year, almost ripe for picking. Granny says we must have been naughty because nature is playing games with us. If it rains it sweeps down from the mountains and lasts all day. An owl swoops across the back yard every night when I'm sitting reading. He doesn't know I can see him. I sit so still. My granny says I'm too thin and she keeps giving me stew and dumplings and steak and kidney pie with masses of potatoes. It doesn't make any difference though. She says almost every day:

"Bear, your body is like the rake I use in the yard, so it is. If you turned sideways they'd mark you absent. You're a slim Jim in a bone yard."

I'd forgotten how strong her accent is. Mammy says I now sound like the Irish boy I am and not the cockney sparrow living in London is making me. I don't think I sound like a Londoner, do I? Please keep writing to me at this address, Amy Lee. Two weeks have gone already and I'll soon be home. Every night at ten, sit outside and look at the moon and know that I'm looking at the same moon as you. Don't climb trees without me, remember?'

I wrote back, telling you that the summer was dragging for me. I was riding my bike in the street and playing tennis with my sisters. I told you I looked over at your bedroom every night, even though you weren't there and I would gaze at the moon every night too.

One morning when the sun was high and white around the edges, I burst into tears in my bedroom. I had tried so hard to keep it in but that day it just poured out of me. It did little to help my aching heart, Bear. Your absence was filling every corner of my life and ruining every single moment. I tried very hard to conceal it. My mother knew though because I caught her watching me continually.

I missed you and your romantic soul and I longed for you, with a longing that was far deeper than a pre-teenage crush. It was so deep it hurt in my chest and made me feel despondent. I felt only half there most of the time and the other half was with you. What I missed most was talking to you. I missed telling you everything. I hadn't realised that I told you everything, until you were no longer there to tell. So I wrote everything to you.

What rubbish I put in those letters about my dad being unwell with an ulcer and in quite a bit of pain, and how Mrs Duncan up the road had been accused of shoplifting. I told you how Betty two doors up was as thick as two short planks. At least my mother called her that. I described how stiflingly hot it was in London but mostly I told you that I was stretched out on my bed listening to music that *we* loved and how weird it was without you there.

I had no idea when you were coming back and for a couple of days I suddenly felt sick with anxiety that you might not. But one day, when the close weather finally broke into an electric thunder storm and rain bounced off the dry and sticky pavements, you were standing at my front door. Your skin had turned a golden brown that only comes with being in the fresh air of the countryside and you looked more robust and healthy. Your grandmother certainly had put roses in your cheeks. You were still as thin as her rake and your hair was longer and streaked with gold from the sun. You were soaked to the skin but we just looked at each other in silence.

'Is that Bear at the door?' Ava called. She was two years younger than me and had idolised you from the beginning. 'Amy, is that Bear?'

'Yes, it is.'

'Come in, Bear,' my mother called, rushing up the hall. 'You'll catch your death standing in the rain like that.'

'You don't catch a cold from rain,' Isabelle said firmly behind her, always a know-all.

'Amy, bring him in. Don't stand there like a silly arse.'

'Don't swear, Mum,' Ava told her, mortified, as you walked into our house once again. 'Bear never swears, does he, Amy?'

I couldn't speak. I couldn't believe you were actually there in front of me, under the same roof. Everyone wanted to talk to you and you were polite and answered all their questions and had a cup of tea. My sensible, intuitive mother ushered us upstairs and told us to have a chat about what we had been doing all summer. We sat on my bed and you appeared tense and unable to say much. I rambled on about stupid, childish subjects and your eyes sparkled as you looked at me fondly.

'School next week then,' you eventually said. 'The summer has flown, hasn't it?'

I wanted to scream, no! It hasn't flown! It dragged by so slowly, without you here. I wanted to yell loudly, don't you ever go away again without me! I didn't though. All I could mutter was, 'Yeah, I suppose so.'

'I love Ireland and I love Granny, but I missed you, Amy. Maybe one time your mammy will let you come with me. That would be so grand, don't you think?'

I nodded but listening to your voice, I couldn't help laughing and when you asked me why I said, 'You're a real Irish boy now, Bear.'

You glanced at me as if you knew instinctively that I had become a little shy with you in your absence. There was a little awkwardness between us because we were children after all. We weren't exactly sure how to express ourselves but you wouldn't be put off.

'Would your mammy let you come one year, when you're sixteen maybe?'

'I'll come,' I said, jumping on and off the bed pretending to be a ballerina. Then I showed you how I had learnt how to walk on my hands like a circus performer. I had spent the summer holidays perfecting it. 'Do you think I could learn how to walk a tightrope too? I reckon I could.'

'I reckon you could do anything you set your mind to, Amy Lee, even walking on a tightrope.'

'Mrs Kelly up the road has gone barmy.'

'How do you mean, barmy?'

'Oh you know. She's gone nuts! She thinks trees are from outer space and that they spy on us. She was out in the middle of the road the other night ringing a bell.'

'So why was she ringing a bell?'

'Dad said because she's gone barmy. He said it's very sad and we shouldn't stare at her or laugh.'

'Your daddy is very wise and very kind, so he is.'

We looked at each other for a moment and I felt my mouth begin to curl up as I stifled a laugh. For a second you tried to look disapproving, but then you did the same and we were both shuddering with laughter as the shyness from the six weeks we were apart fled to the waiting hills in Ireland and never came back.

Through our school days we continued to be inseparable. We both had other friends but I can't remember their names now. They weren't close friends and they never came to my house and certainly never to yours either. I hadn't even been in your house, which my mother thought a little strange.

You loved studying and devoured novels and poetry, often describing them to me on the bus home. Mrs Nichols had us acting out Shakespeare's plays in the classroom and we were both in the choir. I couldn't take it seriously though. I was just messing about most of the time and trying to make you laugh by singing the wrong words on purpose. You would nudge me to behave and then get ticked off by Mrs Smith who had breasts almost to her knees. You said your granny loved to hear you sing but that your brother Danny was the one with the superb singing voice. He sang so beautifully it would move your old granny to tears.

I would often find you in the school library, poring over poetry books, with your nose near the page. I would watch you for a few minutes, taking in your long legs and your thin body and how your hair would shine under the sun streaming through the windows. Then I would sidle up to you and say something daft to make you laugh. Miss Williams, who resembled a corpse wearing a shroud, would call my name in a stage whisper.

'Amy Lee, you are talking! Talking, I tell you! Leave Bear Flynn alone! He, at least, is trying to study and you are disturbing him with your idle chatter.' You hated me being told off and always spoke up for me. That day you looked over at her and spoke politely.

'Miss Williams, she's not disturbing me, really she isn't.'

'You always stick up for her, but it doesn't wash with me. I have eyes in my head, Bear Flynn. If you don't find another best friend, you'll under-achieve. Out, Amy, right now before you get detention!'

You would then put down whatever book you were enjoying and leave with me and Miss Williams would just shake her head as if I was a lost cause, which I was. I always wondered if my lack of interest was within me or whether it was because the teaching was so poor. I suppose it was the former because you achieved everything expected of you and more.

'She's so ugly, she looks as if she's been dead for forty years,' I whispered to you that day as we walked out.

You just about kept it together until we were in the safety of the corridor. We then both collapsed and slid down the wall with helpless laughter. I had a raucous, powerful laugh that would stop everyone in their tracks and you had a sweet, high pitched one that you did your best to suppress, but without success.

One morning in autumn, when the sun was golden and lower in the sky we were walking through masses of fallen leaves. You spoke about how your daddy expected you to go to Cambridge University. It had to be Cambridge because it was the best. You said he would be mortified if you didn't go. The thought of you going away was like a knife piercing my chest, but I dismissed it because it was years away.

Those years flew by and when I reached sixteen my feelings began to change. Do you remember how we danced in my bedroom that spring? As with everything else you danced as if you had been taught by an expert. You moved your body in such a fluid way, with ease and without embarrassment with your arms by your side and your hips moving gently. It was as if the music flowed through you. I would just stare at you with undisguised adoration. You pulled me up off my bed.

'Dance with me, Amy Lee.'

I tried to copy you but instead of looking like a natural as you did, I looked like a rag doll. You taught me how to waltz one evening. Why on earth were we doing that? I can't remember, can you? Then we would then fall on my bed, our heads touching. You had a unique smell, Bear. Did I ever tell you that? Nobody had the same smell as you. Lying on my bed one day, I felt an unexpected energy moving through me, as if I'd been asleep all my life and now I was suddenly waking up. It took my breath away. I went to touch your face with my fingers but you jumped up and said you had to get home to help your mammy before your daddy arrived.

I had never been to your house for tea, you were always at mine, but a few days after you spoke about going to Cambridge, I was invited to Sunday lunch. We had been friends for four years by then. I had seen your brothers from the other side of the street and your mammy would wave you off to school when I knocked for you, but I had never met your daddy. He worked away much of the time. Your mammy was very kind and had made roast beef and seven vegetables to go with it. I know there were seven because I counted them. Her Yorkshire pudding was golden and crisp and before we ate we had to say a prayer. I had already picked up my knife and fork.

Your mammy said, 'We'll say grace, shall we?' Your three older brothers, none of whom resembled you, sniggered quietly and I quickly put them down again. She flashed her dark eyes at them. 'Will you stop your laughing?'

'Amy,' you whispered kindly, 'my mammy likes to thank God for the food.'

I had no idea that people prayed at the dinner table. I didn't know that God gave us our food either. I thought farmers did. We didn't pray at home and we didn't do it at school, but then I noticed a small statue of the Virgin Mary on the mantelpiece and a painting of Jesus on the cross on one of the walls.

Lunch was eaten mostly in silence except for your mammy telling all of you to take your elbows off the table and not to speak until you had all finished eating. There was none of that in my house. We were just as noisy at the dinner table as we were the rest of the time. After apple pie and custard your brothers all began speaking at once and I only caught a few words of the conversation. If Patrick wanted your attention, he would knock hard on the table twice to make you look up. Tommy and Danny were noisy and whacked each other round the head a few times and your mammy looked at them fondly. You were the quiet one, the gentle, intelligent one and the baby of the family.

There was a subtle change in the atmosphere when the front door opened. Everyone sat up straight and there was a sudden, taut silence hanging in the air in front of my eyes. Your daddy was a handsome man for his age with black, wavy hair, a heavily lined face and sallow skin. He was carrying a newspaper under his arm and he was dressed in a suit, even though it was a Sunday.

'Hello, who have we here?' He wasn't from Ireland and he had no accent to speak of. 'It's not often we have a pretty girl in our house. Is this the infamous Amy?'

'Yes, Daddy, this is my friend, Amy Lee.'

'It's very good of you to visit, Amy. I'm told my clever boy helps you with your homework, doesn't he?'

'Yes, Mr Flynn, he does. He's very patient. I'm not a good student.'

Your mammy was flapping round him, taking his jacket and newspaper. 'Would you like some lunch, Zachary?'

'Is there some left?' His voice was very loud for such a small house and it seemed to fill the whole room and bounce off the walls. 'You haven't eaten it all?'

'Of course there's some left, it's in the oven. Tommy, get up and let your daddy sit down. Bear, you get your daddy a knife and fork, would you? You're early, Zachary, I wasn't expecting you yet.'

Your daddy sat next to me and he stank of whisky. He was sweating slightly and the smell seemed to be coming out of his pores. His eyes, a cold, penetrating blue, were bleary and unfocussed. You offered to get him a cup of coffee or some water but he waved you away.

'With your friend Amy here, Bear, I'm sure you don't want to sit and watch me eat. Take her upstairs to your room, but behave like a gentleman now. My boy is going to Cambridge, Amy. Did you know that? My boy, from a tiny village outside Dublin, will be going to the best university in the land, won't you, Bear?' He leant towards me and the smell of drink was overpowering.

'Yes, I will, Daddy. I need the grades first though,' you added nervously, watching him carefully.

'I don't know what they will make of the name his mother gave him there. It's not exactly a good old Irish name, is it? Will *you* be going to university?'

'I doubt it, Mr Flynn. I'd rather be out cycling or running.' He frowned and I felt his displeasure and your anxiety, Bear. 'I'm only good at P.E.'

'That won't get you far in life, my girl. What do your parents say about that?'

'I don't think they mind,' I said, quite innocently. 'They just want me to be happy.'

He frowned again as if that thought had never entered his head. I felt a kind of tightness in everyone as if a violin string had been stretched too far and you were all waiting for it to snap.

'You're a sweet, pretty little thing, aren't you, Amy?' The expression in his eyes had changed. 'I bet my boy finds it hard to keep his hands to himself.'

'Here we are,' your mammy said loudly, saving the day by bustling in with the plated beef dinner. 'Here you are, Zachary, eat it when it's hot. Boys, give your daddy some space. Bear, will you be showing Amy your room, darling?'

You took hold of my hand and led me out and your brothers followed. They went in the front room and started to wrestle together but we escaped upstairs. You shared your room with Patrick but it was sparse and bare and old-fashioned. There were no posters on the walls like in my bedroom and it was too tidy with nothing out of place. Jesus was on the cross again above your bed, looking down at you.

'I couldn't sleep in here with Jesus looking down at me,' I had told you, but you hadn't appeared to hear me at first. I thought you would laugh because you always found me funny, even when I didn't mean to be. You told me to sit on your bed beside you and you looked unhappy. You began whispering to me.

'I have no chance of living how I want to live. You see how strict he is? He doesn't really care what my brothers do. All the expectation is on my shoulders. Sometimes the heaviness of it all weighs me down, so it does. Now you know why I'm always at your house. Your family is so happy. My family is always on edge, waiting for him to come home and lay down the law.'

'You aren't like him at all, are you? Your brothers look like him a bit, but you don't.'

'I don't want to be like him,' you said, shuddering. 'He isn't gentle, he isn't kind to my mammy and he makes us all anxious. We never know when he's going to explode. Now you know why I haven't invited you before. The only time we are free, is when we go to Ireland to my granny's farm. Then we can all be ourselves, our *real* selves. He favours me above the others for some reason and it's so unfair. He's tough and hard and his masculinity is in your face and gets in your brain. He makes me sick, so he does. Patrick needs his approval and deserves it so much more than I do, but he gets none because he's deaf. Tommy dislikes him and doesn't hide it and Danny pretends he doesn't care but he does, very much so.'

'Why isn't he kind to your mammy?'

'He isn't kind to her because that's how he is. When I was much younger I would hear her crying after he had shouted at her. It was always about the same thing.'

'What thing?'

'I don't know but it was always something to do with me. I would put my head under the bedclothes and dream of living in a place where there was *only* kindness and love and compassion. He has a brutal tongue when he gets going and he belittles her because he knows he can. I look at daddy and I think, I want to be the furthest away from how you are that I can be.' You clutched at my hand. 'I watch him carefully and he thinks it's because I admire him and want to be like him. I will *never* be like him! I watch him to detect when the next explosion will be and how I can diffuse it so mammy won't get it. I'll go to Cambridge alright. I'll go to get away from him.'

'What do you mean, "get it"?'

'I saw him try to slap her face once. He brought his hand back to strike her but I sensed it was coming and jumped on his back and screamed at him to leave her alone. He was so shocked and ashamed that I had witnessed it that he never did it again. It's always there though, hovering inches away, ready to boil over. She fusses around him, belittling herself for him. Sometimes I want to shout, for God's sake, Mammy! You're so much more than him in every way. When he's around, I can't feel her love. I don't know why I can't feel it, but I can't. Do you ever feel that your mammy withholds her love from you, Amy?'

'No.'

The tears ran silently down your face. That was the first time I saw you cry and it made me cry too. We both stood up and moved forward simultaneously. We wrapped our arms around each other and you clung to me as if letting go would see you falling off a cliff to your death. Feeling your slim body next to mine made me wake up to the fact that I wanted you, *all* of you, whatever the circumstances.

I wanted you to quote Rumi to me for the rest of my life even though I didn't understand half of it. I wanted you to describe the morning mists, the glorious autumn colours and the night stars. I wanted to hear from you how the trees I was climbing were spreading their branches out especially for me because they loved me being there. I wanted to hear you call out to me: 'Amy, catch the snowflakes. Every one of them is so exquisite and intricate.'

I wanted to be curled up next to your slim body every night, before we went to sleep. I would complain that I wasn't clever enough and you would sigh so deeply.

"'Amy, you were born with wings, why prefer to crawl through life?'"

'Rumi was a clever bastard, wasn't he?' That was always my answer because it made you laugh and your answer was always the same: 'Amy Lee, will you stop your swearing now?'

I had no idea at that moment, when I could easily imagine my life mapped out in front of me with a smooth path that always led to you, that you were trying to work out how to explain to me that *your* path was full of rocky stones and hazards and wasn't as straightforward as I hoped.

That day, in your room, after we had clung to each other, I told you I had felt uncomfortable when your daddy had leant towards me. I said he stank of whisky and that I never wanted to be that close to him again. You had nodded quickly.

'Amy,' you whispered, 'I promise I will never let him hurt you or allow him that close to you again.' You kept your promise.

After the summer term ended, when I turned sixteen, I was going to Ireland with you for the first time. We began planning what we would do and my happiness felt like a balloon flying free above the rooftops. I could think of nothing else. We had been studying together every evening but you were worried about my lack of concentration.

'Amy, you have to concentrate. What will you do if you don't pass?'

'I'll come and live in Cambridge with you, Bear,' I replied and I thought you would laugh but you simply turned your head. I had no idea what you were thinking because I couldn't see your eyes.

I had been dreaming in lessons so much, Mr Thompson told me there wasn't much use in me attending. I was thinking what a blast that would be, to stay home, until I realised you would be at school without me and at the mercy of all the other girls who adored you. My thoughts were interrupted by Mr Thompson again; he was looking at you and frowning.

'Don't let Amy distract you from your studies, Bear. These are of great importance for you if you want to go to university.'

'Yes, sir, I know, thank you. I'm grateful for your concern, so I am.'

Our shoulders were touching and I felt the sadness seep from your body into mine as your shoulders drooped. I thought it was because I was being childish and you wanted me to act maturely. I only found out later it was because you wanted to run as fast and as hard as you could, away from that school, away from London and away from your daddy's cruel and relentless expectations. Passing exams and going to university were still your daddy's dream, not yours. You would have been just as happy living on a farm and writing stories about owls and thunderstorms.

After the exams were done and dusted, we would stretch out on my bed and listen to the rain pounding on the pavements and lashing against my bedroom window. We were having a week of heavy rain storms that year and the air was close and still and thunderous. Our heads would be together and I longed to touch you and run my fingers through your hair. It had been cut short ready for your holiday and it accentuated your expressive eyes.

I had deep feelings stirring inside me that sometimes bubbled up and threatened to ravage my body. They were setting me on fire and burning me up and they wouldn't be quenched, especially when I was near you. I dreamt of what you would feel like when we eventually gave in to what I imagined were our mutual longings. In my imagination you always felt warm and soft and comfortable, as if I was coming home. I noticed your body was changing. You were losing your boyish figure and becoming more muscular and lean rather than stick thin. I would ask you to tell me about Ireland and you always answered, 'Amy Lee, it's a place where angels live.'

There were a couple of end of term parties where many of our classmates had drunk too much and smoked something that smelt like burning sugar. At the last party before going to Ireland, the music was deafening and Dominique Fraser was annoying me intensely by monopolising you. She tried to kiss you, but you turned your face away and appeared disgusted with her. She wasn't to be put off though. She grabbed your hand and led you outside. You resisted at first and glanced over your shoulder at me. In your eyes I detected a look of longing and discomfort.

I followed you both and stood at the patio doors. She had pulled you into some bushes and had her hands either side of your face. I couldn't hear your conversation but she was doing most of the talking. Your arms were hanging limply by your sides and because I knew every inch of your body I could tell it was stiff with tension.

Dominique took hold of one of your hands and put it on her breast. I immediately felt a wave of nausea wash over me. I wanted to scream at her and pull her off you by her hair. You grabbed her face and kissed her roughly as if you detested her. You then jumped back as if touching her had caused you immense pain. I hid behind the curtain as you rushed in and picked up your jacket from the banisters in the hall. I followed you out into the deserted street and watched for a moment as you were looking up at the moon. Your lips were moving and I thought you were praying.

'Bear,' I called, 'Bear, are you going home? I'll come with you.'

'Stay if you want to, Amy Lee. Don't leave because of me.' Your face was full of confusion and your eyes were flicking from side to side as if you were having trouble keeping them still. 'I don't want to spoil it for you.'

'I don't want to stay if you aren't there. I'll be bored without you to talk to. Shall we walk home?' You stopped and looked down at me with such a tortured look on your face that I had to ask, 'What's wrong, Bear?'

'Why can't I be like everyone else?'

'That's an easy question to answer. It's because you're unique.'

'I don't want to be unique.'

'*I* want you to be unique. I don't want you to be like all of them.' Your body began to relax a little and you gave me a small smile and put your arm through mine. 'I like you being different from them.'

'Well, that's good because I'm not like any of them. It's a beautiful night, so it is. We should have been looking at the stars rather than trying to fit in.'

'I don't want to fit in and I don't want you to either.'

'I'll *never* fit in.'

'You fit with me.'

'I know I do and I'm grateful for that. But I don't fit in the world very well.'

'Who cares about the world? I certainly don't and I never have.'

'My daddy wants me to fit in, so he does. My daddy wants me to be a great success and get a first at Cambridge. Can you imagine what it will take to get a first there? He wants me to be strong and full of alcohol fuelled testosterone like him and marry a suitable woman and give him perfect grandchildren. He wants me to be a good Catholic and I can't be. I just can't be.'

'Don't think about that now. We have *six* weeks to do and be what we want. Think about that and don't be unhappy, *please*.' You didn't answer and I felt fearful for you although I couldn't work out why. 'Bear, why are you unhappy? Is it because of Dominique? I'll tell her to get lost. I'll tell her to shove off, you know I will.'

You stopped and looked at me again. I had never seen you look like you did in that moment. It shocked me and made me tremble.

'I'm in pain, Amy Lee, so I am but I can't tell you about it.'

'You *can* tell me, I won't judge you. You can *always* tell me. I love you, Bear, you must know that. Don't be in pain, *please* don't be in pain. I'll take all of that pain out of your body and into mine. This should be the time of our lives. We are *so* young and we have years to spend together.'

'But we won't always be together.' Your words made me feel

like I could barely breathe, as if someone had their hand around my heart squeezing hard. 'Life has a way of not panning out as you want it to.'

'Don't say that, don't. I won't let you be in pain, Bear.' You put your hand by my cheek. You were shaking and your fingers felt like a butterfly's wings kissing my face. 'I'll spend my life making you happy, if you'd let me.'

'Listen carefully to these words, Amy Lee.' You paused for a moment and then took a long, deep breath. 'Listen carefully, *please*. "I said: What about my eyes? God said: Keep them on the road. I said: What about my passion? God said: Keep it burning. I said: What about my heart? God said: Tell me what you hold inside it. I said: Pain and sorrow. God said: Stay with it. The wound is where the Light enters you."'

You then held my hand tightly and we walked home in silence. I was beginning to feel you slipping away a little, not physically but emotionally. There was something inside you I didn't know about because you were keeping it a secret from me. I was terrified of that feeling. I made myself a solemn promise to stay by your side whatever life threw at you. I knew I could deal with what the world hurled at *me* because for me, life had always resembled a light comedy film. For you, it was slowly turning inwards and would soon resemble a tragedy.

On that last week at school, life began to change for me. Dominique Fraser had obviously felt your rough kiss was a green light, even though anyone with an ounce of common sense could have told her otherwise. She would wave at you in the biology laboratory and smile demurely. A demure smile didn't quite work when she had already grabbed your hand and placed it on her breast a few nights before. It was a bit late to be acting demurely. She eventually drew your attention from Mr Howard and ran her hand through her long, wavy blonde hair and pouted. Pouting made her look like a dead fish. I could have picked up a book and chucked it at her, but you were completely oblivious to her flirtatious looks. I frowned at her and shook my head as if she was a naughty child and Mr Howard caught me.

'Amy Lee,' he said wearily, 'you may win every race, play tennis beautifully and kick a football as well as any man, but that won't get you far in life.' I stifled a laugh but he wasn't having any of it, not even on the last week of term. 'Let's see if you are laughing when your results come through, shall we? Now stop pulling ridiculous faces and try to concentrate just a little.'

You glanced at me with such a look of admiration that I was determined to pull as many faces as I could from then on. Dominique had only just started her not so subtle pursuit of you though and slipped her arm through yours at every opportunity despite my giving her looks that I wished could have killed her stone dead in an instant.

'She's getting right on my nerves, Bear,' I told you one day.

'Mine too.'

The next day she tried to sit on your lap in the playground and you appeared weary of it all when everyone else was egging her on. On the last day of term we were sitting at our desks just before the bell for home when Stanley Richards tapped me on the shoulder and shattered my world into millions of jagged pieces.

'Are you worried you'll lose your boyfriend then, Amy?'

'He's not my boyfriend.'

'No, he wouldn't be, would he? She's barking up the wrong tree, silly idiot.'

'Who is?'

'Dominique is, who else? He's not interested. He'll never be interested. Has he tried it on with you yet?' I felt my face burning with indignation and rage. I didn't want to talk about our friendship with anyone. 'I bet he hasn't.'

'Mind your own business,' I snapped and I wanted to put my fist in the middle of his pasty face.

'I thought not,' he said, smirking. 'He should have by now, the amount of time you spend together. Ask yourself why.'

'Just shut up, will you?'

'Ben in the upper-sixth has a better chance than you or Dominique.'

My stomach dropped to my knees in an instant and I started to sweat. I felt the perspiration run down the back of my neck and I was desperate for air. As soon as the bell sounded, everyone ran for the door, except you. You turned, smiled and beckoned to me because we were going to your beloved Ireland together. You slung your bag over your shoulder. Dominique rushed over and perched seductively on the edge of your desk, her summer dress showing off too much of her milky white legs. She whispered in your ear but there was no response from you, so she whispered again. This time you shook your head and whispered something back. Her face then darkened and she swore at you under her breath.

'Fuck off then, Bear Flynn! Just fuck off. I won't ask you again.'

You ignored her and dropped your head. I watched as your shoulders drooped.

Stanley kissed my cheek quickly. 'See what I mean. A girl who looks like Dominique throws herself at you and you tell her to go away, you aren't interested. He's the only bloke in the room who would have done that. See you, Amy, have a good holiday.'

You came over and your colour was high with embarrassment. I wished Stanley had kept his big mouth shut about Ben in the upper-sixth. You were *my* Bear! Mine! You always would be.

'Are you ready, Amy Lee?'

'Yeah, I'm ready. Let's get out of here, shall we?'

'Six weeks in Ireland,' you whispered with a deep sigh.

My mind was all over the place, running ahead towards the shared future that I longed for and running backwards, trying to pick up clues in our past. I was determined that you wouldn't be able to tell from my eyes that I was dying inside. 'Where angels live,' I added and you beamed at me.

'Yes, where angels live.'

## Chapter Two

*Words are a pretext.*
*It's the inner bond that draws one person to another, not*
*words.*
***Rumi***

Ireland stole my heart. There were lush fields, high hedges full of wild flowers and ash trees and the still summer evenings. The distant, jagged mountains sometimes appeared to be tinged with blue and at other times mauve. I asked you why and you replied that they were magical because the little people lived there and they could weave spells and use sorcery to make them even more enchanting than they were already. I even loved the waves of rain that swept down from the hills filling the sparkling rivers to the brim. They drove across the countryside sending the swifts flying into the cherry and blackthorn trees.

There were crab apples around the old farm and in the ancient woodland and I tasted the crab apple jelly your granny made when the fruit was ready to be picked. There was honeysuckle, and wild berries growing that the birds would swoop down to eat and vast stretches of golden corn drenched in hot sunshine. When the heavy rains came though, it would sweep across in one great grey mass and beat against the windows in such a rhythmical way your granny said it was the devil himself wanting to come in.

We roamed for miles, watching pheasants and thrushes and when we were stretched out on damp grass by the river, a kingfisher flew by us in a flash, low and fast. We heard cuckoos and woodpeckers and in the evenings, sitting outside the back door in the yard a barn owl was calling to us. You said it was a comforting sound and that magic was about when the barn owl spoke. Every night as a gentle dusk fell around us the clouds would turn pink and orange in turn. A golden light would set the skies on fire and you found it so beautiful and moving, you told me it made you long to fly into it and disappear for a while.

'Why do you want to disappear for a while?' I asked, a ripple of anxiety running through me.

'I don't know, Amy Lee, that's the problem.'

'Well, I won't let you disappear! I'll bring you back, wherever you are. Do you hear me?'

'I hear you. Don't you be worrying about me now.'

'Let's talk about something else. Tell me what it's like here in the snow or in the spring. One day, when we're older, maybe we'll come then. I love hearing you speak about what you love, Bear. I don't want to hear anything about disappearing.'

You hadn't needed any more encouragement to tell me more about Ireland and the countryside around granny's farm. I often felt that maybe you were made up mostly of Irish heather and moist, dark earth with storm clouds as your hair and soft rain as your blood. Perhaps you were actually one of the little people yourself, weaving magic around everyone who knew you and casting your spells on us. You had certainly cast a spell on me, a spell for life.

'In May, the evening skies are light blue for so long you

imagine night has forgotten to fall. Every morning there is misty dew on the grass like jewels and birdsong so glorious you could listen forever and never tire of doing so.'

Your eyes were dreamy as you spoke and I was quickly and easily caught up in that dream, listening to your every word and watching as your face changed constantly with each memory you spoke of.

'I want to come in May then.'

'I'll bring you, Amy, so I will, I promise you. There are so many little creatures that creep out at dusk. It's a time when mystical stories are told by firelight as the sun goes down and the weather turns colder. When it rains in the spring, it's like a soft mist, not heavy and brutal like the storms that come in August. I used to walk barefoot when I was a little child because through the moist earth I could feel the very heart of Ireland beating. I thought if I left I would die.'

'And what about if it snows? I love snow.'

'We don't get snow that often down here, but when it does come you remember it. We used to come to Granny for Christmas when we lived near Dublin. Daddy never came with us, he stayed at home and mammy was so different here without him. Granny would roast chestnuts on her open fire and we'd sing round the piano, so we would. Daniel would sing with our grandpa and our granny would cry. One February, when the schools were shut for half-term, we came here for a week and it snowed heavily. It was silent, so very silent and frighteningly cold and the wind would blow through the snow making it fly up in the air like the icing on a cake. I didn't want to leave, Amy. I was in a paradise of my own making, so I was and I longed to live where it was always peaceful and not tainted by Zachary's aggressive manner. He was putting pressure on me even then because my teacher had told him I was exceptionally bright.'

You took a deep breath and let the air out slowly. Whenever you spoke about your daddy your face would change. 'His voice has never been heard here though. He has never come with us. He couldn't stand my granny and all her funny sayings and all the crossing herself repeatedly. He thought her stupid, can you imagine? I'd ask the angels in the sky to whisk me away and let me live with them rather than go back to where his dirty, lecherous hands covered everything.'

'What does lecherous actually mean, Bear?' I had never come across the word before.

'It's not a grand way to be, Amy Lee, so it isn't. It means he looks at mammy and other women in a certain way when he's in drink, mostly mammy though. If he's not in drink, he doesn't do it. There's something in alcohol that turns his head inside out and makes him offensive. When he looks at mammy like that it makes me sick to my stomach, so it does and I know she'll suffer for it. This is my haven. He's never set foot on granny's land and I pray he never does.'

I slowly came to love your granny who was a tiny, bent-over lady with kind, twinkling blue eyes and a face so lined her skin resembled crumpled brown paper. She had what looked like blue worms on the back of her hands and a sweet smile.

'Holy Mary and all the saints,' was said by her so often, I thought she must be in the room with us. In fact, she *was* in the room with us, in *every* room, as little china statues and faded paintings. If your granny spoke of someone who had died, she would cross herself quickly twice and look up at the ceiling as if she could see them in Heaven. She would kiss your face every time she passed you and to her you were always, 'Baby Bear.'

She fussed over us, feeding us up and telling us old folk tales in the golden evening light. She believed in the little people and magic and the afterlife and spoke about Deidre of the Sorrows and the search for crocks of gold. She told tales of leprechauns and assured me that wishes came true if you prayed hard enough. She adored you with a passion that swept all other passions aside.

'Baby Bear,' she would say to you every day, 'you'll end up here when you're done with London and its shallow ways. You'll be living here when I'm in my grave and you'll write books, so you will.'

'Maybe I will one day, Granny.'

'I'll leave you this farm and this land. The Angel of Mercy will see to it. The path isn't smooth but she'll look after you.'

I became very fond of your brothers too, who all had such different personalities, I wondered how you all came from the same parents. Tommy was strong willed and a little argumentative at times, but he had an enviable sense of humour and when he laughed it was loud and infectious. He had a girlfriend who lived in the next village so we rarely saw him but when he was at the farm he would pick up your granny and hold her in his arms until she cried for mercy.

'Holy Mary, will you be putting me down, Tommy Flynn! I'll be having a heart attack, so I will.'

Danny was much quieter and wasn't one for conversation but he sang all the time and played the old piano that was sitting in the corner and hadn't been tuned in forty years. It even had cobwebs hanging off it. My favourite, apart from you, Bear, was Patrick. He taught me more signing with such patience and with a shy smile that made me feel warm inside. He was gentle, like you and he would shake his head at your granny.

'Patrick,' she would tell him often, 'the good Lord took your hearing but gave you the kindest nature.'

One evening, just after she said those words, Patrick knocked the table twice to get your attention and signed something to you and you smothered a small smile. Later you told me what Patrick had signed.

'I wish the good Lord would give it back, but only when our granny isn't talking.'

'My Baby Bear,' she often said to you, 'the Lord has given you brains, so He has, and the good looks of your grandfather, but he's taken away so much, a part of you, the part you long for most.'

One night when she said those words you didn't smile, your body stiffened and you dropped your head. Your mammy let go of the dish she was holding and it crashed onto the table causing your granny to cry out, 'Sweet Jesus, Mary and Joseph, Marie, has the good Lord given you dropsy?'

'Granny,' you told her kindly, 'that's not what dropsy is so the good Lord has it wrong if He thinks it is.'

'Well, you'd know, Baby Bear, you're the cleverest boy in the whole of Ireland, so you are.'

Tommy and Danny did quite a bit of wrestling and even more whacking each other round the head. They didn't do it to Patrick because of his hearing aids. They occasionally did it to you, but your mammy would turn on them when they did, her eyes blazing with anger. 'I've told you so many times, you're not to whack Bear round the head! You'll dislodge his brain if you do. You can't be dislodging his brain. He has to go to Cambridge. That's what his daddy wants.'

Your mammy was the hardest to get to know. On the surface she was very kind to me and cared whether I was enjoying my holiday, but she held part of herself back. She was often guarded and distracted. It was obvious to me she had been beautiful in her youth with dark hair piled on top of her head, a creamy complexion and the most beautiful green eyes I had ever seen. After a couple of weeks she did relax a little and the constant frown across her forehead began to fade away. She often went walking on her own, always in the same direction and when she returned, her cheeks were flushed and her demeanour completely altered. I knew she loved you but she wasn't tactile or affectionate towards you at all. I would watch you go to kiss her cheek or take hold of her hand but she would shush you away.

'Jesus, Mary and Joseph, will you stop that, Bear? Kiss your granny if you want to, I can't be doing with all that softness.' I couldn't understand her, my parents were always affectionate, but she was the same with all of you. Then she would feel guilty and she would stroke your hair quickly. 'You're going to make us all so proud, aren't you, sweetheart? He's so bright, Amy. He's so bright and gorgeous in every way. All the girls at Cambridge will be falling at his feet.'

'Stop your nonsense, Mammy, will you? Nobody will be falling at my feet. I'll be working too hard for any of that.'

Your slightly uneasy response had given me an uncomfortable knot of anxiety. I didn't want to think about all the beautiful girls you would meet. They'd be clever too, like you and not daft like me.

Granny's house had originally all been on one level, with just a kitchen and one bedroom and a living room for when visitors came. In her youth there had been no running water and all the cooking had been done on an open fire. Fresh water was collected from a mountain spring a mile away and it was the purest and clearest water anywhere. The house had been thatched originally but now had a tiled roof and an upstairs had been added at the same time with bedrooms and a bathroom. The barn and byre were no longer used and looked desolate and dirty. Your granny said that if a strong wind came across the fields from the mountains it would see them fall down.

One morning when the heat of the day had begun even before sunrise and my room was stifling, I crept downstairs to find a cool place to sit. Your granny was up already, making a pot of tea with a strange net on her head that looked like something you would catch fish in. She poured me some tea and she spoke about her childhood in the next valley and how she had married the handsomest boy in the school. She then reached over and took hold of my hand. Hers were thin and bony and felt like sandpaper.

'Do you love my Bear?' she asked me, straight out with no palaver. The intensity in her eyes made it impossible not to tell her the truth. Not that I would ever have denied loving you. 'Do you love him, Amy?'

'Yes, I do, very much.'

'Amy, if you love him then you'll need to know the God's honest truth. Bear isn't like his brothers, he's different. Tommy is easy going and not very bright and he doesn't care much about anything. Danny is carefree and quite happy as long as he can play his music and sing. Patrick accepts life as it is and doesn't feel the need to ask for much more than he has. But Bear can't accept what or who he is. Bear is complex and has trouble in his mind. If you're going to love him and stick by his side, you'll have your heart broken time and time again.'

'I don't understand. He won't break my heart, he couldn't.'

Your granny shuffled over to the window where a new, bright and magical dawn was breaking in the far distance. Sunshine filtered into the dark room bringing with it a deep, clear freshness and a promise of another warm day on the farm. I could see particles of dust dancing in the sunlight. She was gazing out of the window and gave a deep sigh.

'I look at those mountains and pray to our Lady and all the saints to watch over him. Bear is like a hot flame. It holds your attention and you can't take your eyes off it, but you don't want to creep too near because you'll get burnt. The look of it will keep drawing you in and you'll think, I'll just get a little nearer, so I will. I can stand the heat. I can quell the fire before it burns itself out, but you can't. You'll be scarred, Amy, if you get too near.'

I swallowed hard. 'I'm already too near. I haven't been burnt.'

'I know I'm just a foolish old Irish woman who knows nothing of the world, but I know Bear. I would watch him from this window as his brothers ran and tumbled and jumped in the rivers. Bear would sit and talk to the flowers. He would put his arms around the knobbly, hard trunk of that ash tree out there and put his face next to the bark. I heard him once asking the angels to make him like other boys, to take away his troubles and the black beast that haunts his dreams. You have to face that black beast too if you're going to stay by Bear.'

'I'll face it and I'll fight it too,' I declared, with bravery that I didn't actually feel at that moment. Your granny gave me a fond smile but it contained a hint of disbelief, making me add, 'I will, I promise you. I'll keep Bear from any harm.'

'You're a force of nature, Amy, so you are and I hope one day you will both stand over my grave and tell me the black beast has fled to the hills.'

'We will, I give you my word.' She sat down again and rubbed her lower back. 'Are you okay, Granny?'

'Yes, yes,' she said, waving her hand. 'You're a force of nature, so you are, young Amy. You're a force of nature with courage and compassion. If he pushes you away, and he probably will, don't stray too far.'

Later that morning she made us a picnic of ham and homemade chutney sandwiches and we wandered through the meadows with the warm rays of the sun on our faces. There were cornflowers and poppies growing in the shimmering heat and dragonflies and bees flew around us as light as fairies. It was as if we were the only people in the world. We ate our lunch and then relaxed on some long, thin grasses. The breeze moved through the distant corn fields making a soft whooshing noise and we spoke about what we would do when you came back from university. You seemed content, we laughed all day and I noticed your forearms were turning a golden colour and that your chest and shoulders appeared broader. We were both changing slowly but you stayed as slim as you had been when I first saw you across the classroom.

We roamed too far that day and found ourselves in a field facing a bull that was breathing heavily and had us firmly in his sights. You grabbed my hand and it felt like a whole new world was opening up as soon as your flesh touched mine in that moment. Because it had rained in the night, the grass was sparkling like white diamonds under the strong early morning sunlight. The wheat in the fields surrounding us danced and swayed elegantly and the air felt fresher and more invigorating. The bull had sweat across his back making his hide glisten.

'Amy! Don't move. He's seen us. He's wondering whether to charge.'

I felt no fear. My senses were on full alert, but not because of the huge, shiny black and potentially dangerous animal a few feet away. Your hand gripped mine and I could feel the vitality and spirit surging through you.

'Shall we run?' I asked, hoping we would and that you would hold on to me forever.

'No, we walk slowly backwards.' You stared into the bull's dark eyes and you were murmuring sweetly as you pulled me gently back. 'Good boy, you're such a brave and beautiful animal and we're in your field. I'm sorry we walked into your space but we won't hurt you. We'll leave you in peace, beautiful creature.'

The bull blinked and stared as if he was sizing us up but you, with your soothing voice and innate gentleness, calmed his aggression and he slowly turned his heavy, lumbering body and wandered away. I was transfixed.

'How did you do that?'

'Kindness wins every time with animals *and* people. That's how I calm my daddy when he's in drink.'

It was high summer, but the weather proved unpredictable and storms raged across the mountains bringing with them heavy rain, rumbling thunder and angry, silver lightning crackling across the sky. One day, we had walked for hours, just talking and I had climbed some trees with you watching from below.

'You'll be falling, Amy Lee, if you're not careful and should you be wearing a skirt when you climb?'

'I won't fall, you know I won't. I *never* fall. Will you still talk like that when you're back in London?'

'Will I talk like what?'

'Like your granny does,' I called down to you, laughing.

'No, I'll be a cockney sparrow, just like you, so I will. Aren't you getting too old to climb trees now? Shouldn't you be wearing high heels and be painting your face with make-up?'

'I'll climb trees until I die.'

'Will you now? And don't talk of dying, Amy. You'll be an old, old lady like my granny.'

'Do you think so?'

'Yeah and I'll die a long time before you.' My foot missed the branch of the tree and I slipped forward. I managed to cling on but I had scraped my leg quite badly. You cried out, 'Jesus! Are you alright? Amy, answer me, are you hurt?'

'No, I'm not, it's just a scratch.'

'Come down now! Please, come down.' I made my way through the mass of branches and leaves until I jumped the last few feet. You bent down and examined my leg, shaking your head sternly. 'You've never done that before.'

'I missed my footing because you spoke of dying a long time before me! Don't say stuff like that.'

'You've hurt your leg, it's bleeding. Don't climb trees anymore. You aren't eleven years old now.' I put my hands on my hips in defiance but you were equally defiant. 'Do you hear me, Amy? You could fall and crack your head open.'

'I'll climb trees as long as I can. The only time I won't climb is if you're not there to catch me and you will be. You *will* be! So no more talk of dying.' I could feel the fear moving through my body and into my throat. I tried hard not to let the tears that were blinding me fall onto my face, but it was no good. It all came bursting out of me in a torrent. 'Don't say I'll live to be an old woman. I don't want to be an old woman if you have gone and left me years before. What will I do if you aren't here? Why say you're going to die young? It's just a bloody stupid thing to say. Bear, don't ever say that again.'

Your face fell and you took hold of me, placing your hand at the back of my head and pushing it against your chest. 'Feel my heart, Amy Lee. It's yours, always yours. I'm so sorry to talk of dying. I won't ever say it again. You can climb trees as much as you want for as long as you want.' As you put your hands either side of my face you whispered, '"Close your eyes. Fall in love, stay there."'

'I am, Bear, I am, but you aren't.'

'I can't, I can't. I want to, but I can't. It isn't fair on you.'

'What isn't fair on me? Let me decide what's fair on me and what isn't.'

'I *will* tell you, soon I will.'

We clung to each other for a long time until the sky turned dark with more storm clouds. When we passed a trickling stream, you took out your handkerchief and bathed my leg with such gentleness I hardly felt it. You then took my hand and we walked slowly towards the farm. When forked lightning flashed above us we didn't run, we continued to amble, both lost in our own thoughts. Were they the same thoughts, Bear? I doubt it because mine were scrambled, trying to work out your secret and dreading it at the same time.

Ben from the upper-sixth came sharply into focus. He was a beautiful boy with a face like chiselled marble, golden hair and a muscular physique from playing rugby every spare minute. Every girl in the school was half in love with him, except me, of course. He wasn't a patch on you and yet you had such similar qualities of gentleness, kindness and an unusual, delicate way of speaking. But Ben was quite vain and always checking his hair in every window or mirror which you never did.

Perhaps I was wrong, maybe you *were* thinking of Ben too. Perhaps when you looked at me so fondly it was Ben's face you longed to see or Ben's hand you wanted to touch. Was that why you had rejected Dominique's kiss with such disgust? Was this the secret you were keeping hidden inside you, deep down inside you never to be revealed to anyone? Were you terrified I would push you away because you were different from everyone else? I longed to tell you then that I would love you even more *because* you were different.

I didn't want men who were aggressive, tough and fuelled by

their clumsy desires. I wanted someone with a fine brain who could fill the gaps in mine. I wanted someone who would care about me scraping my knees and passing my exams. I wanted someone who signed to me out of his bedroom window every night and wrote me poetic letters. I wanted somebody who recited Rumi poems so beautifully and perfectly I almost understood them. I wanted somebody whose expressive face and watchful eyes I could gaze at for the rest of my life without tiring of that.

I wanted *you*, Bear. I wanted you and only you and at sixteen I had my life mapped out ahead of me with you at every corner guiding me.

A few days later the rains came again with a vengeance, sweeping across the wheat and corn fields in one quickly moving mass. We'd sat in your bedroom and listened to it beating furiously against the windows. You would read novels to me with great understanding and knowledge that I could only marvel at. The distant mountains were shrouded in mist and appeared even more mysterious. We curled up together on your bed and you told me about Irish folklore that your granny believed in as much as she believed in Mary, Mother of God.

'There's the Witch of Kilkenny, Deidre of the Sorrows and Tristan and Iseult. They're always tragic and full of lost love, love betrayed and deep, dark secrets. Granny loves them all. They are mythological tales handed down, generation to generation.'

'Do any of them end happily?' I asked, with the naive romanticism of a young teenager.

'Does there always have to be a happy ending with you, Amy Lee?'

'Yes, there does, otherwise what's the point? I don't want unhappy endings.'

'Alright, alright, I won't burst your bubble of romantic endings. I'll tell you about the mythical creatures that live beneath the lakes and the sea over here, shall I?'

'Yeah, mermaids sound better,' I said eagerly.

'Well, mermaids often lured sailors to their death with their beauty and wickedness, did you know that?'

'No.'

'You see, Amy, nothing is what it seems in life or in mythology. I'll tell you about the Merrow of Ireland, a half human, half underwater fish like creature with green skin, webbed fingers and seaweed for hair, with a tail like a mermaid. But this mythical creature wears a red cap which gives it the ability to breathe underwater.'

'That's weird.'

'It is, but Irish folk tales *are* all weird. There are stories of men falling in love with these Merrows and taking their red caps so they have to live on land all the time.'

'Isn't that a bit cruel?'

'It *is* cruel, to try and make someone or something how you want them to be and not who or what they really are. But love can be cruel. It can be cruel if you want to change the person you love.'

I moved closer to you. Your distinct smell made me long to pull you over on top of me. 'If it's cruel then it isn't love.'

'You think? I hope you're right, Amy Lee.'

'Tell me another one, please.'

'There's an Irish sea spirit that looks like a horse.'

'That sounds better.'

'Hold on, it sometimes takes the form of a huge dark bird or a man with hooves for feet and seaweed for hair.'

'Why have they all got seaweed for hair?' I turned my nose up in distaste. 'It sounds very odd.'

'Ah, not so romantic for you, is it? It has a fiery temper and you wouldn't ride it if it was in a temper, but it can be tamed by someone with special powers of gentleness and kindness.'

'I like that.'

'Amy,' you whispered, casting a spell, 'you mustn't let it near the ocean though because if it gets one tiny glimpse, it will charge as hard and as fast as it can to get to the sea. It will drown you if you don't jump off. You can't change its true nature. It would destroy you if you tried.' We were silent for a few moments. You had taken me into a dream land with your dark Irish folk tales. Your soothing voice and the rhythmic sounds of the rain had made me lose myself in your eyes as you continued. 'They are fierce creatures, fierce and unpredictable, so they are. There is a tale about a young woman befriending the horse spirit who had taken on the guise of a handsome young man. She befriended him and they were sitting in a meadow, his head on her lap and all was calm and still, until she looked down at his feet.'

'What did she see?' My heart was beating furiously. 'Bear, what did she see?'

'She saw the hooves of a horse sticking out from the end of his trousers.'

'Oh my God, that's terrifying,' I shuddered and you began to laugh at my reaction.

'I knew you'd like that one. Not the happy ending you thought was coming.'

'You're rotten, do you know that? She thought she'd met a handsome young man but he turned out to be a wolf in sheep's clothing.'

Your laughter stopped abruptly. 'No, a mad sea spirit horse in a man's clothing.' You then turned your face away from mine. 'Don't jump on its back, Amy Lee, if it glimpses what it longs for.'

'Bear ...'

'Shall we go walking in the rain? I don't mind getting wet, do you?'

'Bear, wait a second. Are you happy?'

'Come on, Amy, let's go.'

We dressed in the waterproofs hanging on the back of the kitchen door. Danny was playing the piano to your granny and singing. Patrick was reading and didn't even look up from his book and your granny was crocheting baby clothes for the poor in the village. She told us not to catch our deaths and to be back for tea.

We walked along a different path and you always said after that day, that fate and the little people had led you along it deliberately. The rain had eased a little but the earth was sodden and the rivers full and sparkling. You held my hand lightly and spoke little but your shoulders were relaxed and your eyes alight.

'There's an unknown track around here somewhere that leads to a lake called Muckross Lake.'

'That's not a very romantic name.'

'Everything has to be romantic for you, Amy Lee. I hope you stay that way when we're older.'

'I will, you know I will.'

'This way, it's not far. I want to take you somewhere magical where water sprites live.' When I laughed at you again, you laughed back at me. 'You don't believe me?'

'You and your water sprites and fairies, you're just like your granny.'

As we wandered on I heard water gushing over rocks and a spectacular waterfall suddenly appeared before us, as if out of nowhere. Cool spray touched our faces. The sight of the thunderous water tumbling furiously down into a calm, foamy pool below was mesmerising. The river it ran into was full from the recent storms and the flowers and bushes around us had delicate raindrops falling from every petal. It all looked and smelt so fresh and clear. I imagined the water sprites you spoke of dancing and swimming underneath it. The power of the water made me feel excited and expansive and I longed to feel it surging over my body.

'I can see why you call it magical,' I said, glancing at your profile. 'I want to swim in it. Am I allowed to?'

'It'll freeze your whole body, so it will. It's pure water from the mountains.'

'I don't care. I can jump in and swim right under the waterfall.'

'I knew you'd say that. I'm sure you could.'

'Can I jump in? Please, say I can.' You were laughing at me once more. 'Oh, Bear, can I?'

'Your eyes are sparkling, Amy Lee. I'm not going to stop you jumping in, but just be careful now.'

'I'm soaked from the rain anyway, so I might as well.'

'Do it then. But take off my favourite sweater first otherwise granny will be angry. She says it matches my eyes.'

'This is dark blue and your eyes are hazel green.'

'That's granny for you.'

I took off my waterproof jacket and my boots and socks. I was wearing cotton trousers and a cream blouse under your sweater and without thinking much about it, I took them all off too. I had no embarrassment in front of you because I knew you would avert your eyes. As I put my feet in the icy water I trembled with joy. The feel of it made me lift my face to the sky with pleasure. I slowly waded further in until the water was up to my neck.

'Bear, come in with me, it's lovely.'

'I'll be catching my death, so I will.'

'Oh come on, I'm not going any further without you and I want to swim under the waterfall and watch it from the other side.'

'And will you save me if my heart stops from the shock?'

'I'll always save you, you know that.'

You were smiling as you removed your clothes until you were down to your blue underpants. They resembled tiny shorts that ended half way down your thighs. Your body was slim but muscular for your years and I tried my best not to stare at you, without much luck.

'I'm not taking off anything else. I'll be struck down by granny's Mother of God.'

'Mother of God would admire your body,' I called to you.

'Amy, you'll be making me blush and you can't be saying things like that about our Lady.' You came towards me slowly, your shoulders hunched against the cold and your eyes closed. 'You'll be struck down by lightning, so you will.'

'I don't care about our Lady or your granny's Lady. Bear, I'll take everything off if you will.'

'No, no, you're too young to be doing that. When you're over eighteen you can do what you like. I won't stop you then, but you're still a child, Amy Lee, so you are and I have to look after you for your parents.'

'I'm not a child!'

'So you are, don't be daft now. You're a child until you reach eighteen, so be good now.'

I splashed water over your face and pulled you further in. You did the same to me and I screamed in delight as it took my breath away. 'You're always so sensible and so old-fashioned.'

'I know, I know, it's the strict Catholic in me, so it is.'

'Follow me then, I'm going underneath.'

The pureness of the mountain water felt like silk against my skin. I took a deep breath and swam down under the waterfall. The noise of it was thrilling and when I surfaced on the other side in a small recess, the beauty of the wall of white water was exhilarating. You surfaced thirty seconds later, your hair flat against your forehead, your eyes shining. It was the happiest I'd ever seen you. It was only then that I realised fully how often your eyes didn't shine.

You were holding my hand and squeezing it tightly, and I shouted to you, 'It's deafening.'

'Let's just listen to it, Amy. The power of it is overwhelming. It makes my heart sing.'

'Mine too, Bear.' We stood still and watched in silence. I was continually glancing at you because your face was animated with wonder as you enjoyed the power of nature. We quickly began to shiver uncontrollably. 'My legs are turning numb now.'

'Let's go back. You go first, Amy, I'll follow.'

When we climbed out of the pool, we attempted to wipe ourselves down with our jackets. My teeth were chattering and you told me to dress quickly to avoid getting a chill. We were both laughing at our foolishness and I felt, in that moment, that our intimacy had reached a new level.

'Let's do this every day, can we?'

'You'll kill me off, Amy Lee, so you will. I think you're a wicked fairy in disguise.'

'Do fairies walk on their hands or swim under waterfalls? They'd get their wings wet.'

'Fairies can do anything, but maybe you're a water sprite instead.'

'It's weird putting these clothes on when your bra and pants are still wet.'

'They'll dry soon enough, the summer air is warm.'

'Do you want your sweater back now?' You had stopped speaking suddenly and were looking beyond me. Your mouth was open as if you had seen a ghost or the Merrow that your granny was always talking about. 'Are you cold? I'm not, so you can have your sweater back, Bear.'

'Amy, stand still.'

'What?'

'Stand perfectly still, will you?'

'It can't be another bull here. What is it?' I followed your gaze to where a couple were wrapped in a loving embrace about a hundred yards away. The woman was slim and dark, the man much taller with a mass of silver hair. The woman had her back to us and was kissing the man's face feverishly. 'Who's that? Shall we go the other way?'

'Holy fuck!'

I was shocked because I had never heard you swear before. I didn't think you did and I was going to laugh at you and tell you off, but your body had stiffened and your face was grave. You pulled me down behind a gorse bush and said again, 'Holy fuck!'

My heart had begun pounding with excitement. You had your hand round my shoulders, pushing me gently further behind the bush. 'What's going on?' I whispered to you. I had no idea why we were hiding but I was enjoying every moment of being so close to you. 'Bear, what is it?'

'Look, over there, look!' I then saw the woman turn her face to one side and she brushed a tear away from her eyes. Your fingers were squeezing my shoulder hard. 'Stay down, Amy!'

'It's your mammy,' I gasped, although there was no need to state the obvious as you had recognised her immediately even from behind. 'What shall we do? Who *is* he?'

'She mustn't see us. She mustn't! Keep down for a minute. Let me think.' Neither of us could move. I could hear your shallow breathing above the sound of the water cascading over the rocks. You continued speaking very quietly. 'My mammy, look at her, she loves him.' In the time it took you to utter those few words your whole life changed. Your mammy was in the arms of another man. We had no idea then what this would mean to you. 'Look at how she's kissing him, Amy, how she's holding on to him.'

'I'm not sure we should be,' I replied, unsure of witnessing such an intimate moment between two people who had no idea they were being watched.

'This is where she comes every day when she goes walking. Sweet Jesus, no wonder she comes back with roses in her cheeks.'

I wanted to laugh at your comment and the absurdity of hiding beneath a gorse bush with our knees in the dirt. But one look at the confusion on your face stopped me. Your eyes were darting around from side to side, your mind working overtime and sweat appeared on your forehead and top lip. Since that day, I have often thought how quickly and irreversibly everything in your life altered. One minute of pure happiness, holding onto the hand of the girl who loved you deeply and watching nature display her strength and artistry, and the next, the profound and shocking realisation that your mammy loved another man. Luckily, we had no concept of what that meant for you at that moment.

'Who is he? Do you know him, Bear? Everyone around here seems to know everyone else.'

'I don't know. I almost recognise him but I'm not sure. There's something about him that looks familiar. How does she put up with my daddy's shenanigans and cruel ways when she loves another man like *that*?'

'Are you upset?' I was studying your face because I knew every expression that moved across it but I couldn't read it then. 'Bear, answer me, are you upset about this?'

'I don't know what I feel. Keep still, she's coming this way.'

Your mammy and the unknown man had hugged again, a long, heartfelt embrace and she then walked quickly away from him in our direction. We were crouching even lower, our faces together and some gorse scratched your cheek slightly. You didn't appear to feel it. I wasn't watching where your mammy had gone because I was looking closely at your frown and your troubled eyes. I felt increasingly apprehensive as to how your sensitive nature would react to this discovery.

We didn't move a muscle until she had passed by us a few feet away. We then watched as the unknown man dipped his hands in the clear pool of water and splashed his face with it. There was something in the way he moved that made me feel warm inside, like being near the dying embers of a fire. He was light footed, lithe and almost graceful.

Dark, menacing clouds began to form above our heads as we walked in silence back to the farm and they seemed to match your mood. There was a distant rumble and heavy rain once again swept towards us from the mountains. We didn't quicken our pace because you were so deep in thought, I honestly don't think you'd seen or heard any of it. I said your name a couple of times but you didn't reply. Once back at the farm we took off our waterproofs and went upstairs to my room. There was no sign of your mammy, only your granny who was dozing in her favourite chair and Patrick still reading.

'Bear,' I murmured, 'what are you thinking?' You shook your head slightly, still in a dream. 'What are you going to do?' You appeared perplexed by my question.

'I'm not going to do anything.'

'Will you ask her about it?'

'No, no, I won't embarrass her.'

'Are you upset? I don't want you to be upset.'

'There's something about him, Amy Lee. He's familiar to me, but then he's not.'

'I don't understand.'

'Me neither.' You sighed heavily. 'Come here by me, please. Is your underwear still wet? Take it off if you want to. I'll look the other way.'

'No, it's dry, don't worry.'

'Don't get chilled now. What a malarkey! Fate nudged us that way today, for sure.'

We climbed on my bed, lying together with our heads touching as we had so many times before. Your hair was still wet and plastered flat against your forehead so I ran my hand through it and moved it back. You did the same to me. I remember wishing then that I could get inside your head to help ease your anxiety and chase away any troubled thoughts. I would have crushed them in my hands, replacing them with serenity and peace of mind. If only I could have. If only I'd had that power.

'What shall we do tomorrow?' I asked you, hoping to halt your train of thought. But that train of thought wasn't to be derailed, it was moving too fast. Still, I tried again. 'Shall we go for another walk, a different way?'

'Did you see how she kissed him? Did you see how she loves him? Why does she stay with a man like my daddy? This man looks so much gentler, so he does. I need to think this through. I'm sorry you saw it. Don't think badly of her. She doesn't have it easy with my daddy.'

'I won't think badly of her. I don't, I promise.' You moved your body closer to mine and we held each other as tightly as we could. 'She did seem happy with him, didn't she?'

'Amy, perhaps mammy is trying to touch the sky.'

'What do you mean?'

"'Only from the heart can you touch the sky." Perhaps mammy is trying to touch the sky.'

'Rumi was a clever bastard.'

'Will you stop your swearing, Amy Lee?'

'Well, *you* said holy fuck! I've never heard you say that before.'

'I'm sorry you heard that, but it suited the occasion, so it did. It isn't every day you see something like that.'

We stayed in each other's arms until your granny called us all for tea. Tommy was at his girlfriend's house and Danny was out running. Patrick was just putting down his book when we sat down at the table and your mammy floated in as if she was on a cloud. She had changed her clothes and her hair was brushed neatly and fastened in a bun with a gold clip. I stole a glance at her face and she looked years younger than when in London. Her complexion was healthier and she had lost the constant worried frown. You couldn't look at her for the first few minutes until she began to talk about her walk that afternoon and how the thunder had frightened her.

'Did you walk far, Mammy?' you asked quietly.

'No, not that far, not that far, the weather was changeable, so it was and I hate the thunder, you know that.'

'It's the wrath of God, so it is,' granny added, shaking her head.

'It's your fault I'm afraid of the thunder. Amy, when I was a little girl, my mammy here told me God was angry at me when we had storms, or angry with her. Can you imagine?' Patrick signed something to you and you smothered a smile. Your mammy tapped his hand. 'What are you saying to Bear?'

'Nothing, Mammy, nothing of importance,' Patrick said quietly in his faltering, flat way.

You smiled faintly and explained. 'He's saying, Irish superstition will be the death of you.'

'You can mock,' granny scolded, wagging her finger at Patrick and shaking her head. 'Now, let's say grace, shall we?'

Your mammy and granny closed their eyes, but you were

studying your mammy closely. It was as if you couldn't comprehend that this woman afraid of thunder was the same person with her arms around a stranger, kissing him fervently with apparently no concern about who saw her. For the rest of that day I noticed you repeatedly studying her and frowning. You just could not reconcile the mother you thought you knew who fussed round your difficult father, with the actions of someone who looked like a young woman in the throes of a passionate love affair. But there was something else too.

You appeared to be trying to remember something, something just out of reach, something you *should* know. At about eight o'clock that evening when another electrical storm raged above us and your granny was crossing herself continually and praying to the statue of Mary above the fire, your expression changed. It was as if a veil had been lifted from your eyes and you asked me to go outside with you.

'Don't you be going out in this,' granny cried. 'Lord help us, the lightning will strike you down. That wind is blowing right off the sea and howling like a wild animal. It'll strike you down, Bear and wipe your brains out.'

Let them be,' your mammy told her crossly, 'they'll watch the storm from the barn, won't you? They're not nervous like us. They're young and fearless and leave his brain out of it.'

'Amy is fearless, but our Bear is sensible,' granny declared. 'Amy would run through the storm, she's a force of nature, so she is. This storm will take the roof off the barn. Someone has angered our God, so they have. You can mock, Marie Flynn! If the roof comes off the barn the boys will be mending it in the morning.'

You kissed her cheek. 'A storm like this makes me feel alive, Granny.'

'You'll be struck down. Then what use will your brains be to you then, Bear Flynn?'

'No use at all, Granny, but they'll never be any use to me.'

'Don't you be saying things like that! That's tempting fate too much.'

'Fate has already been tempted,' you replied as your mammy waved us away.

'Let them go if they want to. They can't go far without moonlight.'

'You're a terrible mother to say that to Bear, Marie Flynn, so you are.' She crossed herself twice and glanced at the statue of Mary. 'A terrible mother you are.'

'Well, that's as maybe but I won't have him terrified of storms like I am.'

'Ungrateful you are, Marie, ungrateful to your boots ...'

'Amy, come on, if you want to,' you said to me, interrupting your granny's flow.

You took my hand and we did indeed run to the old, disused barn with the corrugated roof on the other side of the yard. Forked lightning lit up the darkening sky in sudden, silver flashes. The wind was blowing like a gale and as it rushed through the trees behind the barn it made a sound like the roar of the ocean. Your eyes were alight as if it reached the depths of your soul. You kept hold of my hand as the rain came down in torrents. The ferocious wind was blowing over the buckets and plant pots in the backyard. When you began speaking I could hardly hear you.

'Amy, I think I was supposed to see my mammy today with that man. It was fate, so it was.'

'Why do you think that?'

'All my life I have looked at my daddy and thought, I wish you weren't my daddy. I wish I wasn't your son. I can see nothing of me in him, *nothing*! Tommy and Danny are like him in some ways. They can be rough around the edges and selfish. Patrick resembles him in looks, but not in nature, but me? I used to think I had been dropped into my family by a witch and that the witch had made a terrible mistake.'

'Bear, I don't understand.'

'Don't you see, Amy Lee? Think on him, that man today who loves my mammy so dearly. Who did he remind you of?'

I thought hard for a moment. The graceful way he moved, the way he turned his head, the way he bent down and splashed the water over his head and the way he took your mammy's face in his hands. The resemblance was extraordinary and I felt my heart quicken. 'You don't think …?'

'Sweet Jesus, all these years I've known something wasn't right. The way she fusses round *him* at home and caters to his every whim. It's her guilt, Amy, *her* guilt, not love. The way she is when she's here! She's so different, more carefree but slightly guarded at the same time, as if she's terrified someone will find out. Even my name! Where did that come from? Daddy hates it, he's *always* hated it. I once heard him say to her that only Nancy boys have a name like mine. That was said to hurt her and I never forgave him.'

'It's a horrible thing to say.'

'All this time, I've been tortured by the fact that I detest the man he is but that I shouldn't because he's my daddy and he provides for us and I have his blood in my veins. But he *isn't* my daddy, he isn't! I think that man by the waterfall is my daddy. That tall stranger with silver hair who holds my mammy so tenderly in his strong arms, *he* is my daddy.' I opened my mouth to answer you but no words came out. 'Can you see it, Amy? I could see myself in his every move.'

'Are you sure? What are you going to do?' I didn't think you'd heard me. You were looking up at the murderous sky, almost in a trance. 'Bear, what will you do?'

'My whole life is a lie. The man who is pushing me to go to Cambridge shouldn't be pushing me at all. What will I do? I have no idea. That stranger today, would he want me to go to university or would he just want me to be happy, as your parents want for you? I haven't a clue. How could I when I don't even know him? What's his name? What is he like? Have they been having this love affair since before I was born? Stupid question, they must have.

How long have they loved each other?' You paused for breath and put your hands over your face for a moment. 'Why did she marry my daddy? No, I can't call him that anymore. Why did she marry *him*? Why did she marry the selfish bastard who turns nasty and lecherous in drink and not the man with the silver hair and strong arms?'

'You'll have to ask her, Bear.'

'But then she'll know I know. If she wanted me to know surely she'd have told me.'

'But maybe she's ashamed.' Another crackle of lightning shot across the sky and again you didn't seem to hear me. 'It's quite a secret to keep, isn't it?'

'Does the man by the waterfall have the same black beast haunting him? Perhaps that's where it comes from.'

'What black beast? Who is haunting you? Don't say that, I'll fight it for you, I'll kill it. You know I will.' Your eyes softened then and you squeezed my hand even tighter. 'I will never let anyone or anything hurt you, Bear.'

'You'll save me, won't you, Amy Lee?'

'Yes, I'll always save you, but save you from what?'

'The beast that has threatened me, threatened me my whole life, for as long as I can remember. The beast I have inside me that I fight constantly. The beast that tries to get inside my head and haunt me every single morning when I first open my eyes, that beast! Does that come from the man at the waterfall? Is he who I get my love of learning from *and* my despairing thoughts?'

'Bear, let's run through the storm together, come on. It'll be fun and exciting.'

You didn't move. Your thoughts were still running amok in your brain. The heavy rain was lashing across granny's yard and beating against the back windows of the house. The thunder was still just overhead, loud and angry and I wondered what your granny was doing at that moment. When you spoke again, you spoke of nature.

'In spring and summer here nature sings to us and opens its arms. It's like the whole world is waking up, so it is. In autumn and winter it whispers and travels inwards to rest and renew. I feel like that right now. I feel I need to travel inward and make sense of what I saw.'

'Perhaps you're wrong though. Perhaps he's just her secret lover.'

You looked down at me with a frown, perplexed at my words. 'Did you see the way he moved? Who did it remind you of? Did you see his straight back and his shoulders and the way he leant down and touched the water so gently before splashing it on his face? I'm not wrong, Amy, I know it. It was almost like looking in a mirror, so it was. I have always looked at Zachary and wondered how the hell ...'

'Perhaps we can find out for sure. If we can't ask your mammy, maybe we can find out another way.'

'I have to know. I have to know for sure. We'll have to find him. He walked away towards the next village. There aren't many villages around here. We have to search for him, Amy.'

'We will, we will.'

'Jesus, I wonder if my granny knows.'

'Surely not ...'

'I'm not so sure. She has a quick brain and eyes that look right into your soul, especially when you're trying to hide something. She knows me inside and out, so she does. She says the little people tell her things. She knows many secrets, believe me.' You then turned your face away. 'She knows about me, so she does.' A huge clap of thunder exploded above us and made us both jump. 'We should go in, granny will be worried.'

'What does she know?' My heart had begun to pound, missing beats, and a feeling of anxiety crept through me. 'Bear, tell me, what does she know?'

'Never mind, never mind, we should go in. I'm getting chilled now and so are you. You need to sit by my granny's fire.'

'I'm not chilled.'

'You're shivering, I can feel it.'

'I'm not shivering from the cold. I'm shivering for you. I'm worried about you. I'm *always* worried about you.'

'I know you are. It isn't fair on you to always worry about me.' You touched my face where my freckles were and I instinctively moved closer to you. 'Your life shouldn't be about me and my complexities and troubles. I don't want that for you, I don't. I want you to be free and find a great love that will treasure you and give you what you need.'

I felt, in that moment, that my pounding heart had frozen and turned to a block of black ice. I imagined it like an enormous icicle that slowly began to crack and break. You had never mentioned me finding a great love before. In my head *you* had always been waiting at every bend in the road that led me to my future. In my frequent dreams about us, you were always holding my hand, walking in front of me, beckoning and smiling. Sometimes you only appeared fleetingly, but you were constantly by my side. There was no future without you, no life without you and no happiness.

'What do I need then? What do you *think* I need? I don't want or need a great love. I already have a great love. I have you, Bear.' You shook your head and tears filled your eyes. 'Bear, did you hear me? I have you!'

'You break my heart, Amy Lee. You break my heart with your devotion.'

'I don't want to break your heart.' My voice sounded like a strangled whisper. 'I just want you to be happy.'

You glanced across the yard where your brother Danny had appeared at the back door. He was gazing up at the lightning as it flashed above us. You turned to me and wiped your tears with the back of your hand.

'"The beauty you see in me is a reflection of you." Come on, let's go in. Tomorrow we'll search for my daddy, my *real* daddy, if that's what he is. Then I have to tell him who I am, don't you think?'

I nodded in encouragement and we dashed across the yard. A flash of forked lightning hit the tree behind us causing a loud crack like a whip and we heard your mammy scream in fear. It felt like a weird kind of omen. I silently hoped the nature spirits and angels you believed in would keep your delicate heart safe from any harm or rejection when you told the truth to the stranger your mammy loved.

# Chapter Three

*What do I long for?*
*Something that is felt in the night, but not seen in the day.*
*Rumi*

Looking at your face now, it is composed, despite the intervention of medical science and clothed in the trauma of trying to end your life. My eyes have always been reflected in your eyes, but what do I do now they are tightly closed and hidden from me? What do I see? I see a deep trench of despair because I can't hear your voice and the walls of that trench are so high I can't climb out.

Do you think I'll stop loving you because of this? I love you as you are because I don't know any other way. We spent so much time together, my body moved in the same rhythmical way yours did. We walked as one. We thought and felt as one too. That's the only reason I experienced your pain in my chest on the morning you decided oblivion was less painful than being here. I felt you moving away somewhere as your heart stopped beating.

How can that be, Bear? You believe in destiny and angels and nature spirits. Do you think it was destiny that brought us together on that first day at school, so I would save your precious life? I think it was and I hope it was too. Your soothing, smooth and gentle voice was so bold when you corrected our teacher. That was the moment, right there, no turning back.

'You want to be my friend, Amy Lee?'

But with you as you are now, I don't know how to reach you. I'm fighting so hard for you, Bear, so very hard. But you must fight too! Don't go to the next world without me. You are the only man I've ever loved, the only one who loves me as I am; the daft, noisy, scatty and energetic, Amy Lee. Promise me you are fighting in there. Promise me you'll stay. Promise me you are telling the other world they can't have you yet because Amy needs you more than they do.

Wake up, Bear! *Please*, just wake up!

The day after the lightning split the tree, the morning had started bright and warm with sunshine lighting up every corner of the farm. The fierce storm had left us with a fresh breeze whispering its secrets through the ash trees behind the back yard and across the wild meadows beyond. It had raged for most of the night, howling around us like a wolf in pain and the relentless rain had been beating at my windows.

When we ate our breakfast with the rest of your family, granny was looking over the table at you with her inquisitive eyes, almost as if she could read your thoughts. The sun pouring in from the back windows lit up your face and hair like a probing spotlight.

'What are you two doing today, Baby Bear?' she asked, fixing you with her steady gaze. 'Have you taken young Amy up onto the moor yet? Ah, Amy, I roamed those moors as a child and as a young girl, I can tell you. I was hardy and free and nothing could hurt me. Now my bones ache and the cold wind gets so far into my joints I reckon it'll finish me off one day, so it will.'

'You'll outlive us all, Granny,' Tommy muttered into his tea cup.

'Mary, Mother of God, I hope not!'

You reached across the table placing your hand on hers. 'Don't say that, Granny, please. You have years in you.'

'Of course she has.' Your mammy raised her eyebrows. 'Take no notice of her, it's all just said for attention.'

'Attention? I'll give you attention, Marie Flynn! I can feel the Mother of God calling to me at times.'

'What's she saying to you then?' Danny asked, laughing. 'Why does Mary call to you especially? Why doesn't she call to all of us?' Your mammy tapped the back of his hand with her knife. 'What's that for, Mammy? What have I said?'

'Don't you be rude to your granny, Daniel, show some respect.'

Your granny was crossing herself repeatedly but still reprimanded Daniel. 'Don't you be calling her by her name, Danny, she's Our Lady. She calls to me because I listen, because I believe, so she does. She won't be calling to you, Daniel Flynn, mocking as you do or you, Tommy Flynn with your fly-by-night ways, sneaking out of the house like bold Jack Leary to visit Janie O' Flannigan when her daddy's not at home. Anyone out after midnight is up to no good. You'll get the reputation of being a ne'er do well, so you will.'

'I don't sneak anywhere,' Tommy declared, indignantly, 'and I don't go to her house when her daddy's not at home.' He lowered his voice so your granny couldn't hear him and turned to Danny. 'I don't have to. We meet in the hay loft. It's much more fun.'

'Don't you be speaking like that at the table,' your mammy said sternly. 'It's not respectful.'

'Mammy, ignore him,' you told her, kindly. Patrick must have signed something along the same lines because she smiled benignly at both of you and her displeasure was gone in an instant.

You then looked across the table. 'Granny, to answer your

question, I *will* take Amy on the moor and show her how beautiful it is and where you spent most of your childhood, but we have to go somewhere else too.'

'Amy, look out for the King of the Birds and the grouse and you'll hear the skylarks singing and maybe a curlew, so you will.' Granny gazed wistfully out of the window behind you. 'I wish I was there now. How I wish I was there. I never thought I'd be this old. Make the most of being young, Baby Bear, it won't come again.'

Danny's mouth turned down in distaste. 'Granny, you're giving me the maunge this morning, all this reminiscing and talk of being too old. You have years in you. You're as strong as an ox.'

Tommy laughed and added, 'If all the crossing yourself and praying to the Mother of God doesn't wear you out first.' When your mammy scowled at him again, he sighed. 'What's wrong with you, Mammy? What have I said now?'

'I've already told you, Tommy.'

'Yeah, I know.'

'You have a bloom in your cheeks, Marie,' granny said, smiling to herself. 'Are you sickening for something?'

'No, I'm not sickening, it's the fresh air.'

'Well, you're out for long enough,' your granny commented. 'I sometimes wonder if you have a fancy man.'

Your mammy immediately looked slightly uncomfortable, but recovered her composure in a split second. Danny and Tommy both threw their heads back and roared with laughter with their mouths wide open, as if the thought of your mammy having a lover was beyond them.

You dropped your head slightly but I noticed Patrick staring at you. He then knocked the table twice to get your attention and signed something so quickly nobody else caught it. You shook your head and frowned at him. Your mammy was looking up at the ceiling and lied perfectly.

'A fancy man, she says, my sainted aunt! Who would want me

after giving birth to four boys? A fancy man, she says! Where would I be finding a fancy man in these parts?'

Granny narrowed her eyes. 'Well, you're my daughter, so you are and you just look so much happier when you've been here a few days. I suppose London sucks all the life out of you.'

'Or our daddy does,' Danny muttered into his hand. He received a whack around the ear from Tommy for his comment and a scowl from your mammy. 'I know, we aren't allowed to say that but it's true.'

I felt the tension around the breakfast table pick up like a sudden wind off the ocean and it crackled like a fire. You snuck a look at your mammy's face. It was completely blank. She was obviously used to keeping secrets because there was no hint of embarrassment or concern at that point.

'Your mother has four sons!' your granny retorted. 'That's enough to suck the life out of anyone, especially you two, but not my darling Patrick or you, Baby Bear. You two have been sent by our Lord to keep your mammy sane and comforted in her old age.'

'Well, I'm glad it isn't me who has the job of keeping you sane, Mammy,' Tommy said bluntly.

You stood up. 'Have you finished your coffee, Amy? Shall we take our walk?'

'Yes, I'm ready,' I replied eagerly, longing to get out in the fresh air and be alone with you, however much I liked listening to the harmless banter between your family. I knew instinctively that you felt uneasy by the mention of a fancy man, even though your mammy had only reacted for a split second and seemed to take it in her stride.

Your granny gestured towards the kitchen. 'Take the ham I've put aside for you and the bread and butter. If you stay out all day you'll need a picnic. You need fattening up, Bear Flynn, so you do and there's a flask too.'

You bent down to kiss her gently on the top of her head. 'Thank you. You'll be spoiling me, Granny.'

'You're worth it, Baby Bear and so is Patrick. Not like these other two scallywags. I'll take the hairbrush to your legs you two, so I will.'

Tommy and Danny just laughed at her and you then said something in Patrick's ear that sounded as if you were offering for him to join us. He just shook his head and indicated he was going to read a book. We escaped into the back yard after you had picked up the food from the kitchen and put it in your rucksack. Then, slinging it over your shoulder, you took my hand. 'I think my granny suspects something, don't you?'

'I'm not sure she does. I think she was just fishing.'

'Patrick knows.'

'What does he know? What did he sign to you?'

'When granny mentioned a fancy man, Patrick signed that he lives in the next village, by the church. Patrick is very observant, he's had to be. I couldn't believe nobody else saw him, but they're not as quick at understanding his sign language as I am. Tommy and Danny could never be bothered to learn it. They said he should speak like the rest of us and granny doesn't understand it at all. It was just a good job mammy wasn't looking up at that point because she's picked it up over the years.'

'She didn't react at all.'

'There was a slight flicker in her eyes. She's been hiding it for so long she must be very practiced at not reacting. Lying well is an art, Amy, so it is.'

We wandered out of the farm and into the lane that led to the narrow, overgrown footpath across the fields. The corn was high and waving gently in one great mass and the swallows were swooping and playing above us. The air smelt sweet and fresh and the silence seemed to relax you because you lifted your face to the sun. You were still holding my hand and I felt ridiculously happy and content in a way I never had before. We shared the secret of your daddy being a stranger with silver hair and it had brought us even closer, if that was possible. I wanted to stay like that for the rest of my life, just you and me and the rawness and purity of the Irish air with no Ben from the upper-sixth looming large in my mind and no aggressive Zachary to put relentless pressure on you.

You turned to me, your eyes troubled. 'Let's go up on the moor first, Amy Lee. I can clear my head and decide what I'm going to do about my mammy loving another man. I need to accept the truth of it and let it settle into my bones.'

We walked quickly for a couple of miles and you pointed out some of the fresh water springs flowing at speed down from the hills. They were turning the ground marshy and wet with delicate, bright green ferns growing beside them. There were lowland meadows with masses of colourful wild flowers and the mauve heather spread into the far distance like a vast ocean. The air became even clearer the higher we went as a keen wind picked up suddenly and the sun went behind the clouds. It became much cooler and you were immediately concerned I was feeling the cold. You took off your dark blue sweater and urged me to put it on again. It smelt of you and my heart quickened with delight.

'Are you warm enough now, Amy Lee?' You tipped your head to one side to study me. 'You know, it kind of suits you.'

'Can I keep it?'

'Your eyes are smiling, so they are. Yeah, you can keep it.'

'I'll never take it off, Bear, never till I die.'

'That's a long time to have something. You'll get plenty of other gifts in your life, so you will and some expensive ones too no doubt, like jewellery and perfume from all your admirers. You'll prefer those to my old sweater.'

'I won't! I really won't. I'm not having other admirers anyway. I've got you and you'll do for me.' You looked away then and gazed across the rolling hills. 'What are you thinking, Bear?'

'Amy, I'm thinking we're so young. You can't know what you'll want or need in fifteen years' time or even ten years' time. People change, you'll see.'

'I won't change,' I declared, with as much force as I could without sounding angry.

'"You were born with wings. Why prefer to crawl through life?"'

I didn't understand what you meant then. But I knew who had said it and in my young, teenage brain I felt fear creeping insidiously through my body. I suspected you were trying to warn me that someday you might not be enough for me. Bear, you were *always* enough. 'Rumi was a clever bastard, wasn't he?'

'He surely was.'

'I'm not going to crawl through life. I *will* fly, but you'll always be there to catch me and if you aren't there, I won't fly or climb at all.'

'Amy, you *will* be able to fly and climb without me. You can do anything you want to. I might drag you down one day. Loving me might be much harder than you think. Remember, bears can be ferocious underneath all that soft fur.'

'You will never drag me down! Don't say that. It's easy loving you, so easy.' I had begun to feel increasingly frustrated with you. 'Come on, let's run through the heather. I bet you can't catch me.' I took off at speed because I needed to clear my head of the tortuous thoughts of living without you. 'Catch me, come on.'

The heather was rough and coarse and the earth sodden and like a bog, but I was so quick and athletic, I flew over the boggy patches with you running hard behind me. I did a cartwheel and some handstands and jumped over a trickling stream. I felt completely free and spirited but I wasn't only running ahead of you. I was running *away* from you and the fear of not always having you close behind me. You were calling to me and the wind took your words spiralling up into the changing skies.

'I give up, Amy Lee. Let me catch you, I'm puffed, so I am. You're so quick. Let me catch up.'

I stood perfectly still and held my arms out wide. 'You can catch me if you like. I won't run from you.' You had walked towards me, breathing hard, your expression a mixture of excitement and concern. You took hold of my hands and I looked up at you. 'Are you okay, Bear? You look frightened.'

'Amy, I'm fearful of meeting him.'

'I know you are.'

'I keep telling myself that I could wait a while, pluck up some courage. But the longer I wait ...'

'I'll be with you.'

'Amy Lee, you're my Guardian Angel, so you are.'

'I always will be,' I said, my heart pounding furiously because you were absentmindedly running your thumbs on the back of my hands.

The sound of a man whistling and calling his dog reached us and he gave us a cheerful wave. I wondered what his life was like and where he lived. Did he hold secrets in his heart? I waved back, but you were staring up at the sky in a dream.

'"Beyond what we wish and what we fear may happen, we have another life, as clear and free as a mountain stream." Rumi knew, Amy. He knew about love and fear.'

'Does that mean we're going to find him?'

'Yes,' you replied softly, 'we are. I just hope he wants to know me.'

'Oh, Bear! How could he not want to know you? At the moment, he has no idea how empty his life is without you in it. But he will, he will.'

We walked away from the top of the moor hand in hand with the morning sun flickering on our faces as it played hide and seek behind the clouds. I could feel your tension moving into my body. I was sure the silver-haired stranger would love you instantly and I felt alive with eager anticipation. This was going to change your life. This was going to rid you of the heavy cloak of anxiety you always wore, that wrapped itself tightly around your shoulders and restricted your life so badly. I had no doubt he would take you in his muscular arms when you told him your name.

'My son,' he would whisper as he held you, 'my beloved son.'

We made our way towards the waterfall and round the deep pool of water where we had witnessed the embrace of two people so obviously in love. Once again I experienced a rush of delight as the water surged over the rocks and the cool spray hit my face. I was remembering your slim, muscular legs as you stood by the water in your underpants. A brutal and fierce sense of longing had rushed through me and taken me by surprise. The moment you'd turned and bent down to throw your shirt away from the edge of the pool, my hunger for you had been overwhelming.

We wandered along the muddy river bank and then a little further on around the edge of some wheat fields. After making our way along another narrow public footpath overgrown with prickly bushes, the next village came into view. It was a tiny, forgotten looking place with the church steeple as the focal point. It all looked abandoned and unloved with broken fences and gates and whitewashed, thatched stone cottages.

'Not many people walk this way, do they, Bear?'

'No, it looks like a secret pathway. Perhaps it's only used by lovers who don't want to be seen.'

'How romantic,' I whispered and I knew you hadn't heard me because you didn't reply with your usual teasing about me liking everything to be romantic.

Tension was building in you slowly. I could see it across your shoulders as you moved ahead of me. I could see it because I knew every inch of your body. I had gazed at it long enough with a heady mixture of desire and love.

When we arrived at the village, there was a single shop with a large black and white dog lying in front of it, squinting up at the sun. You were walking towards the quaint little chapel where weather beaten gravestones were leaning over at odd angles as if craving the light trickling through the trees branches. Long, thin grasses grew between them, hiding some of the inscriptions from view. It felt as if the people beneath them had been long gone and easily forgotten. A couple of people called out to us and waved cheerfully and one old woman even knew your name. She looked similar to your granny, bent over and arthritic with a heavily lined face and white hair pulled back in a clip. Beyond the church was a small, flat fronted pub whose sign was swinging gently in the summer breeze and creaking loudly.

You were frowning hard and looking into the far distance when I asked, 'Shall we go in the pub? Publicans always seem to know everyone. Bear, did you hear me? Shall we go in the pub?'

'We're too young, so we are and don't forget we don't even know his name. We can't ask for a man with silver hair, they'll probably all have silver hair at his age. This looks like a place where everyone will be elderly. Let's just sit in the churchyard, it looks so peaceful. My mind is racing to so many places. I need to sit and think, so I do.'

You sat on a wrought iron bench by some lemon and pink roses and closed your eyes. I stood a few feet away reading some of the worn names on the graves. It was a tranquil place and soothing for the nerves but I had never felt at ease in graveyards.

'I find churchyards a bit chilling,' I called to you, shivering for effect.

'Do you, Amy? I find them comforting,' you replied, looking a little lost.

'Don't say that,' I scolded, feeling the anxiety that had always rippled through me whenever you spoke like that.

'Imagine all their worries, all the pain, all the despair they ever felt quieted forever.' I sat next to you and took hold of your hand as you murmured, 'Peace, Amy Lee, peace.'

'Is that how you see life?'

'Not when I'm with you, I don't. But often when my daddy, or who I *thought* was my daddy, is breathing down my neck to be the hero of the family, I can see life as a battle. It's a battle I'm not sure I can fight.'

Tears stung my eyes at your words. 'Don't say that, I'll fight it for you. *Bear*, did you hear me?'

You tried to smile but your eyes looked impossibly sad. 'It's not your job to fight it, Amy. I won't let you.' I was just about to argue and tell you it *was* my job, my role in life, when you suddenly gasped. 'Angels of Mercy, there he is.'

The stranger with the silver hair and broad shoulders was walking into the chapel. He was wearing old, dark brown cord trousers and a white shirt with the sleeves rolled up. You clutched at my hand. One of your feet was tapping the ground as if you couldn't keep it still. Even in those few moments as we watched him, I was astounded at how he walked like you.

I whispered, 'What shall we do? Shall we follow him?' I don't know why I whispered this because in truth the stranger couldn't possibly have heard me but a whisper suited the occasion.

'Yes, come on. We'll pretend we're looking round the church. Amy, my heart is beating mighty fast, so it is. I'm not sure I can go through with this.'

'You can, Bear! I'm with you, come on.'

The chapel was cool and smelt of wet stone and dusty books. The wooden font at the back had an angel at the side of it with large, open wings. The stained glass windows were deep red, yellow and blue and there were candles flickering in the many recesses. The few wooden pews had tatty, claret coloured cushions on them and every seat had a Bible in front of it, many with rough, well used and torn covers.

We were half hidden behind the font and the stranger was sitting in the front just under the raised pulpit. He had his head down, as if in prayer and one bare arm resting on the end of the pew. We watched as he occasionally glanced up at the altar a few feet away. Then he'd drop his head again. This was repeated several times. To me, his body language denoted a deeply religious man, talking directly to his God.

You were trembling slightly. I could feel it. I longed to throw my arms around you. I wanted to assure you all would be fine. This attractive looking man would be overjoyed to learn who you were and give you the unconditional paternal love you craved. I didn't though because, in truth, I had no idea how he would react and I was terrified by that thought. I pulled you down a little to whisper in your ear.

'Shall we go talk to him?' You shook your head. 'Are we just going to stand here then?'

'What do we say? I can't just blurt it out.'

'I'll go, shall I?' I went to move away, but you grabbed my arm and I tried to reassure you. 'Bear, don't worry, please. I know what I'm doing.'

'Amy, don't give anything away yet. I'm not ready.'

Your vulnerability was pulling my heart out of my chest and making me ache all over. I felt so protective of you I could hardly keep still. My pulse was beating in my temples and I was left wondering whether that was dangerous. Would I die before I spoke to the silver-haired stranger? I felt as if I might. You would have to give me the kiss of life and bring me back and with that thought my pulse quickened even more.

I slowly made my way up the aisle and away from you. My light footsteps were silent on the stone flags. It was as if everything else in the church moved backwards and became blurred at the edges. I could see him and only him. You were flesh of his flesh, bone of his bones, and his blood was moving through your veins.

The stranger half turned to glance at me as I sat in the opposite pew, but then dropped his head again after giving me a quick, welcoming smile. In those few, fleeting seconds, I saw you in his hazel eyes and I felt an overpowering sympathy for your mammy.

Words were struggling up my throat, fighting their way out. I felt sweat forming on my top lip. Eventually I summoned all the courage I had, for you. I needed to be able to tell you I had actually heard him speak and what his voice sounded like. I had to find out if he had the same inflections in his speech or maybe mannerisms identical to yours. I couldn't possibly have walked back down that aisle where I knew you were waiting in the shadows holding your breath and told you nothing.

'I don't mean to disturb you, but it's a beautiful little church, isn't it?' He looked up and gave another half smile. He had a kind face and a gentle manner. There was a tremor in my voice that I felt he would hear. 'I really love it.'

'For sure, it is.'

'Do you live here? It's a lovely place to live. I'm from London so it's very different.'

'You're a long way from home then.' His accent was very strong, like your granny's. His voice was soft with the same tenderness yours had. There was no harshness at all, very different from Zachary. It almost had a lyrical quality. He then asked, 'Are you on holiday?'

'Yes, a long holiday, on a farm near here.'

His direct and watchful gaze was very reminiscent of yours when I first met you, Bear. 'And do you like Ireland?' he asked, as if he truly cared whether I did or not.

'Yes, I love it and I love the people too. I won't want to go back to London.'

'I'm very happy to hear that. We like to think we're hospitable to strangers here. What's your name?'

'Amy Lee.'

'Well, I'm very pleased to meet your acquaintance, Amy Lee.' In that moment, as he said my full name, the resemblance was undeniable. 'When I was very young, many years ago, I thought perhaps I'd be a priest, but God had other plans for me.' He gazed up at the altar and ran one hand through his thick hair. 'All the years that have passed since then, where did they go? How the time flies when you're not taking notice. Your life rushes by and suddenly you're older and wiser. Well, maybe not wiser, not all the time.' He acted in such an open, welcoming way, I felt moved to ask him the next question bubbling up inside me.

'What other plans did God have for you?'

'I think He knew I wasn't suited for it very early on. I was a farm labourer for a while, but it didn't satisfy me, or I felt it didn't. I wanted to be a teacher. I loved book learning so much, so I did that for years, in Dublin, but I'm home now. You don't always know what you want when you're so young. I still come most days to pray. I feel the need to be close to God at times.'

'What do you speak to God about? I've never spoken to God really.' He looked at me fondly, just like you do when I'm being daft and funny but I have no idea that I am. 'Sorry, if you don't mind me asking you that.'

'I don't mind you asking at all. I ask Him to keep someone safe for me until we can be together one day.' I heard him sigh as he looked up at Jesus on the cross. 'It isn't much to ask for, but it's important to me and comes from my heart.'

'I'd better go. I don't want to disturb your prayers. It was lovely to meet you.'

'And lovely to meet you too and you weren't disturbing me at all.'

As I passed him, his bare arm was still resting on the edge of the pew. It was a muscular, tanned arm with silver hairs and I caught sight of a tattoo. I managed, in that second, to recognise the Harp of Erin in faded, blue ink and two names either side of it. Your mammy's name and yours too, Bear. It made me catch my breath.

I had only just passed him when he jumped up and offered his hand. It was as if he had suddenly decided that he hadn't been polite enough. His hand was warm and strong, but he shook mine very gently.

'You mind how you go now and I hope our changeable weather is kind to you while you're here, Amy Lee. Ireland in the sunshine is a beautiful sight, so it is.' He momentarily glanced past me to where you were still half hidden. 'Your friend is waiting for you.'

In that second, I almost told him. I don't know how I didn't. I almost told him because he smelt like you. Nobody has ever smelt like you, before or since, only him. It was that unique smell that I loved so much, the unique smell I would know anywhere in a crowded room with hundreds of people in it and the smell that clung to your sweater when I put it on and made my stomach turn over with pleasure. I walked towards you trembling uncontrollably because he had no idea his son, whose name was tattooed for eternity on his arm, was only a few feet away.

We took one last look at him, with his head bowed again and you grabbed my hand and pulled me towards the door. I went to speak once we were outside but you shook your head. 'Wait! Wait until we are away from here,' you urged me and we ran towards the open countryside again like two little field mice searching for safety.

The sky had darkened a little and a fresher breeze had picked up. We walked quickly back through the thorny footpath where gorse scratched our faces and along the bank of the full, almost overflowing river. The water was bright and lively as it tumbled away from the waterfall and the spray once again felt cooling and refreshing as it hit my burning face. You were perspiring, but your skin was a little paler than usual from emotion and anxiety. I repeatedly said your name, but you couldn't speak and continued pulling me along behind you.

We climbed to the top of the moorland where you let go of my hand and sank to your knees, your hands covering your face. I knelt in front of you and kissed your hands repeatedly. Your turmoil at that point was immense and all I wanted was to take it from you and ease your pain.

'Bear, what is it? What is it? I spoke to him, did you see me? He has your name tattooed on his forearm, so he can see it every single day. He knows about you. He must love you to have your name where he can look at it whenever he wants to. Look at me *please*, Bear.'

You let me pull your hands away and you appeared so agitated and disturbed, it was as if you had reached a point of no return emotionally. You leant towards me and shook your head quickly.

'I feel my mind is in chaos, Amy. What was he like? I just need one word from you, just one.'

'What word do you need? I'll say it for you.'

'Gentle, the word is, gentle. Dear God, let him be gentle. *Was* he gentle? Tell me he was, Amy Lee.'

I threw my arms around you. 'Yes, yes, he was. He was *very* gentle, Bear. You'd like him, I know you would. You look so alike, so *very* alike.' We both began to cry and clung to each other as if we were weathering a mighty storm on top of that moor. You were sobbing, catching your breath. 'There's no need to cry. Everything is fine.'

'He's not cruel then, he's not harsh and masculine like all the men full of drink who leave the pub. He doesn't smell of booze that drips out of his pores and disgusts everyone who comes anywhere near him. He wouldn't force you to do something you have no desire to do. He wouldn't reject you if he knew your true nature. He'd love you unconditionally, even then.'

'He doesn't smell of booze, no. He smells like you, Bear. He talks like you and he's polite and kind like you. Honestly, he does smell like you. I promise.' You began to laugh through your tears and I sighed. 'What's so funny *now*?'

'Don't be daft, how can he smell like me, Amy Lee? What do I smell like then?'

'I don't know, you just smell like *you*. He has such kind eyes and a lovely smile.'

'Did they love each other forever, Amy, do you think? I have to know. Shall I ask my mammy or him? There are so many questions.'

'I don't know, but I reckon he'd be less embarrassed by your questions than your mammy would. He's more approachable somehow than your mammy. Bear, I'm so happy for you that he has your name on his arm. I think he prays for you every day.'

You looked into my eyes and tenderly wiped away the tears from my cheeks. 'How do you know that?'

'I asked what he prays for. He said he prays for God to keep someone safe.' You were staring at me with such fire in your eyes, I felt as if I would burst into flames. 'He must mean you, he *must*!'

'You're so brave, Amy Lee, so you are. Talking to him like that, so bold, so courageous, my Guardian Angel.'

I moved forward to kiss you. It was such an intimate moment, both on our knees in the dirt, the only two people in the world who knew your story. We were the keeper of each other's hearts and lives, but as my lips brushed yours, you froze. I felt it and you knew I had felt it. The look of pain in your eyes was raw and as deep as the lake nearby and you grabbed my shoulders hard and pushed me backwards into the heather. To feel the weight of your body on mine was an exquisite moment I can never forget. You kissed my face feverishly and ran your hands through my hair, but you couldn't look at me. Your eyes were closed and you repeatedly turned your face away when I said your name.

'Bear, what's wrong? Something is wrong, what is it?' You tried to pull away but I wouldn't let you. I wrapped my arms tightly round your chest and my legs around your legs. 'Don't go, please stay.' Your face was inches from mine.

'I can't, I'm sorry, Amy, but I can't. This isn't right, it just isn't right.'

'It's right for me! Why isn't it right for you? I love you, you know that. I'll always love you. I won't *ever* stop loving you, you know that, Bear. I'm old enough for this, aren't I?' You were struggling and trying to take hold of my arms. 'Don't you love me?'

'Amy, you have to let me go. Loosen your arms, please. I can't do this.'

'Say you don't love me then.'

Your hot tears dropped onto my face. They mingled together

with mine, indistinguishable and merging like two spring streams that flow separately but inevitably end up as one.

You pushed my hair away from my face saying agitatedly, 'You know I can't say that. You know I can't. You know you hold my heart in your hands. But I can't be who you want me to be.'

'I just want you to be *you*.'

'You don't because you don't know who I am. Remember, bears look soft and sweet but they're ferocious underneath.'

'Don't keep saying that, you *aren't* ferocious underneath. I know you aren't.' I was now sobbing uncontrollably.

'Oh sweet Jesus, don't cry, Amy. You'll break me, so you will.'

'You can't fool me, I know you inside and out. I know your true nature.'

'But you don't, you *don't*!'

You managed to struggle free and jumped up, leaving me with my face in the coarse heather. You dusted the dirt off your clothes and began to stride away, but the sound of my sobs stopped you in your tracks. You ran back, bent down and took my hands, pulling me up to face you. You wiped my tears away gently as we stared at each other, both breathing hard, our hair awry.

Bear, I wanted to scream at you. I wanted to punch your chest. I wanted to hate you. But I could do none of it when you said you were sorry for hurting me.

'Amy, I'm so sorry. Please believe me when I say I love you, more than my life. I'll love you to the death and beyond. Maybe one day I can give you what you want, but I can't right now. I don't know who I am. I don't know if I want to be who I *think* I am. My life is in chaos. I don't fit anywhere. If we love each other we're going to have to love each other despite everything.'

'I will, I *do*.'

'Will you? Will you really though?'

'You know I will.'

'But you're so young. So many men will love you in the future.'

'They won't if I won't let them and I won't!'

'Let them. *Please* let them. They might be worthy of you. They'll make you happier than I will.'

'No! I don't want anybody else and they could never make me happier. They can all fuck off in the future!'

'You can't be swearing like that, it's not right. You can't be saying *that* word!'

You were so shocked I wanted to laugh. 'I'll swear if I want to,' I said petulantly, even though I had never used that word before and haven't since either. 'Well, *you* said, holy fuck! So I can swear too.'

The corners of your mouth began to twitch because I could always make you laugh. 'Is that so, Amy Lee?' You rubbed your hands over your eyes and seemed emotionally exhausted. 'I can't be fighting like this with you, especially not today and I'm not sure you can be serious with your hair looking like the haystacks on the next farm. Forgive me then. Please forgive me for not being the person you want me to be.'

'You *are* the person I want you to be. One day you'll believe me when I say I don't care who you are or who you *think* you are. I just love *all* of you.'

Your face then, you're beautiful, expressive face with the watchful, hazel eyes always focused on me, was full of confusion and distress. How selfish I'd been that day, Bear. How selfish to cause that heated argument just after you had watched, shaking in the shadows, as I spoke to the silver-haired stranger. All because you didn't return my clumsy kiss when I felt you should have. You still apologised, even though you had done nothing wrong. You never did. You never have.

'Forgive me then, Amy.'

'I do forgive you. What does Rumi think about forgiveness?'

'He says, "start your life over. Everyone is totally forgiven, no matter what."'

'He was right, Bear. I'd forgive you, no matter what.' You were stroking my cheek carefully with your fingertips. 'Forgive me too.'

'There's nothing to forgive, Amy Lee. You're perfect, so you are.'

'Rumi was such a clever bastard. He knew everything, didn't he?'

Your little high-pitched laugh was a comforting sound after the emotional storm we had just passed through. 'Thank you for having the courage to speak to him. I have to decide what I'm going to do and I will, I *will*.'

'I know you will.'

'Shall we go sit somewhere quiet for a while? I can't go back to the farm yet. Look at the sun moving across the mountains. It's like a golden flame, so it is. That's where the angels and the little people live. Amy, let's fly towards a secret sky.'

I heard you but my mind hadn't taken it in. I was distracted by remembering the feeling of your body on top of mine for the first time. I knew the memory of it would stay with me for the rest of my life. It was a memory that would sustain me when all else was in turmoil and you were thousands of miles away. I had no idea that even then your black beast was in danger of overwhelming your whole life and that one day it would bring you to your knees.

# Chapter Four

*This is how I would die into the love I have for you,*
*as pieces of cloud dissolve into sunlight.*
**Rumi**

That night we had sat around your granny's small, tiled hearth as Danny played the piano and sang to us. She was explaining to me that her favourite song was written especially for her and sung to her many times by your grandfather, especially when he had drunk a few too many.

'I'll take you home again, Kathleen,' she cried, clapping her hands. 'Play it for me, Daniel, you know I love it.'

'It wasn't written for her,' Tommy whispered to me, 'but she says it was, so we indulge her. It's better that way. You're on a hiding to nothing arguing with my granny.'

There was a little fire burning in the grate because some evenings, when the wind turned and blew straight down from the mountains, it was too cold for your granny's bones and she would sit warming her rough, gnarled hands by it. Danny began singing and the golden light from the flames flickered across her wistful face. Her sadness, remembering your grandfather's love, was difficult to watch that night because I was imagining my life without you in it. All the songs were about separation and the desperate longing for that separation to end.

'Why are they all so tragic?' I asked Danny. 'Can you play something light-hearted and happy?'

You had laughed quietly, glancing at me fondly. 'Daniel, there has to be a happy ending. There can't be any tragedy or longing or despair for Amy.'

'There was no happiness in Ireland in the old days and these are songs from that era passed down to each generation,' Daniel informed me, quietly amused at my forlorn face. 'It was all about famine and desolation and how people left to get jobs to send money back to their loved ones.'

'The potato famine, so it was,' granny chipped in. 'How about, "I'll be sitting on the stile, Mary." Play that for me, Daniel. My mammy used to sing that outside the pub.'

Tommy was smothering a laugh. 'Now we really are going back into the dark ages, aren't we? Jesus, I'll be slitting my wrists at this rate.'

Patrick was watching you, Bear, watching you carefully and a couple of times he knocked the hard cover of the book in front of him to catch your attention and quickly signed to you. You just shook your head.

I continually glanced across at you but you were lost in your thoughts for much of the evening. You repeatedly studied your mammy's face. She appeared relaxed enough to me and I was trying to imagine how her affair with the silver-haired man had started and how long they had loved each other. Had they grown up together like us? Did he originally reject her and had she married your daddy on the rebound and regretted it ever since?

So many questions and no answers yet. I had my doubts you would ever be brave enough to find out because you feared rejection. You excused yourself early from the family gathering, kissed your granny and mammy lovingly and beckoned to me to follow you. At the top of the stairs, outside your room, in the darkness, you hugged me tightly. Those hugs made my stomach turn over with delight.

'Tomorrow, Amy Lee,' you said into my hair. 'Tomorrow we'll go find him and tell him my name. That's all we'll do. He can decide what he wants to tell me. Yes, tomorrow it must be.'

I felt you tremble and was frightened for you. 'Are you sure? We can wait a few days if you like. We aren't going home yet.'

'No, it has to be tomorrow or I'll chicken out, so I will.'

'If that's what you want.' You pulled back from me and looked into my eyes. It was almost as if you were trying to find something. 'Why are you looking at me like that, Bear? *Is* it what you want?'

'Yes, it *is* what I want. I need to sleep now. I need to shut off the voices in my head. See you in the morning.'

'See you in the morning.' I reluctantly left your arms and walked up the hallway towards my room, but you called my name. Without the lights on, your face was covered in darkness. 'What's wrong?'

'I hope I'm not a disappointment to him, Amy.'

'Bear, you never could be.' The fact you even felt that for a second broke my

heart.

We rose early to an overcast morning, with a mass of grey cloud covering the farm. To avoid the family breakfast time we grabbed some soda bread your granny had made the night before; you buttered it and we both ate it quickly, washed down with some hot coffee. Your granny was up already but dozing by the heavy, black range in the kitchen. She didn't stir because we were as quiet as the creatures that ran around the yard at night, avoiding the watchful barn owl.

It was raining heavily and the mountains were shrouded in a low, dense mist. It seemed to reflect your sombre mood. You hardly spoke but it was a comfortable silence. We didn't need words. Holding your hand tightly then was enough for me. More would come, I told myself repeatedly. More would come when we were old enough to handle the strength and power of our love. It was just too soon for you and you were concerned for me and my immaturity.

You had always been an old soul. I was still like a wild horse, stampeding through life with my hair flying behind me, energetic, strong and free. You were quieter, more introspective with a future as bright as the flames in your granny's fire. Whether it was a future you actually desired was another matter but I knew whatever you did, whatever you decided to do, I would trail behind, adoring you.

We were up on the wild, deserted moor again. The weather that day made them more desolate. I was wondering when we would make our way down towards the winding lanes and overgrown pathway that led to the village where the stranger lived. You were gazing towards the distant hills, your wet hair flat against your head and I watched as you wrestled with your emotions.

'Do you know why we're out here so early, Amy Lee?'

'I thought perhaps you needed to clear your head without your brothers around.'

'No, their chatter doesn't bother me. I love them all, especially Patrick, even though we aren't at all alike. I wanted to get up here before my mammy got out of bed. I didn't want to lie to her if she asked where we were going today. I know I'll have to lie later, but I couldn't face it this morning. I thought maybe, after talking to him, it might be easier. I'm just summoning some courage now.' You looked up at the low cloud and your lips were moving as if muttering a prayer. Then, inclining your head towards me you said, 'What a soft day it is, soft and warm even though the rain and mist is cooling me. I want to feel the earth on my skin and the heather in my hair again.'

We laid on our backs with our faces to the sky and feeling the mauve heather underneath us, springier and softer because of the weather. With the wind breathing through it, it sounded like urgent whispers. It was all I could hear, apart from the skylarks, until you began speaking softly, your voice full of its own urgency.

'Water sprites, fairies and little people, help me, help me, *please*. Angels of Mercy fly over me when I tell the stranger my name. Bear Flynn, is who I am, Bear Flynn to the death and beyond.'

'Bear, stop talking about death, will you?'

'It's just an Irish phrase, so it is. But I'm not Bear Flynn, am I?'

You then turned onto your stomach and rubbed your face in the wet earth. I turned over too and watched as you raised your arms over your head and clutched at the heather so tightly your knuckles went white. You then turned your face and looked at me, your forehead, nose and mouth covered in the dark soil.

'What are you doing? You can't meet your real daddy like that! He'll think you're mad.' Your eyes held a dreamy quality, almost as if you weren't in the here and now but somewhere else entirely.

'There's such beauty and peace in nature, so there is. I wish I could just sink into it, be a part of it, mingle with this rich earth and disappear for a while. I'd let it seep into my flesh and my bones. I want to stay here in Ireland and live simply, live nobly in tune with nature. I'd fly into the burning sunsets and to the end of beautiful rainbows.' You touched my face with your fingertips. 'My dear, sweet, Amy Lee, have I done a terrible thing letting you love me like you do? Is it selfish to be the keeper of your heart and resign you to a life in that kind of prison?'

'It's my decision to love you. I can't stop loving you now.'

'Why stay in prison when the door is wide open? Walk through if you want to, walk away.'

'I can't, you know that. It's too late for me.'

'Then stay, Amy. "Close your eyes. Fall in love, stay there."'

'I will.'

'Will you, even when it gets tough? And it *will* get tough.'

'Why does it have to get tough?' You didn't answer so I asked if you were happy. I often asked you that but you avoided the question every time. 'Bear, please tell me you're happy, just once.'

'Happy?' you whispered, almost as if you didn't understand the word at all. You jumped up, brushing the dirt from your face and clothes and I did the same. You then reached for my hand. 'Let's go meet my daddy, Amy Lee.'

We strolled towards the waterfall and along the river bank and I was watching the jaunty birds darting in and out of the hedgerows. There were masses of blackberries growing there but not yet ripe enough to pick and colourful butterflies resting on all the wild flowers opening their wings hoping to catch any sun. Some of the flowers in the deserted lanes were shaped like stars and there were masses of watercress and honeysuckle with white elderflowers nestling in between them.

I had been trying to distract myself from how hard you were clutching my hand. You looked pale and your teeth were clenched. I began to wonder if this meeting was a sensible idea and whether I should stop and beg you to turn back. But once the steeple of the church came into view, it was as if we were at the top of a roller coaster waiting to plunge downwards. You began talking quickly, your nervousness causing a slight stutter every now and then.

'Did he say he came here to pray every day, Amy? He did, didn't he? Does he really pray about me? Where shall we wait? We're drenched already and you may get too cold in the church. I don't want you to get a chill. Granny will tell me off, so she will. Where shall we wait for him? What time is the early mass? It'll be the lazy man's mass soon. Do they have regular mass here? It's such a tiny church. Yes, they must do, it is Ireland after all.'

'I'm not cold at all, Bear. It's lovely and warm out here.'

'It's a soft day, so it is.'

'Let's wait on the bench again, shall we? The scent of the roses is so lovely and we can see everyone coming and going from here.'

'Yes, yes, we'll wait there.'

You sat beside me, jumpy and agitated, your foot continually tapping on the ground again. An elderly man shuffled out of the church with a walking stick. He occasionally stopped and gently tapped a headstone, as if he knew everyone buried there and he was greeting them silently. Then a young woman hurried out, carrying a baby wrapped in a shawl, glancing around her furtively.

'Confession,' you said quietly, as though you had to explain the comings and goings to me.

We waited almost an hour and the rain cleared as the dark clouds flew away into the waiting skies. Hot sun began beating down on our heads. You lifted your face, as you always did and took deep breaths to calm yourself. I was completely content just to sit with you in silence. I could have done it for hours.

I spotted him before you did, walking quickly and purposefully up the lane towards us. This time he was wearing a green mackintosh over the same cord trousers and white shirt. He walked like you, Bear, his long legs striding out and his back straight. His hair was thick, slightly wavy and such a lovely silver colour rather than grey and I wondered momentarily if your hair would be like his when you were older.

'Bear, he's here, he's here.'

'Angel of Mercy and daoine maithe, give me courage.'

'What does that mean?'

'It's just Irish for the little people, so it is.'

'Are you ready?' You nodded and stood up. 'Hold my hand then.'

As you stood up, you urged, 'Stay close, Amy Lee. I need your strength.'

The musty, dank smell hit me again as we crept in behind the font. The stranger was in the same place, his head bowed once more but the closing of a door somewhere drew our attention away from him for a moment. A priest was walking towards us, with long, dark robes down to his feet. He was elderly and smiled at us in a fatherly way.

'Good morning, children,' he said softly. I said nothing but you replied politely.

'Good morning, Father.'

'Have you come for quiet prayer? Please feel free to pray.'

This time you said nothing and I spoke for you, my voice quite bold. 'Yes, we have, we will and just to take a look if that's alright. We're from London so ...'

'Please do. I would show you around and tell you some of the history but I have to visit a very ill old lady in the village and give her sacrament.' He then turned to you and frowned a little. 'I didn't detect a London accent in your few words, young man.'

'No, Father, I grew up just outside Dublin, but we moved to London a few years ago.'

'Ah, yes, good, good, that was quite a change for you then. Now I must get on. Enjoy your time in this church. Say your prayers and make the most of the silence here. Goodbye and God bless you both.' We both thanked him and you sighed as he wandered out of the heavy, oak door.

'I couldn't say I was coming here to pray if I wasn't, not to a priest.'

'I know, I know. Will I be struck down for telling fibs to him?'

You didn't answer because you were looking over to where the stranger continued to sit quite motionless, his head still bowed. He had taken off his coat and his sleeves were rolled up again.

'Amy, he's still there. I wonder if he *is* praying for me. I'll go up and you follow, but stay behind a little, will you?'

'Bear, good luck. Only do what you feel is right.'

'My heart is beating mighty hard, so it is. I'm surprised you can't hear it.'

I laid my hand on your chest for a second and gave you the most encouraging smile I could muster. You walked slowly up the aisle and I could hear your light footsteps on the flagstones. My heart was pounding too and I could see you had your fists clenched tightly. You stood beside him looking up at the altar and he turned his head slightly because he had heard you approaching. In *my* head I was urging you to say something to him, *anything*, but you appeared to have been struck dumb. I began muttering to myself.

'Bear, talk to him, just talk to him.'

I heard his first words to you quite clearly.

'Can I help you, son?' His deep but mellow voice made me feel warm inside, as if he were already a friend. 'Have you come to pray? If so, don't mind me. I'll move away and give you some space. This is a peaceful and soothing place if you need it to be.'

Did he detect your anguish in those first few seconds? Had he immediately recognised a troubled soul who needed tranquillity in his life? I always hoped so and I believe he had because he continued to look at your face as if he could feel some of your distress. I only just heard your reply.

'I've not come to pray, sir. I'm very sorry if I'm disturbing you though.'

'You aren't disturbing me. I come here every morning. It's a lovely church, don't you think?'

'It surely is.'

I had inadvertently moved a little nearer to you both. I could sense the tension in your body and I wondered if he could too. Very intuitive people can sense the distress in other people almost as if it is solid matter in front of their eyes. He caught sight of me standing just a few feet away.

'Ah, hello again, Amy,' he called, giving me a genuine smile. 'Good to see you back here and you brought a friend with you.'

'You remembered my name.'

'Of course.' He smiled at me and his weathered face wrinkled like screwed up paper. His smile was unmistakably yours and I felt an indescribable urge to creep towards him and feel his arms around me. 'Where did you two meet? You have a local accent, young man, but I believe you are a Londoner.'

'I lived in Dublin mostly, but I go to school with Amy in England.'

I wondered if something would click with the man on hearing that news. I detected a slight frown and an indefinable alteration in the atmosphere, as if he was trying to work something out. The tattoo was exposed and you appeared to be mesmerised by it because you weren't looking at his face at all. What a peculiar feeling it must have evoked in you. There was your mammy's name and yours too forever cut in the flesh of a strange man's forearm. The blue ink, dark still and not faded, reminding him every day of a son he didn't know.

He had a rugged quality to him, broad shouldered and athletic but with a casual elegance. He was the kind of man you could lean on if in trouble, the kind of man who would hold you up, support you and soothe your nerves.

In my head I was screaming at you to engage with him more. I noticed your hands were shaking slightly and I wondered if he had noticed too. You must have heard me somehow because you started to speak and your voice was bolder, more definite.

'Do you know this church well, sir? Can you show me around very quickly, if you have a few minutes?'

'It would be a pleasure, son.'

With that reply your stiff shoulders relaxed a little and you turned to me. 'Will you stay here, Amy? We won't be long.' I fully understood that you wanted to be alone with him for a few precious moments, to hear him speak, to watch his expressions, to take in his intelligence and innate gentleness.

You wandered up towards the altar, side by side, the resemblance from the back quite startling. It was the way you stood, your erect stance, your fingers interlinked behind your backs. You had often done that when deep in thought and he did it too. It was all so obvious to me and I was left wondering how *he* couldn't see it. He was pointing out memorial plaques on the walls and the stained glass window at the back where Mary was weeping at the foot of the cross. You were watching him, his mannerisms and his expressions and listening to the way he spoke. I knew you were taking it all in, holding it all in your heart. This man you didn't know, whose existence had been kept from you your whole life, the silver-haired stranger who wasn't really a stranger at all.

I could read your thoughts because I knew you so well. You were wondering what your life would have been like if you'd had this softly spoken man with the gentle manner as your father. How different would it have been without the constant tension in the house and the relentless expectations? Would your mammy have been less anxious and guarded? Would she have radiated happiness and joy instead of being so subservient all the time, tortured by her Catholic guilt? If you had been under this man's care would you have to fight the black beast every day? Or maybe this man had the black beast inside him too and could advise you how to deal with it.

You walked towards me after a few precious minutes, side by side and you appeared a little more relaxed, but in your eyes I could see a steeliness and determination I had never seen before. I knew immediately you were going to tell him your name.

He smiled at us both. 'Well, good to talk to you both. I might see you again, I hope.'

'Thank you for the tour, sir.'

'Not at all, son, it was a pleasure.' He offered his hand and you took it readily. 'I'm Nathan Carroll by the way, but my friends call me Wolf. It's a strange nickname but it kind of suits me.'

'Yes, wolves are complex and highly intelligent creatures, devoted to their family, so they are.' As you said those words, my pride in your knowledge was full to the brim. 'They take care of the injured in their group and educate their young.'

'You are right, son, they do.' He appeared moved by your description. 'I'm retired so I have plenty of time to chat with people and, as I said, it's been wonderful chatting with you two. I might see you again.'

You were still holding his hand. It was as if you didn't want to let it go because the feel of it gave you strength. 'I have an equally strange name, sir, but mine isn't a nickname. It's my real name, so it is. I'm Bear Flynn. My middle name is Nathan.'

The man seemed too shocked to speak and he blanched a little as his eyes took in your face and your body. He blinked rapidly a few times. He appeared to stagger backwards slightly, but you hung onto him and steadied him by taking hold of his arm with your other hand.

He whispered, 'I'm so sorry, I just felt a little light headed then. I must need to eat.'

The atmosphere was on fire and I was getting burnt by it.

He went on, 'That *is* an unusual name to have. But why be the same as everyone else? Unusual is a fine place to be.'

You let go of him, reluctantly I felt. 'My mother wouldn't ever tell me why she named me so.'

'She must have had a good reason.' He touched your arm lightly and his eyes softened. 'You've had no bullying at school because of it?'

I jumped in and answered for you, declaring proudly, 'Bear would never get bullied. Everyone wants to be his friend.'

You smiled shyly, slightly embarrassed by my words. 'I'm not so sure about that, Amy. But thank you for saying it.'

'Yes, they do! But if anyone did try to bully him, I would see them off pretty quick! They wouldn't get near him again, I promise you.'

His eyes were darting from your face to mine and he gave me a broad smile. 'So you're his protector, his angel. I'm glad, I'm glad you are. Everyone needs someone in their life like that.' There was an awkward silence for a moment and he glanced down at the stone aisle beneath us as if he was struggling to find the right words. He then fixed his eyes on you. 'Whatever you do in life, make sure it's what you want, Bear Flynn. The same goes for you, young Amy.' Still staring at you, unblinking and direct, he began to whisper, '"The mass of men lead lives of quiet desperation ..."'

'"... and go to the grave with the song still in them."'

He smiled quizzically at you. 'You know his work then?'
'Yes.'

You both appeared delighted and there was an instant connection. The electric current running between you was so heavily charged I could have reached forward and touched it.

'Is that Rumi?' I asked, looking up at you.

'No, Thoreau, a philosopher.' You took my hand gently.

'Why do they always have to talk about death, Bear?'

'It's part of life, Amy Lee, so it is. It's just a phrase anyway.'

He had been watching our gentle banter. 'It's been lovely to speak with you. I'll let you both get on and explore. Perhaps I'll see you again before you go home. I do hope so.'

'This *is* my home, sir. It's in my blood and in my heart to the death …'

'And beyond,' he added, quietly. He then glanced up at the altar, his eyes shining and whispered, 'You answered my prayers.'

'One day I'll come back here, when my education is done and I'll take over my granny's old farm. That's my wish, my *song*, so it is. Before that I have to make everyone proud.' You turned to me and squeezed my hand. 'Let's go, Amy Lee, I have a lot to think about.'

'There's a sacred chord between you two,' he said suddenly, as we turned to leave. 'Don't let anyone break it.'

I knew he had felt our deep connection and I was intensely and strangely grateful that he had.

As we walked down the aisle away from him, you repeated his name over and over again. 'Wolf! Wolf! Wolf!' That's all you said on the long walk back despite my asking you a couple of questions.

Back at the farm everyone was out, except your granny. She was in the kitchen listening to an old radio that looked as ancient as she was. We went straight upstairs into my room and sat on the bed side by side. The weather had changed once again and the strong white sun had disappeared. Rain was sweeping across the yard and lashing against the windows. You eventually spoke.

'Amy, it was like looking in a mirror, but not only like looking in a mirror.'

'How do you mean?'

'I don't know, it was just a feeling, a feeling of being near someone who thinks like you, who has the same emotions inside him and loves the same things. I can't call Zachary my daddy anymore. I'm nothing like him. Wolf is my daddy. I didn't want to leave his side. I wanted to stay with him. When I said my name I could feel his love. I could actually feel it. I've never felt anything as strong before, except from you.'

'Did I make a fool of myself thinking he was quoting Rumi? I'm sorry if I did.'

'Don't be saying that, Amy Lee, of course you didn't make a fool of yourself.'

'Do you think he'll tell your mammy he met you?'

'No.'

'Are you going to tell her?'

'No.'

'Why?'

'She'll tell me if she wants to. If he wants to get to know me, he can tell her he saw me and ask her if he can meet me again, don't you think?'

'I don't know. I don't want you to be disappointed.'

'He thinks like me. He thinks like *me*.' You lay back on the bed and curled up in a ball on your side. I did the same and moved as close to you as I could, hugging your back and stroking your hair. You said nothing more and we stayed like that until your granny called us down for lunch.

We had only one more week left in Ireland because September was looming. The sun took on a more hazy quality at the end of August and the early morning air was considerably cooler. There were some stunning sunsets where the sky caught fire and the evening air smelt different.

You didn't speak of Wolf again. It was as if it was *your* secret and yours alone. You were holding it very close to your heart. I was left wondering whether it was safe there or whether it was eating away at you bit by bit and that you would end up in torment and pain. If Wolf didn't pursue your relationship further, would it catch hold of you like a grief without a death? Would meeting him but not *knowing* him cause you heartache and distress? Knowing you as I did, I suspected it would but I had no idea then how long it would take for that distress to manifest itself in your life.

The day before we left for London, your mammy was quiet and distracted. It was obvious she was dreading our departure because she would be leaving behind the man she loved. I saw you studying her every day after meeting Wolf, watching for any sign that he had told her about meeting you. There didn't appear to be any. Your granny had been repeatedly shaking her head and sighing at your mammy's forlorn face on our last evening tea around the table together.

'Marie Flynn, you look like the death's head at the feast, so you do.'

'Ah, I love that expression,' Danny declared, laughing hard. 'What exactly *is* a death's head and why would it be at a feast? You talk in such a funny way, Granny.'

'I know what I mean, so does herself. So that's an end to it.'

Your mammy sighed. 'I just always feel sad when we go back to London, that's all.'

You and Patrick glanced at each other briefly. Your granny was frowning and kept her direct and intense gaze on your mammy's face. I thought she might comment further but Tommy diverted her attention for a moment by jumping up and excusing himself.

'I'm off out.'

Your mammy pointed at him. 'Tell your young lady you can't stay out late, Tommy, we are up and away early tomorrow.'

You watched Tommy leave before turning to your mammy. 'Are you going out for a stroll this evening, Mammy? You normally do.' Your question was so loaded with meaning I was surprised she didn't hear it in your voice.

'Yes, Bear, I'll take a walk in the evening sun. I love the late summer weather. I'll miss my walks when I'm in London, so I will.'

You turned your gaze to me, asking, 'Amy, shall we go to the waterfall for one last soaking? Or shall we go up on the moor and watch the sun going down behind the mountains?'

'The moor is wonderful on a night like this,' your mammy commented hurriedly.

Quite innocently I asked her, 'Are you going to the waterfall?' As soon as the words left my mouth, I realised that she wouldn't want us going anywhere near Wolf's village if she was going that way.

'I do go that way, yes,' she replied, sounding slightly concerned. 'It's a beautiful walk.'

You were looking straight at her once more. 'Shall we come with you, Mammy?' When she gave a little gasp, you added, 'What's wrong? I thought you'd like us with you.'

'Good Lord, no!'

Your granny gave a croaky laugh. 'She won't want you with her. Is it your Anam Cara you're meeting, Marie Flynn?'

'Don't be ridiculous!'

I had asked what she meant as I always lost the thread of the conversation when you all used words and names I didn't know. You had to translate when we were on our own, do you remember, Bear?

'I'll tell you later, Amy. Let's go up on the moor one last time and watch the sun go down, shall we? Mammy doesn't want us with her.'

Your mammy showed no relief at your words, but said only, 'Don't be too late now, early birds catch the worms.'

'We'll be home before you, Mammy. You'll be late, I've no doubt.'

Was there something in your voice then that made her frown? I thought so because she was staring hard at you as we left the room. 'Bear,' I whispered as we put on our jackets in the hall, 'she was watching you as if she knew.'

'She doesn't *know*, but she might suspect. I think he might tell her tonight, that he's met me.'

'Why do you think that?'

'Because we're going home tomorrow and there's no time for us to meet again, that's why I think that, Amy.' The distress in your eyes was difficult to witness. 'If he'd wanted to meet me properly it would have happened before now.'

It was a still evening on the top of the moor, warm and balmy. It was as if nature had saved her richest display just for us on our last time there. The sky was ablaze with a deep orange glow as it stretched into the distant countryside. I heard a cuckoo and its song appeared almost plaintive that evening because our holiday was over. The mountains appeared to be shimmering under the sunset and I watched you struggling to make sense of your life, your family and your past. It wasn't easy for you. Your fragile nature was taking a battering already.

I had no concept of how Wolf didn't feel a burning desire to get to know you intimately. How could he not, Bear? I couldn't understand it. Everyone who had ever known you longed to be close to you. Your gentle, unforced charisma, your soft voice and kind, watchful eyes were all an addictive force that drew people in, inch by inch and moment by moment. The fact that you were completely unaware of it had made it even more compelling. We sat together in the soft heather and after a long silence you turned to me.

'You are my Anam Cara, Amy Lee, so you are.'

'What does it mean then?'

'Soul friend is a correct translation.'

'I like that,' I whispered, leaning against you. 'I hope I always will be.'

'But for them it's not quite accurate, is it? *They* are lovers, so they are, we saw that and I'm living proof that they've been lovers for a long time. It can be translated as soul lovers or soul mates too, I believe.'

'I like that too.'

'I hope you'll always be my Anam Cara.'

I wondered which Anam Cara he meant but said, 'I will be, you know that.'

'You're so young ...'

'What does that matter? I won't change, you know I won't.'

'I could fly into that sunset and be with the angels.'

'Is that what you want to do?'

'Sometimes I do, when it's as beautiful as it is tonight. I could just disappear into its flames and forget about all the drama of my mother's secret life and all the expectations weighing me down. Perhaps that would silence the black beast.'

'Bear, don't go there again. Don't fly off anywhere. I've *told* you, I'll fight the black beast for you.'

'You can't, Amy, he's in *my* head not yours. I thought perhaps Wolf would have the black beast too. I thought maybe he'd tell me how to fight it. But he won't because he doesn't want to know me.'

'I'm sure he *does*. It's just a pretty strange situation. Are you very disappointed in him?'

'Not in him, no, I don't think so. Well, maybe a little, but I could feel his love for me. I suppose I'm disappointed in my mammy for keeping this from me my whole life when she knows how much I dislike Zachary.'

'Does she know that then?'

'Does she know I dislike him? Oh yes, she does.'

'I'm so sorry, Bear.' I touched your face with my fingertips. 'I'm so sorry.'

'I know you are, Amy Lee.' You took my fingers from your face and kissed them softly. 'Anam Cara, to the death and beyond, so you are.'

I had no idea why what happened next happened just then, except to say that it was such an intensely intimate moment at a time when you were probably the most vulnerable I had ever seen you. We put our foreheads together and moved backwards into the heather. Slowly, without any embarrassment or reticence, we took our clothes off. Lying naked together with our arms around each other was blissful for me as the gentle, late summer breeze that evening stroked my skin. Our noses were touching as you spoke.

'Is this enough for you, Amy Lee?'

I couldn't answer at first because as soon as I felt your skin touch mine, my heart ached and broke apart with wanting you. But its pieces, shattering more each moment, then began moving slowly back together again to make it whole once more. For me, it wasn't ever about what *I* wanted, it was only ever about you.

'It's enough, Bear. *You* are enough.'

I felt your taut muscles relax immediately and you whispered, '"Close your eyes. Fall in love, stay there."' Nothing could touch us. Nothing could harm us. Nobody would ever be able to take away that moment. I asked what you were thinking and you answered in your usual way by quoting your favourite poet. '"When you feel a peaceful joy, that's when you are near truth."'

'Rumi was a clever bastard,' I said, smiling and you laughed that distinctive high pitched laugh that was so you.

This was my truth, *our* truth, but I was still longing to hear you say you were happy in any given moment. You never did. You were whispering into my hair.

'I hope it will always be enough, when you're a little older I mean.'

'Will we ever ...?'

You quickly put your hand across my mouth. My thoughts were careering towards Ben in the upper-sixth and your rough kiss on Dominique Fraser's mouth. I pulled your hand away and told you I was sorry.

'Can you feel that soft wind on your back, Amy? Can you feel it on your legs and your shoulders? If only life could always be like this, softness and gentleness and silence with us here together. My anxiety would fade away then.'

'It can be, it *will* be.'

'I wonder what my mammy and Wolf are doing now. Do you think they're in each other's arms?'

Before I could stifle it, I laughed inappropriately.

'Why are you laughing?'

'I bet they are, but not like this.'

You understood my comment and you smiled tolerantly. 'You're terrible, Amy Lee, so you are. They're old enough to withstand the force of their love. They can cope with disappointment and struggle and a long distance love affair. My mammy is strong enough to climb into a bed with a man she doesn't even like, let alone love, every single night. I couldn't do that and you are too young to know your own mind yet.'

I felt indignant at your words. 'No, I'm not! I'm really not,' I declared as forcefully as I could. You hugged me even tighter and I imagined the feeling of ecstasy then would carry me through every disappointment I might feel in the future.

You looked at the sky. 'We should go back, the sun is going down. We'll be covered in darkness soon.'

'Not yet, not yet.'

'There'll be other moments.'

'There might not, not like this at any rate.'

Dusk had fallen silently and stealthily without us being aware that it had. There was just one thin strip of light turquoise and pink above the mountains that looked like a sparkling jewel.

'We had better go, Amy, you'll get cold.' We stood up and I did my best not to stare at your perfect body, but my best was not good enough. You picked up your shirt and quickly put it on. It came down almost to your knees but when you turned your back to me and bent over to pick up the rest of your clothes your nakedness filled me with a burning longing to touch you. I don't know if you sensed it but you urged me, 'Amy, get dressed now, you'll catch a chill, so you will.'

'Nobody will ever have a bum like yours, Bear, nobody! I mean it.'

You looked momentarily embarrassed. 'Stop that, Amy Lee. You'll be making me blush.'

I started to laugh and you couldn't help but join in. I was secretly delighted that my words had halted the chain of difficult thoughts churning in your head about Wolf and your mammy. I was hoping they would help me forget the feel of your skin against mine because I had no idea when it would happen again or indeed if it ever would.

'Bear, can we just ...?'

'Amy, I ...'

I then made an absurd and ridiculously ill advised lurch towards you, flinging my arms around your waist and then sliding my hand downwards towards your backside. It was so soft, but I could feel the tight muscles underneath. I looked up at your face, hoping your expression would be one of relaxation, pleasure or even desire. But your mouth was firmly closed and from what I could see in your eyes through the dim, pink evening glow, I was unsure whether you were feeling pleasure or pain. You took hold of my hand roughly.

'Amy, don't!'

'Bear, can I just ...?'

'No!' You jumped away from me as if I had electrocuted you. 'Now get your clothes on.'

I wanted to cry, to shout at you, to punch you because it was all too much for my immature emotions and childish way of thinking. But one glance at your anguished face stopped me. You were right of course, Bear. We *were* too young emotionally and you had enough to deal with in your life at that moment. You were struggling with the knowledge that the man who had made you knew who you were, but hadn't asked to see you again. You knew you were travelling back to London to be under Zachary's iron will when you wanted the softly spoken and gentle Wolf to be the father under whose roof you lived.

I had expected, even hoped that my lunge would have produced an overpowering sexual urge in you but I had simply just added to your misery and anguish by pushing you to do something you knew neither of us was ready for. I didn't cry though, I didn't shout, I didn't punch you in the chest, I simply muttered an apology that you kindly accepted by kissing my cheek. You muttered an apology too.

'Did I lead you on? I only wanted to be comforted by someone who loves me. I wanted you to hold me because *he* never will. Let's go back, London tomorrow.'

'You didn't lead me on,' I muttered. 'I know my own mind. It was wonderful, Bear.'

'I *am* trying, Amy Lee. I am trying so hard to be who you want and what you want.'

I opened my mouth to reassure you that you *were* who and what I wanted even then, but you had begun dressing quickly and I felt it was the end of the conversation for you. Once we were fully clothed again, you put your arm around my shoulder and we walked all the way back to the farm like that. I welcomed the gentle pressure of your fingers against my arm but I couldn't shake the memory of touching you.

When we got back to the farm on that last evening, Tommy was out with his girlfriend and your mammy hadn't come home yet. Danny played yet another Irish ballad and your granny sang it before asking me, 'Do you like this song, Amy? It's called "She Moved Through the Fair." Ah, I love it, I do. It's about a man losing something he cares about deeply.'

You glanced at me and there was a faint smile on your lips but a deep frown across your forehead and such sadness in your eyes. Were you thinking about us, Bear? Were you thinking about our future and anxious about whether you would lose me at some point when I found out the truth? There was a feeling of melancholy in the air; the melancholy felt like separation and longing and regrets.

I was constantly distracted by your thoughts. You continually glanced at the door looking more and more dejected. You were secretly hoping Wolf would be with your mammy when she returned, longing to speak to you. By eleven, when she came home alone, you looked over at Patrick and both shook your heads. Your mammy appeared flushed; the top of her cheeks resembled two little red balls and her hair was windswept and loose past her shoulders. She looked the happiest and most fulfilled I had ever seen her and I couldn't take my eyes off her.

Your granny cried, 'Mother of God, Marie, you look like Bridget Cleary, so you do.'

'Who's Bridget Cleary?' Danny asked, laughing at your granny's indignant face and he received an abrupt reply.

'She was the last witch, who turned into a changeling and don't you mock, Daniel Flynn, she existed, so she did.'

Your mammy ignored your granny's superstition. 'I'm off to bed, it's an early start boys, so don't keep your granny up.'

Patrick knocked on the table and signed quickly to you. Your mammy caught his eye. 'What are you saying to Bear, Patrick?'

Patrick gave one of his shy smiles and looked a little embarrassed, so you spoke for him. '"She loved him so much she concealed his name in many phrases, the inner meanings known only to her."'

When I heard what you translated, I was so proud you had said it out loud and I held my breath for her response but it was Danny who reacted.

'Rumi,' he cried, striking a chord once on the piano, 'it's always and only ever Rumi for my baby brother.'

Patrick shook his head and I guessed he hadn't signed that at all. It was you, Bear, who decided to let your mammy think that you knew.

As she left the room to go to her bed, your mammy said sharply, 'I have no idea what that Rumi is talking about most of the time.'

The next morning, with early sunlight flooding through the kitchen, your granny kissed us all goodbye. Nobody knew then that it was the last time you would all be together and I had always thought that a blessing because it was difficult enough for her. When she bid you farewell, she took your face in her bony hands and tears ran down her weather-beaten, aged face.

'You'll be back here one day, Baby Bear and this will all be yours.' You hugged her tiny frame with as much tenderness as you could. 'All yours, my darling, troubled boy, don't forget now.'

'What about the others? It's not really fair on them, Granny.'

'They don't want it, but you do. You'll need it too. Don't forget to stand at my grave and tell me you'll look after the old place.' She turned to me, placing her hands on my arms. 'Amy, please remind him to stand at my grave and I'll rest in peace in the arms of Our Lady.'

'I will, I promise.'

The two taxis arrived to take us to the airport. We sped through the countryside taking us away from the farm, the waterfall and the narrow, overgrown lanes full of wild flowers. I felt your sadness at leaving it all, Bear. We were in one car with Patrick, behind the taxi where your mammy was sitting with Tommy and Danny. The moor in the distance, an ocean of wild, mauve heather made me recall our intimacy and my stomach turned over with that delicious memory. The hot, white sun was sending shafts of light across the mountains, lighting them up with magic.

You tapped me on my hand before pointing out the window. 'Look at the fairies dancing, Amy Lee. Can you see them?' When I told you that I could, you took hold of my hand, linking your fingers through mine and squeezing gently. 'The fairies and the nature sprites are keeping us safe for our travels, so they are. I'll miss it all so much. Every time I leave is like a grief.'

While you had been saying those words, our taxi had slowed right down because of some stray sheep on the road. A man with silver hair standing at the side of the road caught my attention. As we passed him, he raised his hand in a farewell gesture, the deep sadness on his face quite plain to see. I had no idea if your mammy had seen him but I doubted it. From where I was sitting, I could just about make out that she was looking straight ahead of her.

You had been looking in the opposite direction towards the moors but you turned your head just in time as I cried, 'Bear, look, it's him!'

Your smile, so delighted, so warm, as you watched him out of the back window as we slowly moved further and further away, must have captured his heart. You raised your hand in exactly the same way.

'He came to say goodbye,' you whispered, almost in disbelief. 'Amy, he came to say goodbye.'

## CHAPTER FIVE

*Your heart knows the way,*
*Run in that direction.*
***Rumi***

THE NEXT TWO YEARS AT SCHOOL HAD BEEN CRAMMED with studying, for you and anyone else who wanted to go to university, but not for me, obviously. After school we would escape to the silence of my bedroom and I helped you every evening with your work by testing you. Those days were very precious and carved deeply into my heart. Your memory was phenomenal and I was often left speechless by how many passages from books you could instantly recall and quote.

When testing you on Chaucer or Shakespeare, I would turn my nose up and ask you, 'Bear, what does all that actually *mean*?'

'You're funny, Amy Lee, so you are.'

'But what's the point of Chaucer? It sounds like a load of old cobblers to me. I don't understand one word, honestly I don't.'

'It's in rhyming couplets and it is difficult to understand

because he kind of twists his sentences around. He's considered one of the greatest poets in the English language, so he is.'

'I'm glad you understand it.'

'And I'm glad you aren't studying it, otherwise ... '

'Oh I'd fail,' I declared. Every time we had a similar conversation we would both end up laughing and you would beg me to stop messing about because you needed to concentrate.

Then you'd become serious. 'Zachary has worked out a study timetable for me, so he has. Two hours every evening I have to have my nose resolutely in a book.'

'That's nice of him,' I said, with disdain. 'How does he know we aren't up to no good over here?'

'He's already told me that if he finds out there are any shenanigans going on and I'm not studying hard, we'll be in trouble.' My face must have shown my indignation at that thought. 'Why are you looking like that, Amy?'

'I'd like to see him try and tell *me* off!' You looked at me proudly and I emphasised, 'Well, I *would*!'

'Ah, so would I. He wouldn't get very far. But his words don't worry me like they used to. They have no power over me now. He's nothing to me, *nothing*! I still shudder at his key in the door because I know my mammy will be acting like a servant and he can hurt her just with a hateful glance, but I can look at him and know that his ice cold blood is not in my veins. How she sleeps in the same bed as him when she loves another man so much is a mystery to me.'

You spoke about Zachary quite a bit in those years and I knew it was because you wanted to rid yourself of him, like shrugging off an unwanted flu that was hanging around too long and talking about him worked like a vaccine.

The pressure put upon you at that time was immense and I watched helplessly as you struggled to cope. I often watched you at school when that pressure showed itself time and time again. It was like heavy, restrictive armour that you longed to be free of.

The teachers' comments came from all sides like a burst of gunfire: 'Bear Flynn, we expect great things from you in the future at this school; Bear Flynn, you can do anything you want to in life, you are *so* gifted; Bear Flynn, don't let Amy distract you from your studies, you are on course for straight A's and a wonderful future.'

They always made a point of adding that they had no idea what would happen to me.

One afternoon, Mrs MacDonald stopped us in the corridor. She clapped her hands together and told you, in no uncertain terms, that you were the cleverest student she had ever taught and she wanted you to achieve all your dreams at Cambridge and in life.

As we walked away you sighed deeply and your shoulders dropped. 'What if all I want to achieve in life is happiness? What if all I desire is peace of mind and for the black beast to retreat and leave me alone? Is that too much to ask, Amy? Why don't any of them ask me what *I* want to do with my life?'

I had no answers for you. 'I don't know, Bear but I guess they think if you didn't go to Cambridge it would be a waste of your brain?'

'But it's *my* brain to do with what I want, so it is, not theirs.'

'Then do what *you* want.'

'The problem is, I do want to study the genius of Keats and Shelley and Shakespeare but I want to do it without the incessant pressure. I want to do it for the love of it.'

All I could do was empathise and agree with you and then make you laugh by doing a quick cartwheel in the corridor before anyone caught me. Sometimes I succeeded and often I didn't and there would be a cry of, 'Amy Lee what *do* you think you're doing? That's a very unladylike thing to do with a skirt on, showing off your underwear like that. Bear Flynn, you must avert your eyes and if you want to get to Cambridge you'd do well to find a different best friend!'

We would whisper to each other. 'Never!'

It had often been on the tip of my tongue to inform any teacher who implied you should find another friend that we had already seen each other naked, but when I confessed that to you, you were horrified and banned me from giving out that piece of information.

'Amy, they won't understand. That's *our* secret. They'll think we were up to some kind of malarkey, so they will.'

'Well, we were, weren't we?' When you didn't answer, I muttered to myself, 'It was the best malarkey ever!'

You were still a dreamer, albeit a highly gifted one and neither of us had changed very much since our first few months walking home together from school. You would still stare at the sky, commenting on the different cloud formation and how nature would change constantly all through the year. You spoke of Ireland with such longing in your voice it saddened me to hear it. You quoted poetry and long passages from your favourite books that you said eased your soul and I would be jumping over the cracks in the pavement and still climbing trees despite your warnings.

The following June, we were messing about in my bedroom, dancing and laughing at each other and it was a rare moment of relaxation for you. It was a Sunday, all our exams had finished and you were about to share our roast beef. The moment was broken by both my sisters calling up the stairs for us to come down and I knew immediately there was some kind of problem by the tone in their voices.

'Bear, Amy, come down *quickly*.'

You looked worried. 'Why are they both shouting up the stairs? Your family never shout.'

'Something's up,' I told you and we both went down to find out what the hurry was.

Your mammy was standing in our hall, her face white and pinched. There was a slight tremor in your voice when you whispered, 'Mammy?'

'Bear, it's your granny, she's got a stroke. I have to go to Ireland tomorrow.'

'Will she live?'

'No, I don't think so. It's a major stroke, but I have to go. Will you come home, please? I need to talk to you and your brothers before your daddy comes home and wants his tea.'

You followed her with only a quick glance behind you, where I stood shivering with shock.

I hardly slept that night because you hadn't signed to me across the street. My dreams were full of you walking away slowly, glancing over your shoulder at me and silently mouthing, 'Goodbye, Amy Lee.'

Your mammy wanted you with her for support and you both travelled to Ireland early the next morning. I only found out you had gone when I found your note on the hall carpet before breakfast.

'Amy,' you had written, in your familiar neat handwriting, 'my mammy needs me. I think we'll have to stay awhile, whatever happens to granny. Tommy and Danny are working and Patrick has to finish his college term, so it's just me. I'll write every day. Remember now; don't climb any trees without me, Amy Lee.'

I didn't see you again for two months.

My parents missed you as much as I did. You had charmed my mother over the years with your soft way of speaking and your polite and respectful manner. My father would sit and chat to you for hours in front of the fire because he liked male company and he didn't have any normally. He told you he was ruled by a petticoat government and it was such a change to hear another man's voice in the house. The pair of you discussed politics and history and sometimes philosophy. You ended every conversation with the same words.

'Thank you, Mr Lee, I've learnt such a lot from you today, so I have. So much, so much and it's grand to speak with you like this.'

My father always smiled at you. 'I think it's the other way round, son. I learn from you.'

Your sudden departure left me bereft. There had been no warning. One minute we were hanging on to each other as we were waltzing round my room together and the next, your granny was gravely ill and you were gone. We had practised the waltz before and I still can't remember why on earth we were doing that. There was no possibility of us ever being anywhere that would require either of us to do it. But I simply enjoyed every single moment of being so close to you.

I had been going with you to Ireland with your mammy and Patrick for the summer, but your granny's stroke had changed everything. Patrick did join you when his course had finished, but you wrote that you didn't want me to see your granny so changed. You wanted me to remember her as she had been the year before; funny, daft and talking nonsense.

One muggy July morning, when the sky was an unusual purple colour and threatening thunder, I received another letter from you: 'Amy, yesterday we brought granny home because she had made some progress and the doctors felt she would be happier in her own surroundings. We gave her a light tea and she pointed to the piano as if she wanted Danny to play for her. Mammy said she thinks Granny saw my grandfather and that he *was* there. Her speech is greatly affected by the stroke but she repeatedly called his name and told him she was coming soon to be with him. Mammy says he did come for her. I think he did too.

Later that night, Mammy went in to check on her in bed and granny had slipped away. Earlier, just before she went to sleep for the last time, I had gone up to say goodnight and she was talking softly, sometimes quite clearly but sometimes rambling. Her last words were for me. She said my name four times quite urgently. I told her I was there beside her and if I had known those were her last hours and we were soon to lose her, I would have stayed by her side and held her hand as she moved on to the other place. She deserved that, so she did. She struggled to make me hear what she was saying to me but I put my ear to her lips and just made out the words.

"You, come home here."

I promised her that I would keep the farm and look after it one day and she let out a long, deep sigh. I hope I was the last voice she heard in this life. She loved me so much. I hope she knew how much I loved her. I must go now, mammy is very upset. What actually is the point of life? You'll need to remind me of that. Remember, Amy Lee, don't climb trees without me.'

I longed to join you in Ireland, knowing by the tone of your letter that you were struggling to make sense of the last few days. I wanted to see your face, touch your hair and throw my arms around you, but you were miles away and across the sea and I missed you so much it became almost like an illness I couldn't shake off.

You wrote to me describing the morning of her burial and what happened at the wake. As I read your words my hands began to shake.

'Amy, Zachary came with Tommy and Danny and I shuddered when he arrived at the farm. It's the one place I didn't ever want to see him. He's never been before. I didn't want any memory of him here in a place I love so deeply. He thought granny a fool when she visited us years before in Dublin and she thought him an interloper. She hated the way my mammy changed when he was around and she told mammy once he was cruel and controlling and she could have done so much better. Mammy asked her never to speak of it again and she didn't, except to me. I don't know why he came to the funeral, but Patrick said it was to save face.

The burial was over so quickly, as if her precious life had meant so very little in the scheme of things and as she was lowered into the rich, Irish soil, I asked myself repeatedly, what does it all actually *mean*? What use is the struggle, the hard work, the heartbreak, the grief, the love? It all turns to nothing, Amy, except a cold, motionless body in a box and a few Catholic prayers said for her. The mass could have gone on for hours but granny had asked for a quick but meaningful service to spare me the pain of it all. That was so like granny to know the fragility of my mind.

She used to say, "Baby Bear, my Baby Bear, you have trouble in your mind enough already without having to go through a long Requiem Mass for me. I don't need it. I have had the Mother of God with me my whole life. She has been my guiding star."

Zachary drank too much at the wake and he seemed disinterested in everything going on. The day was so warm and close, he was sweating profusely and red in the face. Patrick signed to me that he had drunk enough to sink a ship and there would be trouble if he drank any more rum. Rum makes him rotten, foul and very vocal so I hid the bottle from him. I watched him sidle up to mammy and pretend to be concerned about her. He put his arm around her waist and pulled her roughly towards him. His face was blotchy, his expression severe and lecherous. That's the face of his I hate the most. I know what it means for mammy when he has her on his own. She tried to move away but he has an iron grip, so he has. He planted a drunken kiss on her pale cheek and I was just about to intervene and save her when the priest began talking to them both. Patrick told me later that Father Looney had been watching Zachary for a while and obviously disapproved of his behaviour. What a name for a priest to have! Tommy and Danny laugh into their hands every time someone says his name. Zachary then asked Tommy to go and buy some more rum in the village, but Tommy refused and the atmosphere turned dark and threatening. Again the priest calmed the rough waters and whispered in Zachary's ear. Whatever he said, Zachary slumped in a chair heavily and said no more the entire time. But his steely eyes were on mammy constantly as she thanked a few of granny's old friends for coming. I knew what it meant, so did my brothers and we formed a protective circle around her for the rest of the day.

I longed to escape onto the moor and go swim under the

waterfall to freshen my body and my mind. I would have thought of you, Amy, of you and me and our happiest moments, but the dark cloud of Zachary's lustful and hateful thoughts bound me to the farm. I'm the only one who can calm his violent tongue and turn his aggression into passivity. Do you remember the angry bull, Amy? Zachary is that angry bull in human form, just about to charge if you get too near or cross him when he's in drink.

Later that evening, I knew instinctively that mammy wanted to take a walk in the moonlight towards the next village. She appeared restless and watchful and often gazed out of the window at the waiting fields. I knew she longed to feel the strong but gentle arms of Wolf around her. I could actually feel her emotions in my body as if they were my own. But how could she leave? And was her lover watching for her from his window? What must *he* have felt, knowing she needed his love and affection so badly that day and not be able to comfort her? My mind was in turmoil as Danny began playing granny's favourite tunes on the piano and tears streamed down mammy's face.

As dusk fell and our family was missing one irreplaceable person, the black beast reared up inside me and I felt hopeless and despairing. I wouldn't ever see my granny again sitting in her chair wearing her hair net, with her crocheting and her weird and wonderful tales of the little people and the angels. I began to cry quietly and Patrick soon followed until Zachary spoke to us sharply.

"Don't be Nancy boys now, you two. Tommy and Daniel aren't crying." He set his dark eyes on me. "Bear Flynn, stop that snivelling, will you? Someone with your brain should know that old age and dying go hand in hand. You're almost eighteen, be a man now. You too, Patrick, come on, shake yourself out of it. Bear, did you hear me?"

Mammy shouted at him so loudly we all jumped out of our skins. She told him to leave me alone and Patrick too, but her words were directed mostly to me. She told me to cry as much as I liked. Zachary yelled back at her that no son of his was going to be a Nancy boy. When she yelled at him to defend me, I realised that was the only time I actually ever really felt her love. She started to say more but stopped herself. Amy, she actually put her fist in her mouth and bit on it.

Zachary turned his flashing eyes on her and pointed at her accusingly. "Don't you shout at me in front of the children and make me look stupid, don't you dare! Especially in this God-forsaken arsehole of a place! I'm the man of the house."

He was turning blood red and purple and as he spoke he spat everywhere. It was disgusting and vile and I hated him so much in that minute, I could have confessed my parentage myself. He took a step towards mammy and all four of us boys jumped up, but I was the only one he ever listened to. I was the one he seemed to idolise and the only one he appeared to feel ashamed in front of. How ironic is that, Amy? I'm the only one not his. Well, I *think* I'm the only one not his, but who knows? Sometimes I wonder about Patrick, although he does resemble Zachary. I grabbed one of his arms and put my face very close to his. I whispered in his ear, over and over again.

"You aren't the man of this house and you never will be, especially not here. Real men don't behave like you do. If you touch her, I'll hate you forever. If you hurt her in any way, I won't go to Cambridge. I *won't* go to Cambridge. I won't make you proud. If you touch her or shout at her again, so help me God, I won't go to Cambridge."

He sat back down again immediately, almost as if I had flattened him with a punch. The evening then wore on as if none of it had happened as the darkness closed in on the farm. The darkness closed in on my mind too as I watched mammy continually glancing out of the window, longing for a gentle man named Wolf and then over at the monster she was married to. When she eventually took herself upstairs, he followed and all I knew was, she would have suffered then without us there to protect her. He wouldn't have hurt her physically, he wouldn't have dared, but she would still have suffered, believe me. That's the man who I thought was my daddy. That's the man I live with. That's the man who brought me up. I feel damaged by him.

Sorry for telling you all this, but I need to try and rid my mind of all the loud, jarring conversations going on inside it. We are home in two days. Don't climb trees, Amy Lee, please. I miss you, but I'm so glad you didn't witness any of those shenanigans.'

I read my mother part of your letter because she could see how much it had affected me. I didn't read the part where you spoke of not being Zachary's son though. I would never have betrayed you like that, Bear. It was your secret and yours alone.

'He sounds an awful man,' she said, shaking her head. 'How on earth can Bear have been brought up by him? They aren't at all alike, are they?' She hugged me hard and added, 'Oh, Amy, you must miss him, but he'll be home soon.' I let the tears flow. It was difficult hiding anything from my mother. 'Let it all out, darling, let it all out.'

'But he'll be going to Cambridge, Mum and he'll be away ages.'

'Cambridge isn't as far though and you'll stay close. I know you will. You two have been best friends for so long.'

'Forever,' I muttered, 'it seems like forever.'

It was hot and cloudless the day you arrived home looking white and exhausted. I watched from the lounge as you quickly unloaded your luggage from the taxis and I saw you glance over your shoulder at our house. Isabelle was watching television and she laughed quietly.

'I'll give him twenty minutes.'

'I hope it's not that long,' I replied succinctly.

Zachary and your mammy walked into your house separately and without speaking. Their body language told a story words never could. I could see the tension in your mammy's shoulders from across the street, made even more obvious by the flowery, sleeveless dress she was wearing. Ten minutes later my heart leapt as you crossed the road.

'There's Bear!'

When I flung open the door, you gave me your unique smile which always floored me, and everything I wanted to ask you and tell you went out of my head in a flash. Did you know? Did you ever suspect that I was lost in that smile like a child searching for the comfort of its mother's arms?

'Hello, Amy Lee, it's good to see you, so it is. Can I come in?' You then looked over my shoulder to greet my mother as she bustled up the hall. 'Hello, Mrs Lee.'

'Amy, stop standing there like a knotless thread! Bear, come in, love, come in. Would you like some tea with us?'

'That would be grand, thank you kindly, Mrs Lee. There's quite an atmosphere in my house, so there is. It's feels so happy in here.'

'We've got ham salad and new potatoes. It's too hot today for a cooked meal.'

'That sounds perfect, Mrs Lee. I'm very grateful.'

'We'll eat in about an hour when Amy's dad gets home. Now, you two go upstairs and catch up. Ava, Isabelle, you leave them to it and stop staring at Bear as if he's got two heads.'

You probably never noticed but both my sisters had a crush on you and Isabelle said shyly, 'Good to have you home, Bear.'

In the silence of my bedroom I could hear my heart thumping as we sat side by side on my bed. You held my hand and sighed deeply. 'Amy, granny is gone to be with the angels. At least I hope she's with the angels. Do you think she is?'

'Yes, I hope so. I'm so sorry I won't see her again or hear her voice. She made me laugh with her funny sayings.'

'I can't quite believe she isn't sitting in her chair right now crocheting and knitting for the poor. The farm belongs to me now. She knew I'd look after it one day. She loved me so much and she knew me too.'

You said no more for a few minutes and I wondered whether I should ask what you were thinking, but I hadn't daren't because your face was a mask of pain. You pulled me down onto my bed and ran your hand through my hair. 'Amy, I need to tell you something. I need to tell you what's in my heart.'

'Tell me then,' I urged you.

'It will break your spirit.'

'The only way you can break my spirit is by being unhappy. Nothing else will, I promise you.'

'You say those words, but I know you as well as I know myself. It *will* break you. It will break the wonderful, energetic and courageous person you are. You'll hate me for doing that to you. No, I can't tell you yet, you're too young to cope with it. But I will, I will.'

'I'm not too young ...'

You put your finger to my lips. '"I closed my mouth and spoke to you in a

hundred silent ways."'

'Rumi was such a clever...'

'Don't you be swearing now, Amy Lee.'

'I'm old enough to swear.'

'I'm not entirely sure you are.'

'I'll swear if I want to.'

'Where have all your freckles gone? You're a force of nature, so you are. Always be that force with me.' We stared at each other without speaking for a few minutes until you sighed. 'Do you think they are lucky, Amy?'

'What do you mean? Who are lucky?'

'Those that are gone, you know, the ones who feel no pain now and no fear.'

'I don't understand that way of thinking, Bear. How can they be lucky?'

'It doesn't matter, don't worry about it. I'm just a little down. The farm won't be the same.'

'I'm so glad we had our long holiday there. I'll never forget it.'

'I won't ever forget it either. I met my real daddy.'

'I was thinking more about being naked in the heather with you.' I began to

laugh and hoped you would too, but your expression didn't change. 'You did like it, didn't you?'

You touched my cheek. 'Oh, Amy, you kill me with your devotion. Don't

worship an idol with feet of clay. Find an idol worthy of your kind and fiercely loving soul. I'm not that boy. I'm not that person.'

'You are! I *have* found an idol worthy of my soul. I just wish you would believe

it.'

'I'm not who you think I am.'

'But I don't care ...'

'You *must* care! You're only seventeen and you have a lot of living to do.'

'So have you, Bear. *We* have a lot of living to do. We can do it together.'

You rubbed your eyes and appeared drained with the weight of all the worries.

Your skin was pale and you had the beginnings of dark, rough stubble on your chin.

'Granny knew me so well,' you whispered and I didn't reply because you then fell asleep in my arms until my father came home.

The weeks sped by and you studied even harder. Your only light relief was being with me and my family. I occasionally saw your mammy walking down our street and she always looked harassed and sometimes anxious. I also caught sight of Zachary returning from work in his smart, dark suit, with his black hair slicked back with a touch of grease.

You told me frequently that your parents were arguing most of the time and that you would put your key in the lock after being at my house and be greeted by him shouting at her. You always let the door slam so he knew you were there and he would stop immediately, but the atmosphere felt so toxic you wanted to flee.

One particular evening before Tommy and Danny arrived home, you had found your mammy crying in the kitchen, her hands covering her face. Patrick was trying to comfort her and had his arms around her shoulders as her body heaved with sobs. You ran into the living room where Zachary was standing with his legs apart and his arms folded across his chest in a decidedly aggressive stance. You punched him hard in the middle of his chest. How angry you must have been to do that, Bear. You said he staggered backwards, gasping for breath. He then put his fist up in a reflex action of defence. Patrick ran between you and tried to drag you away. He was signing quickly to you.

'Calm, Bear, keep calm. He'll hurt you.'

Through grasps for breath, Zachary said savagely, 'You'll cripple me doing that, my boy. You know I have a bad back. I'll let it go as it's you but you won't be doing that again anytime soon.'

'And you won't be shouting at my mammy again either. I told you in Ireland, I'll leave school, so I will. There'll be no Cambridge, no university and no degree. I won't be making you proud if you make her cry! Just leave her alone or so help me God …'

He'd laughed at you, in a quiet but derisory way. 'You'll go to Cambridge, your mammy wants you to as much as I do and you won't disappoint *her*. Besides, your mammy brings this on herself.'

'Fuck you! Fuck you! You're a poor excuse for a man, Zachary Flynn, so you are. I'll change my name, so I will. I don't want *your* name anymore.'

'What will you change it to? Nancy? You need to toughen up, so does Patrick.'

'We don't want to be tough like you.'

Your mammy had come rushing in then and taken your face in

her hands. 'Bear, that's enough! Leave it now, leave it. Don't swear like that at your daddy, *please*.'

You explained to me later that those words ignited something inside you and it was as if, at that moment, it had gone past the point of being quenched and began raging throughout your body until you could contain it no longer. You couldn't say it out loud for fear of Zachary hearing you so you signed deftly.

'He's not my daddy!'

Your mammy hadn't understood though, it was too fast for her and she wasn't expecting it, so she glanced at Patrick to explain better but he was shaking his head.

Zachary declared fiercely, 'You're always signing when you're all keeping secrets from me.'

Your mammy ignored him and said to you, 'I didn't catch that. What did you sign?'

You put your lips to her ear and whispered. 'He is *not* my daddy.'

She had frozen, stunned into silence. Her eyes had flickered quickly from your face to his repeatedly. Zachary had no idea what was going on but again he accused you all of always keeping secrets from him and that you needed to go to your room for an hour to think about what you had done and said to him. You were longing to tell him he had no hold on you now and that you detested the man he was, but one glance at your mammy's forlorn face and the pleading in her eyes stopped you from making matters worse.

You'd finally gone upstairs with Patrick following you, his hand on your back patting you gently like you would a wayward dog. You both sat on your bed and he begged you not to be unhappy. He signed to you, if *you* were unhappy then there was no happiness in the world for him. He asked you to try and deal with your hatred of Zachary until you went to university because it would make your mammy's life so much easier.

You had shaken your head in despair. 'He's getting worse, Patrick.'

Patrick nodded, signing, 'Their marriage is crumbling.'

'She's always loved another man.'

Patrick nodded sadly and you had then hugged each other and stayed like that for a long time until your other brothers came home and caused havoc with their play wrestling and noise and all was supposedly forgotten. You hadn't ever forgotten though, had you, Bear? You could never shake off emotional confrontations like everyone else. You always had such a fragile soul. Your hatred of the man who had raised you stayed with you and festered, until it eventually destroyed your peace of mind.

Your doctor told me yesterday that childhood and adolescent trauma can damage a person for life unless they can deal with it in some way. You never dealt with it because you were already fighting off the black beast, although what you hadn't realised was the black beast and your hidden childhood traumas were one and the same. On top of that, you were keeping your secret from everyone and not being your authentic self.

How you coped during those years I will never know. You told me it was because you had me beside you, but eventually even my ferocious, deep love for you wasn't enough to keep you from sliding into that pit of despair that was slowly engulfing you.

Our final year at grammar school all seems to have been squashed into a few short weeks in my memory. Your parents' marriage limped on, but you were spending most of your time with my family. Tommy got engaged and went to live and work in Ireland and Danny soon followed. They kept an eye on granny's farm but sadly it was shut up and deserted in those years. Neither of them wanted to live there.

You had started to wear glasses, dark-rimmed ones, which made you look even more studious than before as you worked so hard with your face continually hidden in books. You had said Zachary couldn't influence you anymore but, because your mammy was so proud to tell all her friends her son was going to

Cambridge, you kept up the toil for her sake. I longed for the exams to be over so you could be free of all the tension.

Often you seemed to be in another world, dreamy and distracted but there were still flashes of the old Bear who would laugh at my antics and dance with me in my room.

'You are funny, Amy Lee, so you are. There's nobody like you in the whole world.'

'There's nobody like you either, Bear,' I replied as I stared into your eyes. 'Are you happy? Please tell me you are.' You avoided looking directly at me whenever I asked you that and you never actually said you were. 'Bear, just say it once, will you?'

You replied, '"If everything around you seems dark, look again, you may be the light."'

'Is that Rumi again?'

'It is.'

'How come he was such a clever bastard?'

Then that smile that always melted my heart had spread across your face and we spoke of how we would spend all our time together once you returned from Cambridge. I couldn't think about you returning because I dreaded you going.

When we both turned eighteen I assumed something might change between us. We were now adults and we could behave like adults as all our classmates seemed to be doing. You were bombarded with admirers at every turn. None of them interested you though despite their flirtatious looks and obvious advances. A couple of girls in our English group made a desperate attempt to get a reaction, all to no avail.

I was walking behind you in the corridor one afternoon trying to catch you up and Sheryl and Amanda were both hanging on to your arms and laughing up at you. You were laughing back and for a second I was hit by sudden unwanted and fierce jealousy that engulfed me and took my breath away. Sheryl was caressing your back with her hand, not briefly but carefully and consistently. I saw you disengage yourself from her touch by squirming slightly, but it didn't put her off. She was smiling up at you and Amanda then joined in and pulled your face towards her mouth to kiss you.

I intended to protect you from their obvious advances so I ran towards you. Before I could do or say anything you shrugged them both off as if they were vile reptiles winding themselves around your body and I heard what you said to them quite clearly.

'Will you stop your nonsense now?'

'Come on, Bear, you know you like it really,' Sheryl whined with her bottom lip sticking out like a petulant child.

Amanda stood on her toes and reached up to kiss you again before simpering and saying, 'Bear, come round my house later. My parents are away. It will help your studying to have a bit of fun.'

'The studying takes all my time. There's no fun to be had at the moment.'

'You can study after the fun. I've got some wine in my bedroom. I think you need the sort of fun I'm talking about.'

'I told you to stop your nonsense. I don't drink wine ...'

'And he won't be coming up to your bedroom either,' I chipped in angrily as I drew level with them.

Sheryl sniggered. 'Oh God, here's your bodyguard, Bear. He doesn't need you, Amy.'

Amanda whispered to me, 'Amy, have you got him into bed yet? I bet it was good. He's good at everything he does. I envy you if you have but I'm not sure he's that interested. I'd jump on him quick if I was you. Someone else might grab him, he's so gorgeous.'

My face was burning and I wanted to slap her, but one look at you and my anger dissolved. You had heard her and your sensitive nature caused you to blush and you appeared upset and embarrassed but, despite that, you spoke up.

'Amanda, will you stop saying such things to Amy? Amy, don't even answer. It's not your business what Amy has or hasn't done. Don't either of you ever touch me like that again. I'm not your plaything to touch when you like.'

'Hark at you,' Sheryl said, in a patronising way, but Amanda was furious with you and stormed off.

'You think you're so above us,' she yelled behind her and Sheryl followed with her tail between her legs. 'You're a condescending bastard, Bear Flynn and Amy is nothing but your bodyguard!'

'So childish,' you said under your breath. 'Why do they think I want them to keep touching me constantly? It makes me sick, so it does.'

'That Amanda has eyes like a demented cow,' I muttered, making you smile.

'You're funny, Amy Lee, so you are.'

'I mean it.'

'I know you do. Only a couple more weeks and I'll be free of their flirting. Mother of God, we're late for class, come on.'

'You sounded like your granny then, Bear.'

'I know I did and I'm glad.' You gave your sweet little laugh. 'Granny lives on in me, so she does.'

'Did you like it really though?' I asked as we rushed upstairs to our classroom. 'I mean, most boys would like it, them touching you like that and kissing you.'

'I'm not most boys, Amy. I'm not most boys,' you said and I recall your eyes being a pool of sadness.

Momentarily my heart leapt at your words but then I saw the distress on your face and my mood plummeted. Those few words, they haunted me like the black beast haunted you. They darkened my days when we were apart and woke me in the middle of the night.

'I'm not most boys, Amy. I'm not most boys.'

## Chapter Six

*You had better run from me, my words are fire.*
***Rumi***

WE HAD WALKED OUT OF SCHOOL ON OUR LAST DAY AS we did on our first, side by side. Exams were over and you had done your best, urged on relentlessly by everybody who expected so much of you. Teachers clamoured to wish you goodbye and good luck and I stood in the background watching proudly. In our years there you had charmed pupils and staff alike with your soft Irish accent and kind and compassionate nature. Even the school keeper, Mr Reynolds knew your name because you had often stopped and chatted to him because you said he was a broken man. You had recognised his pain very early on in our time at the school.

'How do you know he's a broken man by just looking at him, Bear?' I had asked you early on in our time there.

You appeared surprised by my question. 'Just take a look at his face, Amy. There is sorrow in his every expression and his whole demeanour. I have spoken with him many times and I could drown in his sadness because I recognise it.'

We had both grown up in those last two years, but you had matured much more than I had. You had always been an old soul and I was a whirling mass of hormones, energetic and free from any complexities or anxiety, except for the inevitable separation from you that was looming on the horizon.

You were longing for the freedom of the Irish hills and to be able to breathe in the fresh, unpolluted air. We were travelling with your mammy and Patrick the next morning for three weeks rest before our results came through and we both had to find summer jobs. We had no idea how difficult the next few years were going to be.

Before we escaped to Ireland, however, we spent our last afternoon sitting in the sixth form common room surrounded by our classmates larking about and writing on each other's shirts. Teacher after teacher came to find you.

'Bear Flynn,' Mrs Moore had said with tears in her eyes as you shook her hand and thanked her. 'You have no need to thank me. You are the most naturally gifted pupil it has ever been my good fortune to teach. Now go off and be the brilliant, exceptional person I know you are. Please make me proud. I expect great things from you.'

'I will do my very best, Mrs Moore,' you had replied but as she walked away you muttered to me. 'But what if I don't want to be exceptional? What if I just want to be happy?'

Mrs Wilson was next. 'You can be anything you want to be in life, Bear. You have a fine brain, charisma and kindness in abundance. Go off into the world and shine!'

You surprised me when you replied, 'Mrs Wilson, what if I just want to be happy? What if I just want to live on a farm in Ireland and watch the sunsets? I might do that one day.'

She shook her head and appeared exasperated. 'That would be a terrible waste of your brain, wouldn't it?'

Only one teacher, Miss Miller, said farewell to me. Throughout my time at the school I had disliked her intensely and she had always looked at me as if the feeling was entirely mutual. But remarkably she was the only one who could see inside you and who knew that you needed me just as much as I needed you. I had made you laugh after every lesson with her by telling you she reminded me of a horse with her protruding teeth and wide nostrils.

'Amy,' she cried that day, opening her arms wide, 'I'm so sorry to see you go.'

I was truly bemused by her admission. 'But you don't like me.'

'Don't be ridiculous, I admire your spirit immensely and your devotion to this lucky young man here. Bear, you make sure you look after our Amy.'

'She looks after me, so she does, Miss Miller.'

She gave us a knowing look. 'I'm well aware of that! Amy, stick by his side, he's going to need you.'

'I will, Miss,' I said definitely and, as our eyes met, for the first time I saw in her a human being with insight, shrewdness and emotional depth. As she left us, you turned to me.

'That was very kind of her and very astute too, so it was.'

'I still think she looks like a horse!'

'That's cruel, Amy Lee, so it is,' you told me, trying your best not to laugh.

By the end of the day all the girls had kissed you or signed your shirt. Many scribbled that they loved you and would miss you and they hung around you until the very last minute. I was quietly delighted that I was the only one who didn't have to leave you and pushed the thought of Cambridge to the back of my mind. The boys had messed about with your hair and undid your tie. One of the other boys was a little rough as he tried to pull your tie off.

'Bear, can I have this as a souvenir?'

I gave him a shove as anger bubbled up inside me. 'What do you want a souvenir for? For God's sake, leave him alone.'

'What's up with you, Amy?' he asked angrily. 'I only want his tie, that's all. He won't have you at Cambridge to fight his battles. Bear, you'll need to toughen up a bit, mate.'

I persisted. 'Leave him alone! Just leave him alone. You have your own tie! Why do you want his?'

You pulled me away gently. 'Don't be angry, Amy Lee. Leave him be. He didn't mean any harm.' You called him back. 'David, here have my tie. I don't need it now. Amy didn't mean anything by it.'

'Yes, I did,' I said petulantly, under my breath. My fury had come from nowhere in an instant. I knew its source was the truth in David's words that I wouldn't be with you in Cambridge to fight your battles. But I was more mortified by the fact that you had apologised for my behaviour. 'Are you ashamed of me, Bear?'

'Don't you be so daft now; I could never be ashamed of you. You were just protecting me, I know that.'

'But you won't need me at Cambridge, will you?' I said, tying my best not to sulk but failing badly. 'You won't need me, there'll be other girls.'

You kissed my cheek. 'Oh I think I will. I'll always need you more than you know. Don't worry about other girls, there won't be any.'

With those few kind words that warmed my heart and made me smile, we walked away from our school life together hand in hand, towards what I believed wholeheartedly was our shared future. I had no idea then how difficult, painful and heartbreaking that would be. Thank God we didn't know, Bear.

Being in Ireland on the farm without your granny there was a strange experience. Tommy had been there hours before, opening the curtains and doors to let in light and fresh air. But it smelt musty and there was dust on every surface which your mammy attacked with a damp cloth that very evening. She shed a few tears gazing at your granny's empty chair but then wiped them away when you put your arms around her shoulders.

'She's still here, Mammy,' you whispered, 'I can feel her. I don't think she'll stray very far from the farm. This place is in her soul, so it is.'

'I know, I know. Now, I'm going for a long walk. I need it after sitting for so long. I need roses in my cheeks and the wind in my hair.'

You glanced at me briefly. 'Yes, Mammy, a walk will put roses in your cheeks to be sure. Take a walk to the waterfall. It will refresh you. Take a swim in it too, like we did.'

She didn't bat an eyelid but smiled faintly. 'I love that waterfall. No, I won't be swimming in it. I'm not young and hardy like you two. Now, I'll be back to cook your tea. Patrick, will you be getting some shopping?'

Patrick nodded and signed something to you but you didn't react at all except to say to me, 'Amy, let's go up on the moor and sit awhile. It's such a soft day.'

The sun was high and shed streams of white light across the mountains. It was a cloudless day, hot and with not a breath of wind even on top of the moor. Ireland seemed to be weaving its magic already because your body changed in those first days. Your shoulders were relaxed and you didn't walk with your eyes on the ground constantly. Your headaches stopped and you didn't need to wear your glasses anymore. Studying so hard had sucked the life out of you, but Irish air was slowly helping you come back to yourself again.

We spent every morning walking, eating our sandwiches in the sunshine and drinking coffee from a flask, returning in the afternoon to spend some time with Patrick. Tommy and Danny came over regularly in the evenings and your mammy delighted in having all her boys under one roof again. Your granny was mentioned constantly with reminiscences and laughter, especially when anyone said one of her ridiculous sayings.

Your mammy was so changed I barely recognised her. She wore her long, dark hair loose about her shoulders all the time and there was no tension in her face at all. She wore prettier clothes, not the dowdy ones she wore in London and she appeared years younger. Most days she disappeared in the morning and stayed out all day until she came home to cook our tea. Her eyes shone and sparkled and she didn't seem harassed or uncomfortable. You confessed one evening in your bedroom that you thought she would leave Zachary as soon as you went to Cambridge.

'That's another reason I have to succeed, Amy Lee. My mammy's happiness depends on it. She can't live with Zachary much longer, it's destroying her slowly every day. The brutality of his spirit is wearing her down. You've seen how she is here. It's like another woman has come to stay at the farm. She appears to be in paradise when she comes back every afternoon. *He* does that for her. Wolf does that, so he does.'

'She doesn't appear to be hiding it either,' I remarked, 'not like last time.'

'She knew Granny could see through her, so she hid it. I loved my granny and I miss her, but I prefer my mammy like this, free of guilt and shame.'

The following week the weather changed from still, close and very warm. The winds blew in from the ocean and brought with it storms and heavy rain. That seemed to ignite something in you and you suddenly appeared restless and almost agitated. Patrick picked up on it immediately and continually signed to you, asking if there was something on your mind. You simply shook your head and gave a weak smile, but I was aware too that something was troubling you.

I still have no idea why you chose that day to tell me your secret. The telling of it had seemed to come out of nowhere but you had promised yourself that this holiday was to be the watershed moment you had planned. You wanted it to be the end of all the secrets in your life.

I had asked you that morning, 'Bear, do you want to go to the church again, in the hope of seeing your daddy? We can if you like, I don't mind. We could just sit at the back and pretend we're praying.'

'You can't pretend to pray, Amy, it's not right to do that in a church,' you had scolded gently. 'No, no, I'm not sure I want to see him. If he'd wanted to meet me again he would have told my mammy.'

'But it's still a secret, isn't it? It isn't all out in the open until she leaves Zachary.'

'I know that which is why I don't want to make it any harder for her.'

You were always thinking of other people before yourself, which is why I pushed you to confess *all* that day. Although the exams were over and you were less anxious about them, your deep-rooted, long held secret was eating away at you.

An angry storm was raging across the countryside that morning and it seemed to erupt inside you too. You asked me to take a walk with you, despite the heavy rain and gusting winds. Even the birds were hiding their little heads in the hedgerows and some of the taller trees were bent over like elderly people with bad backs. The loud and chaotic crackles of lightning and thunder exploding above us excited me so intensely, I ran ahead of you and did cartwheels and forward rolls, soaking my clothes and hair even more. I then stood on my hands because I knew - or thought - you loved seeing me doing that, but you smiled briefly.

'You're eighteen now, Amy Lee, so you are. Aren't you supposed to be behaving like a responsible adult?'

'I never will. I will *always* be like this. I intend to be notorious and completely daft all my life, you know that. You wouldn't want me to behave, would you?'

'I want you to be yourself, whatever that is, just yourself. Do you want that for me?' I stopped the cartwheels immediately because there was a tremor in your voice as you asked that question. You were standing a few feet away, your arms limply by your side and your eyes troubled. 'Did you hear me, Amy? Did you hear my question? Can you answer me, please?'

'Do I want you to be you?'

'Yes.'

'I've only ever wanted that, you know I have. What's wrong, Bear? You seemed so happy to be here now your exams are over, but the last couple of days ...'

'I'm frightened, Amy, I'm frightened.'

'I don't understand.'

You said no more but grabbed my shoulders and pulled me close. You pushed my wet hair away from my face and you were trembling violently. We were in such a tight embrace those shaking movements ran through my body too like an electrical current. The sudden change in you made my head spin.

'I must tell you, I *must*. I love you, Amy Lee, I love you so dearly, it makes my heart ache. But keeping it in is causing me such distress.'

I caught my breath. 'I love you too, you know I do, but that's not something to be frightened of. It's wonderful, *you* are wonderful. What are you frightened of?'

'I'm frightened of the depth of my feelings.' I took your face in my hands and tried to kiss you, but you pulled back. 'Don't kiss me like that.'

'If you love me so much, let me kiss you. Dominique had more of your kiss than I ever have.' You looked perplexed. 'When you grabbed her in the bushes, your kiss was ...'

'But I don't love her, so I didn't care what she thought. My rough kiss was designed to put her off me. She meant nothing to me in that moment and I wanted to shrug her off and get rid of her like you would a wasp in your hair.'

'Bear, please don't pull away from me. I want you, I want *all* of you.'

You looked distraught and unhappy and you began to sob. The sobs were so deep and so distressing, I couldn't breathe. I listened as you fought a war within yourself to stem them.

'Don't, Amy, don't. You can't have all of me, don't you understand?'

'No, I don't!' You were pointing to the side of your head. 'What does that mean?'

'I'm so terrified of what goes on in here. I'm fearful of so much. I'm fearful of not succeeding, of not matching all the expectations, of them being disappointed in me. I'm fearful of being a failure and wasting my brain, but most of all I'm fearful of breaking your heart and then breaking my own.'

I held you tightly because you were rocking backwards and forwards as if you were drunk. 'Don't break my heart then.'

'But you need to know who I am. I can't hide it any longer.'

I shouted at you and the wind took those words and threw them away towards the mountains, never to return. 'I don't care who you are!'

'You need to know ...' I put my hand over your mouth. I dreaded what was coming next, even though I longed for your happiness and peace of mind more than my own. You tried to move my hand away. 'Amy, let me speak.'

'Don't say it, *please*.'

'I have to even though I know it will break your spirit.'

'The only thing that can break my spirit is you being unhappy, you know that.'

Suddenly words were tumbling out of your mouth and as they did, the life I had planned melted away into a liquid nothingness. All my hopes and dreams, with you at the end of every single one of them, burst into fragments and exploded.

'Listen to me! You *must* listen! I'm what Zachary calls *bent*. I'm what he calls a *Nancy*.' You put your hands over my face. 'I don't want to be a witness to the pain in your eyes.' I was shaking my head as you cried, 'Amy, I can't ever give you what you want.' I pulled your hand away from my eyes roughly. 'I can't! I just can't!

'Don't say that!'

You closed *your* eyes tightly and shuddered. It was almost as if you were shrinking before me. The bright, charismatic, brilliant and gorgeous boy I knew was shrinking slowly into someone I barely recognised.

'I can't look at you. Don't hate me, I was born this way. I've tried so hard to change for you, so hard.'

I was sobbing too and I just managed to cry, 'I don't want you to change. I've never asked that of you. I just want you to be happy.'

'Sometimes I think I'd be better flying away and being with the angels.'

'You would not!' I was screaming at you then. 'You would not! Don't say that!'

'But you'd be better off.' Terror almost struck me speechless. 'You'd be better off without me here to ruin your life.'

'I wouldn't be better off! How can you say that? I'd die too! I'd shrivel up and fade away.' You shuddered again violently. 'Bear, don't say that. I could never live without you here.'

'You'll shrivel up and fade away loving a man who can't ever give you what you need.'

I struggled free from your arms and hit you hard in the middle of the chest. 'I need *you*! I only need you and not some version you think I need, but just *you*.'

'Amy...'

'Why did you let me ... the last time we were here ... in the heather, why did you let me hold you like that?'

'I thought I could change if we did that. I really thought I could. I tried and I hoped something would change in me, but it didn't. I *could* make myself do it, physically I could, but I don't want that for you. A purely physical act would be terrible for someone as lovely as you. It would mean belittling you, like Zachary belittles my mammy. You are worth so much more, Amy Lee, so much more.'

'Didn't you like it then?' My voice sounded like a cry in the night, a cry nobody was responding to. 'Didn't you enjoy feeling my body against yours?'

'I did, of course I did, but you need more than I can give you. You are a physical, loving being and you need passion, Amy. You need to have sex for the first time with someone who wants you as much as he wants to take his next breath. I'm not that man. Believe me, I'm not that man.'

I ran away from you, not because I wanted to get away but because I longed to shake you out of the dark armour you always wore. You followed and if I had run as fast as I know I can, you would never have caught me. I can run like a high wind through deserted fields. I let you catch me and I stood shaking uncontrollably as you attempted to calm me down by stroking my hair. I hit you again in the middle of your chest without much force. You could easily have grabbed my hands but you simply took the blows as if you deserved it. You never deserved it, Bear.

'So you *did* want Ben in the upper-sixth, they all told me you did. I always defended you, Bear. I always knew you loved me more. Why are you being like this? I thought you were my best friend in the whole world.'

'I am! But I can't stop being this way.'

'Don't you want me then, I mean like *that*?'

'Oh, Amy, Amy, I only wish I did. How is it possible to love someone so much, but not like that?'

The sobs continued to fly out of my mouth in sudden waves. The path I had chosen for myself, with you at every turn, was full of thorns and rocks and quickly disappearing out of view. The intimate moments with you I had yearned for, for years, were becoming confused and hopeless and we were both watching them fly up into the sky to become one with the murderous thunder. But my mind cleared for a few precious moments and I looked up at your dear face. It was the face I knew better than my own.

'What can you give me then?'

'What do you mean?'

'I'll take one tiny part of you, if that's all you can give.'

'No, Amy, don't do this. Stop acting so small, you are the universe in ecstatic motion. You were born for a great love, a fulfilling love. Many men will love you. Let them, let them.'

'You don't mean it. How can I let other men love me when I only want you?'

'Stop wanting me, Amy Lee. It's better that way.'

I sunk to my knees. You dropped to your knees too.

'I can't stop loving you.'

'Then stop *wanting* me. Do you think I want this? I wish I was like Tommy and Danny, who spend hours in the arms of the girls who love them and only ever want to be there.'

You put your head in your hands and cried pitifully from your feet to the top of your head. It all came out in strong, overpowering shudders. My beautiful, kind, Bear who thought I was funny and daft and who stood patiently under trees waiting for me to fall. You didn't belong to Ben or any other man in the future. You would only ever be mine. Tears continued to stream down your face.

'Stop crying now, Bear, *please*. I'll take what you can give me.'

'You'll take it for now, but it won't be enough in the future. You're so young, Amy Lee, so you are. I don't know if I can change. I long to make you happy and every time I take a breath, I ask the angels to take this from me, but they never have. I have to live with it like I live with the black beast and so do you.'

The sky was suddenly clearing and patches of pale blue and turquoise appeared from behind the storm clouds. Thunder was still rumbling in the distance but it had left us in peace. It somehow reflected how you looked then having confessed to me what you had been holding inside you almost all your life. You leant forward and kissed my forehead gently and it felt like a butterfly's wings.

'Amy, do you hate me now?'

'I could never hate you, Bear, *never*! You know that.'

'What will happen in the future?'

'I'll still love you.' You looked relieved and sighed.

'And I'll still love you too, so I will.'

There was nothing more to be said and we continued to wander for hours, with you holding my hand tightly and continually glancing at me. After the rain cleared, warm sunshine flickered on our faces and the birds flew in and out of the bushes and hedgerows. There were swallows and goldfinches playing in the breeze of the fresh Irish countryside. Swooping in the air like acrobats, rising and falling quickly, fearless and free.

We walked through fields with old, broken fences at their edges and passed stone cottages, some with thatched roofs and long low barns with corrugated ones. Did I love you any less because of your confession? No, Bear, I loved you even more, but I didn't tell you that then. It was as if I had been waiting for that moment of brutal truth from you for years and in an odd way it came as a relief, albeit a painful and distressing one. It made me even more determined to be the one person in your life who loved you unconditionally.

We never mentioned that pitiless conversation in the wet heather again. The moor, for me, signified one of the happiest and one of the hardest of my young life. Our holiday continued and we sat each evening looking up at the mass of stars in the black sky and listening to the ghostly sound of the barn owl calling to us.

As the days flew by, your mammy would mention your exam results a few times but Patrick would say out loud repeatedly in his monotone way, 'Mammy, no, leave him be on his holiday!'

Patrick could pick up feelings as if they were solid objects flying through the air towards him and you would sign your thanks to him for his intuitiveness. Each day I asked if you wanted to find Wolf again but you declined. It was if you couldn't cope with any more emotional turmoil. Your anguished confession to me, your mammy mentioning the exam results and the thought of the silver-haired man in the next village rejecting you, it was all too much for your tender and loving heart. The black beast reared up and almost overwhelmed you. You kept most of it inside you though and it began to fester. We had no idea that there was worse to come.

We roamed wherever we wished and when the air was warm and airless we sat in the grass by the river and listened to bees humming by the fast flowing water. In a way we were closer than ever and I managed to ignore any mounting anxiety about your secret. We were always going to be like this.

I pushed to the back of my mind that you longed for someone like Ben more than me. Looking back, I realise now how naive that was. I also know how much insidious pressure that put on you. You had pressure from all sides, in so many different ways and from your perspective it must have seemed as if everyone in your life wanted something from you.

How lonely it must have been in your head. How lonely and alone you must have felt, even more so when your mammy spilled her guts out to you on that holiday. She wouldn't have, but you were determined to make that time in your life the moment when all secrets were revealed and all heartache put to rest. If only, Bear, if only that had happened.

One evening, towards the end of our time on granny's farm, when the sun was slowly setting and leaving a golden glow across our eyes, we were sitting in the kitchen and you signed something to Patrick. That day, I had noticed you were quite reflective and much quieter and you had mentioned Wolf a couple of times. Patrick had shaken his head sternly and looked aghast at you. Before I could ask what you were talking about, your mammy floated in, her long dark hair hanging down her back and her face alight.

'Now,' she said to us, rubbing her hands together, 'what will I be making for our tea?'

You seemed tense and agitated and my heart began pounding as you stared at her. You said boldly, 'Mammy, where have you been all day?' She didn't appear to hear the distress in your voice. 'Mammy, did you hear me?'

'What, darling?' she asked, breathlessly, as if she was still on cloud nine after being with the man she loved.

'Where have you been?'

'I was visiting an old friend.' You appeared deflated by her answer. 'I know so many people here.'

'Don't keep telling lies to me, Mammy, please.'

She turned and frowned at you. 'What do you mean, Bear?' She then began taking food out of the fridge, as if your question was irrelevant. 'I *have* been visiting an old friend.'

'What's his name, your friend?' The atmosphere instantly had an electrical current running through it as Patrick knocked on the arm of his chair twice to divert your attention. You ignored him and took a sharp intake of breath. 'Mammy, answer me, please.'

She shrugged, 'Oh, Bear, don't be ...'

You jumped up and faced her, knocking over the chair you had been sitting on. The noise as it hit the tiled floor seemed to ignite your slowly burning temper.

'Why doesn't he want to know me?'

'I don't know what you mean.'

'Oh, Mammy, you know I know and Patrick does too. You've hidden it so long, *so* long. You hardly know the truth anymore. Wolf is my daddy, so he is. He has my name etched in blue ink on his forearm. Is that all I can ever be to him, blue ink on his arm?'

Your mammy sank into a chair. It was as if someone had pricked her balloon of long held, devastating shame. The skeletons in her cupboard were banging on the door desperate to be set free to dance as they pleased all over your life.

'That tattoo,' she whispered. 'That tattoo!'

Emotion was struggling up your throat and you looked so distressed, I longed to take your hand and pull you away from a situation that I knew was going to injure you badly. Patrick knew too and he began signing furiously. You didn't appear to even see him. Your voice broke as you continued to question her.

'Mammy, why doesn't he want to know me?'

'He *does* want to know you,' she answered, still in a whisper, as if your granny was within earshot. 'He does, but I'm not ready. I'm still wedded to Zachary, so help me God.'

'What does that matter? I hate Zachary, you know I do. This messes with my head, so it does. Wolf is the only person who can make any sense of it. I've watched Zachary all my life with a disdain I could never understand. I detest his aggression, his belittling of you and his brutality. I have no idea how he can't see I'm not his. Look at me, I'm Wolf's son through and through. How long have you loved him for? Zachary must be blind or a complete fool not to be able to see I'm *nothing* like him.' Your mammy hung her head. 'You need to make sense of all this for me.'

'He does see it,' she muttered.

'What did you say?'

'He does see it,' she said again, unable to look at you. 'Zachary knows you're not his son, he does. He *does*! Jesus, have I not suffered enough for my mistake?'

Patrick was reading your mammy's lips and he was signing again frantically. You shook your head at him. 'Patrick, I can't walk away. I need to hear this. I need to hear the truth. Mammy, please look at me. If Zachary knows then why does he favour me like he does?'

Tears fell down your mammy's face and for a moment she was struggling to form any words at all. She began shaking her head quickly, as if she was trying to rid her mind of what was tormenting her.

'He doesn't favour you. He uses you to get to me.'

'I don't know what you mean.'

'Darling, it doesn't matter ...'

'It matters to me, so it does.'

'Bear, please don't make me say anymore. You're too fragile for all this.'

'I have to know. I don't want any other secrets hidden in my life. There have been too many.'

Your mammy appeared deflated, as if all the blood had been drained out of her. I held my breath because I knew whatever came out of her mouth next would hurt you permanently. Part of me was willing her to stand up and walk away but another part of me always wanted for you what you wanted for yourself. Those mixed emotions made my face burn. She began speaking quietly, as if in the confessional, her face flushed.

'He knew right from the beginning. He knew something was different about me when I was pregnant with you. I had been turning away from him because I was still in love with Wolf. I always had been and suddenly you were on the way. Your conception coincided with a long stay over here. I tried to deny it at first but then I couldn't. It would have been like denying my love for Wolf. Bear, you were born out of a deep love. It was a love that had begun when we were not quite sixteen. I can't explain why we didn't marry. It's too painful to dwell on, even now. Zachary burst into my life, charm itself, good looks and with an air of mystery about him. I tried to make it work and your brothers came along so quickly, but it won't ever last if you love another.' She wiped her eyes and continued, without realising how every word cut into you and left a wound that would fester and bleed for years. 'He let me know that he realised you weren't his. Oh yes, he let me know. He favoured you alright, just to get his own way time and time again. He'd say to me, if you don't act like the loving wife you should be,

I'll make Bear pay. He told me he'd turn you inside out, ruin your life and mess with your head. The better I treated him, the better he treated you. And then, of course, when he realised how gifted you were, he wanted to show you off, brag about you in the pub, bathe in your reflected glory as if your brains came from him. When you go to Cambridge, Tommy and Danny are throwing him out. You can't be there that day and neither can Patrick. My dear, sweet, Bear, you are Wolf's son through and through.'

You whispered, 'Did my granny know?'

'Your granny suspected, but she wouldn't ask. The devout Catholic in her dreaded the answer.'

You looked shattered by her revelations. I saw something disappear in you that day. I can't quite quantify what it was, but it left you empty and half the person you had been. The next words that came out of your mouth sent a shiver through my whole body.

'What's it all for, Mammy? He made you pay but he messed with my head anyway. I saw his true nature at granny's funeral, even more than I had before. It's all been for nothing, all of your belittling yourself for him.'

'Don't say that, Bear,' she pleaded, 'please don't say that. It can't all have been for nothing. You're complex, you have a fine brain and a bright future ahead of you that Zachary cannot touch. You're fragile in many ways but you're strong too.'

I wanted to scream at her, how can he be fragile and strong at the same time? You answered my question by what you said next. Your face had turned pale and there were shadows under your watchful eyes.

'You want me to be strong, Mammy, so you won't be eaten up with guilt, but I'm not. Patrick has more strength in his little finger than I have in the whole of my body, so he has. All this time I thought he favoured me because he loved me in his own way.'

Your mammy cried so much she sounded as if she was choking. All her pent up fury at Zachary and her guilt and denial came pouring out. Neither you nor Patrick made a move towards her but Patrick signed something that I interpreted as him telling you he loved you. He patted his chest, then his heart and pointed at you.

I could scarcely breathe as I listened to your mammy's wrenching sobs and watched the enormity of what she had confessed sink into your bones. There was a profound sadness in your eyes I had never seen before and I knew instinctively it would never leave you. Your only hope was to get close to your real daddy one day and hear from his lips the truth of your beginnings.

'Bear, forgive me my mistakes. Please, forgive me. You were born out of love. It was a love that I've held in my heart since I was fifteen. Life is so very complicated. You'll find that out when you're older. People make mistakes, my darling. You'll make plenty when you're older, believe me.'

'But what of my brother sitting here, with his eyes full of sadness? What of Patrick's feelings?'

'I don't know what you mean?'

'What of Patrick when Zachary was favouring me, or pretending to? What disservice has that done to my brother? Tommy and Danny don't care, but Patrick always did when he was small. What of his feelings? It's such a holy fucking mess all of this and it was my birth that made it so.'

Patrick was signing furiously again and shaking his head. Your mammy tried to read it and said, 'Patrick, slower, slower.'

He stopped signing and said in his flat way, 'Bear is the best of us. You are the best of us, the *best* of us.'

'I wish I was,' you replied with a weak smile.

'You are ...'

'I just don't see it. Why did granny leave me the entire farm? Why isn't it left to all of us?'

'Bear, it's because you are the best of us,' she said, wiping her eyes continually. 'Granny knew that.'

'Sweet Jesus, I'm no better than Patrick.' You ran your hand over your face as if ridding yourself of your mammy's words. You bent down and looked into her face. 'Has my real daddy peace in his mind?'

'Yes, he has.' She appeared perplexed by your question. 'Yes, why do you ask?'

'It's not from him then, the black beast. I'd hoped that maybe he has it too and could help me understand it.'

Your mammy tried to hug you but you moved away from her and kissed Patrick's cheek tenderly. Looking in his eyes, I could see you trying to decide what to say to him. You signed and whispered at the same time.

'I'm so very sorry, Patrick, so very sorry.' You then turned to your mammy again and asked, 'Mammy, why can't I feel your love?'

I followed you as you walked quickly out into the back yard. Dusk was settling upon us and there was faint birdsong and a couple of bats flying in and out of the old barn. You were staring up at the summer sky and saying something under your breath. Your lips were moving but I couldn't hear what you were saying. It looked like a prayer, but your arms were hanging loosely by your sides and your eyes were wide open. I took your hand in mine and tears were blinding me.

'Bear, are you okay? I'm so sorry you had to hear all that. Are you alright?' Your eyes were dull and almost lifeless. 'Speak to me.'

'Amy, could they fuck me up any more if they tried?' I threw my arms around you. Your body felt taut and rigid and your face gaunt and white. 'I'm broken by her and Zachary and their mind games, broken.'

'Don't say that, they all love you so much and so do I. Forget it all, forget it. I'm sure your mammy didn't mean to say all that.'

You sighed so heavily, it came up from your boots. '"A wound is the place where the light enters your soul."'

'Is that Rumi again?'

'It is.' I went to say what I always did, but your face was like a death mask. Your eyes held a bewilderment that frightened me.

'What if your soul is so damaged no light can get in? What happens then, Amy Lee? What happens then?'

'Don't say that. I'll save your soul if it's damaged, you know I will.'

You wrapped your arms around me and lifted me off my feet. We stayed like that with our cheeks together until darkness hid your face from mine. 'Amy, let's fly towards a secret sky, you and I ...'

# Chapter Seven

***If your beloved has a life of fire, step in and burn along.***
***Rumi***

The disclosure of all those secrets in Ireland became a distressing memory you wouldn't return to despite my urging you to discuss it all with me to ease your mind a little. But the damage had been done. The few times I was in your house when Zachary was home, I noticed how you seemed to shrink away from him whenever he spoke to you. You couldn't look at him at all and simply dropped your head, staring blankly at the floor. He noticed it too and took to slapping you on the back as if you were one of his mates down the pub and you would squirm and clench your teeth. His overtly masculine manner made you cringe. Now you had learned that he knew you weren't his, it had changed everything and the tenuous relationship between you had, for you, come to breaking point.

I had longed to speak to you about your confession on top of the moor on that stormy day but I couldn't possibly add to your problems. I know now that I was in denial about how you wanted someone like Ben more than you wanted me. I was completely blinded by my love for you.

You had been looking as if you were carrying the problems of the world on your young shoulders already. I didn't want to add to that heavy burden by questioning you and then watch you collapse.

The morning our results came through I was fidgeting at the breakfast table and Isabelle and Ava were laughing at me.

Isabelle was only a year older than me but as my older sister, she had always spoken her mind where anything to do with me was concerned. She grinned at me across the table. 'Anyone would think you were waiting on *your* results to get into Cambridge.'

'I don't care about mine. I've failed them all, I'm pretty sure of that.'

Ever the optimist, my mother said, 'You never know, Amy, stranger things have happened.'

My father placed his hand on mine and chipped in. 'We won't mind what you get, we'll still be proud of the person you are, dear.'

'And as long as you're happy,' my mother added sweetly. 'Isn't that right, Alfie?'

How I always wished your family were like mine, Bear, uncomplicated, supportive and always loving. How different your life would have been without the aggression, the long-held, complex web of secrets and the constant pressure.

The postman delivered to our side of the street before yours and when I heard the letterbox clang, I went to get the envelope and opened it with no particular haste. I stared with incredulity at the piece of paper before calling out, 'Mum, Dad, I passed English Literature! I can't believe it!' I honestly felt they must have made an error and that someone else with a similar name was opening my result somewhere and crying bitterly.

There was a collective cheer and much clapping from the

dining room and my mother rushed up the hall and flung her arms round me. 'Oh, well done, Amy! Well done!'

'That's my girl,' my father said proudly.

'The teachers all said I'd fail them.'

'Well, what do *they* know?' Ava declared, wrinkling her nose, never a fan of anyone in authority.

'I've only passed it because Bear helped me. He'll be so pleased.'

'Of course he will, love,' my father said.

We were all looking out the front bay window, watching for the postman to put an envelope through *your* letterbox. He took such an age, I was becoming quite agitated and impatient. How anyone could walk so slowly I had no idea especially on results day.

My own result came to mind again. 'I can't wait to tell Bear about passing.'

'He'll be so thrilled for you, Amy,' Isabelle said kindly as we all watched and waited with bated breath.

Suddenly the postman was in sight, strolling along without a care in the world and as he posted the longed for results of your hard work through your door, I had my fingers crossed tightly. 'I hope he gets what he wants, Mum,' I muttered as she placed a comforting hand on my shoulder.

'Yes, I know you do, even if it means you'll be separated.'

'I can't wait any longer, I'm going over there.'

My father was laughing quietly. 'Go on then, if you must, but don't be upset if he hasn't ...'

I didn't allow him to finish. 'He will have,' I said, dashing out of the room.

Patrick opened the door and as he did so I could hear Zachary's booming voice coming from the back room. 'Well, it's all done and dusted now, my boy. All that hard work you put in.'

As I walked into the room he was slapping you on the back and you were glancing over at your mammy's face. Zachary's eyes followed your glance. 'Marie, are you not going to say anything?

Where's the brandy? Let's all have a drink, shall we? Aren't you proud of *our* boy?' he asked pointedly. 'Aha, here's young Amy come to congratulate you.'

I wanted you to look relieved, Bear. I wanted your eyes to shine like headlamps on a foggy day. You merely appeared dejected and uncomfortable. I kissed your cheek gently and you showed me the piece of paper. Your hand was shaking uncontrollably. I put my arms around your neck and whispered in your ear so the moment between us could be as intimate as possible. 'Are you happy, Bear? You did it then, three A's.'

'Happy, Amy Lee?' you whispered back. 'This is the easy bit for me. It's life that is hard.'

Your mammy hugged you and, despite your results, the tension in the room was overwhelming.

Zachary was rummaging around in the drinks cabinet and swearing. 'Where the bloody hell is that old brandy? Marie, have you hidden it? I was keeping it for this special occasion. Let's make do with rum then. Here, Patrick, take this and here's one for you, Bear. Marie, are you having one and you, Amy?'

I took the glass because he thrust it at me. You flinched slightly and I felt it and you sighed heavily. Patrick and your mammy both seemed on edge and I wished you had been able to open that envelope in my house.

You told him resignedly, 'I don't drink, Daddy, and neither does Amy.'

Your mammy frowned. 'Zachary, you were drinking before breakfast, I can smell it on you. You don't need anymore.' You mammy said this quite firmly despite knowing there would be an argument if he didn't get his way.

Zachary laughed loudly and ignored your mammy's protestations. 'I was nervous for *our* boy. You'll have a drink on this day of all days, Bear Flynn. Get it down you!' The hostility in the room was swirling around us all like a thick fog and it felt unbearably stuffy and claustrophobic. Now we both knew *he* knew you weren't his, every word he uttered was dripping with meaning. 'Here's to Cambridge University for *my* son, *my* boy, *my* clever, clever boy.'

I sipped it to be polite but it tasted bitter and I turned my nose up. You appeared frozen.

Your face was etched with anger and frustration as you turned to put your glass on the sideboard. 'Thank you, but I won't drink it. I just told you, I don't drink. You know I don't. Even the smell of it makes me feel sick, so it does.'

I could hardly breathe and felt faint as Zachary retrieved the glass and held it up to your mouth, pressing it on your lips hard. 'Fuck, take the drink boy, take it! What are you, a man or a Jesse? This is the day I've been waiting for.'

As soon as the words left his mouth, your mortification and anger burst out of you. Pulling your head away from him, you shouted, 'Don't swear in front of Amy. It's not right. Her daddy never swears in front of women.'

I watched in horror as he lurched towards you and tried again to make you drink it. Patrick grabbed his arm and the glass fell to the floor. The alcohol splashed across your shoes.

Your mammy cried, 'Zachary, you're spoiling Bear's moment. Why do you *always* have to spoil everything when you're in drink? What must Amy think of you?'

Those words seemed to bring him to his senses and he turned to me. For a split second I saw a look in his eyes that made me feel quite nauseous. It was the look I had seen before when I first met him, when the smell of alcohol had been oozing from his skin. I thought he was going to say something embarrassing as he had that day, but then his face changed and he appeared contrite.

'I'm very sorry, Amy. I'm just overcome with emotion. This boy I've brought up ...'

He didn't finish because your mammy interrupted him loudly. 'Why don't we all calm down and have some coffee? I think we are all a bit overcome with emotion on a day like this. Amy, you'll stay for a cup, will you?'

'Yes, thank you, Mrs Flynn,' I replied with a lightness I didn't feel at that point, and desperate for the aggression to subside.

I hadn't wanted to stay but I thought Zachary would explode if I wasn't there and I felt my presence was keeping a lid on his vile temper. I knew your parents' marriage was in its death throes. Every word between them was loaded with the memory of your conception and every look that passed between you and Zachary was full of a barely concealed antagonism on his part and loathing on yours.

Finally, he slumped into a chair and Patrick put his arm round his shoulders, patting him gently as if soothing the temper of a mad dog.

With Zachary quiet at last you seemed to come out of a dream and looked at me expectantly. 'Oh, Amy, what did you get? I bet you passed your English, didn't you?'

'How did you know that? I only passed because you helped me, Bear. Some of your brains must have rubbed off on me.'

You lifted me off my feet and said excitedly, 'I'm so pleased you proved all our teachers wrong. They all told you that you were wasting your time. I knew you weren't, Amy Lee. I'm proud of you, so I am. It's grand that you passed, so grand.'

I couldn't believe your generosity of spirit, Bear. Even at that moment, with the achievement of your three A's and the awful feeling of suppressed aggression in the room, you still had delight in your eyes for my meagre accomplishment. How you did that I'll never know.

Zachary looked up at me and said with a sneer, 'Are your parents pleased? I suppose one pass is better than none.' I doubt he could believe in a million years they would be pleased but I replied as cheerfully as I could.

'Oh yes, Mr Flynn, they're ecstatic. They didn't really expect me to pass any, but even if I hadn't, they wouldn't have minded. But Bear helped me so much. It's all down to him really.'

You were gazing at me so proudly, as if I was the cleverest person in our school. Even just being near you I was influenced by your intelligence as well as your kind and compassionate nature. You dropped your voice to a whisper and put your lips next to my ear. '"Your soul is so close to mine, that what you dream, I know. I know everything you think of, your heart is so close to mine."'

Your eyes resembled those of a bloodhound, sad, lost and weary and I could only whisper, 'I'm so pleased about your results, are you?' You didn't tell me you were pleased, you simply sighed.

'I'll be going to Cambridge then, Amy.'

'I know, Bear, I know.'

That was all I could say as my heart was pounding so hard. You had once told me, your sleeping heart needed to be in Ireland to be able to breathe. Perhaps we should both have been kind to our sleeping hearts and let them out into a vast field in Ireland. You would have been so much happier.

On the day of your departure to university, I was supposed to be at work but I'd taken a day's holiday to see you off.

Since we'd left school we'd both been given temporary employment at the local supermarket. You'd worked upstairs in the office working alongside the manager, Mr Portman, correcting his sloppy paperwork and poor figures and I was on the shop floor, running around like a startled rabbit whenever someone on the till wanted a price check.

We spent our lunch hour together in a cafe nearby or in the park and spoke of inconsequential things rather than stray onto you leaving London or our heated and emotionally charged conversation on the moor. The manager was keeping me on until I found something permanent and he was a kindly, rotund and fatherly man whose eyes lit up when he spoke to me.

My parents were dreading how I would react to you going, especially my father whose health was rather precarious at that time. He was often exhausted and grey and he spent much of his spare time gazing out of the window at the trees in our garden. It was early October and chilly, brisk winds were scattering the turning leaves and making a golden carpet on the lawn.

The day you left, my father said wistfully, 'It's autumn, love, look at the leaves falling all around us.' He shot me a quick glance and added sadly, 'Bear will be going then?'

'Yes, Dad, today ...'

'Amy, don't let him know how upset you are. Pretend, darling, pretend you are happy for him. That's what love is.'

'Dad, I can't ...'

'Yes, you can! Do it for him. You are stronger and braver than you know. You are so much stronger than Bear. He's a fragile lad, always has been, fragile and complex. He feels things so deeply. You aren't fragile, darling. You are tough like your mum. Bear hasn't had the happy, loving family life you have, that's the difference. His father over there is a difficult man.'

'How do you know that?'

'I watch him sometimes, walking down the street, as if he owns it. He has a swagger about him. He isn't kind. I can see that in his face. Bear's mum is downtrodden and full of anxiety and that's because of Mr Flynn. So, put on your bravest face, my dear and wave him off cheerfully and then you can come in here and break your heart. Do it for him. Do it for Bear. He deserves it, don't you think? He's been such a good friend to you all these years, teaching you maths with such immense patience and taking you to Ireland. Do it for him, Amy.'

You came across later that morning with your bags packed and a worried frown on your face. My mother was the only one in apart from me and she deliberately made herself scarce after kissing you goodbye and telling you she would miss you terribly.

'You're off then,' I said flatly, an unknown hand reaching inside my chest and squeezing hard.

'Yes, I have to be quick, I can't miss the train.'

'Write to me, Bear, won't you? Tell me all about it, what books you're studying, the friends you make, you know. Or ring sometimes maybe. Describe everything, even your room and the view...' My words tailed off because your face was clouded with sorrow.

'I will, Amy, I will.'

I could stand it no longer. I wanted to keep you there for as long as possible. I hugged you as hard as I possibly could.

Your thin frame was trembling slightly as you asked, 'Will you be okay? I'll see you at Christmas. It will fly by, so it will.'

'Yes, I'll be fine and you, will you be fine?'

'Yes, I'll be grand. Don't cry, Amy or I won't be able to walk away from you.'

My throat felt as if it was closing with misery as I watched your eyes quickly fill with tears. Our years together flashed through my memory in an instant: The day we met, when I first heard you voice, walking home from school with me climbing on walls and jumping over the cracks in the pavement and you helping me understand maths. And all the times we had danced in my room together with you laughing at my antics. The intimate moments we had shared and how you finally and bravely admitted what your body desired. What on earth was I going to do without you? The last few seconds of having you there in front of me were flying and I could already feel the enormous, empty space opening up in front of me. You put your forehead against mine for a few fleeting seconds.

'Remember, Amy Lee, don't climb trees without me.'

I had no more words as you turned quickly and walked away towards your new life without me by your side. I glanced across at your house and Patrick was watching you from the bedroom window, his face ashen. I blew him a kiss and he blew one back and withdrew. I ran to the kitchen where I knew my mother was waiting for me with open arms. I cried so hard and for so long my eyes were burning and my chest hurt. My mother simply stroked my hair and spoke with her motherly, soothing voice.

'I know, Amy, I know. The heartache is too much. He's such a lovely boy.'

I had felt bereaved by your absence. It was as if the world had turned into a vast mass of grey and white. All colour disappeared in an instant. I existed in a vacuum of loss.

Your Cambridge years had begun, Bear, the years when you grew up and expanded your knowledge and intellect and I tried my hardest to get on with living my life, without you as the very core of every moment. I couldn't settle until your first letter appeared on the hall mat and I devoured it. It was full of descriptive passages and I felt as if I was actually seeing it through your eyes. You began with Rumi, of course.

'"Your deepest presence is in every contracting and expanding." Amy, Cambridge is a beautiful city which is a great relief to me. I couldn't be anywhere that wasn't aesthetically pleasing because it would be difficult to study superb and deeply affecting literature and be somewhere that didn't lift my emotions. My tutors are so bright they make me feel inadequate, so they do.

'My main teacher is a kind, brilliant and softly spoken man called Eddie Baker. But more than that, he has an old soul and we have become firm friends already. Apart from you, he's the only *real* friend I've ever had. He's very young for a post with such responsibility. I would guess he's forty-five although he looks much younger and I feel grateful he will be my mentor for the entire course. I feel he understands me. Not many people do. He has a compassionate nature with great depth of feeling. I could listen to him speaking for hours because his voice is deep and rich and he uses such clever words that light me up.

My room is tiny with just a bed, a desk and some shelves for my books. I get up early to read and as I look out of my window I see the dawn rising gracefully over the rooftops opposite and as light floods the cobbled courtyard below, I think of all the students who have studied here before me and wonder what they have done with their lives and what I'll do with mine. The buildings are mostly built with light-coloured stone and in the late afternoon as the day fades away, yellow and orange lights come on in the little rooms opposite me as students begin to study or to gather to socialise.

It feels strange not to be looking across at your house and signing at you. How is life in London? Did you see anything of Tommy and Danny when they came over from Ireland? Zachary has gone, Amy, thankfully and left Mammy and Patrick in peace. It was ugly though, ugly and violent apparently. I don't mean physically violent, my brothers wouldn't have allowed that. I mean he said some pretty nasty things to mammy about me and my conception, but she is free now. Tommy and Danny had no idea, of course, but mammy's deepest secret is out in the open now.

I think of the sun coming up in Ireland every morning, filling my granny's house with its golden rays, and how you can see the mass of silver stars and how the mountains rise out of the early mists. I think of the silence too and of standing over granny's grave and letting her know I've come home. I wonder what my daddy is doing and whether he ever thinks of his son as he prays in that little church. I miss you, Amy Lee.'

With each letter you wrote, I could feel you easing into your life there, easing into the world of academia and leaving this world behind you. You mentioned Ireland in every letter and how you loved the lyrical beauty of W.B. Yeats because he seemed to be writing just for you. You appreciated the emotional violence of Sylvia Plath and could identify with her black moods and depression, the dark eloquence of the war poets and the romance of Byron, Keats and Shelley. Rumi was still your favourite, you said.

Eddie Baker was mentioned constantly and a couple of other names of young men in your group who would come to your room most evenings, drink coffee and encourage you to write. Occasionally I would wonder what else they were encouraging you to do. I felt a stirring of jealousy because of these faceless people, knowing that they would all be enchanted with you and imagining the quality of the conversation that would have flown over my head. It made me wonder how on earth I had ever been enough for you with my scatty, daft ways. I felt frightened when I imagined I might not be in the future.

You asked me to go and stay with you for a weekend, but not until the summer when we would be able to sit on the banks of the river Cam or go punting together. I held on to that invitation, hoping to meet the wonderfully talented Eddie Baker and judge for myself whether he was a threat to our close friendship. But I never did visit you, Bear. You were completely overwhelmed with your studies and I didn't want to encroach on your life in any way. I was also worried that I would embarrass you with my lack of knowledge when everyone else there was so obviously brilliant.

One letter you sent, soon after the first, turned my stomach over with fear. 'Dear Amy,' you wrote, 'Zachary came to see me. I opened the door to my room and he was there, glowering at me but pretending to be friendly and cheerful. He came in and sat on my bed and unburdened himself without a thought for my feelings. He'd been drinking and told me things I didn't want to listen to, like how he forced my mammy to be affectionate towards him because of me. I detested him then and I told him so. He appeared shocked by that and tried to backtrack by saying he'd been a good husband and father before I was expected. He had cursed my birth, he said, because it ruined his life, but he professed to having a deep love for me despite everything and despite not wanting to. I listened and said very little even though I longed to tell him that I didn't want that type of love because using me to get to mammy was the furthest from love you could get. I was so desperate for him to go, I told him what I knew would force him to leave in disgust. I told him I was nothing like him even though he had brought me up. I told him my secret, Amy. I watched as his face registered my words and he just stared, with his mouth open, like a dying fish. I revelled in his astonishment, his distaste and ultimately his revulsion. I know I shouldn't have and I regret it now. He called me some awful names that I don't care to repeat, but I will tell you one of them. He said, "I always knew there was something, but I didn't imagine you were *bent!*"

I'm not sure where my reply came from, it just kind of burst out of me. I said, well, what's so interesting about a straight line? He then told me not to be so damned clever with my words but I answered, it was always *him* who wanted me to be so damned clever.

As he left, he uttered these words. "Well, you would be one of *them*, because you aren't *my* son. A son of mine, from *my* blood would never be like that!" I watched him leave and as the door closed I collapsed on my bed. I'll never see him again, thank God. Later that day I had a tutorial with Eddie and he sensed my despair. He was so kind and he put his arms around me and hugged me. Tonight I'm going to his sitting room to chat with him. He said he can help me come to terms with everything in my life, even the black beast. He has it too, can you believe it? I miss you, Amy Lee.'

I imagined Zachary with his belligerent manner and sweating face, spitting alcohol all over you as he lost his temper at your confession. I can only guess at what a terrible, degrading encounter it must have been for a gentle soul like you. I was more concerned though at your tutor putting his arms around you.

Eddie Baker had slowly begun to take Ben's place in my mind, especially when your letters became less frequent and yet contained more and more praise for him. You apologised for not writing so frequently but blamed your workload and said it was horrendous. When you came home after that first term you had changed a little. You were still my Bear, my best friend, my confidante, but your life was opening up and different characters were entering it and expanding your horizons. You encouraged me to find a job that would suit me, even though neither of us could think of one that would.

You'd asked me, 'What employer will put up with your shenanigans, Amy? Who could contain you in one place?'

'I don't know what you mean,' I'd replied, knowing exactly what you meant.

'You need to think about your future, your life, you know. Eddie says I should teach in America one day when I leave Cambridge, so he does. He says they'd love me over there. He said he'd always wanted to teach there and perhaps we could go together and support each other.'

'America!' I had gasped. 'That's so much further than Cambridge, Bear.'

'It's a long way off, so it is and I'd need a top grade to go there. It's a long way off, don't think about it.'

'Is that what you want then, to go there with Eddie?'

You didn't answer and I cursed Eddie bloody Baker for planting the seed in your mind where I suspected it would stay and grow. I knew why he wanted to go with you too. It was blindingly obvious the man was falling head over heels in love with you and the thought of being separated from you by thousands of miles was already making him feel bereft.

I imagined him hugging you after Zachary's visit. I imagined his arms around your shoulders and feeling your slim body against his and I wondered how tightly he had held you. Was it a hug so hard against his body that it had awakened your hidden desires? Were you so close inside that embrace that Eddie could feel those desires surfacing in you? I knew Eddie was hugging you because *he* held those same desires inside him too and your lithe but taut body and beautiful spirit was just too overwhelming a mix to resist. I had to banish those thoughts because I was becoming increasingly concerned about Eddie Baker and his influence on you.

Each time you had come home for the holidays we reconnected instantly and yet I could sense a change in you. Looking back, I realise now you were simply maturing. You appeared more comfortable in your own skin and yet less at peace in your mind. You were more confident outwardly and yet more anxious and distracted. I asked you about it but you didn't seem to understand my observations.

Zachary was out of your life, but you still felt a mountain of expectation from your mammy because she had given up so much for you. Your granny had left money in her will too for your higher education and you felt you owed it to her memory to succeed.

Whenever she could your mammy fled to Ireland leaving Patrick alone but she didn't stay at your granny's farm, she spent all her time with Wolf, the silver-haired stranger who continued to be a stranger to you, despite your mammy's impending divorce. That weighed heavily on you and you began to speak of it often.

Although I'd missed you continually, the years had gone by fairly quickly and your finals soon came upon you. Before you returned to Cambridge for these exams we were together in my bedroom every evening when I came home from my shift at the supermarket. We talked endlessly and listened to music and you were still the boy I had always known and loved. I would pull you up and make you dance with me and I could still make you laugh with my erratic and daft behaviour. My heart would swell when we lay side by side.

You would whisper in my ear, 'Amy Lee, you're my Guardian Angel, so you are. There's nobody like you in the whole world.'

'There's nobody like you either, Bear.'

You spoke about the joy of learning and how much you admired the writers you were studying, but Rumi continued to shine brightly above the rest. Eddie had taught you how to understand the hidden, powerful meaning behind many of Rumi's most difficult poems. You said you would be eternally grateful to him for that because it made you understand life so much better. I tried so hard to tell myself I didn't care how close you seemed to be to your main tutor, but I began to dread hearing you speak his name.

It was because of the fabled Eddie Baker that we had our first and only slight disagreement. He was moving insidiously and snake-like into your life, slowly winding himself around your body and squeezing tighter and tighter. I take full responsibility though, Bear. I was envious of your ever-deepening friendship with him and envy is an ugly emotion that taints everything it touches. I regretted it immensely as soon as the devil clothed in green had reared up inside me and spilled over into my shallow words, and still do regret it. We had no idea what would follow our conversation when you returned to Cambridge.

One night, just before you travelled back to sit your final exams, you had told me something that made me fearful. I had asked you what happened to Rumi and how he had written such wonderful, affecting poems about every emotion we feel in our lives. I have never forgotten one word of your answer.

'He became obsessed with a young man and all his love poems are thought to be about the friendship they had. His children were thought to be jealous and worried about this close relationship, so they killed the young man. It's so sad, why couldn't they allow their father to love who he wanted?'

'That's terrible, but you can hear it in his poems, his sense of loss I mean.'

'There's one quotation of his I have written on a note on my wall, so there is and I look at it every night before I go to sleep. Eddie encouraged me to do that at the beginning of my degree and I still do it now.'

My voice had shaken when I asked, 'What does it say on the note?'

'"Tear off the mask. Your face is glorious."'

I knew exactly what Eddie had meant when he encouraged you to read those words every night. I knew what he was referring to, but *why* he was, was another matter. Did he sense in you a desire to cast off your old self and who you *had* been and embrace your true nature, to become more of who you wanted to be in the future? Was it altruistic on his part and did he want the best for you or was he in love with you and did he long to feel your slim, muscular body against his? I prayed it was the former but I suspected it was the latter. You asked if I liked that quotation and when I answered, I could hear the lie in my words clearly. 'Yes, it *is* lovely, Bear.'

'You didn't say what you always say, Amy. Rumi really was being a clever bastard when he wrote that, so he was. He knew so many of us wear a mask in our lives, but we don't need to. We should show our true, glorious selves to the world, wouldn't you say?' I couldn't answer because my throat felt tight and my words stuck in it. You looked at me curiously before asking once more, 'Amy, would you agree with that? That's what Eddie says, so he does.'

'Eddie is wearing a mask though,' I observed, my voice just above a whisper.

You looked intrigued. 'You haven't met him so how could you know that?'

'It's in the way you describe him to me, I can feel his adoration for you, his passion and his ...'

You immediately pulled back from me, shocked, with your eyes full of bewilderment. 'He's my teacher, so he is and my friend. You can't be saying that, it's not fair to him. He's so kind and he cares about me. He says I'm the most gifted student he's ever taught. He wants me to get a first in my finals and he's working so hard to make it so. Amy, he gives me extra tuition and spends so much time with me, more than any of the others. It's not like you to be unkind.'

'Oh, Bear, you're being naive. It isn't kindness that's driving him, it's his lust!'

'Mother of God, you don't even know him,' you gasped, in utter disbelief. 'How can you say that?'

Anger was beginning to burn inside me and looking back now, with more mature eyes and emotions, I know how I hurt you with my jealousy. As soon as the next words had escaped from my mouth, I wished wholeheartedly I hadn't spoken them. My only defence is youth. 'Do you talk about me to *him* as much as you talk about him to me?'

'I do, I promise I do.' You appeared unsettled and confused. 'He calls you the *infamous* Amy Lee.'

'Why haven't I ever been to stay with you in Cambridge?' I demanded, my anger quickly turning into childish tears. 'All this time you've been studying there and I don't even know what your room is like or your friends. All I ever hear is Eddie! Eddie! Eddie! Why can't I come up and meet him? Are you ashamed of me, Bear? Is it because I'm not clever like you and Eddie?' Your face fell and I could have bitten my bitter tongue.

'I haven't asked you to stay because I'm consumed with work. I didn't realise I spoke of him all the time. I'm truly sorry if I do but he's opened my eyes to so many things. He's the first close friendship I've made apart from you. He is the only person who understands me apart from you too. He has no side to him, he just wants me to achieve what I'm capable of, Amy. He admires my intellect, so he does.'

I felt frustrated by your answers and your blind defence of the compassionate and benevolent Eddie and even though I knew my outburst was hurting you, I carried on regardless. 'Oh, Bear, he's in love with you, I just know he is. He'd have to be blind just to admire your intellect. You're so gorgeous, so talented and hard working, he must bless the day you walked into his classroom.'

'He does, he told me that. He says he's been waiting all his working life for a student as gifted as I am. But it's the literature and my understanding of it that he is passionate about. He knows I feel like he does about it. He spends time with me to discuss ...'

'He spends time with you because he *wants* you,' I declared, my voice rising with exasperation. 'Is he married? Does he live with his family or does he live alone?'

'He lives in the university grounds; he has no family.' I could see how my sudden flare up of temper was affecting you. You had sweat on your top lip and your eyes were moving so rapidly from side to side, they made me feel queasy. You appeared deflated and defeated. 'I can't be thinking like this, I can't. He's my friend, my teacher, my mentor, so he is.'

'Well, maybe he is, but I know he wants to get you into bed. I just know it. Didn't you feel that when he hugged you after Zachary visited you?'

You paused before answering and I knew you were thinking hard about that heartfelt hug because your expression changed. It was as if my words had lifted a veil from your eyes and you were now seeing clearly. It hurt you though, Bear, didn't it?

'I don't know, well maybe I wondered, but I wasn't sure. He ran his fingers down my face after the hug and I did think that was a little too intimate, for a teacher I mean. He's so kind to me, so kind, so he is. I did feel ...'

'Look, just be careful. Just be aware, that's all. I'm sorry I brought it up. I guess I'm just envious of the time he gets to spend with you. I know that's wrong of me and childish, I'm really sorry.'

You didn't answer, your head was reeling and I longed to take my words back. I thought perhaps you would shrug them off and even laugh a little, but they had damaged you in a way I could never have expected.

You suddenly grabbed your sweater from the end of my bed and muttered, 'I have to go ...'

'Bear, what's wrong? Please don't go.'

You didn't appear to hear me and opened my bedroom door. As you left, you glanced over your shoulder. 'I could never be ashamed of you, Amy Lee.'

I heard you call out to my parents that you weren't staying for tea and the front door then closed behind you. I sat completely motionless for a few minutes. I felt so startled by your negative reaction it was as if I had been slapped round the face. The space on my bed where you had been lying felt brutal. It was empty and soulless and I cursed my quick, insensitive tongue because without my outburst you would still be there, curled up beside me. I shivered as I realised that in the future, that space would probably seem like a vacuum, an abyss, with no way out.

My parents picked up on my distress at the tea table that evening. Knowing glances were exchanged between them and when I jumped down Ava's throat, it was patently obvious there had been words between us. She was the baby of the family so she often said what others were thinking, knowing she could get away with it. There was no malice in her, she was just very open and often spoke before thinking.

She had said quite innocently, 'I thought Bear was having tea with us.'

'Well, he isn't!' I snapped.

My mother reached across the table and touched my hand. 'Amy, what's wrong?'

Isabelle nudged me. 'Is Bear your boyfriend now? You spend all your time with him when he's at home so I guess he must be.'

'Shut up, will you? He's my best friend, always has been.' My anger deepened and I repeated, 'Just *shut up*!'

My father gave me a disapproving frown. 'Amy, don't speak to your sister like that.'

I couldn't breathe, I felt as if I was suffocating. I jumped up and ran upstairs and flinging myself on the bed, I whispered your name over and over again until my voice sounded hoarse.

All I could see was your forlorn face when I'd I said Eddie felt only lust for you. Even when I shut my eyes you were there, perplexed, disturbed and saddened by my outburst. I could see your worried look when you admitted he had run his fingers down your cheek. I was shouting into my pillow. 'Oh, Bear! Bear! Bear! Eddie is right, your face *is* glorious.'

My door opened slowly and my mother came in, perching lightly on the end of my bed. She began speaking softly. 'Amy, sometimes I feel you'd be happier in yourself if you let Bear go a little.'

'I can't let him go! I just can't, don't you understand? I'll never be able to.'

'But perhaps you *should* for a while. Look, people change and grow up and leave their past behind. Maybe Bear needs to do that for a while. It doesn't mean he doesn't feel the same as he always has about you. Perhaps you need to let him fly away for a bit. I think of him like a homing pigeon, flying to other places because he needs to stretch his wings, but always returning. He's a very clever, popular young man and he can't stay in these streets forever. The world needs to know of Bear Flynn.'

'But he doesn't want that, Mum. Everyone thinks that of him but I'm the only person who knows his true mind. He can't cope with it. I know him, the *real* him and he's too fragile.'

'What does he want then?'

'He just wants to be happy and look up at the night sky in Ireland. He can't cope with too much, he gets anxious.'

'Have you had a bust up? It isn't like him not to stay for tea.'

'Yes, I opened my big mouth and said something that shocked him,' I snivelled, wiping my hand across my nose.

'I'm not surprised at that. Amy, you have to give him some freedom. Like I said, he needs to spread his wings. University changes you, it'll change Bear.'

'Bear hasn't changed. His bloody tutor fancies him,' I cried, sobbing out loud.

My mother stroked my hair and laughed quietly. 'Of course he does.'

'What do you mean? You were supposed to say, of course he *doesn't*.'

'Bear is a beautiful young man, inside and out, who wouldn't want him? University is like its own little world. But he'll be leaving university soon and his tutor will have to let him go. Bear will forget all about him, I promise you. He'll never forget you though.'

'How did you get to be so wise, Mum?' Her words were making me feel a little calmer.

'I've been around the block a few times, darling. All I know is this: that you and Bear have a close friendship that will probably last for most of your lives. It may not end up being the physical relationship you want, but if it isn't then you'll find someone else and so will he.'

'But I won't, Mum and neither will he,' I told her, knowing that was the truth, *our* truth even at that young age.

'Then if you don't, it means you will end up together, in some way.'

I thought of your mammy and Wolf and how, despite the many seemingly impossible twists and turns of their romance, they could now reveal their love to the world and be together. But I didn't want to wait that long. I didn't want to be married to someone else and hide how I felt for you and I couldn't imagine you in the arms of someone else. 'I couldn't marry another man, Mum,' I whispered, as if talking to myself. My mother appeared perplexed and opened her mouth to ask me a question, but initially thought better of it.

She paused for a moment before finally plucking up the courage from somewhere. 'Amy, I wonder about Bear sometimes. I think he might be ...'

I jumped down her throat before she could finish. 'Don't say it! Please, don't say it!'

'Alright, alright,' she said, soothingly, 'I won't, I won't, darling. Come downstairs now and eat your tea. Dad is worried about you.'

I couldn't settle after our argument. I can't really call it an argument because you need two angry, opinionated people for that and there had been only me. I watched for you to sign later that evening but you didn't appear. I felt completely overwrought and imagined you were brooding on my outburst or perhaps telling Eddie on the phone you were so disgusted and disappointed in me, you wanted to return to Cambridge straight away. I had no idea you had already forgiven me and that you were sitting quietly in your darkened room, remembering all the moments in the past three years where Eddie had singled you out for praise and for private tuition and unburdened his soul to you. Your defence of his character against my volley of unbridled criticism was, in truth, your unspoken fears coming to the surface.

I remember you told me eventually that he had placed his hand on yours so many times, letting it rest there just that bit too long, his arm around your shoulders and his fervent looks a little too obvious. You admired his brain, the way he thought and you were immensely grateful for his tutelage and his faith in you. You had indeed been very fond of him, but there were no feelings of desire or love on your part. Eddie had finally confessed his unrequited love to you in a letter shortly before you left Cambridge and it had made your last few weeks there difficult, unhappy and stressful. But my jealousy of someone I hadn't even met had contributed so much to that misery.

When you had returned to university for your final exams, you avoided Eddie and stayed cocooned in your room, concentrating solely on getting through the final few weeks and obtaining the best grade possible. You fought for that high grade not for yourself but because everyone had expected that of you for as long as you could remember.

My world meanwhile was crumbling into an unedifying nightmare and our happy family life changed beyond all recognition.

As you wrote your answers eloquently and with depth, I watched as my father's life ebbed away. That week he had been very tired and listless and he couldn't remember how to use the oven when my mother had gone out for the evening. I thought nothing of it, although there was a fleeting sense of concern when he jokingly mentioned the blood from his heart not reaching his brain quickly enough, but it was said in jest. When I listened to his breathlessness as he climbed the stairs that night, I thought it was merely a sign of age. If only I had known that those breaths were the last I would hear from him. If I had known, I would have sat on the edge of their bed and told him how much I loved him and how grateful I was that he was my father. I would have spent those last few, precious moments of his life just making the most of his kind, sparkling blue eyes and the feeling of always knowing I was deeply loved by him.

My mother's screams in the early hours of the morning told a different story and sent ice through my veins as I rushed into their room. I fought to save his life as his lips turned blue. Isabelle and Amy stood paralysed with terror, clinging to our mother and shaking uncontrollably. I begged him to stay, begged him not to leave us because we couldn't live without his love. But he had already gone. He was already waking in the next world.

Is that where you are going now, Bear as I sit and pray for your cherished life? Don't go into the next world without me.

We were stunned by Dad's loss and our collective grief was a despair that seemingly had no end. My mother was half the person she had been and not quite in this world with us. He was no longer there to support and adore her. He was no longer there to laugh at her funny ways and her loud singing and swearing in the kitchen. At times she looked as if part of her skull had been blown away. When she walked into a room, I glanced behind her expecting him to follow. Life became a blank and hopeless blur as we all struggled to confront our deep grief. I didn't tell you at first because of your exams and because you were dealing with the loss of Eddie's friendship.

Through her tears my mother had urged me to let you know about losing my father. She understood that I needed you at this awful time and that you would want to know. She said your exams were finished and you would be upset if I didn't tell you. I tried to pick up the phone so many times, but when I imagined saying the words, I collapsed in a torrent of sobbing that lasted for hours, and I never made the call.

Crying so hard and for so long meant I went to work the next morning with red-rimmed eyes that were so sore I could barely see out of them. The kindly, fatherly manager did his utmost to comfort me and told me he couldn't wait for you to be back by his side when you came home. He said it to cheer me up, Bear, but he also missed your gentle presence and your polite ways.

During the early days of bereavement, I had received a long letter from you. It caused immense guilt on my part, although that was never your intention, I know that. You don't have an unkind bone in your body. Your mind just doesn't work that way.

'Amy,' you wrote, 'I was looking for Eddie after my first exam, to let him know how it had gone. I thought it the kind thing to do after all his hard work. I had avoided him for the previous few weeks because I now realised the truth in your words and I was embarrassed because his deep feelings for me weren't reciprocated in any way. I also felt they were inappropriate, with him being my tutor. I'm so sorry I reacted so badly, you were courageous to tell me, but you've always been brave and I know you were trying to protect me. So I waited until I had finished completely and I was thinking of coming back to London, to earn some money.'

You had then got sidetracked from Eddie and your tone was a little more cheerful when you said, 'Do you think the supermarket will take me on again until I decide what my next step will be? I do hope so because lunch with you every day, Amy Lee, is a wonderful thought, so it is.'

But Eddie wasn't far from your thoughts and you continued. 'I had no idea that Eddie had resigned from his teaching post and left Cambridge for good after putting a note through my door. Amy, you forced me to open my eyes, but he has left his passion, his career, his calling, all because of *me*. I don't know how to even start dealing with that. I feel forever in his debt but I also feel such guilt. I thought we were friends, I thought he'd written to wish me well, but no ... Oh, Amy, I wanted to show you everything he wrote;

perhaps I shouldn't but I feel abandoned by him and let down. You'll probably guess he started the letter with a Rumi quote.

"My love for you has driven me insane. I wander aimlessly the ruins of my life, my old self a stranger to me. Because of your love I have broken with my past. My longing for you keeps me in the moment. My passion gives me courage. I look for you in my innermost being."

'I felt a deep wrenching disappointment, Amy, because he hadn't said goodbye in person, but he didn't end there. I suppose he couldn't help himself and he wanted to force me to inspect my own feelings, my own life. He quoted more Rumi: "Look for the answer inside your question. Tear off the mask. Your face is glorious."

'If all that wasn't enough, he went on: "Please think kindly of me, Bear. I have been humbled by your intellect, the sweet, generous person you are and the experience of knowing you and teaching you. You will get a first and I will bask in the reflected glory. I send my deepest love and best to you, Bear Flynn. I will never forget you because you are simply unforgettable. Eddie."

'Can you imagine how I felt, Amy? I hadn't meant for any of it to happen. I hope he didn't think I led him on, I don't believe I did. Oh I don't know what to believe!

I'll be home soon to wait for my results but there are a few parties first. I don't have to go to them, but it would be grand to relax for a bit. I'm utterly exhausted. I miss you, Amy Lee.'

As I read your letter, I felt some sorrow for the brilliant, pining Eddie and I regretted greatly my jealous, harsh words about him. What I didn't know then was that Eddie had watched you helplessly from afar throughout your university life, as other students, younger and more sexually adventurous, were drawing you into unfulfilling, short but intimate encounters. You were examining your true nature, but they left you unsatisfied emotionally and increasingly dejected because I still held your fragile heart in my hands. You held my heart in your hands too, Bear. In those years we were both imprisoned by our love for each other.

The evening before my father's funeral, I was shaking with fear. The thought of seeing his coffin in the car outside was terrifying. Isabelle and Ava were trying so hard to be brave and I wanted to support my mother as much as I could. She had lost the man she loved and her life would never be the same again. I longed for your presence so much it began eating away at me and I was wondering about the sense of my decision to not inform you of Dad's death when our doorbell rang.

There you were, Bear, with tears streaming from your eyes and your face clouded with such heartache, it didn't look like you. You grabbed hold of me. Feeling your arms around me at last was like the soothing balm I had longed for. Your familiar smell washed over me once more as I moulded my body into yours as we cried together.

'Patrick rang me when he knew my exams were over. Oh, Amy, Amy, why didn't you tell me? Your kind daddy, your wonderful, loving daddy, how can you bear the pain? You must be heartbroken and I'm heartbroken for you. You loved him so much and I loved him too.'

With those words we both dissolved into a paroxysm of more tears and clung onto each other grimly as if we were drowning. The difference between us was that you never came up for air.

# Chapter Eight

*Life is a balance between holding on and letting go.*
***Rumi***

You stood by my side throughout my father's funeral, your hand firmly in mine. You trembled uncontrollably all the way through the short service and as the coffin disappeared behind some nondescript curtains, we held each other up. The pain was only bearable because you shared every bit of it with me. My grief was your grief, my anguish your anguish, my loss your loss. I only navigated my way through its brutal and unforgiving path because you were there at every corner.

You had left the Cambridge years behind you and began to plan your immediate future. We walked to our job at the supermarket together just as we had walked to and from school. Outwardly we hadn't changed that much, but inwardly you were struggling with the black beast more than ever. I continued to jump over the cracks in the pavement when nobody else was watching as you gazed at the clouds and spoke to me of your longing for Ireland and peace. But you didn't go to Ireland that summer after your finals because, as you explained to me, 'If I go this year, Amy, I won't come back.'

When your results came through you we were in your kitchen. You were clutching my hand as your eyes scanned the piece of paper. 'I did it, Amy Lee, I did it. I got a first.'

Your mammy cried tears of joy and Patrick hugged you, but I had no idea how to react because I expected to see relief on your face, but your eyes seemed quite vacant. I kissed your cheek softly. 'I knew you would.'

Despite your achievement, as always your first thought was for someone else: *my* father. 'I wish your daddy knew; he'd be so pleased. We used to sit on either side of your fire and he'd tell me, "Bear, you can only do your best, my boy. That's all anyone can ask of you." Amy, I wish I'd had a father like yours but instead I have two, one who disgusts me and one who doesn't want to know the man that I am.'

We settled back into our close friendship as if the last few years and Eddie Baker hadn't existed. You spoke of teaching in America and I did my utmost to put your possible departure to the back of my mind. I imagined America loving your soft, Irish lilt, your sense of decency, your kind and charismatic character and your intellect. My mother urged me to encourage you, even though she too loved you deeply and didn't want you to leave.

'Amy,' she told me endlessly, 'you have to let him go willingly. He needs to spread his wings and so do you. He's trying to be sensible. He wants to give you the chance of finding someone else.'

'I know, Mum and I will let him go. I only want his happiness.'

'And he wants yours,' she replied wisely, 'which is why he has to go.'

I was finding it hard coming to terms with my father's death and the fact that my mother was so changed and I leant on you heavily at that time for emotional and physical support. Emotionally you were the rock on which my heartbreak sat comfortably. I had no outlet for my grief other than holding you as closely as I possibly could. This must have weighed you down mentally because you were always so tuned in to others emotions, especially mine. I couldn't cry in front of my mother or my sisters because they would then join in and it often became virtually impossible for any of us to stop.

It happened that night, Bear, do you remember? Of course you do, why wouldn't you? That night, all my long-held dreams that had shattered into a million fragments that day on top of the moor, came rushing back in half an hour of ecstasy with you. I couldn't believe you were in my arms, allowing me to hold you and touch you. We had been lying on my bed, our heads together as usual and I had begun to cry because I missed my father so badly. You had pulled me towards you, to comfort me and kissed my face repeatedly.

'Don't be sad, Amy, I can't stand it.' I could feel your heat thumping in your chest as you asked how you could ease my heartache. 'Just tell me what to do and I'll do it for you.'

'You must know what I want. I want you, Bear. I want *all* of you. It's the only thing that can comfort me, especially as you're going away.'

It felt like a fantasy as your skin touched mine and I repeatedly asked if it was what *you* really wanted. Your face was inches from mine, your body warm and muscular and your soft voice in my ear.

'Amy, I want so much to make you happy. It's all I've ever wanted.' You closed your eyes tightly but you couldn't prevent the tears falling onto my face. I wrapped my legs around yours because at every exquisite moment, I thought you would jump up and run away. You sighed and murmured softly, 'If this makes you happy then it makes me happy too.'

'But please, *please* tell me *you* want this.'

'*You* want it ...'

'That's not enough. You have to want it too.'

'I do, I do, it's all I've *ever* wanted, but it's just so hard for me.'

'I know it is, but you might change. It might help you change.'

What a ridiculous notion that was, but I was so young and I firmly believed anything was possible. Our love for each other could battle any storm. We saw it through, the fumbling, the intimacy, the long awaited union and we allowed our suppressed emotions to come to the surface. All my hopes, dreams and longings since I first heard you speak burst out of me in those precious moments of ecstasy. To feel you moving on top of me was all I had ever wanted.

You felt how I always knew you would feel. You were like coming home to a place of refuge from the outside world and from a cruel and sometimes difficult life. I had rehearsed those moments in my head so many times. The only difference between the thoughts and reality were your anguished tears. I asked you to stay there, with your legs intertwined with mine and your head buried in my shoulder. I could feel the wet of your tears against my neck and I knew, even with my naivety and constant denials, that this would possibly never happen again. I would have held on to your forever. If I could choose a way to die, I thought, it would be with the feeling of your body on mine, your arms around me and your face inches away. I was with you, Bear, body and soul.

But where were you? I couldn't tell. I just couldn't tell. Perhaps you were recalling your sexual experiences at university and if you were, at that moment I didn't particularly care. I just wanted you to be happy. I longed for that, even if it hurt me.

'Amy Lee,' you whispered, 'you're my Guardian Angel, so you are. "Dancing in ecstasy you go, my soul of souls. Close your eyes. Fall in love, stay there."'

'I will, Bear, I will. I am!'

Even at that moment, you were thinking of me before you. 'I'm sorry if it wasn't what you hoped it would be. Was it a disaster for you?'

That was so typical of you, unselfish, kind and anxiously trying to please in every area of your life. I still don't know how you could ever have thought that you weren't enough, that you weren't completely and utterly bloody wonderful, that you weren't loved so deeply by me that everyone else simply paled into insignificance and relegated to the outer reaches of my life. Your eyes were open and you were studying my face with a worried frown.

'Oh, Bear, it was everything I hoped it would be. I can't describe how I feel right now. There's nobody like you in this world for me but you, *no-one*. There never will be. I just wish you'd believe me. If this never happens again because you don't want it to, I'll keep it in my heart forever how you felt. It was perfect, Bear. *You* are perfect.'

'So are you, Amy, so are you. One day, when we've had enough of everything and everyone, we can live in Ireland, on my granny's farm.'

'Where angels live ...'

'Yes, where angels live.'

When I look back at that night now, I know you were trying your very best to be the person I could have a long-term physical relationship with but unhappily it simply magnified our sexual differences at that point and widened that gulf between us. That knowledge caused a battle within you, as monumental as the other battles you were already fighting bravely.

Zachary and Wolf were so hard for you to shake off. They continued to wage war inside your head, both absent but for different reasons. Throughout your life Zachary had been verbally aggressive and had pushed you continually but Wolf appeared in your dreams as a shadowy figure, always standing apart, a lone, emotionally absent parent you only discovered by chance.

You didn't even feel that your mammy loved you unconditionally and you should have been able to feel that, Bear. She had kept so much from you, lied continually and often shrugged off your need to be closer to her.

Your departure for America was looming and you seemed almost excited, but often anxious about teaching there. I dreaded it, but my mother was urging me to hide my feelings for your sake, as she had so often before.

'Amy, he's doing it for you. He wants you to find your way in life without his influence. You must know that, darling.'

'I do know, Mum, but that doesn't help how I feel already about his absence. Two years is *so* long, so bloody long. What will I do without him?'

'You both need this, believe me. You can travel, make other friends. Sometimes I feel you two are *too* close.'

'Why do you think that?'

'Well, because there's no room for anyone else, for either of you. Think about it, Amy. Who did Bear make friends with at Cambridge? He made some acquaintances maybe, but not real friends and most people do.' She was watching me carefully for a reaction and then added, 'I don't mean sexual relationships either. I mean mates, that kind of thing.'

Eddie Baker came strongly into my mind. You had cherished a long-lasting and close relationship with your mentor built on friendship and a shared passion for classical literature. But then you had been sadly disappointed when you found out the man was hopelessly and secretly in love with you. And it was I who had revealed that to you by voicing my opinion, underpinned by my ferocious jealousy. It caused you to withdraw from him through concern for his unrequited feelings and through embarrassment. Was it me who ruined that for you, Bear? Looking back with more mature eyes, I now see clearly that I did.

My mother's continued kindly spoken words broke into my thoughts again. 'I worry about your lack of friendships too, darling. A woman your age usually has lots of mates, like Isabelle and Ava have and they're not even as outgoing as you. Bear has been your whole life since the age of eleven and he knows in his heart you need to meet new people and widen your experiences.'

'But, Mum, he needs me to fight his battles for him. He really ...'

'Amy, it's not fair on him *or* you and he knows that. Let him go, allow him to grow up, to fight his own battles, allow him space. That's what he's doing for you.'

'I don't want space.'

'He knows that. Try and remember, he's doing it for you.'

Do you remember how we decided to say farewell in my room, Bear, in private, where I had experienced the longed-for feeling of your warm body on mine. There was a tension crackling between us, caused by suppressed agony and dread. Sitting beside you on my bed I knew we were bound together by our shared past, your long-held secret and our few minutes of intense intimacy. Our bond was about to be broken though by thousands of miles and possibly two years of living apart. Wolf had called it a sacred bond. He was right, Bear. It was sacred. It *is* sacred even now when I look at your lifeless face.

Those were my feelings that day, were they yours? I recall how you were jittery and ill at ease, perched on the edge of my bed, your right leg moving constantly as if plugged into an energy source. It reminded me of how you had been the day we searched for your daddy. You repeatedly glanced at your watch until I could stand it no longer. 'You'd best be off then. Don't be late for your flight.' Our shoulders were touching and I felt as if I was being wrenched apart from you forever.

'Yes, it is time I went, so it is.'

'Will you be okay, Bear?'

'Will *you*, Amy Lee? I'm going because we need to find ourselves. Do you understand? Please say you do.'

My father's words had appeared clearly in my head, urging me to pretend that I understood but after his sudden death and my grief, I had no strength left in me. Your departure felt like a death too. It was going to be like a slow death, where all your internal organs fail and you simply fade away. 'Why do we need to find ourselves? I don't know why we have to.'

You leant your head against mine. 'Oh, Amy, you know why, so you do.'

I tried to sound a little more cheerful. 'I'm going to Paris and the south of France and maybe Italy.'

'What country could contain you with your shenanigans? They won't know what's hit them when you arrive.'

'Will you write?'

'Yes, as frequently as I can, until you go travelling and then you make sure you write to me. Will you keep an eye on Patrick and my mammy, please? She's not here that often now, but Patrick will be lonely without me.' I nodded and clutched at your warm hand. You were shaking from head to toe. 'Maybe we can go to Ireland when I come back and my daddy will ask to meet me.'

'I'm sure he will, Bear.'

We both began to cry at the same time, catching our breath and shuddering. I couldn't hide my despair. I was trying so hard to be encouraging and pretend I was delighted for you, but it was beyond me. I didn't feel as strong as my father had told me I was. I was only strong with you by my side.

You sought reassurance once more. 'Amy, please don't be upset. I need to set you free to live your own life and meet a man worthy of you who can give you what you need. I can't leave until you promise you understand.'

I nodded dumbly again because no sensible words would come out and I could almost hear my father's words in my ear. Pretend! Pretend! Pretend! I gasped and when I found my voice it was so small and insignificant, it sounded as if it was coming from at the end of a long, dark tunnel. I *was* in a long dark tunnel where you were slowly walking away from me into the distance. I forced out the words, 'I promise.'

'I'm going then.'

Through my tears, I muttered, 'You have a wonderful time.'

'Amy, *please* ...'

'I'm only crying because I'm so lucky to know you, Bear. I'm crying because I'm grateful you're my friend, my *best* friend and only mine. I'm crying because you helped me learn fractions and because you did my homework for me when I was busy messing about and being daft. I'm crying because you were there to catch me and worry when I climbed on walls.'

'Amy, don't ...'

'Let me finish, *please*. You need to hear this. I'm crying because I didn't have to explain how deep my grief for my father was because I knew you'd feel the same and that you'd comfort me and support me despite your own feelings. I'm crying for every time someone you love has hurt you and disappointed you badly because you never deserved it. I'm crying because you are the first person I want to tell good news to and because you celebrated more when I scraped a pass in English than you did at *your* wonderful results.'

'Amy, I can't be your idol, I have feet of clay.'

'But you don't have feet of clay! I know you don't. Why can't you see that? I'm crying because you gave me what I'd longed for despite knowing it would hurt who *you* are. I'm crying for the times you sat with my father for hours on end because you knew he liked you to. And I'm crying because of the person you are, the generous, deeply loving, compassionate person who is forcing himself to go away for two years, not for his own sake but for mine. I'm crying because you have no idea about any of this and no notion of how downright bloody wonderful you are. That's why I'm crying, Bear.'

You appeared frozen, unable to move, your eyes full of unspoken tragedy. You then took my face in your hands and said through your tears, 'Amy, listen to these words and never forget them: "I am yours, don't give myself back to me."'

You wiped my eyes gently with your fingers and turned away without saying any more. You closed my bedroom door behind you. Your light footsteps on the stairs echoed in my head. I leant against the door and my legs gave way. I slid slowly to the floor.

Two years! Two years without you, Bear! Two years without hearing your voice. Two years without seeing your smile. Two years without feeling your hand in mine.

Long after your departure many mornings I had woken up and for the first few seconds had been unable to remember whether it was my father who had died, or you. The feelings of loss were so similar. Losing you felt like a slow, lingering death. I cannot count how many times I stared at the space where you had been during those last few moments together. It became like an enormous black hole and I found myself turning away from it because of the pain.

Neither of us had any idea at that time that those two years would stretch into three and that life would change dramatically by the time we saw each other again.

My year of recklessness, of escaping my heartache and trying to forge a new life without you, began. I couldn't stand walking to work without your voice saying, 'Amy, look at the clouds, they're angels in disguise, so they are. Will you look at their beautiful white wings flying behind them? They're watching over you, Amy Lee because they love the person you are.'

'Do I need watching over then?' I would always ask you and you would laugh, as if the question was ridiculous.

'You surely do.'

Eating lunch on my own in the park was soul destroying and I would cry into my coffee, asking those angels you loved to keep you safe and bring you back home. I gave my notice in at the supermarket and began planning my trip to France.

Before I went, my mother decided I needed some kind of distraction. She paid for me to have a crash course in driving lessons. I knew you'd find that funny, Bear. Me in a car behaving calmly and rationally and concentrating for more than an hour! When I passed first time, my family were incredulous and my mother bought a second hand car. The only person I wanted to tell regarding this miracle was you. I imagined your face lighting up and the pride in your voice when you would say, 'Amy, well done for passing first time, I'm made up for you, so I am.'

After a couple of weeks without you, I felt a burning need to see Patrick. He was your brother after all, the nearest person to you. His face lit up when he saw me and I asked after your mammy. He explained, in his faltering way, that your mammy was in Ireland and wasn't coming back any time soon. I asked if he was joining her.

'I won't go without Bear,' he said.

I decided to be bold. 'Patrick, why do you think Bear's daddy hasn't asked to see him?' His eyes filled with sudden tears. I put my hand on his arm. 'Don't answer if it upsets you. I don't need to know.'

'Mammy doesn't want to share him yet.'

'*What*? Why?' I was completely flummoxed by his words. 'Bear loves her and that won't change even when he knows Wolf better.'

He seemed perplexed and frowned. I wondered if he had read my lips correctly because he took a few moments to respond. 'No, I meant she doesn't want to share *Wolf*.'

I let his words sink in and although I was shocked, I instinctively knew it was the truth. The sight of the silver-haired man at the side of the road, waving at you as we passed in the taxi had appeared rather upsetting and odd at the time, but Patrick's opinion made complete sense. Many of your complexities and much of the damage done to you in your life were ultimately caused by your mammy and her secrets, not only by Zachary.

An overbearing, verbally aggressive man who brought you up and who you disliked intensely and a mammy whose life was full of contradictions and untold jealousies, had turned you inside out and left you with a gaping hole where unconditional love should have been.

I must have looked aggrieved because Patrick added hastily, 'Mammy does worry about him too. Don't think badly of her. She knows Bear is sensitive and that he'll build meeting his daddy up so much in his imagination, it could never match the reality. Please try to understand, Amy and please don't say anything to Bear.'

I promised I would never divulge anything that I thought might cause you pain, Bear. You were fighting so many emotional battles and I hope I didn't add to them in any way, although I suspect I did.

While I arranged my travels, you wrote regularly. Your letters were like poems for my soul. 'Dear Amy, Boston is an interesting city. The public library is the largest I've ever seen and there is a museum dedicated to the Boston Tea Party, can you imagine? There are beautiful parks and public gardens, unusual apartment buildings and the whole place is a mixture of old and new architecture, depending on where you are. I'm enjoying the teaching, more than I thought I would and the students are polite and respectful and eager to learn. They find my accent difficult sometimes but we get along, so it's grand. But I miss you, Amy Lee and I miss the hills of Ireland.'

The last couple of letters I received before leaving for Paris left me slightly anxious because you described making some friends amongst the other staff and at the end, you told me you were seeing a therapist. Fear for your health gripped me but I could do nothing for you. You were so far away. I convinced myself that a medical professional would be better placed to help and that perhaps, the therapy would conquer the black beast once and for all. I did wonder what a therapist would think about all the complexities in your life.

After a tearful farewell with my mother and sisters, I left the security of the grubby London streets and, I thought, my memories of you but it didn't quite work like that though. Those memories were locked inside my head and heart, never to be forgotten or removed or escaped from. They were etched there as deeply as your name tattooed on your daddy's forearm.

Travelling to France had initially taken my mind off everything that had happened since we left school. I felt excited and energised by Paris with its little flea markets, tree-lined squares, cobbled alleyways and historic buildings. I found a cheap hotel in Montmartre whose decor was rather loud and vivid with bright red and gold walls and little, ornate lamps placed on every surface. The noises from the streets were so different from the London suburbs with loud car horns blasting constantly and artists calling out to tourists to have their portraits done. It was very hilly, with hundreds of steps and narrow alleys leading to the Sacré-Coeur. Yet, no matter how different it all was from London, every sight, every experience, however small, led me back to you and how you would view it, what you would say or think about it.

One bright morning I walked into the Sacré-Coeur, hoping some quiet reflection would ease my aching soul. I found the deep stillness comforting and I sat for a while and watched the candles flickering in small recesses. I thought of your granny.

'My Bear is troubled, Amy. He's like a hot flame.'

I soaked up the Bohemian atmosphere in that part of Paris and wandered into a small art gallery one morning simply because it intrigued me. I had been having a coffee in the bistro next door and the tiny windows and purple shutters of the gallery had caught my eye. There were many artworks on display and I found them quite bizarre but interesting and strangely engaging. Staring at them from the street, I struck up a conversation with the owner who was standing in the doorway. She was an elegant Parisian woman, perfectly dressed in a short, tight skirt and cream blouse, smoking thin cigarettes. She asked me to stay and have a drink with her because she loved everything English.

She drank strong black coffee from a miniscule porcelain cup and for some unknown reason we hit it off immediately. Her name was Josephine and her husband Matthias was upstairs painting in his studio. She took me up the narrow, steeply winding stairs to meet him; he was scruffy and had blue paint in his greying hair and under his fingernails. They both had kind smiles and were amusing, warm people with a generosity of spirit I admired greatly. They had a passionate, mutually supportive marriage and she believed wholeheartedly in her husband's talent.

It was important to Josephine to improve her English because of the tourists, and so she offered me a job there. I was to clean the gallery every morning, after a fashion, make coffee for anyone browsing and serve drinks on the many regular open evenings. I did explain my domestic skills were non-existent and rather slap-dash but she merely laughed and said hers were also.

Josephine and I became very close, she was easy to talk to, had travelled widely in her twenties and now in her forties, she was experienced enough about life to know I was running away from something or someone.

Most evenings we sat in the bistro next door. She hated cooking and the owners were her relatives, so we ate there regularly for free while Matthias painted furiously long into the night. She encouraged me to try a few white wines to go with the fish they served and I listened to her and learnt from her. She wanted to know about my life and listened intently when I spoke about you, Bear, and about us. But whether there was an 'us' at that point in our lives I didn't know, but who else would I talk about? You were my whole life and always had been.

I moved into the attic room at the top of their tall, decrepit building. It had rough, lumpy, cream-coloured walls and contained only a single bed, a round table covered in a lace tablecloth and a small, electric fire. Despite the sparse furnishings, I found it cosy and I loved the view over Montmartre with all the cafes and street artists. The smell of French coffee and croissants filled my senses as soon as I opened my eyes each morning. It was so different from home and I would close my eyes each night wondering what you were doing.

Josephine made me laugh with her exaggerated, typically French mannerisms and her unwavering support and love for Matthias was obvious. She would look at him the way I look at you, Bear. You could see the adoration in her eyes and often I would have to turn away from witnessing their mutual desire because it hurt too much.

I had stayed two months and almost felt like a Parisian, but I had promised myself I would travel on to Provence and then to Italy. Josephine understood my need to move on and begged me to stay in touch and to bring you to the gallery one day. She said she felt she already knew you. You would have liked them both, Bear. They were good people with kindness in every cell and they treated me like the daughter they had never had.

Paris was turning colder and I felt the need to feel the sun on my back, so I took a train southward. As it raced towards Provence, I was able to view ancient hill towns, castles and churches and there were vineyards stretching across the open countryside. The air was noticeably warmer and smelt entirely different from Paris. The sweet smell of juniper, pine, herbs and lavender had a calming effect on me and during the months I spent in the south I would often sit under the shade of old olive trees and look up at their welcoming branches. You would fill my mind completely then, Bear. I could hear you calling to me.

'Amy Lee, will you come down out of that tree? You'll be falling, so you will.'

Many of the beaches in Cannes and Nice were privately owned and belonged to the expensive hotels so you couldn't just wander along them, which disappointed me. I found St. Tropez such a contrast with the harbour full of large, impressive yachts but then inland just a half a mile away there were people living like peasants.

On my first afternoon there I met a group of hippie types sitting in a circle by the crystal-clear, turquoise, Mediterranean. I was paddling in the soothing water and thinking about how different it was to the freezing springs and rivers that ran into the waterfall in Ireland, when one of them called me over. I envied them their relaxed and laidback approach to life and their easy-going, charming personalities and so, when they invited me to stay with them in their campervans, I accepted. I felt I should be sociable, a first for me. I had never wanted or needed any other company other than you, Bear.

I would listen avidly to their conversations and how, in their eyes, everything was fun and would always end up in a positive outcome. It slowly rubbed off on me. I felt myself begin to unwind and I became more at ease in their company and with life in general for a while.

I enjoyed watching the elderly French men in their dark berets playing boules in any spare piece of ground, shrugging their shoulders and laughing loudly. They had large bellies, lined faces and white hair. There were elderly women too, often huddled together, chatting, knitting or just watching the world go by. I wandered through narrow streets in the old part of each town where washing was hanging outside across the streets to catch the hot sun and watched people sitting in cafes and bars. I found it all colourful and interesting but I longed to share it with you.

After weeks of glorious weather, the mistral arrived suddenly one afternoon, gusting and chilly and it swept up the dust from the ground and scattered the falling, autumnal leaves high in the air. The hippies took it as a sign from nature to move on and we packed up and made our way even further south. They told me they needed to earn some money and were heading for the vineyards of Italy for some part time work.

They were all very in tune with the natural world and it made me think of how on our way to school you would describe the wonder of the clouds, the hazy early morning sun and the stark beauty of winter. You had found enchantment and angels and wonder even in the dirty, dusty streets of south London.

'Amy, would you look at this hard frost, glistening like diamonds in the morning sun?' I'd watch your breath floating upwards. 'I love it like this. It's grand, so it is. I wish you could see the beauty of an Irish winter.'

'One day I will.'

'Look, shooting stars. They're exquisite, sent by the angels, so they are. Make your wish, Amy Lee, quickly now.'

My wish was always the same, Bear, but I never told you. It hasn't come true yet and sitting by your bed now, I wonder why the angels you believe in have deserted you. If there was one person in this world who deserved happiness it was you. I always wished for your happiness and for us to be living together happily on your granny's farm. I hope your beloved angels know how desperately unwell you are and that the little people are weaving their magic even now, to bring you back to me. Is this all part of their plan? I will reserve judgement on their mystical powers for now, but I hope they know what they are doing. If they do exist how could they possibly desert someone who believed in them so completely?

My hippie companions and I journeyed through the wavy, undulating fields of Italy and in Tuscany the evening light was golden, soft and enchanting. The landscape was crowded with cypress trees, solitary farmhouses, barns and yet more vineyards. At the end of each afternoon the olive groves were bathed in gentle sunlight and I imagined Matthias sitting in the fields painting, with a chain-smoking Josephine by his side drinking strong, black coffee from a tiny china cup. I missed them both.

The men I encountered were mostly tender hearted and tactile and in the group itself, nobody appeared to be partnered with one person. It was all a bit of a collective love-in and although it took me a few weeks to change my way of thinking and feeling, I gradually became more like one of them.

In the many months I spent in their company, you were always there in the background, Bear. Your presence dominated my days; you were like a faint ghost, often hovering in the distance and appearing most nights in my dreams, just out of reach. I felt this most when I saw couples holding hands or gazing lovingly at each other. My heart would often pound with frustration and longing that I wasn't holding *your* hand. My whole body would ache with a sense of loss and it was the loss of your company, the loss of you physically and emotionally and the loss of a future together that I continued to yearn for.

At times I would despair of ever feeling at peace because I needed *you* to feel at peace. I needed you to talk with me about everything under the sun. I needed you to cry with over the sudden death of my lovely father. You were the only person who understood it all and the only one I *wanted* to tell. Nobody else came close, although they did try. Every time I let go for a few hours and slept in the arms of another man, I would convince myself I was moving on, but into my memory you crept, sometimes silently, sometimes just whispering to me.

'Amy Lee. Amy Lee. You're my Guardian Angel, so you are.'

My longing for you would cut like a sharp blade into every corner and crevice of my life. I would bleed profusely and that blood would stain all my waking moments and disturb my nights. The memory of you would seep into every area, every pore and every cell. You would turn me inside out and rearrange me, until I was someone I didn't even recognise. I became someone else completely because I only knew who I was in relation to my friendship with you.

I loved your memory but I hoped perhaps you would fade, slowly and gracefully into the distance, but you did not. Not one bit! Did I for you, Bear? Did I fade at all? Did I, at any time, simply turn into a girl you once knew, no better than any other girl?

I had hoped that a new environment, somewhere with no memories of you would help me and initially it did. But after about eight months, I lost my way and the path was covered in thorns once more, dark and lonely. There was and is only ever you at the end, only you. Only you could bring me home to myself, only you. *Only* you! You would torment me, standing just out of reach, half in darkness, afraid to come out of the shadows because of the black beast waiting for you.

The men in the group told me I was only half there, even during our intimate moments. How could I tell them, without being unkind and denting their egos, that sex with them was just a physical act, not an emotional one? How could I explain I had my eyes closed tightly, not through passion but because I was pretending it was you? I was trying to create new experiences and memories, as you told me I must, but I have no memory now of the men I met. They're faceless and I can't even remember their names, Bear. Is that awful of me?

That year of endless wandering and reckless relationships with unsuitable men were as transitory as the clouds passing across the moon. Trying to forget you was just a waste of time. I began to wonder why I was even bothering. Every time I tried to give of myself wholly to one of those men, I could see your face above mine.

"'Amy Lee, close your eyes. Fall in love, stay there.'"

I would yell into my hands, 'Bear, I'm trying for God's sake, but I can't because they aren't you! Come home!'

I often sat by the calm, benign sea and listened to water lapping gently onto the white sand and I would think of Ireland and how the rivers would sparkle because, you told me, the nature spirits were swimming across them and making them so. I found it increasingly difficult to look at the beauty of a pink sunset because you had explained that the summer sunsets were the world set on fire.

The longer I travelled and the further afield I wandered the more and more distracted and reflective I became. I no longer had the urge to run or climb or stand on my hands. That wasn't because I was maturing; it was because you weren't there to watch me. I wasn't being myself because I could only be my true, authentic self with you.

Some nights I would sit outside until late with a shawl around my shoulders under the stars and imagine you were across the ocean signing to me.

*The breeze at dawn has secrets to tell. Don't go back to sleep.*

The missing you wasn't romantic; it was messy, painful and

often unbearable. I smiled, I laughed and I joined in with all the heady socialising and partying and various town festivals, enjoying the riot of colour and loud music. But underneath my outward humour, my carefree and at times careless behaviour, was a yearning for you so profound, I couldn't even put words to it.

I thought of the hapless Eddie Baker and felt such an affinity with him and how he had written to you quoting the Rumi poem that matched his feelings for you perfectly. They now matched mine too.

"My love for you has driven me insane. I wander aimlessly the ruins of my life, my old self a stranger to me. Because of your love I have broken with my past. My longing for you keeps me in this moment. My passion gives me courage. I look for you in my innermost being."

I wondered how Eddie was coping with the loss of your presence and whether he thought of you every day. I knew he did. How could he find anyone else who compared to you? There was nobody else like you in the world.

The men I spent time with had such a mellow, casual and at times blasé attitude to life in general, dedicated to the pursuit of pleasure with not much thought for tomorrow. I often wondered if it was all quite natural but I soon realised most of their behaviour was a result of smoking so much marijuana. At first I thought them fun but as the months went on I began to find them shallow. It brought home to me sharply how difficult you must have found it, being surrounded by people who didn't view life like you. I had spent all my growing up years with you and the way you looked at the world had affected me. Your deep emotions were, at times, unfathomable but they were heartfelt, honest and always sincere.

Two of the men in the hippie group professed to reading philosophy and classical literature and would often spout off about poetry and the meaning of life while under the influence of red wine and drugs. At times, while sitting under the stars listening to them when *I* was the only one stone cold sober, I became bored very quickly and irritated by their drug induced ramblings. They had never heard of Rumi. Can you believe that, Bear? That was the last straw for me and I began to plan my route home.

As I had not been able to give you an address to which you could send letters to me, I wrote to you, but not being able to receive letters from you agitated me. One morning I woke up fearful; I just knew you were in trouble. I had always sensed that you were attached to me somehow, in some way, by an invisible thread and whatever you felt, I would also feel. I couldn't concentrate on anything and even the vivid beauty, colour and fascinating history of Florence wasn't enough to quieten my mind. I had to get back home to feel closer to you. The group were going on to Venice and I couldn't possibly have gone with them. Venice was a place for lovers, for romance and the thought of it sharing it with any other man made me shudder.

These memories of our few years apart seem a lifetime ago and feel quite senseless, and now I'm here by your bedside desperate for you to live. I'm praying voiceless prayers hoping that if I sit here for long enough my life force will flow into your motionless body lighting it up with warmth and energy and a longing to live again.

There was something else I had to tell you when you returned home, Bear. My year of intense soul searching and reckless behaviour had culminated in a pregnancy I didn't want. I had absolutely no idea who the father was and worse still, I have no desire to know. Bear, I cannot count how many times I've wished the baby was yours but you would instinctively know that, wouldn't you? I dreaded telling you about the baby, I didn't want to burden you with more emotional turmoil.

I left the hippies after ten months of an erratic, nomadic lifestyle with a few fond kisses and no sorrow and then stayed a few days with Josephine and Matthias on the way back to England. They welcomed me like their long-lost, wayward daughter who had found her way home and listened eagerly to my adventures. A couple of times they offered me a glass of white wine and when I declined, Josephine studied my face closely.

'Amy, you're having a baby!' she declared loudly. 'The south of France was great fun then, yes?'

When I burst into tears and sobbed on her shoulder, Matthias sensibly made his exit and left us alone. I didn't have to confess how I wished the baby was yours, Bear because she knew. She said she could read my face like her favourite book.

She kissed my cheek softly, gave me her flowery handkerchief that smelt strongly of French perfume and spoke some comforting words to me I'll never forget. 'Amy, why are you trying so hard to forget him? Why are you trying so hard to stop loving him? Your father died, but you don't try to forget him, do you? He will always be there, so just accept that Bear will too. Love can be difficult to find, especially love like yours for Bear, so accept it and treasure it. Stop running away. You can't run away from a love like that.'

We talked long into the night in their kitchen, with Parisian sounds and colourful street lights outside the window, and Josephine drank copious amounts of coffee while I ate her sweet biscuits. I honestly felt she was the first real friend I had made in my life except for you.

Paris was bitterly cold in late spring that year with some unseasonal snow showers and a cruel wind blowing the pink blossom from the trees but Josephine was warm and delightful and motherly. I left them again reluctantly with promises of sending photographs of the baby and you.

I arrived back in England after a fierce storm in the channel which saw me curled up in a ball in my seat trying desperately not to be sick. My mother and sisters had no idea I was arriving home and all flew at me when I opened the front door. I had glanced briefly at your house and there was a light on in your front room. That made me catch my breath in case it was you come back early but finding two recent letters from you on the kitchen table made me see sense.

My mother looked tired and world weary and glancing at my father's empty chair that evening, I could only imagine what it had been like for her looking at it every day. But seeing me again unexpectedly perked her up considerably and she bustled about in the kitchen making a welcome-home meal and humming happily.

'Did you meet anyone?' Isabelle asked as I settled into the sofa. Her long, light brown hair had been cut into a neat bob and she appeared to have matured quite a bit in my absence. 'I bet you met some handsome French men, didn't you?'

'I met quite a few people,' I told her lightly, wondering if the change in her appearance meant *she'd* met someone. 'They weren't all French, they were different nationalities.'

Ava was sitting crossed-legged beside me. 'Tell us about Paris, Amy. Did you go up the Eiffel Tower?' She had matured quite a bit in the time I'd been away and I wondered momentarily where my baby sister had gone. Her long mid-brown hair was pulled back off her face in a ponytail and she had lipstick on. 'I'm going travelling when I'm older, aren't I, Mum?'

Isabelle butted in. 'Can you speak French and Italian now?'

My mother, intuitive as ever, called through the serving hatch. 'Girls leave Amy alone for a minute to read Bear's letters. We have all evening to hear her news.'

'Patrick comes to tea most days,' Ava called as I scooped up your letters to read in private. 'He fancies Isabelle, doesn't he, Mum?'

I heard Isabelle scolding her as I ran upstairs to the privacy and silence of my room. I devoured those letters and at first glance they appeared to be the same as they always had been, but I sensed some anxiety within their pages and a longing to be home. You spoke of a couple of new friends, Dean and Adam and a girl who worked in the library called Lizzie whose father was a clinical psychologist. It bothered me greatly why you had felt the need to mention his profession, but I dismissed it from my mind for the time being. You had been to some concerts and mixed with some intellectual types at a couple of parties and discussed politics and literature and art. In both letters you had ended with the same words.

'Amy, Ireland is calling me, so it is. I feel a burning within me to breathe Irish air and to walk in the rough heather. I need to look across at the mountains rising in the early morning mists. Do you remember the mass of stars? My soul aches for it all. I need to come home but my contract here is for two academic years and I won't let them down. It wouldn't be right to do so. They have all been so kind and welcoming.'

'Is Bear coming home soon?' Isabelle asked, almost plaintively. 'I hope he is, it's not the same round here without him. Patrick misses him terribly.'

I tried to hide the despair in my voice. I have no idea why, because they all knew how I felt. I guess it was because I had spent so long trying to forget I had those feelings at all, it had become second nature. Your mammy came fleetingly into my mind.

'Not yet no, his contract is for two years.' My mother brought in a pot of tea.

It was the first thing I had asked for. 'I'm dying for English tea, Mum. The French can't make a cup of tea to save their lives.'

'Darling, the couple in Paris sounded lovely and they were so kind to you, weren't they?'

'Yes, they were *really* kind and generous. One day I hope I can take Bear there, he'd love them. He'd get on great with Matthias. He's like this mad, passionate painter.'

'And what about Cannes and Italy, what were they like?' Ava asked excitedly. 'I've always wanted to go to Italy.'

Before I could answer Ava, my observant mother commented airily, 'You've put on a bit of weight, Amy, but you needed to, you were always so thin in your teens. You look so healthy now. France and Italy obviously suited you.'

'I'm having a baby.' I blurted this out like a long-held confession. 'Sorry.'

There was a stunned silence that went on for so long you'd have thought they had been struck by lightning, until Ava giggled with embarrassment. My mother had gasped and then put her hand over her mouth and Isabelle was staring at her, trying to gauge her reaction. Eventually and thankfully Ava broke the impasse.

'When is it due? Are you getting married then?'

'I'm about sixteen weeks and I'm definitely not getting married!'

My mother seemed to be in shock and asked shakily, 'Does the father know? Is he coming over?'

'No to both of those questions, Mum. Can we talk about it later? I'm very tired from travelling and the crossing was so rough, it made me feel quite ill. I'd like to have a sleep if you don't mind.'

'Of course, darling, of course, you go up. I'll call you later for tea.'

I left the three of them there to discuss my predicament and as soon as I walked out of the room I could hear Isabelle and Ava talking quickly in hushed tones, but not actually what they were saying. But they sounded almost excited and I felt relieved by that because bringing a baby into the house was going to change their lives immensely.

Opening the door into my room after all that time away was a rather peculiar and singular experience. In one respect it seemed as if I had only left the week before and in another it was like entering into another world. The sounds and sights of Paris in autumn seemed years away and the warmth and sweet-smelling herbs and vineyards of Provence and Italy belonged to another lifetime and that lifetime knew nothing of Bear Flynn.

I sat on my bed and stared for a long time at the space where you had been before life wrenched us apart. That space was just as huge and just as empty. There was at least another year to go before you were home and in my low moments, I imagined you staying even longer, which you did. I put my hand on my swelling belly and wished you were there with me.

I slept for an hour until my mother tapped gently on the door. She appeared quite apprehensive when she came in and sat on the end of my bed. We looked at each for quite a while. I think she expected me to speak first, but I had no idea what to say because this was such an unexpected turn in my life that I couldn't ever have predicted. Eventually she spoke, very quietly.

'Amy, is this really what you want, darling? Is this baby what you want?'

'It wasn't planned, Mum. I was irresponsible and foolhardy, I know that. I'm sorry if I've disappointed you, but it's happened and I have to live with it.'

'Oh, Amy, you could never disappoint me. I only want your happiness and I know how unhappy you've been. You can't hide it from me, I'm your mother. I'd hoped your travels would have made you forget him, but they haven't at all, have they?'

'No, Mum, not one bit, but at least the baby will give me a focus until he comes home. I still want him as much as I ever have.'

She leant down and kissed my forehead. 'Don't tell your sisters, but I'm secretly quite delighted.'

In that moment I realised that I hadn't even asked how she had been and whether my father's absence still weighed as heavily on her. At times, I could be selfish in my love for you because there was little space for thinking about anyone else and how they were feeling. That's what you would have said to me, Bear. I could hear your voice in my ear so often, urging me to think of others more.

'How have *you* been, Mum? Really, how have you been?'

'Well, I've missed you dreadfully, but I'm not too bad. I can't sit and look at four walls all the time, so I keep myself busy and I work part-time in the corner shop. I like meeting all the customers and chatting to them. I have to make a life, Amy and I am, I *am* and now I'm going to be a grandmother and that new life will give me a focus too. If you concentrate on grief and loss all the time, you miss the present moment.'

'But you loved him so much,' I said, tearfully. 'How do you do it? You're so strong.'

'I do it because I have you and Isabelle and Ava and I can't give up. You'll understand that when this baby makes an appearance, I promise you.' She looked thoughtful for a moment and then added, 'I wonder what Bear will think when he comes home to find ...'

'I don't know, I don't know.'

'He wanted you to make a future without him. He was only thinking of you when he went to America, wasn't he? I wonder how he's been. I do worry about him. He's such a sensitive lad. I'm not entirely sure America is the right place for him. I think a Buddhist temple would be better for dear Bear.'

'I have a feeling he's struggling a bit. Now I'm home I think I'll call him. It's been so long since I've heard his voice and I miss it so much. Perhaps if I call him I can tell him about the baby so it won't be such a shock.'

'If you think so, dear, then do that. Now, tea is ready and you need to eat properly now.' She went to leave but I called to her.

'Mum, thank you.'

'Amy, don't be daft,' she replied with a loving smile, 'you're my daughter.'

A few days later I found your number in Boston and my hand was shaking as I dialled. I had worked out the time difference and thought I'd catch you before work. It rang for what seemed like ages and eventually an unknown male voice answered. It was a voice with a hard edge. I asked to speak to you and he called you. He didn't use your name though and my heart fluttered because you were obviously close.

'Bubba, there's someone on the phone for you, a woman.' I heard you reply that you were coming and as he handed the telephone to you, I heard him add something else. It was said under his breath but I heard it clearly. 'Don't talk for long. Do you hear me?' You didn't reply to that so he repeated it, more firmly. 'Don't talk for long!'

I had rehearsed in my mind all I was going to say to you, but when I heard your voice it all flew out of head, my eyes filled with burning tears and I could barely speak.

'Bear, it's me ...'

'Amy,' you whispered, as if it was a dream, 'Amy.'

'I'm home, so I thought I'd call. How are you?' There was a pause and I thought at first you hadn't heard me. 'Bear, can you hear me?'

'I'm so pleased to hear your voice, so I am.'

'Are you about to leave for work?'

'No, I'm off sick for a couple of weeks.'

Fear gripped my throat and it continued to squeeze hard throughout my conversation with you. I had known something was wrong. It was a knowing I couldn't quite quantify and I could never explain it to anyone except to say, you were a part of me, such a huge part of me that when you were in trouble I felt it inside my chest and always had.

'What's wrong, Bear?'

'I had a few anxiety issues and they were overwhelming me, so the college doctor told me I had to rest. Don't you be worrying about me, Amy Lee, I'm grand, so I am.'

'Bear, I have something to tell you.'

You gasped, 'Is your mammy okay?'

'Yes, yes, she's fine, she's fine. I'm so sorry. I didn't mean to scare you.'

'Sweet Jesus, my heart almost stopped then. What is it you have to tell me?' Silent tears streamed down my face and I went to speak but nothing came out. I felt as if I was going to choke. 'Amy, are you still there?'

'Yes, I am. It's nothing really.' I tried hard not to put any pressure on you because you had been so courageous in leaving behind all you knew, for my sake. But my next words were burning my throat like acid and had to come out before they ignited into flames and set me on fire. 'Bear, I just wish you'd come home.'

There was silence and then I could hear you breathing. I now know you were crying too, but you wouldn't admit it for fear of upsetting me even more. I heard the other voice calling to you, harsh and impatient, but you ignored it.

'It won't be long now, but I have to work my contract. They're very kind to me here, so they are and I want to repay that kindness. Dean wants me to go to Canada with him too. It would seem a shame not to go, to experience it all, but I miss you, Amy Lee. I really miss you and it's so thoughtful of you to call me.'

Your voice, your light, beloved Irish voice, with the gentle lilt and soft edges, seemed so far away, across a vast ocean of separation and if I thought hearing it would comfort me I was wrong. It made me even worse.

'My mother sends her love and so do Isabelle and Ava.' I was trying to bring the conversation back to normality. 'They miss you coming round.'

'Ah, give them my love and have you seen Patrick since you've come back or my mammy?'

'No, but I will go over, I will, I promise.'

'Tell them ...' You couldn't finish and I cursed my selfishness in calling you. It had stirred up so much.

I asked quickly, 'Are you sharing a place with the man who answered the phone?'

'Yes, that was Dean and we have another housemate called Adam. They're both teachers and they've helped me so much.'

The faceless Adam did not ignite any jealous response from me, unlike Eddie Baker had. You were too far away and I didn't know enough about him, but Dean did ignite it because he had a pet name for you after all and he was close enough to feel he could hurry you off the phone. I wondered fleetingly if he was in love with you, but it *was* only a fleeting thought.

'I'll let you go, Bear. It's lovely to hear your voice. I worry about you. I hope you feel better soon.'

'It's the black beast, so it is. I think only the peace of Ireland can defeat him now and I need to see my daddy and feel his love. Thank you for calling me. I'll write soon now I know you're home. Look after yourself, Amy Lee.'

'Bear ...'

'Amy, please remember this, "I miss you so much that I would fly to you faster than a bird, but how can a bird with a clipped wing fly?"'

'Rumi was such a clever bastard,' I replied, in my usual way, to make you laugh, but I could hear someone shouting at you and the phone went dead.

# Chapter Nine

*These pains you feel are messengers.*
*Listen to them.*
*Rumi*

My son was named Alfie Wolf Lee Flynn on his birth certificate. He therefore had both our fathers' first names but we always called him Wolf because it suited him so much. He came into the world running, almost as if he couldn't wait to get here and his birth changed all our lives. You had told me years before that the wolf is known as Mac Tire in Irish mythology which meant, 'Son of the Countryside.'

It was a strange experience becoming a mother without you knowing I was. I had always imagined you being a big part of it. I lost count of the number of times I had picked up the telephone to call you again but couldn't see it through. Patrick had seen me across the street when I was obviously heavily pregnant, but he'd been sworn to secrecy. When I told him Wolf's name, he appeared touched beyond words and simply nodded. He then signed, saying at the same time, 'Perfect!'

My mother blossomed into the role of grandma as if she had been waiting all her life for it. It was as if nobody else existed for her and it was Wolf's birth that eventually helped to heal her deep grief. She would sit for hours with him cradled in her arms, talking endlessly to him and kissing his forehead every few minutes.

'Wolf is the future,' she told me many times. 'I'll never get over losing your dad, but I have to focus on the future now. Dad would want that, Amy.'

My sisters were almost as bad and Wolf was ruled by a petticoat government as my father had been. His birth did change me in so many ways, I wondered if you would recognise the woman I had become as the girl you once knew who had climbed trees and performed cartwheels in the school corridors. I still had an overpowering urge to do that sometimes, but I had to grow up pretty quickly even with the loving support of my family. Wolf's happiness depended on me and I wanted to give him the upbringing I had enjoyed, not one as complex as yours.

Did you have similar feelings about me, Bear: that my future happiness depended entirely on you? If you did then what a cross to carry through your young life and as if I wasn't enough, you had the burden of so many other crosses on your young shoulders.

Occasionally I would wonder if I should have put the name Carroll on Wolf's birth certificate because you had mentioned changing your surname to rid yourself of Zachary. I realise now I should have asked you first about using the name Flynn, but I was headstrong and I had decided not to tell you about Wolf until we were together again. A phone call was too impersonal.

When Wolf was eight weeks old, I met the redoubtable, incredible life force that was Annie. Annie had long, grey and silver, Titian curls below her shoulders and optimism and experience in spades. She was instantly likeable and loved life, grabbing it with both her hands, talking quickly and swearing often. Annie was in her fifties, bubbly and attractive and unintentionally funny. She taught me more about love and desire and the complexities of human nature than anyone else. She had the greatest capacity for happiness of anyone I had ever come across. Every morning I thanked my lucky stars I had met her, not only because she became my generous, kind and considerate boss, but because she opened my eyes to so much, particularly about so many problems I *thought* were facing me. She was the close female friend I had always needed, the close friend my mother had always longed me to have and the only person, outside my family, I allowed myself to love, apart from Josephine and you.

It was certainly fate that brought Annie and me together. Her bright, rosy outlook and her enthusiasm became addictive and knowing her changed me irrevocably. She encouraged me to talk about you. I did often and she listened patiently and intently.

I first met her when I applied for a job at her riding stables-cum-small holding after I had noticed the advert in the local library. It was only a forty minute train ride into the Kent countryside and I loved the idea of working in a rural setting.

My interview, which wasn't like an interview at all, but more like a chat with an old friend you hadn't seen for years, was quite amusing and illuminating on so many fronts.

She had greeted me with a cry of, 'Amy, hello, fancy a coffee?'

Her house resembled an old shack, half shed, half caravan but inside it was delightfully unorthodox, arty and surprisingly comfortable. She was eccentric to say the least and definitely a free spirit. We clicked instantly and instead of asking me relevant questions, she spoke about her life and her love of literature, art and living in nature. The best part for me, Bear, was she had a poster on her wall. I had to smile when I saw it. I read it out loud. "'I want to sing like the birds sing, not worrying about who hears or what they think.'"

Annie was making the coffee and she turned and smiled. I read it out loud again because it made me feel closer to you. She laughed quietly and asked, 'Do you like Rumi?'

'Yes, I do, very much. I'm not sure I always understand his poetry, but I appreciate its quality. He's Bear's favourite too.'

'Look at that one over there then.' She pointed to the wall above her tatty, worn sofa. 'It's actually my favourite.'

'"Forget safety. Live where you fear to live. Destroy your reputation. Be notorious."'

She'd listened as I read this out loud too and then said, 'I live my life by those two sayings. I've never given a toss what other people think, why should I? The one thing you can't control is other peoples' thoughts. You'd drive yourself nuts if you thought you could. Sit down here, Amy, make yourself comfortable. Let's have a chat about the job, shall we?'

'Is this actually a farm then? Do you keep animals?'

'Yes, but it's a very small farm. I grow vegetables and keep chickens for the eggs. I sell them at the local farmers market. There's also a small orchard and I sell the apples too. That doesn't bring in enough money, so I keep horses and I teach riding for the disabled. Disabled children get a hell of a lot from being with animals, especially horses. It's the gentleness of the beast they respond to and when they get on their backs, the kids feel that innate gentleness.'

'How many horses do you have?'

'There are eight at the moment and they're stabled just over that hill there, about half a mile away. We use them in a kind of rota so they don't have to work every day. Normally four are working at one time, but I hope to expand the business because it's so popular and the demand is high. I want to meet that demand, for the kids' sake. I bought the horses with my divorce settlement. My husband was minted, but unfortunately an arsehole too.'

'That must be hard work, dealing with eight horses.'

'Ah well,' she cried, her eyes lighting up. 'I have a kind of groom who helps me. He lives just a mile up the lane. He's pretty much an expert with horses. When I bought this land and moved here after my divorce I couldn't believe my luck to find him. I'd been married for twelve years. Twelve years! What a bloody terrible mistake that was! I'm not designed for marriage, Amy. Some people are, but not me! My dear husband wouldn't allow me to be who I wanted to be and I did try to conform but fuck that! I'm no domestic goddess as you can see.' She let out a peal of laughter and I couldn't help but laugh with her. She was so amusing and honest. 'So, after leaving him I found this and I'm like a pig in muck here and I absolutely love it.'

'So the groom looks after the horses? Would I have to help with that, if I got the job?'

'Oh no, well, only if he's sick or something, but I leave him to it really and that's what he prefers. He doesn't like me sticking my nose in. He can be a pain in the arse sometimes, but he's absolutely bloody gorgeous, so I forgive him his funny ways.' I had to smile but I couldn't have guessed what she was going to come out with next. 'He comes over twice a week in the evenings to chat about stuff and we have a bloody marvellous roll in the hay without any hay and then he goes home again. He's about fifteen years younger than me but he makes an older woman very happy and immensely grateful.' She let out another peal of laughter. 'Oh you should see your face! Well, I'm a free spirit and so is he, so what's the problem? I don't want him living here, God no! He'd get on my nerves I reckon, but you should see his muscles. It's all a bit like Lady Chatterley's lover!'

I felt my face flush. I had never heard anyone speak like she did but I was enjoying every second of our conversation. She appeared so carefree and irrepressible, I liked her instantly. 'I don't know what to say.'

'You didn't expect an interview like this, did you? Look at that

Rumi quote again. "Destroy your reputation. Be notorious!" I do and I am! I don't think men and women should live together if I'm brutally honest. I think women should help other women bring up the kids and then the men should come over for a bit of the other, bond with the kids, be a positive role model and then fuck off again. What do you think?'

'I don't think I'm experienced enough about life and love to comment, I'm really sorry. But I'm really enjoying listening to you.'

She pulled her knees up onto the sofa and hugged them. 'That's good. Oh and we aren't exclusive either. I don't care what he does or who he sees when he isn't here and he doesn't care what I do either. So, if you don't mind me asking, what have you been doing with your life then, in the last few years?'

'I went travelling for a bit …'

'Wonderful, did you have a great time?'

'I went to some beautiful places and met some interesting people. But I …'

As my voice trailed off she was staring hard at me. 'Why are you sad, Amy?'

'I'm not exactly sad, not now anyway, but I have been. I was pregnant when I came home from Italy and my son has made me a lot happier than I was.'

'Don't tell me the father didn't want to know when you told him, bastard!'

'The father doesn't actually know because I don't know who the father is, I'm afraid.' I couldn't quite believe I was telling a stranger the intimate details of my life, especially in an interview. 'I was careless and reckless when I was travelling. I was trying my best to forget about …'

She'd frowned for a moment and her light blue eyes were studying my face. It felt as though her eyes were piercing my every thought. 'Were you running away from someone when you went travelling?'

'Yes.'

'A man has got to be involved somewhere in this,' she remarked knowingly. 'You mentioned someone called Bear a few minutes ago. But your story can wait until you know me better. Whoever he is, he's a fool for not wanting you. You're bloody lovely.'

I knew her remark was meant to be kind but I couldn't let her think you were a fool, Bear. I just couldn't. 'No, he isn't a fool, far from it. He's the cleverest, gentlest and most compassionate person you could ever meet. He's complex and sensitive and fragile and we love each other deeply. There's only ever been him for me. I know I'm very young, but it's just complicated.'

Her sparkling eyes had softened. 'Oh you poor love, you poor, poor love.' She then sat upright and shook her hair again. 'Right, we'll no doubt tell each other all about our secrets, but enough for now. You must think me rude to be asking questions about your private life. Is your mum looking after your baby?'

'Yes, she is, is it a problem to have a young child and work here?'

'No, not at all, I was just going to say that you can bring him sometimes if you like. I wouldn't mind. This is a lovely place for children, especially in the spring and summer. Do you like kids? Silly question really as most people pretend to, but we only really like our own, don't we?'

'I haven't really any experience with children, except for Wolf, of course. I feel at times as if I'm still a child myself.'

'Is that your son's name? Oh how bloody wonderful, what a fabulous name for a child! I love it, I really love it. It's better than all the silly, boring names people usually give their kids. Right, I'll explain your duties. You've got the job, by the way!'

'Oh, have I? Thank you very much. I'm *so* grateful.'

'So, you'll help me with the riding for the disabled. I want to expand it, offer more classes because, as I said, it's so popular and there's a need for it. You can answer the phone, take bookings and deal with any other queries if I'm outside. What else? It's quite a job picking the apples, so I'll need help with that too. Just kind of act as my number two really, if that's alright with you. You'll need some training for a week for working with the kids and the horses but I can teach you that. I'll introduce you to Max, but no stealing him!'

'Sorry, who's Max?'

'He's my gorgeous, sexy, muscular groom!'

I immediately thought of you, Bear. I thought of you because you had such a tight grip on my heart, Annie had no reason to be worried about me being attracted to her fit, sexy, gorgeous groom.

She shrugged and spoke more to herself than me. 'I don't know why I say "my" really because he can love who he wants to, it doesn't affect me or our relationship in any way.' She grinned at me, turning to the mundane once more. 'We'll take turns making the coffee, but when I make it I'll put a tot of brandy in it because it gets quite raw out here in the winter months. That's my excuse anyway.'

'I'm sorry, Annie, I don't drink.'

'Don't you? Oh bugger, if you don't then I won't. Mind you, I bet you've never tried a tot of brandy in your coffee, have you?'

'No.'

'Well, you can always try it. You might like it. A little of what you fancy does you good in all aspects of your life.' She grinned again and added, 'especially with a sexy, gorgeous, muscular groom! I'll try not to lead you astray, Amy, I promise.'

'Well, I think having a baby and not knowing who the father is ...'

'Yes, you're right! You've already gone astray. Yes, fair point, fair point. Now, I must get on. Have a wander around if you like.' She stood up and held out her hand and when I took it she pumped it hard. 'It's been lovely to chat, see you next Monday, if that's good for you.'

'It's great with me, thank you, Annie.'

'I hope you'll be able to put up with me. I'm a bit of a handful. Bye, love.'

And put up with her I did, but more than that, I became increasingly fond of her and her scatty ways. She was like nobody I had met before and she certainly *was* fearless and notorious. I loved every minute of being in her company. I helped her with the riding for the disabled and because of my help she doubled the classes. It was such a relief being outside all day and not confined to a stuffy building. Even on colder days I appreciated the freshness of the air, the changing trees and the deafening birdsong. I spent some days in the orchard, picking the apples and wandering between the low branches of the trees on my own. You were constantly by my side though, Bear; by my side and vividly in my imagination, commenting on everything.

The horses were tender, gentle beasts with eyes that held the wisdom of the whole world in them and the disabled children taught me so many lessons about life. They smiled and laughed the whole time and some were so excited about being on horseback, they would screech loudly and wave their arms about wildly. Many of them would arrive looking pale with dull eyes, but that would often change during their session.

In our lunch breaks, Annie told me all about her life and I spoke about you. She had travelled extensively in her youth, living in a kibbutz for a couple of years in Israel and then moving to New Zealand and working there. She had done a variety of jobs including working for an airline as a stewardess, modelling and owning a market stall that sold crafts and vintage clothes. She had even been a waitress in the restaurant in the House of Commons but she had been sacked for accidentally on purpose pouring gravy on a politician who was engaged in a very public extra-marital affair.

We were very similar in so many ways, it astonished me. She was active, athletic and loved climbing and skiing. It wasn't walls and trees she had climbed but mountains and she still did that whenever she could get away. Some days I was speechless with laughter at some of the stories she told me and I asked if she was making them up. She assured me she wasn't, but a few of them were so incredible, I still wonder.

'I have no idea why I got married,' she told me one day as we sat together in her garden having our coffee. 'I suppose I loved him, I can't really remember now, but I knew it wouldn't suit me. It might have if he'd allowed me more freedom to go off and do my own thing, but he wouldn't. So I fucked off!'

The way she spoke and the way she lived was highly unusual and at times I envied her emotional freedom. But then I thought of you, Bear and I reminded myself that I didn't want emotional freedom from you. I had tried it in France and Italy. It just didn't work for me.

The riding lessons took place even if it was pouring with rain and gale force winds. She wouldn't dream of letting the children down and they always turned up. She loved being in the open air as much as I did, especially that first winter when it snowed. It transformed her farm and the surrounding countryside into a winter wonderland and turned the noses and cheeks of the children bright red and glowing.

Annie would wear a woollen hat pulled right down to her eyes with her mane of flowing hair tucked up inside it. She resembled a kind of Boudicca rampaging around or a goddess. Everything about her was larger than life, loud and sometimes hilariously vulgar, but kindness was at the core of her being and I responded to that wholeheartedly.

She had taken me to meet her groom, Max, during my first week. She'd said that we ought to get to know one another as we'd be working together but I think she couldn't wait to show him off to me.

I soon settled into the routine of the three of us walking the horses to the farm every morning to work with the children and then returning them to the stables in the afternoon. Often it would just be Max I walked with and I began to love that walk, Bear. It was down a quiet, narrow lane with high hedgerows either side of it stuffed full of flowers, similar to the one in Ireland that led to the moor where we'd wandered together.

Sparrows, blue tits and nuthatches would fly across in front of us and throughout the year the flowers changed constantly. Masses of jaunty daffodils, purple and white crocuses and miles of bluebells and orchards spread into the distance. There were wild pears and damson as well as the apples and the hedgerows seemed to create an intimate feel to the landscape, preventing strong winds damaging the various crops and rows of hops. Annie and Max pointed out the hawthorn and holly bushes, the dog roses and other shrubs. I took it all in and described every detail of it to you in a letter. Do you remember that, Bear?

On those short walks with Max, I slowly got to know him although he wasn't easy to get to know. He held part of himself back for a long time, but gradually he let me in. He was indeed muscular and gorgeous and he had a gentle, non-threatening masculinity about him. He was so different to you, Bear, in so many ways but he was also intelligent and well read and he taught me patiently about the horses and their various characters. He had a rugged quality, similar to your daddy in Ireland and his face, in repose, was quite stern. When he smiled, which wasn't often, it was as if he was bestowing a wonderful, rare gift on you and when I spoke he listened intently, just as you did. His black hair, tinged with grey streaks, didn't appear to have been anywhere near a hairbrush for months and he always had dark stubble on his chin. He wasn't bothered about his appearance at all and cared more for animals than he did for people. He spoke about the horses as if they were his close friends.

One afternoon, the three of us had been walking the horses back and Annie had made a funny, rude gesture behind Max's back as if she was grabbing his backside. I wasn't expecting it and couldn't stop myself from laughing quietly. Max simply turned and wagged his finger at her.

'I know what you're doing, Annie,' he declared, with an exasperated look, 'so stop it right now! You'll embarrass Amy. You're supposed to be acting like a boss.'

'Max, my darling boy, I can't act like a boss when I'm sleeping with you.'

'Amy, take no notice of her, she does it to shock,' he said, shaking his head as if she was a naughty child.

'Oh don't be a bore! Amy knows all about us.'

There was an intimacy between the two of them, a frisson of desire in all their looks and words and part of me found it too painful to witness because the intimacy reminded me of us, Bear. But for them there was much more. I could feel the mutual physical attraction buzzing around them like a live wire. I realised, in those first few moments of seeing them together, that we had never experienced that. I hadn't ever felt desire flying towards me from your body or felt it when you held me. I had felt love, tenderness, a deeply held intimacy without any physicality and sometimes desperation but not a raging, unstoppable desire. The realisation that I never would was a painful thought to have.

I had told Annie all that very early on in our friendship. She guessed the rest and had shaken her head, muttering sadly and genuinely, 'Amy, you poor sweetheart.' Then she rocked with loud laughter and said, 'I will lend you my sexy, gorgeous groom for a night, shall I? He'll do you a world of good.'

I had to laugh with her and even though the suggestion of borrowing Max was said in jest, I felt a sense of poignancy and sharp stab of regret about my situation. It was a hankering for something I hadn't experienced in France or Italy. I could only name it as, a longing for a relationship that encompassed all the depth of feeling we already enjoyed and the closeness, warmth and shared past but with a mutual passion thrown in. At times, those sudden moments of truth left me with waves of hopelessness and I knew the only way to rid my mind of them was to see you again. I needed to touch your face and hear your voice and remind myself that you were worth every minute of those melancholy and sombre flashes of truth.

When Wolf was a little older, I took him regularly to Annie's farm to give my mother a break and to let him toddle about in the fresh air. The first time he sat on one of the horses with me, I held him tight as he shouted with delight and excitement. Stroking the solid, muscular body of Shadow, the most docile of all of them, his little face lit up as his chubby hands gently touched the shining mane. Max was standing near, holding Shadow's noble face and urging Wolf on. 'There's a good boy, that's so gentle of you, thank you for stroking Shadow's neck, he loves it and he'll remember you next time you come.'

Max and I had taken a few weeks to get to know each other because he was quite a reserved man who preferred to be with animals, but we were slowly becoming firm friends. He was what you might call the strong, silent type and often, when near him, I felt the need to talk all the time to fill the gaps, but he just seemed amused by me. He would run his hands through his dark hair and shake his head as if I was daft.

On another afternoon, when we slowly walked the horses back to the stables in the sunshine, Max suddenly declared, 'I'm a free spirit, Amy and so is her Ladyship. Jealousy doesn't exist between us and it never will. She's the woman I've been waiting for all my life and the feeling is mutual. I'd marry her if she wanted me to, but that isn't going to happen so there *is* room for other people in both our lives, please remember that.'

I was so young and naive, I flushed up with embarrassment because I knew what he meant and I had to turn away because a shot of desire and unexpected lust was rippling through my body. It shocked me so much, I almost bolted. He then moved a little closer and squeezed my arm. There was nothing lecherous in what he had said or the way he touched me at all. He was simply very honest and he had a caring, empathetic manner that I responded to. I imagined a few hours in his arms would be a wonderful memory to have, but your dear face and velvety voice, Bear, loomed so clearly in my mind, I almost gasped.

'Amy Lee. Amy Lee, you're my Guardian Angel, so you are.'

Without meaning to I blurted out, 'I'm in love with someone else.'

Max merely gave me a knowing smile. 'I know you are. I can see it in your eyes.'

'Can you?' I asked plaintively.

'Yes, I can see it clearly every time I look at you. You have this sadness that hovers around you. The only time it goes is when you're looking at your little boy, but even then there's a kind of wistfulness. Whoever he is, he's a damned fool. Does he love you?'

'Yes.'

'Then what's the problem, if you love each other?'

'I can't tell you and he isn't a fool, far from it.'

He was scrutinizing my face as you would a map. There was a sudden look of recognition and a knowing. He paused for a long time before he said any more and I almost poured out our whole history to evade the scrutiny and fill the silence.

'Amy, if he's married ...'

'He isn't married!'

There was another long pause in which I could almost hear his brain working and then another look of recognition crossed it. I felt he probably thought me an idiot and I was preparing to justify our relationship to him. His honesty when he next spoke was brutal.

'Ah, I get it, I get it. Well, you're on a hiding to nothing, I'm afraid. He won't change, unless he likes both.' He thought for a moment and then carried on regardless with his personal comments. 'Mind you, if he does like both, you can have half of him but that won't help you if you're desperately in love with him.

You won't want to share him. There aren't many like her Ladyship.'

I shuddered and went to walk away. 'I can't talk about him like this.'

He immediately looked mortified. 'I apologise, I really do.' His face had fallen. 'Perhaps we don't know each other well enough yet for you to confide in me. I can be a little blunt but I always try to mix it with kindness. Bring him to the farm one day. I'd like to meet the young man in question.'

'He's working in America.'

We were almost at the stables and Max took hold of the reins of the two horses I had been leading. 'Well, just remember, he'll be having a right old time of it there. Why can't you do the same?' I must have looked disapproving and annoyed because he put his hand up. 'Sorry, sorry, that's enough from me. I'll finish off here. I think you've had enough of me for now. Sorry to have upset you, but I didn't mean to. You're only young once. Don't waste a minute of it with misplaced loyalty. You'll regret it in the future. I know what I'm talking about, believe me.'

As he turned to walk away, his muscular, broad shoulders and arms could be easily seen under his pale blue shirt. He had attractive, charismatic qualities and I admired his honesty even if it was difficult to take when in relation to you. I went over our conversation in my head a few times and for a moment I wondered if he was right in his assumption. Were you having a right old time of it in America? Was my loyalty misplaced? You were so far away from me, so far, and yet, I could feel you inside me *and* beside me constantly, like a shadow hovering inches away.

At times the urge to yell your name into the sky was overpowering. Your absence continued to be overwhelming and I only found solace in the unconditional love I had for little Wolf. I only found out much later that you *were* in a relationship at that time but it was destroying your self esteem and damaging you so badly, you were slowly disappearing into a vacuum of despair with no way out.

On the train home that day, I continued to scrutinise every bit of my conversation with Max. Something was niggling away at me. Why was I being loyal to you when we weren't even in a relationship together? If you were seeing other people in America, why wasn't I? With thoughts and words waging war inside my head as we sped through the sleeping countryside and into the suburbs, I came to the conclusion that it wasn't loyalty at all stopping me. It was because I knew that whatever I did and whoever I did it with, I would wish it was you and the sense of longing and loss might bring me to my knees.

Annie continued to be a great friend to me and a generous employer and some days we laughed so much together we almost choked. She was a brilliant mimic and an amusing raconteur and it hadn't escaped her notice that Max had taken a shine to me. But he was right when he had told me she felt no jealousy. In fact, she even encouraged me to spend a few hours with him.

'Oh why the hell not, Amy, you're a long time dead, aren't you? Don't mind me, I won't care.'

'I've never met anyone like you, Annie,' I told her one day when we were eating lunch outside her shack and watching Max doing some odd jobs around the place.

'Is that a compliment? I could take it either way, I suppose. I'm only kidding you, sweetheart. I know you love Bear too much. I just want you to know that it wouldn't change anything between us and by *us*, I mean you and me and me and Max.' She laughed raucously, throwing her head back. 'Did you follow that?'

'Yes, just about.' I leant towards her and kissed her cheek lovingly. 'Thank you for being such a wonderful boss and a great friend to me. I never thought I'd have a boss like you. I'm so lucky.'

'Don't be daft! I'm just being me and people can take it or leave it. You happen to like me, so that's lucky and I like you. What could be better?' She paused for a moment and then laughed quietly. 'Would you look at that fine specimen of a man? You don't know what you're missing, Amy.'

'I'm sure I don't,' I muttered, laughing back at her.

'You just can't get past him, can you?' she said, studying my face. 'He colours the whole of your life, doesn't he? All I can say is, he must be a beautiful soul.'

'Oh, he is, he is! If you met him you'd understand. There's nobody like him in the world. Honestly, you'd understand better if you met him and heard him speak.'

She put her arm around my shoulders and hugged me. 'You should see your eyes light up when you speak about him. I worry about you, sweetheart, I really do. Your mum must worry too.'

There was nothing left to say because it had all been said before. Bear, you did colour my life. You coloured it with radiance and gentleness and a love so clear and luminous it continued to dazzle me. You spoilt me for everyone else because, beside you, they appeared dismal and shadowy and I could barely see them.

Time flew by without us noticing and through the bleak winter that year and into the following spring and summer, I grew much closer to Max than I had intended. Once he let his guard down, he was easy to talk to, fun to be around and a surprisingly deep thinker. I often spent longer in his company than I needed to, helping him wipe down and feed the horses after the classes. Watching him being affectionate to them had become like an aphrodisiac. I was often lost in my thoughts when watching his well-defined arms and shoulders and sometimes I had to force myself to look away.

When the May flowers began to bloom in the hedges and the bluebells spread across the countryside, I felt a surge in my energy and I taught Max how to walk on his hands. He tried so many times to master it, Bear, but never succeeded and we ended up laughing uncontrollably every time he attempted it. I can't even remember how we arrived at that point. I think I was telling him how different we had always been with you gazing at the sky and reciting poetry and me jumping off walls, doing cartwheels and climbing trees.

I had become intensely fond of him and my mother began to give me knowing smiles whenever I mentioned his name. He spoke constantly about Annie and how she had influenced his life in too many ways to recall and when I mentioned that to Annie she merely laughed.

'Oh, silly sod, he'll be professing his undying love for me next!'

Max didn't love her though. He desired her and admired her greatly, but he began to fall for me. Bear, I hadn't done anything to encourage him, but I felt his love and affection moving slowly towards me more and more each day. His rare smile became more frequent and his sometimes offhand comments stopped altogether. If I glanced his way, his dark eyes would be fixed on me in a way that needed no explanation.

I hadn't spoken about you for a while but he did ask one day when I expected you home from America. I think he'd sensed that I was feeling intensely vulnerable because the day before I had received a letter from you telling me you were staying in America another few months. Dean had asked you to and then he wanted you to travel to Canada with him for an extended holiday. You said he had been planning it for a while. I had cursed Dean and his suggestions, especially when you had added that he was a difficult person to be around, but you thought Canada would be interesting and vast enough for you to lose yourself in nature.

I felt you slipping away, not from me, not from our friendship, but in a way I couldn't explain, even to myself. Your letters had been less descriptive, flatter somehow and without energy. Was Dean controlling your intellect and reasoning? Was he sucking the life out of you? Or was I blaming everything on the faceless American when really I should have realised you were sliding into a depression?

Max had tuned into my anxiety and consequently said nothing more at that time. However, as we walked back to the stables on a hot, airless afternoon that following summer, my silence was enough to make him embark on a rather rash course of action.

When all the horses were rubbed down and fed, he made a large pot of tea for us both and we spoke about the sweet, vulnerable little children in our care. He was describing their delighted faces and their disabilities and how tragic it was for them and their parents and I felt tears burning in my eyes. I was imagining little Wolf being like that and how hard it would be to accept. It also made me think about how you were staying away much longer than I had anticipated and I was consumed with dread that, if you stayed away even longer, my little boy might have to grow up without you or your influence in his life. I couldn't stop myself from crying. It just came out of nowhere and Max jumped up and pulled me to my feet. His tough demeanour vanished in an instant and he took my face in his hands.

'Amy, I wish you'd forget him. Why can't you? You're living half a life. You have so much to give, if only you'd allow someone else in. Let me help you forget! Let me in!'

'How did you know I was crying about Bear?'

'It's *always* about Bear! Look, being with you these last few months has been a revelation for me. You're so full of energy and compassion and you're a beautiful young woman, so full of life, but some days you're only half here. The other half is with him.'

I suddenly felt weary with the constant weight of missing you, Bear. I longed for a few hours of emotional freedom. 'I know,' I whispered, 'I know.'

'I can feel his hold on you. I'd just like to be with you for a few hours where the dark cloud of him hanging over you disappears. Can you do that for me?'

My legs felt like jelly and I longed to collapse into his arms. 'I can't forget him, I just can't. He's my world.'

Max held me close and kissed me. It was a desperate kiss because we both knew it might not happen again. His strength surprised me and the stubble on his face scratched my mouth. He felt so different from you, Bear, it was astonishing. He felt like rock, where you felt soft. His hold was full of desire. Yours had felt warm, affectionate and loving. He felt like a stranger. You felt like coming home.

I have to be honest. I wanted to give in at that moment. Why couldn't I? I have asked myself that so many times since. My answer is, I wanted to feel as if I belonged somewhere and I thought I wouldn't with him. It would feel as if I was just passing through, as I did with the men in France and Italy. I wanted to settle somehow with little Wolf and I could only settle with you.

'Amy, you need to let him go. You *have* to let him go. Let me take you home to yourself. You have so much to give. Let me love you. Let me! I've never met anyone like you, Amy Lee.'

My senses were pulled into sharp focus by Max's words. I had closed my eyes and as soon as he said my name like that, out of the darkness you appeared, running towards me. I could hear you clearly, as clearly as if you were standing behind me.

'"Close your eyes. Fall in love, stay there."'

I pulled back sharply. Max would never know how saying my full name then as he did, broke my heart. It broke with the ferocious longing to hear *you* say it and its shattered pieces fell to the floor and scattered around my feet. Our prolonged separation meant those pieces wouldn't move back towards each other and become whole again until I heard your voice or saw your face. Max was staring at me and seemed perplexed by my reaction.

'What's wrong, Amy? What did I say? What's troubling you? Ah, you see, he's here now, between us, isn't he? I can feel him. I can actually feel him.'

'So can I,' I replied softly, 'but the difference is, I want him here. I'm happy he is.'

'Look, I'm sorry.' He sighed deeply and looked dejected. 'I don't mean to pry but is there *any* chance you could ever love me back, just a little bit? You must have allowed someone to get close to you. You have a son who is proof of that.'

'Nobody got close to me. It was just a fling, nothing more. The relationships I had when travelling weren't relationships at all. They were simply a few hours of relaxation and excitement in a man's arms and a need to feel fully alive.'

'And did it? Did it make you feel alive?'

'No, it didn't but I can't deny it was enjoyable at that moment. To feel fully alive and to feel as if the present moment is a gift, I need to be with Bear.'

Max shook his head as if I was hopeless and sat heavily in his chair. He appeared quite frustrated by my words and my rejection. I wasn't sure what to say next without hurting him even more than I had already. He didn't deserve to be hurt. He was a kind and compassionate man who simply wanted what most people wanted. I was different though, wasn't I, Bear? I was different because I had only ever loved and wanted you.

Finally Max spoke softly. 'I find it incredibly sad. A beautiful young woman like you with a wonderful future ahead of her with her little boy and her family, imprisoned by a love for someone she can never fully have.'

'But this prison is of my own choosing,' I told him, passionately. 'The bars are of my own making and from the windows of that prison I can see the stars in Ireland.'

'There are stars here too, Amy. You just can't see them.'

I could feel the tears choking me and I knew there was no more to be said to Max then. I also felt some embarrassment because after his declaration and his kiss, we would still have to work together. I feared we wouldn't be able to get past this moment and continue to be friends and colleagues in the same way. I didn't know how to react or what else to say, so the only course of action was to flee. I ran all the way back to Annie's farm. Luckily I saw her only briefly before I went home, but she was so in tune with my feelings she asked what was wrong.

'Nothing, I'm fine,' I said, a little too quickly. 'I just need to see little Wolf. It's a long day without him and sometimes I just want to get home and give him a hug.'

'If Max has upset you in any way, I'll kill him, stupid bastard,' she declared, as if she could see right through me.

'No, Annie, it's not Max.' I slung my bag over my shoulder and went to leave, but I felt she deserved an explanation. 'I just want to see my baby and I'm missing Bear today because of this glorious weather. It reminds me of our holidays together. He's staying longer in America because *Dean* wants him to.' I said Dean's name in such a derisory way, it was as if I had tasted something awful and was spitting it out. 'I'll see you tomorrow.'

All the way back to south London on the train you were inside my head. You just wouldn't leave. I knew there was such truth in Max's heartfelt words and I also knew he was trying to be kind. Was he in love with me? Did I feel his love like I felt yours? Yes, I did, but it wasn't as intense as yours, or as deep. It wasn't as devoted, or as intimate or tender. I knew Max thought I had put you on a pedestal but you deserved to be there. I was aware he thought you were an obsession but I was happy to be addicted. I knew he felt I was besotted with you, infatuated even, but I could never use harsh, negative words like that in relation to you. I was consumed by you, consumed by our mutual love and affection even if it meant I had to watch you fall for unsuitable men who obviously didn't deserve you.

I was also thinking about how you would return home and be confronted by a little boy you had no idea existed. But our love could survive all of that, I knew it. Our love could climb mountains, fly across oceans and remain steadfast and *still* steadfast. We could endure emotional storms, floods and earthquakes of our own making and we would still be clinging to each other, fighting for each other and sustaining each other until the world stopped turning and the darkness closed in.

You were the only man who could be a father to little Wolf. I had written your name clearly on the birth certificate. Father: Bear

Flynn! It was there in black and white, on a legal document. I hadn't felt a moment's doubt on that score. It was the truth, *our* truth, but as you pointed out to me later, we were doing to little Wolf exactly what your mammy had done to you.

Secrets, secrets and more secrets seemed to follow you constantly even where I was concerned and they invaded your life. By putting your name on Wolf's birth certificate I was as guilty as your mammy had been when putting Zachary Flynn on yours.

Guilty, Bear and I'm so, *so* sorry.

# Chapter Ten

*You have to keep breaking your heart until it opens.*
*Rumi*

Sitting here every day, watching your impassive face, white and drawn with dark smudges under your eyes, is like a loss in itself. You are here, but not here. As I watch every breath you take, I am remembering your magnetic, timeless energy. You told me you didn't fit anywhere. Bear, you fitted everywhere and with everyone but in a different way, that's all. How difficult that must have been for you.

I was hit by a thunderbolt when I first heard you speak; your voice was soft, as melodious as any song, when you told our teacher that Bear was indeed your name. It was unusual in that it possessed boldness, as well as a certain vulnerability, woven through with charm and a rare lyrical quality, all of which drew me in. It was almost as if I was being shaken by an unknown, invisible hand, urging me to wake-up, take note and to remember this was my future, right there, a few feet away within touching distance.

This was the person who would give everything of himself to me and ask nothing in return. This was the man who would need me to feel his distress so clearly and sharply in my own body as his heart stopped beating, that I would ultimately save his life. How did I know all that as, when it was my turn to say my name, you turned and smiled and looked at me with your intense, curious and watchful eyes?

'You want to be my friend, Amy Lee?'

I could have answered, yes, because we're going to need each other so badly in the future. Even in that first moment I felt it! I knew it! How did I know, Bear? I had been struck with a feeling of: here you are at last, what took you so long to find me?

Don't go without me. Are you running hard towards the next life even now? Are you dancing through forests and bluebells and gazing at clouds in *that* world? If you are, then you need to come back. They don't need you there but I do! Everything in *this* world reminds me of you. It's as if nature is tapping me on the shoulder and whispering urgently, 'Amy Lee, he is here! He is here!'

Every season brings you into sharp focus. The sunshine flooding through the windows makes me think of wandering along the lanes in Ireland where you would lift your face to meet its golden light. That thought fills me with the warmth of your memory. Birdsong is louder, clearer because you loved it so and in the unearthly silence of early mornings when I am feeding little Wolf, I tell him the birds are calling to me, as you did.

'Amy Lee, look at the glorious sunset. I could fly up there. It's where the angels live, so it is.'

In the vicious months of winter the mists and fog circle around me, giving way to a gloomy, moist afternoon that threatens to sap my energy, but I only have to think of your words about old souls to feel some ease.

'Amy, these mists are nature's comfort blanket. They hold us close, so they do. It isn't a mist at all. It's the old souls of thousands of ghosts who walk with us and between us daily. Watch carefully and you'll see them.'

When the snow fell on that last February you were away, its fresh, powdery and pristine beauty lifted my spirits. Little Wolf had been mesmerised by it when I took him to the park to make a snowman and the dazzling, refreshing sight that met me at Annie's farm reminded me of your beliefs once again.

'Amy, snowflakes are a miracle of nature, so they are. Look at them sparkling like the stars in Ireland. Listen to them crackling and you can hear the fairies whispering to each other.'

'What are they saying then?' I had asked you.

'They are urging you to listen carefully. They are saying, quieten your mind, Amy Lee and stay very still. They are telling you, you are deeply loved by millions of them.'

Spring rushed in that year with heavy downpours and gusting winds, but the disabled children always came for their rides. Rainstorms and windy weather seemed to excite them even more and I wondered if they were more in tune with nature because they were different. You would have said that, Bear and you would have felt it too, like they did. We would all be drenched and wading through mud but the smiles and squeals made it all worthwhile.

One morning, when drying off with Annie in her shack, she put a cup of coffee in front of me and sighed. Her natural curls were forming into tight, little ringlets because of the rain and she looked disgustingly healthy and full of life. But she rarely sighed so I knew something was on her mind and I was concerned.

'Are you okay, Annie?'

'I'm just worried about you, sweetheart,' she declared, looking at me over her mug. 'When is he coming home?'

She had no need to mention you by name, Bear. It was obvious who she meant but because the conversation came out of the blue, I wasn't prepared for it. It was always me who would begin talking about you, not her.

'I don't know,' I replied, shrugging my shoulders as if it didn't mean the world to me when it so obviously did. 'I suppose it depends on this Dean bloke.'

'Does it worry you that Bear may have fallen in love with this Dean bloke?'

'No, no, it doesn't.' I caught my breath, which made it so obvious I was being dishonest.

She gave me a faint smile. 'A few weeks ago, I urged you to examine your deepest feelings, do you remember?'

'Of course I do and I have.'

'It was the unavailability of Bear that I wanted you to think about. Someone who is unavailable can be extremely attractive. It's the fun of the chase and the thought that you can conquer him, *make* him available. It would be a shame to wait for him if that was the case when he might be having a whale of a time with this Dean.'

I paused for a moment to listen to the rain beating down on the roof in a steady rhythm and lashing against the windows. It was warm and cosy inside and we were drying off slowly and both still looking quite bedraggled. I loved those days sitting with her and speaking about you but that day I wasn't sure where her questions were heading and answered carefully.

'I've thought about your question quite a bit actually.'

'What conclusion did you come to?'

'Well, let me ask you a question. You're a woman of the world, aren't you?'

'You could say that. Go ahead and ask away.'

'Would you say it was love if I want his happiness more than my own?' She didn't hesitate before she answered.

'Yes, I'd say so, but you must think about your own life and where *you* are heading. Bear can always be there, but you might have to stand by and witness him making mistakes with unsuitable men who will break his heart.'

'But they won't have his heart, Annie. They'll only have part of him. I have his heart. If you saw us together you'd understand.'

'I hope you're right, Amy and what of Max, the silly sod?'

'What do you mean?' I felt my face begin to burn. 'What has Max got to do with it?'

'Do you fancy him? Are you physically attracted to him at all? You must be, he's bloody gorgeous and quite uncomplicated. He doesn't ask much of a woman. Don't be embarrassed, sweetheart. I told you right from the start that I'm a free spirit. I can't very well be like that and expect him to be faithful. Oh I hate that word! Faithful makes me think of an old dog sitting by your feet in front of the fire. For me, faithful means kind, compassionate, caring and honest.' She let out a peal of laughter and shook her curls. 'I think he's fallen for you big time and I'm quite a good judge of character. It won't change what we have together or threaten it in any way, so don't hold back on my account.'

'I don't love him, Annie. I love Bear.'

'Darling, I'm not talking about love on your part! I'm talking about lust! You can't look at that body while he's working with the horses and not want him, surely.' I didn't answer so she laughed again. 'Oh, maybe it's just me then. Maybe it's because I'm a post-menopausal woman who is not shackled anymore by all those awful hormones or concerned about what people think.'

'I don't think it's just you. He is bloody gorgeous as you say, but more than that, he's a lovely man in all ways. But you know I'm not a free spirit like you. This spirit is joined to another spirit for the rest of her life.'

'Fair enough, darling. Just be aware that Max has very deep feelings and most of those feelings are centred on you.' She then threw her head back and laughed loudly again. 'He'll just have to get a grip on himself, won't he, silly sod?' Her face then changed and she appeared a little worried. 'All I ask is you be kind to him. I'm very fond of him really even though he gets on my nerves sometimes.'

'I will be, of course, I promise.'

'Thank you, sweetheart.' She was silent for a few moments and ran her hand through her hair absentmindedly. When she had finished her coffee, she put her feet up on the chair and hugged her knees as she often did. 'Amy, you've had a great affect on me, you know,' she said earnestly.

'Why have I?'

'I've never envied anyone, but I envy you.' She must have seen the bemusement on my face and asked, 'Does that surprise you?'

'Yes, it does, very much so.'

'Well, it's true. I envy you but you break my heart.'

'I'm sorry I break your heart. I don't mean to.'

'I know you don't, you daft girl. Your mother must worry about you terribly.'

'Yes, I think she does, but she knows Bear well so she understands and accepts the situation.'

'Do you want to know why I envy you and why you break my heart?'

'If you don't mind telling me, then yes, go ahead.'

'I always know when you're thinking about the young Irishman who holds your future in his hands because your eyes give you away. They take on this soulful, faraway look. I could dive into them they appear so still and deep. Watching you like that breaks my heart because nobody can help you, except him.' Her face, usually animated and full of life, changed and for a moment I couldn't quite work out what she was feeling. 'I envy you because I have never loved anyone like that.'

'It isn't easy but I don't have a choice. It's there all the time. *He's* there all the time. Max told me the other day that he can actually feel Bear in the room sometimes.' She seemed highly amused by that and laughed hard, forcing me to add, 'He did, I promise.'

'Oh did he now? Silly bastard! What's it got to do with him anyway?'

'I think he was trying to be kind, that's all,' I said hurriedly.

'Yes, probably, I'll give him that. But if he asks you anything and you feel it's too personal, just tell him to fuck off! Now, let's get some lunch and look at the forecast for this afternoon. A break in this torrential rain would be welcome.' She glanced out of the window where a weak sun was struggling through the low cloud. 'Aha, I think we'll be okay, it looks brighter.'

At first, Max acted as if nothing had happened between us. He and Annie seemed just as close and I was left wondering what would have happened if I had let him get closer to *me*. I saw her grab his backside a couple of times and he merely shook his head and smiled as if he was quite used to her doing it. The first time we were alone together, walking the horses to the classes, he asked how I was.

'I'm fine, thanks,' I replied in a casual way, wanting to keep the conversation as light as possible.

'I'm so sorry, Amy,' he said quietly, staring at the ground. 'I overstepped the mark the other day and I thought perhaps ...'

'Please don't mention it again. I didn't mind, honestly.'

'Are you sure?'

'Yes, I'm sure.'

'I would never force my attention on any woman but I think being with Annie all this time, I've forgotten that not everyone is like her. She's so tough and funny and she never takes offence at anything. She can't be bothered with all that nonsense. What you see is what you get with her. You are much deeper, especially where *he* is concerned.'

'I know and I understand.'

One of the horses had stopped to munch at something growing in the hedgerow and it gave Max the chance to stand still and look at me directly.

'I wish I understood *you*.'

'You have no need to. I am as I am. One day, when he comes home, I'll bring him here and you can meet him. Then maybe you'll see ...' I couldn't finish because he jumped down my throat.

'I don't want to meet him and watch you gazing at him with a love that strong when I wish every day it was me who felt that love.'

'Max, I ...' He pulled on one of the horse's reins.

'Let's go, Rory! We'll be late for the kids.'

'Max, wait!' I took one of his arms roughly to force him to stop. 'What I was going to say was, if you see us together you'll realise it isn't one sided. You imagine that this is some kind of unrequited love and it isn't.'

'Of course it is, you little fool!' His eyes were blazing. 'He likes men! He *wants* men! It takes another man to tell you this, Amy. He's never going to look at you with the lust that you crave.'

My face began to burn because I detested people who didn't know you talking as if they did. I hated discussing you with anyone so personally because it made me feel disloyal and uncomfortable.

'I don't want his lust!'

'Of course you do, you're just fooling yourself. At your age lust is all most people think about. If you were in your sixties or seventies it would be different, you'd have experienced a lifetime of lust, but you aren't. You're both young and healthy and full of life. He's never going to want you like *that*. Men like him don't change; he can't, even if he wanted to, he's ...'

'Don't talk about him like that.' Tears had begun to fall from my eyes but I was angry more than upset and shouting at him just burst out of me. His outburst had come from nowhere making my head reel and I began to shout at him. 'What gives you the right to comment on someone you don't even know? I've accepted who he is and I love him even more because of it.'

'Listen to yourself, just listen to yourself. It's all a dream, Amy, all a dream,' he declared, his voice loud and cutting. 'Nobody wants to tell you, not even Annie and she's the most brutally honest person I know. She loves you too much to hurt you, but you break her heart. I've never known her take to someone like she's taken to you.'

The observations Annie had made the day before in her shack

came clearly to mind. 'I know she loves me and I love her, and she *does* understand me.'

'Well, I don't and I think it's a crying shame, wasting your life on him like this.'

After his apology his words were so wounding that I felt a sudden rage fly up my throat. I tried to speak but couldn't utter a single word. Instead, I let go of the horses I was holding and pushed Max hard on his chest. He staggered back a few paces because he wasn't expecting it but I could never have hurt him. He was too strong, too tough and too muscular to feel much. He grabbed my arms and held them down by my sides and I struggled violently.

I yelled at him, ferociously, 'Let me go!'

'Amy, you need to calm down first.'

'How can I calm down when you speak about Bear like that? You don't know him at all. He's worth a hundred of you. He'd never speak about you like that if the roles were reversed. He'd only ever say kind things about you. Don't *ever* mention him again. If you do, I'll leave here and never come back. I can't work alongside anyone who thinks about Bear like that. You said you were sorry, but you aren't at all. Who the hell do you think you are? I don't want *you*; I want Bear and I'll only *ever* want Bear.'

I was kicking him like a mule and my fury showed no signs of abating. Max held me tightly and sweat was trickling down his face. He began speaking softly, as if trying to calm one of the horses when they were skittish in the pen. It reminded me of when you calmed the angry bull, Bear, but that's where his likeness to you ended.

'Amy, calm down, please. Just calm down now and I won't ever speak of him again, I promise you. Calm down, calm down. I'm very, very sorry, *very* sorry. Look, the horses are feeling your distress. They'll bolt if you don't keep calm.'

'Let me go,' I demanded, hoarsely. He did let me go slowly and stepped back reluctantly. I put my hands over my face and whispered over and over again, 'Bear, come back, come back. Bear! Bear! Bear!' I felt sure you must have heard me somewhere or felt it somehow, inside of you.

Max touched my hair and looked so dejected by our row, my anger dissipated quickly. His gentle manner and obvious concern made me feel completely drained and hopeless and I could have dropped to the ground. Instead, I felt compelled to throw my arms around him and he responded immediately.

'Amy, I love you so much. *Let* me, let me love you.'

I couldn't reply, I felt emotionally exhausted and unable to think clearly. Max then took hold of the horses again and I took hold of mine and we simply walked on in silence. Despite our angry words, I felt a new closeness had been forged between us and I knew that closeness would grow.

Your two last letters before you came home were from Canada and they arrived with only a few days between them. They described the vastness and savage beauty of the mountains and wildlife but they lacked any emotional depth. Dean was mentioned in almost every sentence and I began to suspect he was pressing you to stay longer. You hadn't actually written those words, but I definitely felt it. I replayed Max's frustrated words in my head so many times and they were pushing me further into wanting to feel his love.

Bear, I was just lonely then because you were so far away and you sounded so different. It was as if you were sinking into a dark hole somewhere and becoming someone I didn't know. You had been abroad for so long and at times I wondered if I would even know the Bear Flynn who returned. Travel changes and matures people and I even began to imagine that Dean would come back with you and that possibly he would live with you and Patrick. I would then have to witness you walking along our street with him, touching each other briefly and secretly, your hands brushing together and your smiles intimate and loving. I would have to stand by and slowly turn to stone when you were spending your evenings chatting to him and forgetting to sign out of the bedroom window to me.

Your last letter was written like the author had ice in their veins. There was no warmth, no Rumi and no feeling. It made me shiver and when I showed it to my mother, she looked aghast.

'Are you sure Bear wrote this? There's nothing of him in it at all. How very strange, Amy. Could this Dean have written it for him?'

'That's what I thought, but why would Bear let him do that?'

'I don't know, dear. How very worrying. Perhaps you should show Patrick.'

I did show Patrick that night and he studied it carefully, shaking his head slowly.

'This is not Bear,' he said forcefully. I had never heard him speak like that before. Normally his voice was flat, without expression, but then it was alive with anger and passion. 'It's not him, Amy.'

'But it's his handwriting, Patrick.'

'It's not Bear though.'

'What can I do? There isn't a return address so I can't write back. Oh, Patrick, I thought he'd be home by now. I'm sure Dean isn't a good influence on him. I feel somehow he's controlling Bear completely. What shall I do?'

Patrick touched my hair gently, like you used to whenever I was upset or worried and he then placed his hand on his chest and blew me a kiss.

'You can do nothing,' he replied, sadly. 'We just have to wait and be here for him when he comes home.'

That night, as I listened to little Wolf's deep breathing as he slept, I was frozen with fear and I watched as the moon sent beams of creamy white light into my bedroom. To say I felt alone, despite being with my child and my family, is an understatement. It was as if the world had turned into a mighty stranger with an enormous void in the middle of it and I was in danger of slipping into that void and becoming another person. A person who no longer had a close, lifelong friend called Bear Flynn.

I couldn't concentrate on anything the next morning, not even little Wolf who was becoming a bright, chatty, lively child who demanded your attention. His speech was advanced because he lived with four women who spoke constantly. He would even take hold of my face and turn it towards him.

'Mama, you're not listening.'

'I am, Wolf,' I would reply, laughing at his serious expression.

'No, you're not,' he would insist, 'you're looking out of the window.'

During the train journey to work on that warm, late spring day, where the sleeping fields were bursting with life and colour, I spoke to you just as if you were sitting opposite me. There was nobody else in my carriage luckily because they would have thought me crazy. Maybe I was.

'Bear, you need to come home. I know you are struggling, I just know it. I can actually feel it, in my chest and in my guts. Why did you write that letter? It wasn't you. It didn't sound like you at all. Come home to me, Bear, come home to *us.* Come home to yourself. My longing to see you again is turning me inside out. I look for you everywhere and you are here, but not here. You are in every flower, every sunset, every star. But even so, your absence is overwhelming and life feels like a vast, never ending empty space. I need you and Wolf needs you, even though he doesn't know it yet. Come back, Bear, just come back.'

I hope you heard me, Bear. I like to think you did, because, as I later discovered, you had decided to leave Dean and Canada that very day but when I stepped off the train that morning and walked towards Annie's place, I still ached with wanting your physical presence.

Annie was making coffee and she was her usual lively self. 'Aha, there you are, Amy. Max is in the wood near the stables. He wants to see you and apologise. He told me you had an argument and I told him it must have been his fault.'

'It wasn't, Annie, honestly …'

'Don't take the blame,' she commanded, laughing loudly, 'let him grovel. He needs taking down a peg or two sometimes. He's too bloody gorgeous for his own good! Go on with you. Let him say sorry, for me, please.'

I did as she asked and wandered towards the wood. The sunshine was flooding through the branches of the tall trees and there were bluebells nestling in small hollows everywhere. It was a warm day and I remembered you, in Ireland.

'It's a soft day, Amy, so it is. Look at the clouds. They're angels in disguise watching over you.'

'Why are they watching over *me*?' I always asked you.

'They need to watch over you because you're always climbing trees and up to some shenanigans, so you are.'

'Don't they watch over you too?'

'Yes, but they love *you* most, Amy Lee, because you are a child of nature, so you are.'

I spotted Max moving some logs into a pile, his shirtsleeves rolled up and his hair wet with perspiration. As I walked towards him I spoke to you.

'Forgive me, Bear, forgive me, but I miss you so much, my body aches for you and I can't stand it any longer.'

I was only a few yards away from him when he looked up. He was slightly breathless and he wiped his forehead with the back of his hand. His whole demeanour seemed different somehow. He appeared not as confident.

'Did you want me, Amy?'

'Annie said you wanted to see me.'

As I moved closer he smelt of hay and sweet grass mingled with sweat. It was a pleasant, if unusual combination. He appeared a little apprehensive and not the usually confident and self-assured man I had come to know.

'Look, we need to work together and I've made a bloody mess of it so far. I won't *ever* speak about him like that again. It's none of my business who you love and who you don't.' He glanced up at the sky. 'My God, what on earth must you think of me?'

'Do you really love me?' I asked, and my voice sounded small, far away and forlorn.

'Yes, I wish I didn't though. Loving a woman who wants another man isn't an enviable place to be, even if she can't ever have the man she loves.'

'Then you must understand what it's like for *me* then. If you love someone deeply, you don't have a choice.'

'No, you don't and I came to that conclusion last night when I was regretting every word that came out of my stupid mouth. I really am very sorry, Amy. He must be some wonderful young man to warrant such devotion.'

'He is, he really is.'

His sincerity and vulnerability at that moment were an attractive mix and he obviously picked up on my feelings because we both stepped forward at exactly the same moment and clung to each other. I could feel the warmth of the sun on my face and the soft breeze moving through the trees around us sounded like tiny waves crashing onto the beach. I felt completely at ease, more at ease than I had in a very long time and we slowly dropped down to the ground into a small hollow, locked together.

He was immensely strong, but gentle too and it all felt so different from being in your arms, Bear. I could hardly comprehend how different. It felt like being in another world at that moment, another life where knowing you didn't exist. I hadn't heard your voice that day at school or looked into your watchful eyes as you spoke directly to me when I asked to be your friend.

We had not become inseparable or walked home from school side by side where I jumped over cracks in the pavement and you gazed at the clouds. It was a different world from the one we shared through our teenage years where I climbed trees and you told me not to. Where you took me to Ireland and told me the secret you had been hiding. We hadn't met your real daddy and I hadn't felt bereaved by your absence when you studied at Cambridge. Eddie Baker wasn't anywhere in the background and we hadn't signed to each other every night since we first became friends.

*The breeze at dawn has secrets to tell. Don't go back to sleep.*

We hadn't held on tightly to each other in my bedroom, with the weight of your slim body on mine as we cried pitifully together and your tears fell on my face. I had no idea who Rumi was in this world where our destinies hadn't merged.

Was this the moment where two worlds would collide again, yours and mine? Was this the moment where the separate paths we had been forging and all the twists and turns we had experienced, merged together once more and brought us back to ourselves? I closed my eyes to block you out, to pretend we had never met. I was screaming inside that Bear Flynn didn't exist. I longed to respond to Max's tender touch and not wish it was you.

We had not met! We had not met! Even that thought caused a surge of loneliness in me, a complete and utter feeling of emptiness, and a vast, brutal space where you should have been. You were haunting me so completely. I almost didn't hear Max's soft words.

'Close your eyes if you want to. Close your eyes and pretend it's him if it makes you happy, but just be happy, Amy, just be happy in this moment. You deserve that so much.'

I began to feel an emotional outburst bubbling up inside me and the sobs came up from deep within my chest, in the heart space, the aching place where you always are.

'Amy, "close your eyes. Fall in love, stay there."'

As I lost myself in the warmth of Max's arms, in my head I was screaming for you and *at* you. 'I'm trying, Bear, I'm trying *so* hard, but I can't forget you. I can't stop loving you. I won't *ever* stop loving you.'

Being with Max that morning, I realised how devoid of any real emotion my quick, uncomplicated and transient relationships had been in France and Italy, even though one of them had produced Wolf. Those months now felt like walking through an abandoned building and I wondered why on earth I had embarked on them. I was remembering Eddie's letter to you.

'"My love for you has driven me insane. I wander the ruins of my life, my old self a stranger to me."'

Poor tortured Eddie who suffered deeply from an unrequited love for you and left everything and everyone in his old life behind because staying in Cambridge would just be too painful with the memory of you everywhere. He couldn't even teach anymore because no other student would be as gifted and as unforgettable as you. But my love wasn't unrequited, was it, Bear? That's what made those years so difficult to get through. I struggled because I hoped and believed it would ultimately lead me back to you and the only thing that made it any easier was, I knew you felt the same.

Annie had often told me, we change with every year we are alive, as surely as the seasons change. In only one respect had I stayed as constant as the stars in the night sky. Loving you, Bear, loving you had never wavered.

'That was a grand sonnet we read today, wasn't it, Amy?'

'I don't even know what a sonnet is,' I had replied, laughing as we wandered home from school. You were lifting your face to the sun and I was attempting to pirouette around you.

'It's just a poem, so it is.'

'Why isn't it called a poem then?'

'You're funny, Amy Lee, so you are.'

'Who wrote it, Rumi?'

'No, Shakespeare and it's wonderful considering it was written so long ago. His words hold true even now.'

'Okay, if you say so.'

'The Chanting Heart is still my favourite though, so it is. It completely floors me.'

'Is that Rumi?'

'Yes, it is. It's Rumi at his best, so it is.'

'What's that about then?'

'It's about love, Amy, just about love.'

'How does it go then?'

'"Dancing in ecstasy you go, my soul of souls. Don't go without me."' You carried on reciting as I danced around *you* and I was listening despite pretending not to. '"The two worlds are joyous because of you. Don't stay in this world without me. Don't go to the next world without me."'

'It's about death again! Why is it always about death? Look, I'm dancing in ecstasy around you, Bear.'

'Shush now, listen.'

'Sorry.'

'"O ruler of my Heart. Wherever you go, don't go without me."'

You explained its meaning then but I just laughed and swung from the lamppost like a monkey swinging from a branch. I understand it now, Bear, every single word. I am so sorry I didn't then because we could have shared those beautiful, affecting words together. How on earth did you put up with me? I was lost in my memories of you completely as Max was stroking my face with his fingertips.

'I do love you, Amy, please believe that.'

'"Dancing in ecstasy you go, my soul of souls. Don't go without me."'

'What did you say?'

'It doesn't matter.' I smiled and kissed his cheek. 'It doesn't matter. It's a poem I like.'

'Bear's favourite poem,' he said, but he didn't appear angry or disappointed in any way. 'It's Bear's favourite, isn't it?'

'I'm sorry, Max.'

'It's fine.'

'Is it really? Is it really fine?'

'Are you happy? I mean, right now are you happy? I want you to be, so much.'

'I'm happy right now, yes.'

'I think we'd better get back to work, don't you?'

'Yes, Annie will wonder what's going on.'

'Annie will know exactly what's been going on, but that's fine too.'

'I hope you're right. I wouldn't hurt her for the world.'

'Trust me, I *am* right and I wouldn't hurt her either.'

I was brushing earth and grass off my clothes and went to walk away but I paused. I was feeling heat in my face from guilt, guilt that I had been thinking constantly about you when Max was showering me with love and desire.

'Max, thank you for ...'

He was running his hands through his dark hair. 'No need to thank me for anything, now go!'

He was right about Annie. She was her usual self, although she did give me a knowing smile when she saw me emerging from the wood. For a moment I wondered if she had engineered the whole thing in the hope I would forget you.

'Everything okay with you, sweetheart?' I didn't know quite what to answer so I said I was fine even though I knew my face was flushed with embarrassment. 'Did Max apologise to you?'

'Yes, he did and I accepted his apology. We can be friends again now.' I couldn't look at her. I knew she would pick up on my feelings because she was very intuitive. 'We have to work closely together after all, so it's important.'

'You enjoy every minute of his friendship, darling. It'll do you the world of good,' she told me, with enough hidden meaning in her words to let me know she realised Max was now much more than a good friend for me. She checked her hair in the mirror briefly and just before she went outside, she added with a grin and a wink, 'Amy, I just hope he has enough energy to be friends with both of us.'

Max did indeed have enough energy for both of us. I knew Annie was much more demanding on that score than I was though. The three of us were increasingly close, both as work colleagues and as friends and I loved every minute of being with both of them. Occasionally I would wonder about how it had all happened and the wisdom of my actions. If someone had told me a few years before that I would be sharing a lover with my boss, I would have thought it ridiculous and a fantasy, but I was. My mother commented that I appeared much happier and more fulfilled than she had ever seen me, since you had left.

Summer was upon us and spending time at the farm in those months was a delight. All the flowers and shrubs were in full bloom and the trees and fields were a sparkling and effervescent lush green. The whole place was a sea of bright colour and I had a healthy glow from being outside all the time. Little Wolf accompanied me often and watching him playing in the fresh air and spending time with the other children filled me with joy. I often wondered if we would ever take him to Ireland, to your granny's farm. I imagined him running freely where you would have run as a child and those thoughts filled me hope and an inner glow.

In your absence, Patrick had begun to spend much of his time with us. It was almost like having you there when he shared our evening meal and my mother grew increasingly fond of him. So did Isabelle and from watching their long, lingering glances at each other, I realised they were gradually falling in love. She would look across the table at him while he ate and then shy, intimate smiles would be exchanged and my mother would wink at me. Isabelle was even learning sign language which told me she was serious about Patrick, but it also gave them a way of secretly communicating to each other without the rest of us knowing what they were saying. He often knocked on the table to get her attention and it made me reminisce about the times he had done that to sign to you in Ireland. Those days on granny's farm seemed a lifetime away.

One Sunday morning, when Isabelle had gone to visit a friend for a couple of hours and Ava was playing with little Wolf upstairs with more patience than I thought her capable of, my mother asked me to put a note in your door, to invite Patrick for Sunday lunch. It was a hot and airless day, dry and a little humid for July, the streets somewhat dusty and gritty. I glanced up the road, as I normally did but something made me stop in my tracks.

It was a lone figure with long, slim legs, walking slowly and carrying a heavy bag. My heart quickened because there was something I recognised about that long stride. I knew who repeatedly lifted his face to the sky every few seconds, something that turned a short, uneventful walk into a study of nature, and whose every step was thought about rather than rushed, like mine.

'Bear!'

I began to run hard and fast, my hair flying behind me. When you spotted me you immediately stood still, dropped your bag and held out your arms. With every step I wondered if you had changed in any way. Was this the moment when all that had gone before would be wiped out in an instant and our worlds would collide once more? By the time I reached you, tears were blinding me and I could hardly breathe. I jumped into your arms like a child desperate for a parent's affection and safety. You lifted me off my feet and repeated my name over and over again.

'Amy Lee. Amy Lee. Amy Lee, it's grand to see you, so it is.'

We both began to cry and I was being held closely by you, tightly by you, lovingly by you once more. I was overwhelmed by the smell of you and you felt exactly the same as you had when you left over three years before. We stayed clinging on to each other like that for so long, with my legs around your waist and our foreheads together, a few teenagers walking by laughed at us. Eventually I was able to speak and my voice sounded so quiet and hoarse, it was like someone else altogether.

'I can't believe you're here. Don't go away again, Bear. Don't, please ...'

'I won't, I won't, I promise you. I'm finished with it all. I'm home now, Amy, home for good. I missed you so much and I missed Patrick and your mammy and I don't want to be with strangers who don't understand me anymore.'

You put me down and we stared at each other, as you would with someone who looked the same to you but a little different as well. You didn't appear any older but you were unkempt with dark stubble on your chin. Your hair was cut short though which accentuated your large, hazel eyes. They still held the same curious, but intense expression in them, as if you were trying to get inside my head. Bear, all you would have found in there was love and relief that you were standing in front of me again. I wondered what on earth I looked like to you after three years of a pregnancy and motherhood. Probably older and a little rough around the edges, but you touched my nose and my cheeks and looked surprised.

'Where are your freckles, Amy Lee?'

'They've gone, thank God. Do I look different to you?'

'No, you're the same Amy. You can still run like the wind coming down from the mountains in Ireland too.'

Listening to your voice was so soothing; it was like hearing your favourite tune unexpectedly on the radio. I wanted to dance wildly and do cartwheels, or walk on my hands as I used to in my bedroom with you laughing at me. I wanted to sing and shout at the top of my voice and swing round lampposts or climb trees. I wanted us to be younger and naive again, when you had looked intensely happy and alive after swimming under the waterfall.

I did none of that though because you looked weary from travelling and your eyes were a little duller than they used to be, as if your senses were flattened. You picked up your bag and clutched my hand tightly and we walked towards your house in a comfortable silence. I was frightened to let go of you or let you out of my sight in case you disappeared again and this had been a cruel mirage.

You felt for your door key in your trouser pocket and I still had hold of your other hand. It was as if Dean and Max didn't exist and tears were pricking my eyes again because I felt I had been disloyal to you in some way. Ridiculous, I know, because we had been apart for so long but you can't always explain or rationalise deep feelings. Holding onto you and feeling your warm body against mine after missing you so much brought all those feelings and all that depth of emotion rushing back and it hit me like a huge wave, sweeping all sensible thoughts aside.

You broke the silence. 'Amy, I need my other hand a second. I can't get my key out.'

'Sorry, sorry ...'

'It's fine.'

'Patrick is coming to lunch so you must come too. My mum will be overjoyed to see you, Bear. Say you'll come.' Your grateful smile floored me.

'Yes, of course I will. I'll be overjoyed to see her too, so I will.' You opened your front door but paused before going in and turned to me. It was almost as if you had just come out of a dream. 'How have you been, Amy? Do you like your job?'

'I love it, my boss is wonderful. You'll love her. She's heard all about you.'

'And she can put up with your shenanigans?'

'Yes, she's worse than me.'

'I can't believe that, Amy Lee.' I didn't want you to go inside without me and you sensed that, saying, 'I won't be long.'

'I'll come in with you.'

'Let me have a bath and speak to Patrick for a while and we'll be over. I won't be long, Amy, honestly. I'm not going anywhere.'

'Isabelle and Patrick have fallen for each other,' I said quickly, still holding you there beside me and you nodded, as if you knew all along it would happen.

'That's grand for them, so it is, wonderful and uncomplicated. It was always meant to be.'

I felt unreasonably anxious. 'Don't be long, will you?'

'No.'

'I have a surprise for you, Bear.'

'Are you married, Amy Lee?' You were frowning as you said this. 'Someone must have snapped you up.'

'Don't be daft! Who would put up with me? No, but it *will* be a surprise for you.'

'Is it a good surprise? Will I like it?'

'I think so. I *hope* so.'

'We'll be over very soon.'

As you said this, Patrick came rushing up the hall and flung himself at you. You were both crying and he was signing furiously at you.

You signed back, whispering at the same time, 'I've missed you too, Patrick. No, I won't go away again. I'm home now, for good. You must have been so lonely here without me. Let me come in and I'll have a bath and we can go for our lunch at Amy's.'

You were an hour. It seemed a very long, drawn-out hour and I fidgeted about unable to sit still. My mother and sisters had been speechless with delight when I told them you were back. Eventually, thankfully, Ava called from the front room where she had been watching for you.

'Patrick and Bear are here.'

My mother bustled up the hall and I could hear her saying, 'Oh, Bear, it's so lovely to see you. It's not been the same without you. Come in, love and you Patrick. What a day to have you both here. We had no idea you were coming home yet. Isabelle, please stop standing there like a knotless thread and put the kettle on for goodness sake. Bear, you look a little different, is it your hair?'

'No, Mrs Lee, I just need a proper shave. I only had a quick bath because I knew Amy didn't want me to be too long. Where is she?'

There was an awkward silence for a few moments and then my mother's voice sounded a little strange, as if she was keeping a secret, which of course she was.

'Oh, she's upstairs, do go up, she has a surprise for you.'

I heard your footsteps coming nearer and my heart was beating so fast I thought it would burst out of my chest and bounce around the room. Little Wolf had been doing a jigsaw on the floor with Ava and I had told him to take it apart and try to do it again on his own without Ava there helping him. He was concentrating hard on it, even though I had told him someone was coming to see us both. Your faint knock on the door made me tremble slightly and when your face appeared, I couldn't even smile.

'I'm here, Amy, sorry if I was a long time.' You saw Wolf immediately and he glanced up at you briefly before turning to his jigsaw again. You stared at him blankly and just said, 'Amy, who ...'

'Come in and close the door behind you. Sit next to me.' You did as I asked and little Wolf grinned at you as he talked to himself, complaining that the pieces didn't fit. How different we both were from when you had left that space beside me three years ago. We were different but the same. Does that make sense? I smiled nervously as I added, 'I have been keeping my own secret, Bear.'

The atmosphere was charged with emotion but you bent down and put a piece in Wolf's puzzle. You appeared so shocked, your eyes were large and questioning and you struggled to speak. You eventually found your voice.

'Where did he come from?' you whispered, turning to me. 'Is he yours?'

'Yes, he is.'

'You do it for me,' Wolf said, handing you a piece of the puzzle.

'Say please, darling.'

'Please, you do it for me.'

You did as he asked and then took hold of him carefully and placed him on your lap. Wolf gazed up at you, his huge blue eyes taking in all of your face and he then rubbed his finger on your stubble. Seeing him in your arms produced a rush of feelings in me that I couldn't put a name to. It just looked so right to me, as if you had always been there and always been his father and the last few years had happened in another universe.

'What's your name, little man?' you asked him softly.

'Wolf.'

Closing your eyes for a second made it appear as if it was all too much for you. Then you wrapped your arms around him. Wolf was a very affectionate child and always responded to a hug. He was hugged so often in our house, it was a natural occurrence. He put his arms around your neck and I heard you sigh.

'You break my heart still, Amy Lee.'

'Do you mind that he's mine?'

'How could I mind someone as beautiful as this?'

'I need to show you something else ...'

'Give me a minute, please, this is so overwhelming, so it is, I need a few minutes to take it in.' Touching Wolf's dark hair, you kissed his cheek very softly, saying, 'Wolf, it's a lovely name, so it is and it fits. Amy, I just need to process this.'

'I know you do and I'm sorry I didn't write and tell you, Bear. Patrick knew obviously but he was sworn to secrecy. I just wanted to tell you face to face.'

'Who is ..?'

'I don't know and I don't care,' I declared, defiantly. 'I'm ashamed to tell you that, but it's the truth. I was missing you so much. I tried to find love and affection anywhere I could.'

You looked at me, frowning a little. 'And did you? Did you find love and affection, Amy?'

'You know the answer to that.'

'He's lovely, so he is. What's his personality like?'

'He's full of life, he's funny and he's affectionate.'

'He's like you then. Wolf, do you want to do the jigsaw again? You can show me how clever you are.' Wolf jumped off your lap and took hold of your hand.

He looked up at you. 'You help.'

Wolf's birth certificate was resting safely in the drawer. You sat on the floor and handed him the pieces of the jigsaw, all the while stroking his hair gently. His chubby little hands were fitting them in and he glanced at you all the while, looking for reassurance.

I opened the drawer and stood with the document in my hands and as I trembled with anticipation, the paper shook. I was looking down at your two heads close together and having you there in my room once more, after all those years, I was filled with a sense of peace and timelessness. It was almost as if you had walked out of that room only two days before. When you held me again after I had raced to meet you just an hour ago, all those other men faded quickly into the scenery of my life, even Max who I had come to admire and like more than I ever thought I would.

They had all been kind to me, loving in their own way and affectionate and they had all put up with my emotional absence, but they weren't you. Only you could bring out the best in me. Only you could make me feel fully alive. Only you could put up with my funny ways and my faults and still laugh at them as if they weren't faults at all.

'Bear, I need to show you this.' I handed you the paper and as you read the words there, you put your hand over your eyes. 'I only want *you* as his father, only you.'

'But I'm not ...'

'Don't say it! Don't ever say it!' I placed my hand over your mouth. You were scrutinising my face. 'Don't!'

You very gently moved my hand away and held it in yours, squeezing it. 'And you didn't fall in love?'

'You know I didn't. I was stupid and reckless and I missed you so much, but I wouldn't be without him now.'

'They must have loved you though. How could they not?'

'I don't know, missing you clouded my judgement and my thoughts. I couldn't feel their love because I was always wishing you were there.'

'I missed you too and I didn't fall in love either. I had a few problems in America and Canada. I had to see a doctor.' You looked down at Wolf again and touched the top of his head. 'If it's what you want, Amy Lee, then I'll be a father to him, so I will. I can never say no to you. He's perfect, just perfect.' We put our foreheads together and I took in your special smell. 'I hope I'll be up to the job.'

'Thank you. Thank you, and don't ever say that. You are all he will ever need.' I squatted next to Wolf and took hold of his chin. 'Wolf, this is your daddy.' Wolf simply grinned again and stared at you. 'Are you going to say hello?'

'Daddy, help me with this.' He held up a piece of the jigsaw. 'Help me, Daddy.'

My heart felt as if it would burst open as you sat down by his side again and helped him with the infinite patience you had always had. I didn't care what happened to us after witnessing your first meeting with my little boy. Everything else would pale into insignificance.

You repeated what you had said and it was so typical of you and so heartbreaking at the same time. 'I hope I'm a good enough man, Amy Lee.'

'You are! Of course you are!' As you kissed Wolf's cheek and handed him the pieces of jigsaw again, I hoped you were feeling the peace and happiness *I* was feeling at that moment. 'Are you happy now?' I asked you, bending down to look in your eyes and desperate for you to say you were. You turned your face away.

## Chapter Eleven

*__Outwardly I am silent__*
*__Inwardly you know I am screaming.__*
*__Rumi__*

OVER THE NEXT YEAR YOU GREW EXTREMELY CLOSE TO little Wolf and your long absence seemed a million miles away. It was almost as if it had never happened and in fact, I told myself it hadn't. Every morning, when I first opened my eyes, I would remember you were home and just across the street once more. I began the day with a feeling of such inner peace and joy, my mother and Annie commented that I was a completely different person.

Max knew immediately, before I even spoke, that you were back. I had walked towards the stables, the day after your return, humming and running my hands through the hedgerows lightly. 'He's home, isn't he?' he said, with a faint smile as we went to put the horses' reins on.

'How do you know?'

'Oh, Amy, don't be daft, you look so happy, you even walk differently. There's a spring in your step and your face ...'

'Yes, he's home and he's not ever going away again. I didn't know he was coming back, it was a complete surprise.'

'I'm very, very pleased for you.' He squeezed my arm gently. 'I'm very pleased, honestly.'

'Do you mean it?'

'Yes, I do. I know that's hard to grasp, but I do. How is he?'

'He's the same Bear who went away just over three years ago, but perhaps a little more mature and he probably needs a bit of time to adjust to being home again. But he's still my Bear.'

'And you love him just as much, don't you?'

'Yes.'

'What are you going to do?'

'What do you mean?'

'In the future, what are you going to do? Are you going to be able to stand by and watch him love ...'

'I'm staying as close to him as I can. I don't care about anything else or *anyone* else.'

Max turned to me and put his hands either side of my face. 'Stay by his side then if you must, support him, love him, but be prepared to bleed.'

'I will support him and love him and I *am* prepared to bleed.'

'Then so be it, Amy.' He paused for a moment, but then a small smile spread across his mouth. 'I'll just have to concentrate on her Ladyship now.'

'Yes, you will, but thank you and it's been fun, Max.'

'So it's been fun and nothing else then? I had hoped it had been wonderful, exciting and loving, but maybe not. Talk about dent a man's ego.' I felt a little ashamed and more than a little guilty and my face must have fallen. 'Don't worry, Amy, I can take my ego being dented. Her Ladyship regularly puts me in my place. She says I think too much of myself.'

'It was all those things and more, but affection was what I

needed most and you gave that to me. I was lonely and you made me less so. I'll be forever in your debt.' As we walked the horses out of the stables towards the farm, I heard him chuckling. 'What are you laughing at?'

'And what about it being passionate, would you describe it like that?'

'Don't push your luck,' I said, laughing back at him. No more was ever said on the subject and I was grateful for that.

Even when you'd had time to settle, Bear, you didn't appear to be looking for a job and when I queried this, you told me you had earned quite a bit of money teaching in America and felt the need to go to Ireland first.

'I have to find myself again, Amy. I can only do that in Ireland. I want to see my mammy too. Patrick said she's living there nearly all the time now and I feel a need to see her again.'

'What about your daddy? Is there any chance of meeting him again?'

You had seemed dejected when I mentioned your daddy and dropped your head. I wondered if time and distance had helped you think differently about your complex family, but it obviously hadn't.

'He hasn't expressed any wish to see me again yet and my mammy knows I'm home so ...'

'He will, Bear, I'm sure of it.'

We had been sitting together in my bedroom after putting little Wolf down for the night. You had been teaching him letters that week with a patience I could only marvel at. You had lifted him up to the window too and told him when it was dark and he fell asleep, the moonbeams would stream into his room and bring the night fairies to see him. You then placed him in his bed and leant over him stroking his hair and kissing his forehead, speaking softly to him as his eyes grew heavy.

'Goodnight, little Wolf, you're such a beautiful boy. I love you very much.'

We sat side by side with our shoulders touching as Wolf's breathing became deeper. The window was open because of the summer heat and the birds in the trees at the end of our garden were singing their soft evening lullabies. I hadn't asked you much about your time in America or Canada and you hadn't offered the information, but I knew by your last letter you had been struggling. You were watching Wolf that night with a small smile and you seemed more relaxed than when you first came home.

'Bear,' I ventured, tentatively, 'Bear, tell me what happened with Dean.' I felt your body stiffen. 'But only if you want though.'

'Dean was a difficult man,' you murmured, 'very, very difficult. I didn't want to tell you because I know it will hurt you.'

'I'm sorry.' I leant my head on your shoulder. 'Did you love him?'

'I thought perhaps I did a little at first, Amy, but I now know it was a kind of passion I hadn't ever felt before. It was the passion I'd been searching for when I realised my true nature. Does that upset you? I'm so sorry if it does.'

I wanted to scream, yes! I wanted to yell at you, why can't you feel that passion for me? How could I though? I felt my father at my shoulder. Pretend! Pretend! Pretend!

'No, it doesn't upset me now. I just want you to be happy. Why was he difficult? Was he unkind to you?'

'Yes, he was.' Your face crumpled. 'He was very unkind.'

'How could he be unkind to *you*?'

'I can't answer your question, Amy Lee because I don't know the answer. I feel sometimes as if I do something to deserve it.'

'Oh, Bear, you don't, you *really* don't.'

'Shall I tell you about him then? I want to, but it hurts me even now.'

'Tell me,' I urged you, 'please, tell me, it might help.'

You held my hand tightly and your eyes held a look of confusion and anxiety. I moved even nearer to you to help you summon up some courage and we both trembled simultaneously.

'He was very manipulative and controlling, so he was, but it was done in such a way, I didn't know I was in danger of being destroyed.'

'That sounds awful. How could he destroy you?'

'It was like a slow burn and I had no idea I was in danger of being burnt, but I couldn't stop warming my hands on his fiery body. Amy, I know this is going to hurt you terribly and I'm sorry, but I had never felt passion like it.' I must have shuddered because you felt it and tears streamed out of your eyes. 'Forgive me, Amy Lee, forgive me for saying that. It must hurt you so badly, but you have to know the truth. If we're going to move on beyond all this together, you need to know.'

'I do forgive you and whatever you say I'll still feel the same about you.'

'That passion burnt itself out quickly though, for me anyway, but not for him. I was like a little child in a sweet shop for a while, gazing at what I had always longed for but never tasted and it was there in front of me, I just had to reach for it. He was brutal in his passion for me though, so he was. It wasn't gentle, it wasn't affectionate and at first, I told myself, this was what I had always yearned for.'

'Why wasn't he affectionate towards you? How could he not be?'

'Dean is not affectionate in his nature, not at all. He can't be, he just can't. I thought I could change him and make him so, but it wasn't possible, Amy. He was jealous too, insanely jealous.'

Sitting beside you then, in the half dark, with the summer breeze blowing through the open window, I was imagining you in Dean's arms as he let his brutality overpower you and I felt physically sick.

You must have picked up on my feelings because you leant forward and looked intently at me. 'I know this is tough to hear, Amy Lee, but there really can't be any more secrets in my life, especially between us. Secrets have a way of festering inside you and they always surface eventually.'

'Why didn't you run from him? I can't imagine how he must have made you feel.'

'It's difficult to answer that question, but when you are on the inside of a situation you just don't realise it's happening until you're brave enough to step back. Eventually, I found the courage I needed because he was slowly crushing the person I am. He chipped away at me gradually, carefully and cruelly. I don't know even now if I have those pieces of my personality back.' Little Wolf cried out in his sleep and you jumped slightly. 'Is he okay?'

'Yes, he's okay, he often does that. He dreams a lot, like I do.'

'I hope his dreams are better than mine.'

'Carry on telling me. Your last letter from Canada didn't sound like you at all.'

'I wrote it but it was his words.'

'Why? Why did you let him do that?'

'He became intensely jealous of you and he would tear up my letters to you into tiny pieces before I could post them. In the end I was writing them in secret. That last letter, he said I could write it, but if I wanted him, if I *loved* him, he had to dictate it. Oh, Amy, I knew you would know something was wrong. That was when I decided to leave him and come home. I imagined you opening it ...'

'Don't get upset.'

'It was so weak of me though, so weak. I feel something is missing inside me. Anxiety has a tight grip on me, so it has. Being anxious makes ordinary life unbearable. Little problems seem insurmountable and huge. Even speaking to people, having normal conversations, seems impossible and terrifying. The thought of attending interviews is appalling, so it is, like climbing a mountain without any footholds.' Your voice was just a whisper, hard to follow. 'It all becomes like an enormous muddle, an enormous feat and I end up sliding into a black hole. That's why I haven't been working yet.'

'Oh, Bear, how can I help you? I'll do anything I can, you know that.'

'I feel slightly apart from everything, slightly detached and not quite here. I feel remote and introverted, disinterested and almost indifferent to life itself. It's this awful apathy, so it is. I can't shake it off and I feel as if life is all moving past me and I'm watching it from afar. I long to jump in and be a part of it all, but I'm really not sure I can anymore.' I wiped my eyes and you touched my cheek tenderly. 'Don't be afraid, Amy Lee. Please don't be afraid. You're my Guardian Angel, so you are.'

'What did the doctor say? You saw a doctor, didn't you?'

'I have these tablets, but I don't like taking them. They mess with my head.'

'But aren't they supposed to mess with your head, but in a good way?'

You gave a small smile. 'You're funny, Amy. They dull my senses, but the black beast is sleeping for now. I can feel him stirring at times when the anxiety kicks in. He's still there, waiting for me.'

I took hold of your face. 'I'll fight him for you. I'll kill him if he comes near you, you know that. I'll save you. You have me here and little Wolf and we love you *so* much.'

Your eyes were like two deep, dark pools of bewilderment and pain. Looking at you like that was extremely difficult because your face and your eyes always gave away your deepest feelings. I didn't like what I saw in your face then. It was too distressing for me. It felt as if you were on the edge of a precipice and too near the point of no return for me to pull you back and save you.

'You're such a life force, Amy. I don't want to always be a burden to you. I want you to be happy and find a man who ...'

'Don't say it!' I cried, anger bubbling up suddenly and Wolf stirred a little at the sound of my voice. I dropped to a whisper. 'I've been with other men and it's not all it's cracked up to be. That's the end of it, so don't mention it again. It's *my* choice who I love. It's *my* choice who I adore. I love *you*. I adore *you*. I have tried so bloody hard to find another man but there isn't one. There just isn't. With love there is no burden. With love there is no fear, except the fear of losing you all over again, so no more of it, *please*. Say you understand.'

You nodded quickly. 'I understand and it's the same for me, so it is. You hold my heart in your precious hands, Amy Lee. Don't let go of it.'

'I won't, I promise you.'

Downstairs we heard Isabelle open the door to Patrick and my mother called up to us that he was here and to come and eat. 'We should go down,' you said, without moving.

'Shall we go to Ireland and take little Wolf to your granny's farm? I have some holiday to come. What do you say?'

'Yes, I think I need to go home.' Your eyes sparkled momentarily. 'I need to breathe Irish air.'

'Let's do it then. It will be like before, when we were younger, before Eddie Baker and Dean and ...'

'Before knowing my daddy was a stranger with silver hair,' you added quickly.

We sat around the table that evening with little Wolf tucked up in bed and my family talking constantly as Patrick concentrated hard to read their lips. Isabelle was trying out the signing Patrick had taught her and Ava smiled sweetly at you every now and again, her face flushing red each time you smiled back. She had always had a crush on you without you ever being aware of it. I was only half listening to the happy chatter because I couldn't take my eyes off you. Every now and then you would return my gaze and I would feel such a sense of belonging, it was as if the last three years had been erased from my mind. I didn't let my thoughts stray onto your sexual relationship with Dean. It was just too painful and I repeatedly told myself that you had simply been experimenting and now that experiment was over and it had failed miserably.

We booked to go to Ireland the following week. Annie was

delighted for us and said she felt quite envious. 'I could do with a holiday. Haven't had one for years but it's difficult with a business. Mind you, it's so beautiful out here. It's like being on holiday all the time.'

'One day,' I told her excitedly, 'one day, when I'm living there with Bear and little Wolf, you and Max can come and visit. Would you do that, Annie?'

'Sweetheart, I promise we'll come. I bet the scenery is wonderful, isn't it?'

'There are mountains and lakes and fields with deserted, narrow lanes and desolate moorland that's a sea of mauve heather in the summer. Bear has inherited his granny's old farmhouse and it's miles from anywhere. Many years ago it had a thatched roof with no running water. There's a beautiful waterfall nearby and when we were sixteen we took our clothes off and swam under it. It was freezing! Bear is like a different person when he can breathe Irish air.'

Annie was looking at me fondly. 'Your eyes are shining. Little Wolf will love it, won't he?'

'Oh, he really will and Bear can teach him all the names of the birds and the flowers and he can meet the rest of Bear's family. I can't wait, I just can't wait.'

'Amy,' Annie said, appearing choked, 'I had no idea how little of the real you I had seen until now. With Bear home, I now realise how much of your personality was missing when he was in America. My God, you really do worship the ground he walks on, don't you, sweetheart?'

'I've got a surprise for you, Annie. I'm going to bring him to meet you tomorrow. He's heard so much about you and Max and you know so much about him, I thought it would be a lovely idea for us all to meet up. Would that be okay with you?'

She rubbed her hands together. 'It would be a pleasure to meet him at last. I'll warn Max he's coming though. You know how blunt he can be and I suspect Bear is quite a sensitive soul. Bring him a bit earlier than your normal time and we can sit and have coffee together.'

'I will do, thank you.' She looked thoughtfully for a moment and I asked, 'Why are you looking at me like that?'

'Did you hear what you said a little while ago?' I must have appeared perplexed because she added, 'Amy, you said "when *we* are living there together with little Wolf." Sweetheart, is that a realistic ambition to have? I worry so much about you.'

'We *will* be living there together, one day, I know it.'

Annie just gave a slight shrug and said nothing more.

I did take you the following day and you were completely entranced by Annie *and* her farm. The masses of flowers everywhere were bursting with colour and the trees and bushes were a vibrant, fresh green and almost sparkled in the sun. As we walked down the lanes from the station to her shack, you were stopping every couple of minutes and staring at the sky. It was just like being kids again making our way home from school.

'Bear, what *are* you looking at?' I had asked you as I always had. 'I'd forgotten how long you take to walk anywhere. It's just the sky. It's always just the sky.'

'There are angels up there, Amy, angels everywhere.' The wispy clouds were stretching above us and they did indeed look like angels' wings. 'I can't wait to be in Ireland where they live near the mountains. The sunsets in Ireland make me want to fly up there with them and reach another, secret place, so they do.'

'What secret place?'

'There's a secret world beyond the sunrise and sunset, so there is. A secret sky it is. I can almost see it. I can feel it too. Sometimes I just feel the need to be there, Amy Lee. I need to be in a secret sky where everything is possible and where unconditional love exists.'

'You're not going anywhere without me again,' I said, feeling a flutter of anxiety in my chest. 'We're nearly at Annie's now, look. This is her land and there's the little shack type caravan she lives in. Wait until you see the horses, they're so gentle with the children.'

'This is a beautiful place to work, so it is. You must be in paradise working here. And the wood over there, full of nature spirits, no doubt and the little people.'

'I thought the little people only lived in Ireland.'

'Normally they do, but they follow you, Amy Lee, because they're watching over you. Look, over there, at that nuthatch and the swallows are flying across the fields. This is a heavenly place, a truly heavenly place. I'm so glad you were here for some of the time I was away. It must have eased your soul.'

I had felt such a quiet joy to hear you commenting on nature, like you used to and your eyes had taken on the wonder of your youth, where everything was like a magical fairytale to you. I spotted Annie coming out of her shack.

'There's Annie, come on.' I took your hand and we walked quickly to where she was feeding the chickens. I called out to her. 'Annie. Annie.' She looked up and waved frantically. 'You think I'm a life force, Bear, wait until you spend time with her.'

Annie's curls were in a mess and her face was smeared with dirt already. She was wearing old, tatty dungarees on and a T shirt with large holes in it. She didn't ever care what she looked like, even if she had a visitor coming. Everyone had to take her or leave her as she was. She had no side at all. Her eyes were shining as she hugged you tightly.

'Aha, it's the notorious Bear Flynn! So lovely to meet you, sweetheart, I know so much about you.'

'It's grand to meet you too. Amy told me you're a wonderful boss and a kind friend to her and I'm very grateful to you for that.'

Annie gave you a broad smile and clapped her hands together in delight. 'Now that's a gorgeous Irish accent. I had an Irish lover once and as soon as he spoke, I was putty in his hands.'

Your amusement at her words showed in your smile. 'You have a beautiful place here. I'm so relieved Amy works outside here with you. No building could contain Amy Lee. I wish I could work outside, it's so much better for the soul, so it is.'

Annie put her arm through yours as if she had known you for years.

'You're right there! Come inside and have some coffee and then you two can take a stroll around. Amy can show you everything.'

'I'd love to see the horses, if I may.'

'Amy will take you and you can meet the delectable Max.'

We spent a wonderful morning with Annie and the disabled children and you found the horses quite mesmerising, stroking their noses gently and whispering in their ears. Annie was taken by you, I could tell and so was Max. He was almost speechless when you shook his hand warmly at the stables and said you were honoured to meet him.

'Amy has told me how kind you have been to her, so she has. Thank you for being a friend to her and little Wolf. I'm forever in your debt.'

For a moment, Max was so taken aback, he just nodded. He was looking at you as if you had landed from Mars, but when he found his voice he appeared choked by your words.

'Well, it hasn't exactly been difficult. Amy is easy to get on with and she loves the horses. Anyone who loves the horses is a friend.'

You were stroking the head of the horse nearest to you. 'They are beautiful, gentle beasts, so they are. Look at their eyes, Amy Lee, they are so soulful. You can see the whole world in their eyes. They hold such wisdom, such kindness and such depth. I could look in their eyes all day and not be bored of doing so.'

I could see Max watching me out of the corner of my eye and I could almost read his thoughts. The three of us slowly walked the horses to the farm and you helped with the children and their lessons as if you had been doing it all your life. It was the brightest I had seen you since you had arrived home. I wished fervently you had never gone to America and met the cruel, controlling and nasty Dean. I was sure I could slowly put the pieces of your life back together, as long as nothing else emotionally charged happened to you.

I watched proudly as you lifted the vulnerable and uncoordinated children onto the horses' firm backs and with each one, if they cried at first, you spoke quietly to them, soothing their nerves and their fears and looking directly into their eyes. How I wished then that I could do that for you, Bear, to quell your anxiety and your nerves. It made me think of the angry bull again in Ireland and how you had calmed him with your gentle words and manner.

Max was standing beside me at one point and he whispered in my ear. 'Amy, he's so charming and gorgeous I almost fancy him myself.'

'Stop that! It's more likely to be the other way round, unfortunately.'

He squeezed my arm and gazed at me fondly. 'I had no idea though. Really, I had no idea.'

'What do you mean? You had no idea about what?'

'I'll be brutally honest with you ...'

'Do you have to be?'

'Shush and listen for a second, will you? I thought you were suffering from unrequited love and that really worried me because that's an unenviable place to be, but I was wrong. I had absolutely no idea how much he loves you too. It's quite astonishing to watch the two of you. Her Ladyship will have clocked it, believe me.' He shook his head. 'What *are* the two of you going to do?'

I left his question hanging in the air but he was right about Annie, she had *indeed* clocked it and, while you helped Max walk the horses back in the afternoon, Annie and I sat in her shack and drank some tea. It had been a warm day and there was a welcome, cool breeze blowing in her open windows and fluttering through the curtains.

'He's absolutely bloody gorgeous, Amy. What can I say? I can see exactly why you love him so much. He has a kind of gentleness about him and that's rare in many young men. And that voice and those eyes, my God, you poor darling, how do you keep your hands off him?'

'With difficulty,' I said, smiling and she threw her head back and laughed.

'I can only imagine, he's just adorable, so it must be very, very hard. Oh dear, what are you going to do?'

This time I didn't avoid the question. 'I'm just going to keep on loving him. I have no other option.'

'I didn't realise how much he loves *you*. I watched you walk together towards the stables and he reached for your hand. It wasn't the other way round. *He* reached for you. You could warm your hands on the love between you.'

'How could you realise? You'd never met him.'

'Maybe one day, one day, when you're both older...'

'I don't think that far ahead.'

'No, better that way. We'll miss you when you're in Ireland. Max will be quite bereft.'

'I doubt that, he has you, Annie.'

'Yes, I'm enough for him. I'm wearing him out at the moment. It must be the summer weather.' We both laughed and she shook her head. 'You think I'm joking, but I'm not.'

'I believe you!' We laughed again and I blew her a kiss across the table.

You came and drank some tea with us when you had finished washing the horses down with Max and Annie asked you about Ireland.

'Do you think you'll end up living there one day, Bear?' She flashed her eyes at me for a second. 'When you're a little older, I mean.'

'I hope so, one day, yes.' Your eyes suddenly lit up, like a sparkler on a foggy bonfire night. 'The farm belongs to me now and I don't want it to fall into disrepair. For me, there's nowhere like it. You can smell the fresh dew in the mornings and you can hear the earth breathing. You can feel nature at its rawest, at its beginning and at its most spiritual. You can actually feel the vibrations under your feet, of every living thing reaching for life and for the light. It speaks to me, so it does, it speaks to me.'

There was silence for a moment, where Annie was processing your words and enjoying every second of you saying them. You appeared to be in a trance, as if you were there, at that moment.

She finally asked, 'What exactly is it saying to you?'

You didn't hesitate. 'It says, Bear Flynn, come with us. It whispers to me, you are one of us, nourish your soul with our strength, enter the web of life and nature and connect with the universe. I can hear the grey wolves of long ago telling me, we are near, we are near, come run with us and be free for a while. I can hear the wild horses urging me to jump on their backs and hold on to their shining manes. I can even hear the stars speaking as they fall to Earth. It all speaks to me. It's where the angels live, so it is and they ask me to join them and fly into the sunrises and sunsets, to warm my body and ease my mind.'

Annie was completely struck dumb by the poetry of your words, so I jumped in and laughed. 'He's always saying stuff like that, Annie. He's been speaking like that since we were eleven.'

'But he's right,' she replied, not able to take her eyes off you. 'Bear, you're so right, sweetheart.'

As I watched you that day in Annie's little shack, your face, always so expressive and a little more chiselled as you left your boyhood years behind you, was changing constantly as you chatted with her because you recognised a kindred spirit. You were, quite simply, beautiful. There was beauty in every gentle word you uttered, in every small, shy smile, every affectionate look. There was beauty in your every movement as you continually reached for my hand for reassurance and beauty in your curious, intense look as Annie spoke. Nobody listened like you, Bear. It was as if you were examining every word. There was a seductive tranquillity in how you listened and reflected on conversations.

More than this though, there was beauty in the way you made everyone around you feel. I had witnessed it at school when all our classmates clamoured to be your special friend. I had seen it at the supermarket when the manager would look at you with relief in his eyes when you kindly and politely rectified his careless mistakes without making him feel a fool. I had known of it when you spoke of Eddie Baker and how he singled you out for special attention.

Bear, you bewitched everyone without even knowing you were doing it and every time you looked at me I was reminded constantly that I was still under your spell and always would be. There was an inevitability about it that comforted me.

I should have told you all this at the time. Perhaps it would have helped you. Telling you now, without seeing you react to my words, is hell. I want you to open your eyes and smile with embarrassment as I praise you. I know exactly what you would say.

'I think you're a little biased, Amy Lee, so you are.'

Later, when we left Annie's farm, she kissed you and hugged me and told me she would miss me while I was away. 'It's only two weeks,' I told her lightly.

'I know, darling,' she said, as you wandered away, still gazing at the sky as if you had never seen it before. 'But one day I'll lose you altogether. You'll move on and go to Ireland with him and leave me with my gorgeous hired help, but that's fine, you must live your life.' She suddenly took my arm and frowned. 'Amy, listen carefully. He's a fragile young man and there's a bit of depression lurking inside him. I know about depression. My father had it, it was from the war. Max has it occasionally too. Watch over him, won't you?'

'Of course I will,' I said, her sudden, heartfelt words sending a little shiver down my back. 'I'll always watch over him.'

I was such an optimistic person, similar to my mother and it had never occurred to me that I couldn't handle all your various moods, but I couldn't, could I, Bear? I know that now. It was all too deep rooted, too profound and the damage to your precious, gentle soul had been done years before.

Patrick travelled with us to Ireland and when we arrived at

granny's farm, Danny had opened up the windows and doors the day before to let in the sweet, summer air and it had chased away the closed up, musty smell. There were flowers on the living room table which you said your mammy must have put there, some food and milk in the fridge and a crusty loaf of bread in the kitchen. I felt a great weight had lifted from your shoulders because you seemed more at peace and at ease and you even looked different. Your back was straighter, your walk lighter and your face less grave in repose. Little Wolf ran excitedly around in every room, calling to you loudly.

'Bear, come with me. Bear, come here.'

You followed him and I could hear you upstairs explaining what every room was for. 'You'll sleep in here with your mammy and I'll sleep in here. Look this was my bedroom when I was tiny like you, so it was. Look out of the window, Wolf. You can see the fields stretching so far and all the birds flying around. It's grand, so it is.'

'Mama,' he called, as I came up the stairs, 'Mama, this is my bed here.' He was beside himself and jumping up and down on the bed as if it was a trampoline. 'I like it here.'

'Don't do that, it might break. I think the beds here are very old, aren't they, Bear.'

'They are, very old, but if you break it there are others to choose from. Shall I be putting the kettle on, Amy Lee?'

'Yes and we'll eat.' Wolf followed you, like a little lamb following its mother and took hold of your hand. 'I don't think I'm needed here at all,' I called after you, but my heart was full to the brim with happiness and I repeatedly told myself, this was where you would heal.

We roamed the countryside every day, you carrying Wolf on your back or your shoulders and me carrying the picnic we had prepared. We sat by the river and Wolf paddled a little despite the water being icy. Every moment reminded me of us being younger and trying to find ourselves, together and apart. I was hoping for a shared future where our love and passion would overflow and we would be emotionally and physically fulfilled. You were still holding your secret close to your heart and wondering all the while how not to keep breaking mine.

When we took Wolf up onto the moor and he bounded through the rough, coarse heather without a care in the world, I was recalling how we had sobbed together, united by the guilt and shame that was torturing you and the emotions that were moving inside me. But you didn't mention any of it, until we went to the waterfall. Then you glanced over to where we saw your mammy kissing the stranger for the first time and your world as you knew it fell apart.

Wolf was splashing you with the water in the pool and giggling from the spray that was cooling his red face. The weather that year was glorious almost every day and we all had colour in our cheeks.

'Amy,' you suddenly said, 'she's not going to bring him. She's not, I know it.'

I smiled encouragingly and took your hand. 'She will. I'm sure she will. Please don't be upset.'

'I'll need to ask her why. If I don't ask her it'll eat away at me. I want to know him. I want his love. I *need* his love.'

'Do whatever you think is best. You make the decision and I'll support whatever you want to do.'

You clutched my hand very tightly. 'Is she ashamed of me?'

'Oh, Bear, how could she be?'

'I need to see him. I need to know him the man that he is. The black beast is rearing his head again, even here. I have so little strength to fight him.'

Fear shot through me like the sharp, deadly point of an arrow. 'But you have the tablets. I thought they were helping.'

'I don't think they were. They were dulling my senses, so they were.'

'Bear, please don't tell me you've stopped taking them.' You stared at the ground and I repeated, 'Bear, have you?'

'Don't be angry, Amy Lee.'

'I'm not angry with you. I never could be, you know that, but you should have asked the doctor first.'

You turned to watch Wolf throwing sticks into the pool with great effort but no skill and you sighed. 'I had therapy in America, psychotherapy it was. She was a lovely doctor and she asked about my childhood. I spoke a lot about my mammy and how I feel an enormous hole in my chest, an enormous gap where her love should be. Your mammy's love is the first love you feel, the very first, so it is and my mammy always seemed to favour me. It was always, "Oh my Baby Bear, my Baby Bear is so clever, he's going to Cambridge, don't rough him up, you'll dislodge his brains." But I only realised when I spoke to the psychotherapist that I never really *felt* it. You should feel it, you *should,* Amy, but I didn't.'

'But she must love you, she *must*. She's your mother and everyone loves you.'

'Yes, she must, but you have to feel it and I haven't ever felt that unconditional love that you felt from yours. I have searched my soul to find it, but it isn't there. She's very selfish, so she is and she's being selfish now with my daddy, I know it.'

'Did you tell the doctor about finding out about your real daddy?'

'Yes and she encouraged me to meet him and to get to know him, even if my mammy doesn't want me to. She said that he might fill in some of the gap.' You were shaking slightly and sweating. 'But she told me I must be prepared to be disappointed.'

'Why, disappointed, I don't understand?'

'It's because you build it up in your mind to be something pretty wonderful and he's just a man, after all.'

'Bear, he'll love you so much, it *will* be wonderful, it will. Remember when he was standing at the side of the road and how he waved at you.'

Wolf was calling you. You were his favourite person in the world, apart from me and the one he always wanted to play with, the one who had to put him to bed and the one who could console him if he cried. You went over and picked him up in your arms, placing him on your shoulders.

'You're the King of the World, little Wolf, *and* the King of Love. "A thousand half-loves must be forsaken, to take one whole heart home."'

'Rumi was a clever bastard,' I said, very quietly just in case Wolf was listening.

'Amy, stop your swearing now,' you whispered back with a half smile and for a split second, in that moment, you were the old Bear. But that thought made me realise that mostly, you were actually very far from the old Bear. 'Wolf will hear you.'

'Nanny swears in the kitchen,' Wolf chimed in, without really knowing what he was saying and we both laughed quietly.

We turned away from the waterfall and I was left wondering how on earth it was all going to play out. I could never have foreseen what was coming.

Your mammy visited us on our fourth day there and cooked us lunch. She appeared about ten years younger than when she was married to Zachary, full of life and free from any kind of worry. The frown lines had all but disappeared between her eyes and forehead and she was wearing a figure-hugging dress that accentuated her curves. The transformation was completed by her dark hair being worn much longer and loose below her shoulders. You were quiet and subdued at the lunch table even though Wolf repeatedly asked you to feed him his food. You did so, but when he tugged on your shirt sleeve, you didn't appear to feel it.

'Wolf,' I said gently, 'leave Bear alone for a minute, please. Eat your lunch yourself like a good boy.' He looked across at me with his big eyes and did as I asked and you stroked his cheek because his bottom lip had begun to tremble slightly. I tried to console him. 'Wolf, don't cry, just eat your food and we can go and catch some fish later with Bear.'

You nodded a little absently. 'Yes, we'll catch fishes later, so we will, you and me, Wolf.'

I was wondering what on earth your mammy thought of me naming my son after your daddy, but when I had introduced them she had merely smiled and hidden any other emotion behind her carefully constructed mask. That was the point where I began to wonder who your mammy really was inside, as a person.

She was chatting away, full of tales about local people she now knew or ones she had met up with again that she had known as a child and both you and Patrick were silent. I tried my best to fill your silences because I knew what was coming. Patrick's intense, serious eyes were on you constantly and you glanced from him to your mammy countless times.

When we had finished eating your mammy made tea in your granny's large, dark brown teapot and you suggested to Wolf that he go and play with your old train set. Patrick had found it in his bedroom and brought it down for Wolf.

'You come, Bear,' he whined, 'you come with me.'

'I'll come in a minute, so I will but I need to talk to my mammy for a bit. Go on, I'll be there soon and then we can go fishing.'

He climbed down from his chair quite happily and I marvelled at how I could ask him repeatedly to do something without success, but one word from you and he gave in. I was quite aware why you had sent him into the other room, so was Patrick and your mammy's body had stiffened slightly.

She was pouring the tea from the heavy pot as Patrick knocked on the table twice. This caused her to jump and some of the tea missed the china cup and spilt on the clean, white tablecloth. She turned to Patrick and scolded him.

'Patrick, will you stop your knocking, please? Look what you made me do. What are you knocking for anyway? What secret are you two hiding?'

I have often thought it was such a ridiculous comment to

make to you, when she had kept such a profound secret from you all your life. Both you and Patrick obviously felt the same because Patrick shook his head and you began your carefully planned interrogation. I call it that, but it was a soft interrogation and could have been much harsher considering the delicate subject matter.

'Mammy,' you started, boldly, 'when do I get to meet my daddy properly?' She appeared surprised, although she shouldn't have. 'Mammy, did you hear me?'

'I don't know, Bear, I don't know.'

'Does he want to meet me?'

A heavy, taut silence hung in the space between you both and I was praying that whatever came out of her mouth next wouldn't destroy you. She was blinking repeatedly and obviously unnerved.

'Well, it's a bit complicated, so it is.'

Patrick said simply, 'It isn't complicated, Mammy.'

'Patrick, it's not that easy and it's not *your* problem,' she said, rather sternly. 'Life is very complex sometimes.'

You had taken a deep breath in at the tone of her voice. 'Patrick is only trying to help, Mammy, don't be saying that to him. What upsets me, it upsets him too. I don't feel it's complicated at all. Will you ask him, please? Just ask him.'

'You think it's all going to be wonderful, don't you?' she suddenly said and the words had erupted out of her as if she had been keeping them inside a long time and now the lid had been pulled off her emotions. 'You'll build it up in your mind, Bear Flynn, to be something it might not be.'

'But it might be wonderful, Mammy,' you replied, rather sadly. 'And I'm not really Bear Flynn, am I? I'm Bear Nathan Carroll, to the death and beyond. To be honest, I don't know who I am anymore.'

'You're so fragile! Look at you, you look like a shadow of the boy you once were. What happened to you in America? You won't cope with all the different feelings, I know you won't. I'm your mammy, I can tell it!'

I came to your defence as I always had, even though there was some truth in what she was saying. 'He isn't a shadow, he's still Bear. He just needs time to readjust and find his way, but he's getting there.'

'Amy, that's how you *want* him to be.' She was shaking her head at me. 'You can see he's a shadow, be honest now. Are you prepared for disappointment, Bear? Are you prepared for it not going how you long for it to go? Think about it carefully. I know you, you're my son, my Baby Bear and it's always going to disappoint you because you hope for a miracle or a saint. He's just a man like any other.'

'How can you say that about him, when you love him so much?'

Patrick knocked hard on the table and signed to you, but your mammy's eyes flashed at him. 'Patrick! Will you stop that?'

Little Wolf's plaintive cry came from the other room. 'Bear, come and be with me.'

You rose from the table. The way you looked at your mammy then would have cut me into pieces if it had been me. 'It's *not* Patrick's fault, any of this. Keep your anger for me if you must be angry with someone. Just ask him, Mammy, just ask him. That's all I want you to do for me. It isn't much, is it?'

As you left the room, I followed and I heard Patrick say something to your mammy. I can't be sure but I thought I heard him say, 'Bear is the best of us. Don't destroy the person he is because of your jealousy.'

Your mammy didn't reply. She didn't deny it either.

No message came from your daddy the next day and you had been on edge from the moment you had woken up. When I came downstairs with Wolf, you were kissing Patrick on the side of his head and he appeared even more dejected than you. You picked Wolf up and stroked his chubby cheek.

'Patrick is going to take Wolf out for the day to pick flowers for you, Amy. Would you like that, Wolf? Would you like to pick flowers for your mammy?' Wolf nodded in an exaggerated manner as he often did when he was pleased about something. 'That's grand then, so it is.'

'What a lucky boy,' I said to him, 'so be very good for Patrick, won't you? No running off on your own, hold his hand and do exactly what he says, okay?'

I knew what you were going to say to me before it came out of your mouth. You sounded so determined. 'Amy, we are going to the little church. We need to be there soon. He's a man of habit, so he is. He goes to an early mass.'

We both kissed Wolf on the top of his head and walked out into the warm, white sunshine of a soft day to find your daddy.

# Chapter Twelve

*The desire to know your own soul will end all other desires.*
***Rumi***

You had clutched my hand the whole way and I fervently hoped all my strength and steadfast support would seep from my flesh and bones into yours. You were silent throughout the walk to the waterfall and when I heard its powerful surge, I vividly recalled your face when we had swum under the white wall of water. You had looked fully alive and excited in that moment. It was only when I remembered how your eyes had been shining that day that I felt some sympathy for your mammy's words.

'Look at you, you're a shadow of the boy you once were.'

I repeatedly glanced up at you and your profile was like an impenetrable mask and very different from how you normally appeared. I had seen you distraught, anguished and dispirited, but this was something altogether new and it frightened me. You appeared more and more haunted as each day passed.

When the church came into view, the sun was streaming

through the trees surrounding the small, crowded graveyard and the birdsong uplifting. I mentioned it but you appeared to be in a dream or a tunnel and you didn't reply. You glanced at your watch and I felt you tremble. We sat on the same bench by the sweet-smelling roses where we had sat that day when I saw your name tattooed on the stranger's forearm.

'He goes to a nine o'clock mass, so he does. Then he sits for a while by himself to think and reflect, I believe. I wonder if he thinks of me. Does he even know I'm here in Ireland? Why is my mammy shielding him from me?'

'I have no idea, but he *must* think of you. I know he prayed about you. He doesn't know the wonderful, clever and compassionate person you are, Bear. But he will, he *will*.'

'I had hoped being here in Ireland would help heal the wounds of my time in America with Dean. I felt I needed peace, tranquillity and beauty and I usually find all that here, but this time, this time ...'

'What's different about this time then?' You turned and looked at me and I could see fear in your eyes. 'What's different, tell me?'

'I'm frightened I've forgotten how to live, Amy Lee and that maybe, just maybe, the black beast is too far inside my head to withdraw again into his cave. I'm not sure I can live like that every day for the rest of my life. My pills were doing something odd to my memory which is why I've stopped them. Being here, a few yards away from him, I realise that I'm almost home to myself, almost but not quite.'

'You will get home to yourself, I know you will.'

'He holds the key. He holds the key. Let him love me. Sweet Jesus, let him love me.'

'Bear,' I whispered, 'if you get close to him, will you tell him your special secret?'

'No!' You seemed aghast at my suggestion. 'It's not relevant to our relationship or to my life anymore.'

'What do you mean?'

'Oh, Amy, I mean I'm done with it all, so I am. You must know that. It's brought nothing but heartache into my life and not even the physical aspect has fulfilled me. I imagined it would. I *hoped* it would. I wanted to experiment and I thought it would bring me home to the man I truly am, but I'm not actually that man anymore. I'm someone else.'

'You'll always be the same person to me.'

'And you still hold my heart in your loving hands and you always will. I don't want to see his face fall if I tell him. I don't want it to register even the faintest bit of disappointment, disgust or anger. I couldn't stand that. It would hurt too much. I want him to be proud of the man I am. I can't have him disappointed in me.'

I leant my head on your shoulder. 'But, Bear, he might love you unconditionally. Why wouldn't he? There's nobody like you in this world.'

'I think you're a little biased. I can't take the risk.'

A few villagers were coming out of the church and I felt your grip tighten. We watched as they chatted for a couple of minutes and I was wondering who they were and what their lives were like and whether they knew your daddy. You gave him a few minutes but then you stood up, pulling me with you.

'Is this it? Are we going in?'

'Yes, stay close, Amy Lee. You'll bring me luck.'

The church had smelt the same, musty and damp but it was warmer than normal. Sun was streaming through the stained-glass windows like a spotlight. We stood behind the font where we had hidden all those years before and peered towards the front. He was there with his head lowered and his arm resting on the end of the pew, in exactly the same position as before. I felt you shaking and my heart ached for you. Your lips were moving and I just about heard your words.

'Angels of Mercy, hear me. Let him love me. Let him love me.'

I was about to urge you to be brave when you dropped my

hand and began walking quickly towards him. Your light footsteps, moving ever closer to him, seemed to resonate throughout my body and I crossed my fingers tightly. This was your destiny and I felt every emotion you were feeling in my own chest. I will never understand how that is possible, but it is. You stopped just behind and to the side of him, not actually in his field of vision, but you tilted your head slightly and I assumed you were listening to his prayers.

What I heard next made me gasp and my hands flew to my mouth. Your voice was loud and clear. It was as if you had been waiting all your life to say that one word and in that moment, years of sorrow, pain, frustration and longing poured out of you in your plaintive cry.

'Daddy!'

Your daddy turned quickly and then stood up very slowly to face you. From where I was standing I couldn't see your face clearly but your shoulders were hunched and tight and the rest of your body seemed stiff with nerves. He appeared startled, frozen and yet moved. He said your name twice, as if saying it once wasn't enough to convince him you were there inches away or enough to convey how he felt about you being there. His rugged face then crumpled and he grabbed hold of you, his muscular arms around your shoulders. Slowly, one hand moved up and towards the back of your head, as if he was cradling a tiny baby.

For a few moments you stood with your arms hanging limply by your sides. It was as if you couldn't believe he was actually holding you and you were terrified to move in case the spell broke. Your arms then moved up and around *his* shoulders and you were locked in the embrace you had longed for. You appeared so small in his arms because he was taller and broader than you. Or was it simply because you were his lost little boy?

Wolf eventually and reluctantly let you go and you were both wiping tears from your faces. He spoke first. 'Bear, my beloved son.'

Your stiff shoulders dropped and you repeatedly wiped your eyes. Even from a distance I could tell you were falling apart inch by inch, second by second and even being in the arms of the man you had waited for wasn't going to put you back together again. I had always thought it would, but now I know it was too little, too late for you, Bear. I realise now, the damage had been done many years before. Didn't it help knowing your real daddy had always loved you? Didn't it help finding out that he had always wanted a close relationship with you?

When you finally spoke, your question was full of vulnerability. 'Are you pleased to see me? Are you happy I'm here, Daddy?'

My heart was cracking open and your daddy's obviously was too. He put his rough hands either side of your face. 'Don't ever doubt how much I love you, Bear. Don't ever doubt how much I've always prayed for this moment. I have prayed every single day in this church, for the angels to keep you safe until I could be a daddy to you.'

He asked if you wanted to take a walk with him and you said you would love to. You turned to find me. 'Amy,' you called, 'do you mind if we take a short walk together?' I stepped out from my hiding place and walked up the aisle. Your daddy was smiling warmly at me.

'Ah, Amy Lee, there you are again. Please come with us.'

'No,' I said quickly, 'I'll wait in here if you don't mind.' It was only when I stood right in front of you that I saw how much you were still shaking.

You appeared concerned. 'Are you sure? Come if you want to.'

'Yes, I'm more than sure and don't hurry, take your time.'

Your daddy gave me a grateful smile and you reached for my hand. 'Will you stay in here, Amy?'

'Yes, it's so lovely and peaceful.'

I watched as your daddy's curious eyes took in your anxious face and your whole body and he appeared upset. 'Son,' he said gently, 'please, no shaking now. There's nothing to be fearful of, nothing at all. This moment was always written in the stars. Those stars are all now perfectly aligned and nobody is going to keep us apart. I won't reject you, I never will. Don't be afraid, Bear.'

You nodded and I felt, in that moment, that he understood you more than Zachary ever had. I watched as you walked towards the door together, his reassuring hand on your back, his body leaning towards yours.

How long you were out together I can only guess at because I found solace sitting there in the front pew, looking up at the colourful and arresting stained glass.

The angels, in one of the windows, were all staring at Jesus with pale, gentle faces, yellow halos and huge, golden wings. Some were flying, some were standing in prayer, their hands clasped together and some had their mouths wide open as if in awe of Jesus on the cross.

But it was the main window, behind the altar, that affected me most. Jesus was standing with his arms apart in white robes and a cloak the colour of a Burgundy wine. His multi-coloured halo shone above and around his head, sending golden beams of light outwards into the world. It drew me in gradually and made me think of you, the lone figure at the end of our road, holding your arms out to me after over three years apart.

I nearly fell into a trance looking at the windows, and the peace and stillness I was experiencing must have been in stark contrast to how you had to be feeling, walking with your daddy for the first time. I shook my head and thought about your granny's words.

'Holy Mary, you'll come back here one day, Baby Bear, when you're done with London and its shallow ways. You'll come back, so you will.'

While you had been out with your daddy I had been repeatedly glancing behind me at the door, waiting patiently for your return so that I could study your face and attempt to guess at your innermost feelings, and when I finally heard the door open, I spun round. You were standing there on your own and you beckoned to me. You looked wide-eyed, in a dream and I hurried towards you and grabbed your hand.

'Is everything okay, Bear? Tell me what happened,' I urged you impatiently.

'Let's walk, Amy, shall we? I feel I need the fresh air up on the moor to blow through me. Keep holding my hand, you'll steady me, so you will.'

'Bear, how do you feel?'

You replied so quietly I could hardly hear you. 'I feel as if none of it is real.'

The hot sunshine on our faces was welcome and there was a soft breeze that moved almost silently through the grass as we walked along the ancient tracks and lower slopes of the Kerry Way. We gradually made our way further towards the vast expanse of moorland that led to the mountains. The lanes were full of fuchsia and honeysuckle and the sweet scent was overpowering. The purple heather spreading for miles on the moors moved gently and it made me recall what it was like to feel your warm, lean, naked body next to mine. My thoughts were interrupted by you dropping to your knees and burying your face in your hands. I knelt in front of you and tried to pull your hands away.

'Bear, tell me what happened, *please*. Was it what you always thought it would be? Please say it was.'

'He *is* gentle, Amy, he *is* kind, so he is. He's thoughtful and clever and articulate and his love and affection would have been such a wonderful environment to have lived in when I was growing up. He isn't too masculine or aggressive and he asked me what I wanted to do with my life now? He was interested in what I *felt*, what I thought and how I had found Cambridge and America.' You paused looking intensely weary and your eyes were full of regret and bewilderment. You sighed gently and went on. 'I couldn't tell him how unhappy I'd been. It would have upset him too much. His father had the black beast in him, so he did, the same black beast! Can you believe that?'

'Did you ask him that then?'

'No, I didn't have to. He asked me if I had it inside me. He said he can see it in my face. He says I have the same troubled look. He had a little sister, Brigitte and she had it too, the depression, the anxiety, so she did. We spoke of it and he told me I *must* take my pills.'

'Why did he say that?'

'He didn't want to say any more than that, but I pressed him and he said it ended badly for her.'

'I'm scared, Bear. I don't like the sound of that. Did you ask why he hadn't come for you? Did you ask why it has taken him so long to contact you?'

You turned your face to the sky and closed your eyes. 'He wouldn't say, but it's to do with my mammy. He hinted that she wants him to herself. He loves her so much, Amy, it pours out of him. He idolises her, so he does, *idolises* her. Oh, sweet Jesus, how I wish I had spent all my life with him instead of Zachary. *He* wouldn't have pressured me. *He* wouldn't have messed with my head and belittled my mammy. *He* wouldn't have used me to get to her.'

'Oh, Bear, I'm so, so sorry, but you mustn't look back, look forward. Can you do that? *Can* you?'

You stared into my eyes blankly. 'Amy, I don't know. I don't know. I don't want this to torture me, but I can't help how my mind works. Zachary is still in my head, so he is. I dream of him sometimes and he's always pushing me, pushing me to do more, *be* more because I'm not enough as I am. In my dreams he's drunk and punishing my mammy for something I haven't done and I beat the living daylights out of him. I pummel his aggressive, detested face until it's a bloody mass. There must still be anger inside me. My dreams appal me and I wake up thrashing my arms about and swearing.'

'Why don't you see another therapist? I think you should. It's all so deeply buried, it needs a professional to get it out of you and make sense of it.'

You didn't reply to that. We had stopped in one of your favourite spots, sitting side by side on the heather, and you were looking over at the golden heat haze shimmering near the mountains. The soft, benign weather was in such contrast to your demanding, burdensome thoughts. A loud, unforgiving thunderstorm with forked lightning would have suited better.

'He told me he loved me, Amy Lee. He said it continually. He told me he would hide when my mammy would take me and my brothers out for a walk or to visit someone here. He would hide, just to get a glimpse of me. He begged her to allow him a relationship with me, but she always refused. It was so painful for him to watch me from afar and not be able to hold me, so he stopped doing that when I was three. He always thought she was ashamed of being pregnant by a man who wasn't her husband. Catholic guilt is a heavy burden to carry, he says. He wanted to marry my mammy years ago when they were very young, but she refused him. Why did she refuse a man like *him* and marry Zachary? I don't understand any of it.'

I leant my head on your shoulder and I couldn't answer that question. Peoples' lives were complicated, often not straightforward and sometimes tragic. Why had I been so reckless in France and Italy and returned home pregnant when I had always loved you?

'Will you see him again? Will he tell your mammy about today?'

'I'll see him every day, he wishes it so. He said, if she doesn't encourage our relationship from now on, he'll end theirs.'

'He *said* that?'

'Yes, he did. He said he loves her dearly, always has and always will, but he's waited for me all these years and after today, when he held me in his arms, he can wait no longer.' You were now gazing at the cloudless sky, your face catching the heat of the sun. 'Amy, he told me, I'm the person he hoped I would be, but even if I hadn't been, he would still love me. He said he had no expectations about me, only love in his heart from the moment he heard I had been conceived. That's the unconditional love I have longed for all my life. Sweet Jesus, help me.'

The enormity of what you were saying suddenly hit me. 'She'll blame you, Bear, if he finishes their relationship, she'll blame you.'

The despair on your face was terrifying and you whispered, 'Yes, she'll blame me.' We both curled up in the heather, facing each other like two little children about to fall asleep. 'Jesus, what do I do? Tell me what to do, Amy Lee.'

I put my forehead next to yours and my arm across your body. We could still have been the two teenagers who had lain that way so many years before. We looked more or less the same and often acted in a similar way, but we weren't those two people anymore, except in one respect. We continued to love each other and wanted the best for each other, whatever that meant in the future. What I didn't realise then was, you were slowly slipping away into a place where you believed you had no future.

'Bear, tell me the magical stories you used to tell me.'

'What magical stories, Amy?' You looked at me blankly for a moment. 'I don't remember doing that.'

'Yes you do. You know, about the little people and nature spirits, all of that. It will ease your mind a little. It's been such an emotional day for you.'

'They aren't here at the moment. They've gone away and they may never come back. I hope they're not deserting me now. They've been with me all my life, so they have, from when I could first speak and understand.' You rubbed your eyes wearily. 'When I asked granny about them, she told me they were there to protect me because I was a special child who would light up the lives of everyone I met. She said I had magical powers and I could have whatever I wanted. Granny was wrong. They're deserting me, Amy Lee.'

I held you as close as I could and moulded my body around yours. We stayed like that for so long I thought you had fallen asleep because you had your eyes closed and your mouth was slightly open. All I could do was watch you and stroke your hair until some low cloud bubbled up and hid the sun, casting shadows across your troubled face.

For the rest of our holiday we were both preoccupied by what had happened. Making it a wonderful couple of weeks for little Wolf was uppermost in my mind and he continued to monopolise your time and attention. You responded with infinite affection and love. You carried him everywhere on your back or your shoulders, telling him every time, 'I hope you can see the whole world from up there because you're the *King* of the World, little Wolf, the King of Love, so you are.'

Wolf would squeal with delight and call out to me, 'Mama, I can see the whole world! I'm the *King* of the World.'

Those were precious moments for us all, but your face was clouded with tension whenever you thought or spoke of your mammy. We didn't even know if she was aware of what had happened in the church that day. There was no clue in her actions or her demeanour. Not that we saw much of her.

Each morning you would walk alone to the church to spend time with your daddy, slowly getting to know him as a man and learning about his life. You would be together for an hour and it was an hour where he would walk with his hand on your back, patting you gently and talking to you with reassuring words that he had an infinite amount of love in his heart for you. You told me, he couldn't stop touching your hair, or your face and you felt the same about him. It was only because of Wolf's demonstrative nature that you realised neither Zachary nor your mammy had ever been like that with you. You would return to the farm with a small smile on your lips, but with more confusion in your eyes.

Tommy and Danny came by regularly in the evenings after work and they would throw little Wolf up in the air and catch him as he screamed with excitement. There was some wrestling and some hide and seek with him while both you and Patrick looked on with amusement and some concern. Once they had left for the night, it fell to you and me to calm him down by reading to him and giving him a bath. On two occasions, you asked me whether I minded you spending an hour of the day with your daddy.

'Do you mind, Amy Lee? You can come if you'd like to.'

'Don't be daft, Bear, of course I don't mind,' I had told you one morning, 'I'll take Wolf out fishing with his little net.'

'Meet me at the waterfall in a couple of hours then. It's such a hot day and Wolf can go swimming, like we did.'

I watched as you left the back yard on that day, walking quickly and purposefully and I wondered again whether your mammy knew anything about these meetings. If she had no idea, there were even more secrets surrounding you, secrets that would possibly cause you more harm. Little Wolf cried a torrent of tears when you left, despite your kisses and promises that you would both try and catch an enormous fish when we met at the pool. Your words soothed him a little and Patrick took over and played with him for a while, diverting his attention. When we left for our walk with your fishing nets, he appeared a little subdued and I asked him what was wrong.

'Daddy didn't wait for me,' he said, forlornly. I stood completely still for a moment allowing the enormity of what he had called you sink in. He had only called you that once when he first met you. 'Is he there now, waiting for us? Hurry up, Mama, hurry up.'

'He won't be there yet, darling. We don't need to hurry,' I replied, the quavering in my voice caused by the overwhelming emotion of hearing my little boy call you by the name I had always wanted him to call you.

No more was said and from that moment he alternated calling you Bear and Daddy.

We wandered slowly along the quiet lanes and Wolf picked up

sticks and carried them in his tiny hands. I spoke to him of the rolling farmland and the rugged heath and moor and I tried my best to remember the names of the trees. You knew them all, of course and I managed to point out the Alder, Ash and Downey Birch and the meadow sweet plants, the water mint and the marsh bedstraw. They were strange names but they always sounded so right when you said them with your Irish accent.

The hot sun was glinting on the frothing pool of water at the bottom of the waterfall and the spray was cooling down Wolf's eager, flushed cheeks. He put his net in the water and waited impatiently to catch something. Eventually I took off his clothes and he paddled up to his waist, with me looking on. I noticed a Kerry Violet nearby that you had pointed out to me just before we saw your mammy that day.

'They live where it's very wet, in the bogs and the marshlands,' you had explained to me before pointing to another plant. 'This is the Irish spurge.'

'What a weird name.'

'My granny says it treats warts, so she does, but that's a little bit of folklore, Amy Lee. Granny believes in all of that though.'

As I reminisced about the past and our precious time there together, Wolf called out, 'Mama, you come in too. It's cold, hold my hand.' I stripped down to my underwear and joined him. I carried him in my arms and waded further in. 'What's behind that water?' he asked, pointing to the surging wall of white water near us.

'It's a magical place, Wolf, where water sprites and fairies live. Bear took me there once and it's such a happy place.'

'Can I go there? Will he take me?'

'Yes, one day he will, I promise you.' Wolf's face suddenly looked sorrowful. 'What's wrong, darling?'

'When is he coming? He's been a long time.'

'Yes, I know he has, but he'll be here very soon.'

Just as I said those words, you appeared in the near distance and Wolf squealed with excitement. 'Mama, he's here, look.'

Wolf quickly wriggled free of my arms and splashed towards you, calling your name. You took off your trousers and T shirt and waded in to meet him. The unexpected flash of your flesh made me catch my breath and I had to turn away. You had become so much more muscular in the time you had been in America. A few days later when I mentioned it, you had looked quite upset.

'Dean made me do weight training in America. I hate my body like this, it reminds me of Zachary. But the muscles will disappear eventually and I'll be back as slim Jim in a bone yard, like my granny called me.'

'How did it go?' I asked you, as you cradled Wolf in your arms, his little hands around your neck.

'It was fine, just fine,' you replied lightly, with a faint smile.

'And will he tell your mammy yet you're spending time together?'

'She knows She knows and it's causing problems.' Your face was grave and you appeared disheartened by it all. 'My daddy says it's not my problem, it's *their* problem and I'm not to fret over it.' You gazed up at the sky where thin clouds were moving slowly towards us from the direction of the mountains and pointed above you. 'Look, little Wolf! The angels are here, so they are. Look at their wings flying behind them and their long hair.'

Wolf was looking up, his face alight. 'What angels?' he asked, squinting at the sky.

'That's the Angel of Mercy and her helpers, watching over us. There's a blue tit doing acrobatics too and that little bird with the red tummy is a chaffinch, so it is. If we are lucky, we might see the King of the Birds, little man and swallows and we might hear cuckoos.'

'Why are the angels here?'

'They're here because they love you and your mammy and they are watching over you both.'

'Don't they watch over you too?' You didn't reply to his question and Wolf chattered on. 'Mama said there are fairies over there. Can we see them?'

You kissed his cheek lovingly and ran your hand through his wet hair. 'The fairies are everywhere, so they are and the water sprites are too and if we are very lucky we'll see them dancing on top of the water.'

We spent a lovely couple of hours by the waterfall and Wolf was delighted when you told him his mammy was the best swimmer and the best runner in the world and that she climbed to the tops of the trees and swung from their branches. You then suggested I swim under the white wall of water, as we had years before, to show him how brave I was.

'Swim, Mama,' Wolf shouted at the top of his voice.

'Go on then, Amy, you can still do it, I'm sure,' you urged me, your eyes like two deep pools of sorrow.

'I can't, Bear. I can't, not without you.'

'Sure you can, Amy Lee. You can do anything you want to, with or without me by your side.'

Nerves fluttered in my chest. With or *without* you wasn't something I had ever contemplated and I was terrified by hearing you say it. It stayed in my head, unnerving me constantly.

'Okay, I will, but if you weren't holding Wolf, I'd make you do it with me.'

'I can't do such things anymore. I've forgotten how.'

Wolf became a little impatient. 'Go on, Mama, swim under the waterfall.'

I turned and swam quickly towards the surging power of water. It had always made me feel expansive and exhilarated, but that day, I couldn't shake off your words.

'Sure you can, Amy Lee. You can do anything you want to, with or without me by your side.'

I held my breath and felt the freezing water flow through and around my body. When I surfaced the other side, I turned to my left to the exact spot where you had stood, your eyes alight and your face full of delight and exuberance. The deafening, thunderous sound as the mighty rush of the water moved over the rocks and burst into the pool beneath accentuated the space where you should have been and it made me shudder. I swam back to you almost immediately and Wolf was clapping his hands excitedly. You were speaking in Wolf's ear.

'Tell your mammy, bravo!'

'Bravo, Mama!'

'Thank you, darling,' I said, watching you carefully.

'You're so brave, Amy Lee, so you are.'

'I'm not brave at all. We both did it years ago. You could do it now, Bear. I know you could.'

'No, I'm not as brave as you.' I was going to insist that you were brave but Wolf was getting cold and he was shivering. 'You're freezing, little man. Let's get you dry and dressed.'

We walked quickly back to the farm and Wolf was on your shoulders singing a song you had taught him about a leprechaun. He muddled up some of the words and you interjected when he forgot a line of it, but I wasn't really listening. I was thinking about the space where you should have been standing behind the wall of white water and it stayed firmly on my mind until your bitter argument with your mammy made me forget it.

The next morning, with only a few days of our holiday left, your mammy wandered in and appeared at the breakfast table with a freshly baked loaf. As soon as you saw her, you glanced behind her, hoping to see your daddy following. We had sat together in the back yard the night before and you spoke of the precious time you had spent with him. You told me the conversation had flowed freely and easily and he wanted to know all about your life, including how Zachary had treated you. One day he had asked if we were lovers and when you told him no, we weren't, he was surprised and commented that we obviously loved each other very much.

'I did explain to him we had been, briefly, if that's okay with you. I know it was *very* briefly but I didn't want him to wonder why someone as beautiful as you wasn't my...'

When your voice tailed off I said quickly, 'Did he ask about Cambridge?'

'Yes and I explained the pressure was almost unbearable, but the literature had been exquisite. He asked if I'd been happy there and I told him, pressure and happiness don't live in the same place. He agreed, Amy, he agreed and said he was sorry for it, the pressure.'

Did he speak about your mammy much?'

'He idolises her, so he does. I've never known adoration like it, but he knows her true nature.'

'And what is her true nature then? I have known her for all these years but I don't feel I know her at all.'

'You aren't the only one. Before he explained mammy's nature, he asked me not to judge her harshly and he said we are all flawed. He says she is selfish to her bones and she has a jealous streak. It has reared its head over the years and it's rearing its head now, with me. Jesus, her jealousy is killing me, so it is.'

'I don't understand. How can she be jealous of *you*? You are her son. It doesn't make sense to me.'

You had reached for my hand. 'Oh, Amy, don't hate her.'

That was all you had said and there it was left until the red streaks of the sunset spread above us. You then raised your arms murmuring, 'That's where the angels live and that's where they are right now. Angels of Mercy, watch over little Wolf and Amy Lee. They are precious, so they are.'

'I don't want the angels watching over us, Bear. I want *you* to watch over us. You'll do for me, I don't need angels.'

As happened quite often now, you avoided the question and closed your eyes as if all the emotional wrangling in your life was getting too much for you. I could feel a constant pressure in my chest. It was almost as if my heart was aching.

That morning, the morning of the argument, your mammy was sitting opposite you as we ate the breakfast Patrick had prepared and the atmosphere was immediately taut and stiff. Little Wolf was continually pulling on your shirt sleeve and whining, 'Bear, you help me.' You cut up his food and gave him a slice of bread and jam, kissing his head lovingly. At one point your mammy went to speak but Wolf was being persistent in demanding your attention again and said loudly, 'Bear, are we going fishing today?' You had a mouthful of food and didn't respond straight away and so he tried to climb on your lap, crying, 'Daddy, are we going fishing today?'

There was a shocked silence as you took hold of him gently and your mammy glanced from me to you repeatedly. You were so moved, you could hardly speak. Patrick smothered a smile and you simply patted Wolf's head.

'Well,' your mammy eventually said rather smugly, 'it looks like I'm not the only one who has been keeping secrets.'

'It isn't what you think, Mammy, but if Amy wants to explain, that's fine by me, and if she doesn't that's fine as well, so it is.'

'I don't want to explain,' I said quickly, my face beginning to burn.

You sensed my discomfort and turned the conversation quickly, away from my life. I hadn't expected such a blunt question from you though. 'Mammy,' you started, looking directly at her, 'why did you marry Zachary? Why did you not marry my daddy?'

'You can't be asking me that, Bear! It's too personal, so it is.'

'And why are you jealous?' When your mammy scowled, looking furious, you shrugged, 'You can be as angry as you like but I need to know.'

'You're speaking such rubbish, so you are!'

'Why don't you just be honest with me, for once in your life? Just tell me the truth.'

'You speak of honesty when there's a little child here calling you *Daddy*?'

'Don't bring little Wolf into this. This isn't about little Wolf or Amy, it's about you. Just explain to me, *please*. I need to know about your life and about mine. I want to know it all.' Your mammy flashed her blazing eyes at you but you wouldn't budge. 'I mean it, Mammy.'

'You want to hear it all? Okay, you'll hear it. Wolf and me, we were childhood sweethearts, going to school together and spending all our time outside school together too. Nobody could prise us apart. We were joined at the hip, naive and romantic and it was tender and sweet but we had no experience of life, none at all. We lived here, for God's sake, where nothing ever happens except the harvest and folk talking about the weather and how the rains sweep across from the mountains and you're thought a sinner if you go to the lazy mans' mass. God help us, I was bored stiff and I wanted to taste more of what life had to offer. I went to work in Dublin and one night, one fateful night, I was in a bar with some friends and Zachary walked in, all charm and worldly wise, good-looking and with this fiery sex appeal that burnt my willing fingers.'

Both you and Patrick dropped your heads with embarrassment and Patrick knocked on the table twice but your mammy was in full flow and told him to be quiet.

You snapped, 'Don't be telling Patrick to hush ...'

'You wanted to hear it all, Bear, so listen and hear it,' she said, angrily. 'I couldn't resist him. I was a simple country girl after all and one look from his dark eyes and I was lost. I found Wolf boring compared to Zachary, that's the brutal truth of it. Wolf wanted a simple life here, with the moon and stars as his companions. Huh! Just like you, Bear, so like you! I found him too reliable and dependable. Your granny was horrified and disgusted when I fell pregnant with Tommy but for her it was more the shame than anything else.' She gave a hollow laugh and shook her head. 'All the country girls around here were rolling around in the hay but I was the one who got caught and had to get married.'

Her face then changed and she closed her eyes for a moment, as if recalling a painful memory. We waited with bated breath for the next bit. Thankfully, little Wolf was quiet and stuffing his face with the delicious homemade bread and jam.

'I broke his heart, really broke his heart, so I did. But it didn't end there for us. I had Tommy, Danny and Patrick very quickly which kept me occupied for some time, but Wolf and I found each other again. It was always meant to be, it just took us longer than we expected and our path was never easy, but it led us to each other in the end.

'It took me years of grief and heartache with Zachary to realise Wolf's dependability and his kind, sweet and reliable nature wasn't boring at all but exactly what I needed. Passion and excitement disappear when there are little children around your feet. They don't last but Wolf's compassionate and loving nature will last to the death of me.'

As she described your daddy, she could have been speaking about you and Patrick said so in his monotonic but kindly way. 'Bear, you are your daddy's son.'

Your mammy continued as though Patrick hadn't spoken. 'Mother of God, you want to speak of jealousy? I've waited since I was fifteen to have Wolf to myself, but when I admitted to him you were his, it was *all* he spoke of. He would talk about you constantly and it drove me mad.'

'When did you tell him?'

'I didn't actually tell him. He worked it all out. I was supposed to visit him, as I normally did, when we were here on holiday, but I couldn't travel that year. I was too heavy with you, Bear. You were born nine months to the day since I was last with Wolf, to the day. He asked me, with his searching, soulful eyes, is the baby mine? His beautiful eyes, damn them! They were always so full of sorrow and dark with melancholy and suffering. You have the same eyes and you're looking at me now with them, Bear.'

'I'm sorry ...'

With a quick gesture of her hand she brushed your apology aside. 'From that moment on, you were *all* he spoke of and he had your name etched in his arm with blue ink. All I saw was that tattoo, every time he held me, as if I needed reminding. He loves you more than me, so he does. I feel it all the time. He'll love you more with each year too and I'll feel less of it.'

I could see you were bemused by her last words. 'But it's a completely different love. It isn't a competition, Mammy and your name is on his arm too.'

She scoffed. 'That's easy for you to say. Everyone adores you, Bear. You were your granny's favourite, you know it and that's why she left you the farm. She loved you more than she loved me too. Once my affair with Wolf was in full flow again, I lost interest in everyone else. And then of course, Zachary used you to get to me and he used me to get to you. He was twisted in his head, but God took his revenge by taking your hearing away, Patrick. That was Zachary's punishment.'

You were shaking your head. 'I don't understand that.'

'That's what granny thought and I won't contradict her. There is always a punishment in life. Now I'm being punished by the man I love and by you, who looks at me with such disappointment and disrespect and anger. I can see the anger in you.'

There was a difficult, heavy silence in the kitchen until you said firmly, 'I'm not angry, Mammy.'

'No, you are too good for anger, but *I'm* angry, so I am.' Patrick knocked sharply on the table and signed quickly at you, but you shook your head. Your mammy sighed. 'Patrick, don't start with that malarkey. What did you say to Bear?'

Patrick signed more slowly and said, 'It's not always about you, Mammy.'

Ignoring Patrick's comment completely, she went on, 'Now I have to share Wolf with you. Just watch what way he'll go. When you're over here it will be, when is Bear coming? Why are you keeping him from me? Holy Mary, the flood gates are now open and that flood will destroy us all. You are too fragile for all this, too fragile, so you are. Oh, Bear,' she cried, looking at you, with such ferocity, I'm surprised you didn't catch fire. 'You'll break my heart in the end, so you will, I know it. I've always known it. You're breaking it now with that look and you'll break it in the future.'

With those words, she jumped up out of her seat and left us. Both you and Patrick were stunned and staring at each other as if a hurricane had swept through the house taking everything with it. Eventually, you put your hands over little Wolf's ears.

'Patrick, what the fuck happened then?' You were shaking your head despairingly.

Patrick reached across the table and grabbed your hand. 'Mammy is selfish, that's all, just selfish, Bear. You have done nothing wrong.'

'My life ...'

You didn't finish your sentence but I could hear the grief in your voice. It was grief for the loss of the life you could have lived, if Wolf had brought you up and loved you.

Patrick was deeply concerned. 'You're the best of us, Bear. Don't forget that, the best of us.'

'Am I though? Am I? Patrick, do you feel Mammy's love? Do you? *Did* you, growing up? Tell me, did you?'

Patrick paused before answering, for fear of hurting you. 'Yes, but I'm tougher than you. I've had to be. I'm not as sensitive. I don't need that love as much as you do.'

Wolf climbed onto your lap again, his face and mouth smeared with raspberry jam and you wiped it away with a napkin. He put his chubby, little hands on your face, turning it gently and forcing you to look at him. 'Can we go fishing now?'

You stared deeply into his eyes as if you didn't understand the question. I intervened, saying firmly, 'Wolf, come here a second and leave Bear alone for a moment.'

'But, Mama, I want ...'

'Never mind what you want! Bear is a little tired.'

'I'm not tired, but I have to take a walk on my own.' You wrapped your arms around his tiny frame in a tight, almost desperate embrace and he responded and hugged you back. 'I won't be long, little Wolf, I promise. I won't be long.'

You placed him on my lap and I felt apprehensive. I urged you, 'Bear, don't go too far.'

'Don't be afraid, Amy Lee.' Your voice was as soft as a summer breeze moving through the trees behind the farm. 'Don't be afraid.'

A shiver shot down my back at your words. It was almost as if you were warning me not to be afraid at some future time, when you might not be around. Why I thought that, I have no idea, except that I knew you inside and out. I knew every expression that crossed you dear face and every thought that preceded it.

Patrick was frowning hard at me and murmured, 'Amy, I'm sorry about our mammy.'

We left Ireland a few days later without seeing your mammy again. You met your daddy in the church once more and he had been just as loving and affectionate and promised to come to London to see you. He couldn't wait another year before he saw you again, he said. You had parted with his assurance that his relationship with your mammy was solid and unbreakable and he would slowly teach her to be less selfish with regards to you and your relationship with him.

On the journey home you spoke constantly about your daddy and everything that had happened in Ireland. It was as if you were trying to come to terms with it all in some small way. 'He has an enormous mountain to climb to change my mammy. It won't be easy for him. It was a wrench to leave his side. I could stay there forever. He said to follow my dreams, whatever they may be. It was kind of him, but he *is* an immensely kind man. The problem is, Amy Lee, I don't know what those dreams are anymore. I can't find them in this fog.'

'What fog?' I asked, puzzled, but you remained silent.

Within weeks of being home, you had begun taking your antidepressants again. You seemed so lost, Bear. It was as if you were in a tunnel and that tunnel was leading nowhere and had anxiety running down its walls. There was no light, no end and nobody else could penetrate it, not even little Wolf. I had been so convinced that knowing your daddy loved you would slay the black beast, I missed the obvious signs. The last straw came very soon after that when I knocked on your door to tell you little Wolf was missing you badly and could you come over for tea and to read to him. When you opened the door, your face was like a blank piece of white paper.

'Amy,' you said, very quietly, 'I can't come today, I have a surprise visitor.'

'Oh my God,' I gasped, 'is it Zachary?' You appeared so distracted that I had to repeat, 'Bear, is it Zachary?'

'What? No, no, come in.'

An attractive, slim but muscular man was sprawled across your sofa as if he owned the place. He stood slowly as I followed you into the front room. His face lit up.

'Amy Lee, it must be!' He extended his hand and squeezed mine too hard. 'I feel like I know you already. It's great to meet you at last. I know how close you two are. He was always talking about you. I was quite jealous, wasn't I, Bubba?'

You looked completely bewildered and lost for words. I felt immediately uncomfortable with the name he had called you. There was undisguised aggression in his voice. I waited for you to speak and you attempted a smile but it was forced and didn't reach your eyes. You appeared crushed by his presence and that was excruciating to witness.

'Amy,' you said quietly, your body trembling slightly. 'Amy, this is Dean.'

# Chapter Thirteen

*I will be waiting here for your silence to break,*
*For your soul to shake,*
*For your love to wake*
**Rumi**

KNOWING THIS WAS THE CONTROLLING, ABUSIVE DEAN standing in front of me I had been shocked to the core and, unusually for me, I was struck dumb. He had intense, almost disturbing light-blue eyes and I couldn't look away even though I wanted to. They seemed to draw you in, quickly and mercilessly. You seemed jittery and on edge and you couldn't keep still. You were moving constantly, almost as if you were trying to keep warm and protect yourself against the ice in his veins.

'Amy, Dean will eat with Patrick and me tonight. He's come such a long way to visit me, so he has.'

'Are you sure, Bear?'

'I can now see why I was jealous, Bubba,' Dean said to you, eyeing me almost suspiciously. 'She has a way with her and a gorgeous face that's difficult to ignore. Do you run his life now, Amy?'

Before I could answer, you turned to him. 'Dean, don't call me Bubba. *Please,* don't call me that, I never liked it. We aren't in America now and we aren't together.'

Your face was so pale and anxious, I feared for you. Dean had a thick mop of ash-blonde hair that fell over his eyes continually and a baby face. He was so muscular his chest and shoulders were bulging through his grey T shirt. The silence between the three of us felt like an electric current fizzing.

Ignoring his question, you turned to me. 'Tell little Wolf I'll come tomorrow and kiss him goodnight. Tell him to wish on a star, like we did in Ireland and his wish will come true.'

'I will.'

Dean appeared amused by our intimate words. 'Who the hell is little Wolf, if you don't mind me asking? Strange name, whoever he is.'

His words were pronounced in such a derisory way I could have punched him there and then, but I said simply, 'He's my little boy.'

'Now *that* is a weird name for a child! It's even stranger than yours, Bubba.'

He was mocking us both and there was a destructive quality about him. I had decided by then, in those first few minutes of meeting him that even if I hadn't known how vile he had been to you, I would have recognised it immediately. He continued in the same vein.

'I guess people in England do have weird names.'

You were shrinking with each word he uttered and spoke in such a small, apologetic way, I could have cried. 'I'm Irish, so I am. You know that. Irish to the death of me and beyond.'

'The Irish are such a mad but wonderful race, if you're anything to go by, Bubba.'

Rage had begun stirring inside me and it was threatening to

boil over like lava and smother Dean. I felt my back stiffen as I decided to flatten his aggression towards us both.

'Actually, he's *our* son!' You didn't contradict me and when Dean began frowning, I felt euphoric. '*Our* son,' I said again slowly and carefully.

He scoffed and leant towards you. 'Now, why do I doubt that, my beautiful, complicated and tortured, Bear, huh?'

I was horrified as I watched you shrivel up under his compelling gaze. You were my wonderful, brilliant Bear, but you appeared small and insignificant in front of him and his cutting words. You seemed weary of all the emotional complexities that seemed to follow you in life and I now know you were longing to be free of it all. The black beast was attacking you from all sides.

'He *is* my son, so he is,' you said firmly. 'I love him deeply. Why do you doubt it?'

Dean stepped even closer to you and put his face an inch from yours. I was aghast to see you flinch and my mind was racing. What you had gone through in America when locked into a passionate relationship with this revolting individual, I couldn't comprehend. I also couldn't comprehend what you had seen in him either. I didn't want my mind to stray onto the fact that it had obviously been lust and a need to quench those feelings of lust, because that was too painful to admit.

'I doubt it, my gorgeous, sexy, Bear, because I know you intimately, don't I? Or was that someone else in my bed every night in Boston?'

You couldn't speak and watching you become less of the person you truly are and less confident with every word he uttered, ignited my fury once more. This time it caught hold of me so strongly, I thought I would explode. I detested the way he was trying to embarrass and humiliate you. You seemed to be disappearing inch by brutal inch. I found it alarming that this man with the square jaw and American drawl could have that effect on you so quickly and so completely.

Dean appeared so sure of himself and so intent on overpowering you again with his good looks and undeniable sex appeal. I wondered why it had taken someone as brilliant and observant as you so long to see through the obvious, excessive and aggressive charm when you were living together. He reminded me so much of Zachary and how he had looked at your mammy when he was drunk.

Dean's demanding and manipulative behaviour had been insidious and you hadn't seen it crawling towards you until he had all but destroyed the Bear I knew. You hadn't a controlling or manipulative bone in your body and you didn't recognise it in other people either. By the time the relationship had turned abusive, you were lost. His pursuit of you had been carefully thought out and acted out, hidden inside the passion and affection you had craved. You just didn't feel it wrapping its tight, ugly arms around you. Once you had, you'd fled home to me.

At that moment I found the voice I had been using all our young lives to defend you whenever I needed to and I needed it more than ever now. I was fighting for you, Bear, I knew that. What I didn't quite comprehend at that moment was, I was fighting for your life. 'You heard about me, but I heard all about you too. It wasn't easy to hear either.' My voice was quiet but firm. I knew you hated anyone raising their voices because you'd had to live with Zachary being so unbearably vociferous all your life. Dean laughed loudly, rocking back and forward like one of those dolls on the back shelf of a car, but I continued unabashed. 'You won't be controlling Bear here.'

'So, you *are* the person running his life now! He sure does need someone to run it.' You were staring at the floor like an admonished child. 'You're as weak as ever then, Bubba?'

I stepped in again. 'It was interesting reading his last letter from Canada because I knew you'd dictated it. It was so obvious.'

His forced smile fell a little. 'Yeah, right, sure you did. So, the kid *is* actually yours, Bubba?' He looked at me, his eyes full of hostility as he attempted to laugh. 'I'm surprised you've been able to turn him. I didn't think that was possible for my beautiful, complex boy.'

I didn't mean to get embroiled in a conversation like that with him, but he was talking about you as if he knew you better than I did. I wasn't having that. His belligerence wasn't going to frighten me. I sneered at him, shaking my head. 'You really don't know him at all, do you? He's not *your* Bear, he never was. He's his own man.'

Dean narrowed his eyes and I could feel tension flying off his muscular body towards me. He was trying to intimidate me, subtly. As he stared at me I felt as if I was caught in a spotlight.

'Oh, but he *was* mine, Amy. You'd better keep your eye on him because it'll happen again in the future. Boys like Bear don't ever change. He might pretend for you, but he won't change.'

You had been stunned into silence by our controlled but heated exchange and looking back now, I'm ashamed I had taken part in his sordid, unkind conversation at all. You were distraught and your eyes were flicking about rapidly. I knew you were in trouble and I took hold of your hand gently.

You were shaking like a leaf caught up in a hurricane and beads of sweat had appeared on your forehead and around your mouth. I tried to calm you. 'Bear, everything is okay, don't worry. Everything is fine, honestly.' But you were beyond calming.

'Amy, show Dean out, would you, please? I can't deal with this.'

'Jesus, come on, man,' Dean gasped, 'I've come all this way to see you! Can we just talk for a bit? You owe me that, surely. It's cost me a fortune to come over and see you. Come in the other room, I want to talk to you privately. Just for five minutes, Bubba.'

'I don't know what to say to you.'

I told Dean angrily, 'He doesn't owe you anything!' I was trying so hard not to yell at him, but it wasn't working and everything came bursting out of me in a torrent. My voice sounded like someone else altogether. 'Now just shove off and leave him alone. Leave *us* alone!'

Dean deliberately lowered his voice, making it sound gentler and kinder. 'Bear, tell her who would call in sick for you when you couldn't get out of bed! Tell her who lied for you when there was nothing wrong with you, but you couldn't face the students. Tell her, man!'

'I *was* sick, I had depression ...'

'Jesus, not that old chestnut again ...'

'Depression *is* an illness,' I declared, horrified at his lack of compassion. 'He can't help how he feels.'

'But you can't see it, can you? Anybody can pretend they have it, but it's bullshit.'

'You have no idea what you're talking about.' I was shouting even louder now. I didn't want to upset you, but I had no control over my fury by then. 'He's had it all his life. He fights it every damned day. What the hell would you know about any of it? You haven't a bloody clue what he faces every single time he opens his eyes.'

You flinched and closed your eyes. 'Amy, please! Don't let him make you angry. It's what he does. It's how he gets to you. Please, don't shout at him! I can't stand it. It's like Zachary and my mammy. He knows what he's doing. He can wind you up as soon as look at you. He isn't worth your anger.'

One look at your pitiful face was enough to silence me instantly. Dean's voice then changed but his eyes resembled a dead fish.

'Hey, come on both of you. Let's cool down here for a second. Five minutes, Bear, that's all and she can stay in here if you want.' You nodded quickly and he grabbed your arm roughly. Turning to me he added, 'Amy, five minutes on our own, that's all I need from him.'

Your eyes were sunken and dull. 'Amy, stay here. Please don't come out.'

'Bear, will you be okay? Don't go out there ...'

'Stay in here, Amy Lee, *please*.'

I stayed in the front room despite my better judgement and I could just about hear you speaking together. His voice was much louder than yours and he did most of the talking, pleading with you to give him another chance.

'You know we were great together. You know it, Bubba.'

'I don't remember that.'

'You do! Don't give me that shit! You remember us being good together, I know it. Don't look at me with those eyes. You know those soulful eyes melt me. You still love me, I know you do.' There was silence for a few seconds before he carried on. 'Is it *her*? Has she persuaded you that you aren't like me? Well, you are! You never minded before and if that child is yours I'm the President of the United States.'

'Don't speak about him. I don't want his name on your lips. He *is* mine!' You then muttered firmly, 'I never loved you. I was lonely. I was experimenting and trying my best to find out who I am. I've only ever loved Amy. I want you to go now.'

Dean sounded desperate and his voice had lost some of its hard edge. 'Bear, I've flown all this way for you, man. Why did you just leave without even saying goodbye? Let me stay for dinner and a drink. Just let me stay tonight, one last night. You know you want to.'

'No! I don't want you now. I love Amy. I love *her*, not you. I've only ever loved Amy and I will to my last breath.'

'Bullshit!

'It's not bullshit, so help me God! It's the *one* truth in my life. There have been so many secrets, so many lies, but she is the only truth. I love Amy and our little boy.'

'Look, I'm sorry for being tough on you back home, but you needed me to be otherwise you'd have disappeared down a black hole of your own making. I even gave you money, man.'

'I didn't want your money, I told you that. I don't love you, Dean, I'm sorry.'

'You might not love me but you still *want* me! I can see it in your face. You don't want her in there. Jesus, I know she's beautiful but apart from being a female, she's too feisty for you. You know how fucking weak you are.'

'Don't talk about her! Don't!'

Dean's voice changed again then and I strained to hear him. It had a pleading tone and it was as if he was trying a last ditched attempt by appealing to the soft, compassionate and easy-going you I had always known and loved. It was the *only* Bear I had known. It was the one who nearly destroyed himself because he didn't want to hurt me with his secret and the one who loved my little boy as if he was his own.

'Man, I've come all this way. I still love you, you know that. I know I've had my share of men but you were the best of them. None are like you. Bear, come here, please. Don't pull away from me, Bubba.'

'Get off me, Dean. Don't touch me or on my granny's soul I'll knock you down, so I will.'

Dean's savage whisper made me shiver. 'Fuck you, man! Fuck you! Bear Flynn, the high and mighty, clever, complex and pathetic man who can't even get out of bed to teach kids without drugs and therapy. I covered for you, you dick. Time and time again I covered for you. I could make you want me, I know I could, but not with her in there.'

'I don't want you, on my granny's soul, I don't want you.'

'You want her? Fine, have her, but you know deep down it'll never work. You hear me? Never! You can't pretend to be someone you aren't and you sure aren't this. Good luck, you're gonna fucking need it and so will she. It'll be a fucking disaster! You'll drag her down, you'll see, with your fucking pathetic depression every single fucking day. If you love her, let her find a man who'll want her. You sure don't, Bubba. If you love her, walk away from her. You're a fucking excuse for a man! She'd be better off without you!'

His heavy, angry footsteps came up the hall quickly and the front door slammed so hard, the windows rattled. I ran out to find you on your knees on the kitchen floor with your head in your hands. I began crying seeing you there like that. I wanted to stay strong for you, but I could tell you were on the edge of a cliff. How near the edge was and how far you would fall was not evident then, even to me who watched you like a hawk.

'Bear, are you okay? Thank God he's gone. Get up, Bear, please. Get up off your knees. It's over, he's gone. I'm so sorry you had to go through this. You don't need this in your life now, do you? Get up, Bear, come on.'

'Amy,' you whispered, 'I can't move.'

'I'll help you. *Please*, try and get up. I hate to see you on your knees. Come and see little Wolf. He's waiting for you. We both love you. Don't stay on your knees, Bear. It's so awful seeing you like this.' Your mouth moved but no sound came out. I leant closer to you. 'What did you say?'

'I love you, Amy Lee, but when the world pushes you to your knees, you're in the perfect position to pray.'

We held each other tightly, you and I, as we had done so many times before but this was different, very different, and very frightening. We stayed like that until you stopped shaking and Patrick came home. I heard him run down the hall calling your name repeatedly.

'Bear! Bear!'

'Patrick, help him.'

We put you in bed where you shook for hours. I had wanted to call a doctor but you wouldn't allow it so I called my mother instead. We sat by your side, watching you carefully, speaking to you quietly, soothing you and stroking your face and your hair.

'Mum,' I whispered to her, 'I'm staying here tonight with him.

Tell little Wolf that Bear is poorly and I'm looking after him, will you? Don't let him worry though.'

She patted my arm and smiled encouragingly in her motherly way. 'Of course, darling, don't worry about Wolf. If you're concerned at all, call me or call an ambulance.'

Patrick brought me up a sandwich and a mug of tea as you slept fitfully. You were dreaming and mumbling in your sleep but most of it was incoherent, except for my name which you said repeatedly. When you woke briefly, you reached for my hand.

'My mammy said I was a shadow. Am I, Amy? I don't want to be a shadow for you. I thought knowing my daddy loved me would help me step into the light.'

'Hasn't it then?'

'The light is being blocked by the black beast, so it is. He won't go and leave me alone, he just won't, Amy Lee and I'm just so tired of fighting him.'

You looked so lost. I climbed into bed with you and held you in my arms. We put our foreheads together as we had so many times before. Your breathing was shallow and quick and you were sweating but shivering.

'I'll fight him for you, Bear. I'll bloody well kill him. Your pills will help you too.'

'Am I a shadow?'

'No, you are a shining light and always have been. You are the King of Love.'

'Amy, the black beast is so tough to live with. He's relentless, so he is, relentless.'

'I'm tougher, Bear! I'll save you. You know I'll save you. You *know* I'll do it.'

You let out a deep sigh. 'Amy Lee, you're my Guardian Angel, so you are. The sky is falling down and the wolves are at my door.'

You were sweating so profusely I repeatedly wiped your face with a tissue. 'I won't let them in, don't worry. You are safe.'

'You are the stardust, the stardust all around me.'

'I always will be, I promise you.'

You began to ramble, your voice listless and troubled. '"Happy is the moment when we sit together with two forms, two faces yet one soul, you and I." Amy, you and I.'

'Yes, Bear, you and I, always.'

You gave a small smile before you fell into a deep sleep, your mouth slightly open and your breathing growing heavy. You were emotionally exhausted and old wounds, not long healed, had been brutally exposed by the row with your mammy and Dean's sudden and unexpected arrival. It concerned me greatly and made me fearful how intensely fragile you had become. A shadow your mammy had said, a shadow of the boy you once were. I lived in that shadow and I tried my hardest to let the sun stream in on you, but I was failing miserably.

The day before hell opened up and swallowed us all, you had hardly spoken. You seemed depleted and diminished in every way and consumed by your invisible, indefinable black beast. He was slowly ripping you apart with his sharp teeth and stripping you of every aspect of your personality. While we sat together in your living room, I constantly reminded you of better, more carefree times when we were much younger, but every time you would frown.

'Amy, I don't remember.'

'You remember the angry bull, don't you?' But you had looked at me blankly and so I'd tried again. 'Well, you remember swimming under the waterfall, don't you?'

'No, but I remember you speaking to my daddy in the church. You were so brave.'

That day, before our lives changed forever, I had asked you to tea with us. I thought little Wolf's chattering and laughter would distract you from your dark thoughts. You had declined, so that evening I came to your house to sit with you for a while. Patrick was cooking you both a meal and I was trying to engage you in some conversation, but you continued to frown agitatedly at me.

'Amy, being anxious makes ordinary life unbearable. It all becomes an enormous muddle, so it does and I end up sliding down a black hole.'

'How can I help you? Just say one word and I'll do it.'

'I feel slightly apart from everyone, detached and not quite here. I feel remote and disinterested.'

'Keep taking the pills and they'll help you, I'm sure. If they don't, you must go back and tell your doctor.' You didn't appear to hear me and I pressed the point. 'Bear, you *must* go to the doctor. I'll come with you.'

'I'm indifferent to life, as if it's all moving by me and I'm watching it from afar. I want to jump in and be part of it, but I'm not sure I can anymore.'

'You *will* be able to. Just give it time.'

You had looked at me with such fondness then and you whispered, 'Amy Lee, you're such a life force. I wish I had your strength and energy.'

'My life force will flow into you. Just hang on,' I urged you, grabbing your hand.

You had been in another world that night. What I didn't know was, you were planning to move through the veil *into* that other world. Where were you, Bear? Where exactly were you? Were you already running hard towards the next world because this one had become too painful to endure? Did you hear me calling you back? Did you turn briefly and think about changing your mind, for me? Did you think, that's Amy Lee calling me, I must run out of the darkness towards her voice?

I should feel angry I suppose. That's what the doctor told me. He said anger is a normal response. I should feel angry because little Wolf loves you so much, but I can't. How can I feel like that when you must have been suffering so badly to do what you did? How can I feel anger when I should have picked up on how desperate you were? For pity's sake, I knew you better than anyone. I'm the one at fault! That deep pain, those bleeding wounds, weeping inside you for years, festering slowly and full of dark, unfathomable poison, had gradually awakened the slumbering black beast. Once disturbed, it had rapidly taken over once more, sinking its teeth into your waiting flesh.

I had pleaded with you. 'Bear, have your tea with Patrick and then come over and sleep with us. Wolf's breathing will comfort you. It will soothe your anxiety.'

'Amy, I'm just so tired. I can't fight this anymore.'

'Right, tomorrow we're going to your doctor. You shouldn't be feeling this way. I'm worried about you. Come home with me now, *please*. Wolf would love to wake up and find you there. Sleep in my bed with me and I'll watch over you. I'm frightened for you.'

'Don't be afraid, Amy Lee. Patrick is here with me. You go now, kiss little Wolf for me. Tell him I'll love him to the death and beyond.' You showed me to the door and your last words were, 'I just need to sleep. I need to find oblivion. Don't be afraid, Amy Lee, *please*.'

I slept fitfully that night because your words were haunting me. When Wolf jumped on me in the morning, full of life and demanding his breakfast, I decided to stay home from work and take you to the doctor. I called Annie who was her usual understanding self.

'Darling, do what you have to do. Don't worry about us.'

Patrick was leaving for work at nine and I felt I should allow you an hour to perhaps sleep in or be on your own to think. I gave Wolf his breakfast and read to him but my mind was elsewhere. I had a pain in my chest, an ache that I hadn't ever felt before. I took some deep breaths to try and calm my anxiety about you but nothing helped. My mother put her head through the hatch.

'Amy, go over and take Bear to his doctor. Neither of you can go on like this. Tell the doctor it's an emergency.' I kissed Wolf on the forehead and nodded at her. 'Don't let him talk you out of it. He needs help.'

'Mama, can I come?'

'No, Wolf, you stay with nana. I won't be long.'
'I want to see Bear.'
'You'll see him later, don't worry.'

There was no answer when I knocked for you and I wondered momentarily if Patrick had left you in bed. But something was nagging at me, pulling at my guts relentlessly. It was the piercing, ever-present pain in my chest and the feeling of heaviness throughout my whole body that made me look through your bay window, shielding my eyes because of the glare from the sun shining on the glass.

You were lying on the floor curled up in a ball like a baby with a piece of paper in your hand. All I remember of that moment is our lives as we had known them, changed irreparably and the world stopped turning for me. I heard a voice somewhere screaming.

'Oh, Bear! No!'

Luckily the main sash window was slightly open at the top. This was easy for me. I had climbed all my life. I pulled hard on the top of the frame and scraped through, jumping down towards you. I screamed your name over and over again, hoping somehow you would stir at the sound of it. Frozen with fear and my mouth completely dry with terror, I felt the blood draining from my head. I touched your face and it was cold, your mouth slightly open.

'Bear, what have you done? Speak to me! Speak to me! Don't you go without me, don't you dare.'

I grabbed the telephone and demanded an ambulance. The operator had a soothing voice and told me to stay calm, the ambulance was on its way, open the front door. He asked if you were conscious and to start resuscitation if you had no pulse. My body was going into a slow, sickening shock and I ran to open the front door. Your skin was turning the colour of old lace and your lips were going blue. It was just like with my father. I whispered in your ear as I felt for a pulse in your neck and put my ear to your chest. I could hear nothing so I began shaking you.

'Listen to me, Bear, listen to me, you can't leave me. I won't let you, do you hear me? I don't want to stay here without you. The world won't be my home if you aren't here, you know that. Nobody can take your place. Bear, we'll go and live in Ireland where the angels are, you, me and Wolf. I'll save you, Bear, I'll save you.'

Punching your chest hard I started compressions. After every one I was whispering at you. 'Don't die! Don't die! Don't die!'

I heard the ambulance siren coming nearer and seconds later two paramedics rushed in and moved me away gently. They were talking quickly to each other and to me. 'Is he on medication? What's he taken? What's his name?'

'His name is Bear. I don't know what he's taken. Yes, he has anti-depressants.'

One of them glanced around the room and saw an empty bottle of pills. He read the label and said something to his colleague who nodded briefly. They were taking equipment out of their bags and you, like a rag doll, were being pulled about.

'Don't hurt him, please don't hurt him.'

'Was he in arrest when you found him?'

'What? Yes he ...'

'There's a weak pulse now, turn him. We'll get the tube down his throat.' You were then pulled onto your side. I think they made you sick, but I really don't remember. 'That's it, Bear, come on! We've got you now, just relax. You're in good hands.'

They took out a machine and I stood and watched them as if it was happening to someone else. I was frozen with fear as they fought for your precious life. Where were you when your sweet, generous heart had stopped beating? Where did you go? In my head I was communicating with you, calling you back. I imagined you *did* hear me as you hurtled towards the next life and my voice, echoing around you, would make you turn and decide to stay.

'Don't go without me, Bear!'

'I can hear you, Amy Lee, I can hear you and I'm coming back for you.' I imagined you calling to me. I'm sure you did. 'Dancing in ecstasy you go, my soul of souls. I won't go to the next life without you.'

Did you come back for me, Bear? Did you hear me screaming? Hold on! Hold on! Don't die! You know I can't stay here without you. "O Ruler of my Heart, wherever you go, don't go without me."

You suddenly jerked, you shuddered and your eyes fluttered. One of the paramedics was talking and cut through my frozen thoughts. 'Yep, we've got him. Stay with us, Bear. You're okay now, just stay here with us.'

You choked and groaned. Your eyes fluttered again and opened momentarily. I remember thinking what a shock it must have been waking up here, in this world, when you were hurtling at speed towards the next one. It was like some kind of horror film when people try to guess what happens. They're afraid to know what happens though in case the lead character dies and they love him so much they are desperate to rewrite the ending. I was desperate to rewrite your ending, Bear. It was never supposed to be like this. We were always going to walk into the sunset together.

I could feel darkness closing in as they fought for you. Was this another moment where fate and destiny collided again? I had always been able to climb. Did your angels make sure we met all those years ago so I could climb in your window and save your life? I could hear the wolves howling outside and I could feel my heart cracking open.

Rage surged through my veins. Rage and despair were waging war in my body. Despair was winning easily because I can't ever be angry at you. I was angry at myself though, thinking about all the signs I had missed in recent months. You idiot, Amy Lee! You bloody idiot! What were you thinking leaving him on his own last night against your better judgement? You've let him down. You stupid, bloody idiot!

They lifted you carefully onto a stretcher and I couldn't see your beautiful face because an oxygen mask covered it. The paramedics told me where they were taking you and I watched as the scene before me slowed down as if I was in the middle of a dream and your left arm was dangling below the stretcher. Then adrenaline kicked in and I was shaking uncontrollably, my teeth chattering. I picked up the photo of you and me on our last day of school together and hugged it to my chest. I stared at your face, the half smile and the curious, watchful eyes and remembered your words.

'"When the world pushes you to your knees, you're in the perfect position to pray."'

I then picked up the piece of paper you had been clutching as your life was ebbing away and read Rumi's and your words: 'Dear Amy, "Love risks everything and asks for nothing. With life as short as a half taken breath, don't plant anything but love." Thank you for loving me so completely, I never deserved it. Don't be afraid, Amy Lee.'

I whispered to the photo, 'Bear, don't you go without me.'

My mother had heard the ambulance siren and was standing on our doorstep with Wolf in her arms. Her face was in turmoil and I shook my head at her.

'Run, Amy!' She was shouting at me and little Wolf was staring at her with his mouth open. 'Run!'

I ran as hard and as fast as I could towards the hospital a mile away and then down endless corridors that all looked identical. There were white walls, medical equipment, empty stretchers and redundant wheelchairs. The smell of disinfectant and other cleaning chemicals was choking me. I asked at the desk where they had taken you.

'He was in resus,' the woman told me without any emotion and I felt immediately terrified at her words. 'But he may have been transferred to ICU now.'

I found you eventually. They had wired you up good and proper. Tubes were everywhere, machines bleeping, blood-pressure readings, oxygen saturation, charts at the end of the bed, your heart being monitored and the oxygen mask still on your face.

A nurse probably younger than us was checking on your readings and a doctor was shining a light in your eyes. He was asking the paramedics how long you had been *'in arrest.'* How I detested those two short words. It was so quiet in there, everyone spoke in hushed tones and all I could hear were the sounds of those dreaded machines. Bleep! Bleep! Bleeping, continually and relentlessly without a pause, every sound echoing around my head.

The paramedics weren't sure, they said, perhaps a few minutes. They told the doctor I had rung the ambulance and performed resuscitation. They then wished me well and I muttered my heartfelt thanks. Two more doctors came in and they were discussing you and what the pills might have done to your body and the damage to your brain from being *'in arrest.'* Those two words again and they made me catch my breath. I wished fervently that they would stop saying it. One of the doctors discussing your case at the side of your bed was very glamorous with full make-up and high heels. Only the stethoscope hanging round her neck gave away her profession.

Where are you now, Bear as I sit by your bed? Has the pain gone? Has the anxiety, ever present in the pit of your stomach, evaporated? If it has, how can I want you back? Am I being selfish to the last? I can't watch you suffer anymore but I can't let you go. I can't stay in this life without you. You know that. You know my life depends on yours.

Another doctor came in just now; he had all that responsibility on his shoulders and he looks as if he should be in the upper-sixth. He broke my spirit when he said gravely, 'Your husband is very ill. He's stable but critical.'

Do you mind he assumes I'm your wife? I had to ask the doctor what that actually *meant*. You would have understood him, Bear. You would probably have fancied him too. I wouldn't mind if you had. I'm past all that now. I just want you to be happy. I just want you to live. Please, Bear! Just live!

He then added that you might have some damage to your brain due to your heart stopping. They don't know how long it stopped for, that's the problem. He told me you might be a very different man. I nearly told him he was speaking cobblers. You would never be any different to me because when I look in your eyes, I can see your soul.

It made me think of your mammy being angry at your brothers for throwing you in a pile of snow because it would dislodge your brain. How ironic, I thought, how very ironic that was. All the pressure you had been put under because of your brilliant brain and how gifted you were might now all be wiped out.

Your outstanding intellect and your exceptional, rare qualities, the ease with which you understood everything taught to you and your impressive memory might all have been erased, in a few brutal and savage minutes as your heart stopped beating. I didn't care about how clever you were and always had been. I just wanted you to be happy and at peace and it was *all* I had ever wanted.

The compassionate doctor sat and chatted with me for a while and asked how long you'd had mental health problems. I don't know if you could hear my answer, but I said, most of his life, I think. He then went on to explain that suicide kills more men under forty-five than anything else. It was the first time they had used that word and it made me cry out loud. All I could ask was, why?

'There's too much pressure,' he told me, in his soothing way, trying his utmost to console me. 'There is too much expected of men and too much anxiety. Society *still* expects too much of us all. We have to be strong, silent and heroic. What do you do if you feel none of those things? It's a national disgrace! Men need to start opening up, bare their soul to anyone who will listen and they need to ask for help.'

'But he had me,' I muttered, tears blinding me.

He then asked my name and said kindly, 'Amy, this is not your fault. At times the pain is so bad they feel being dead is the better option. They think you'll all be better off without them. Don't feel guilty. His problems may have started from early childhood.' You made a strange noise and he jumped up to check on you while I sat helplessly looking on with my pulse thumping in my temples. My head felt as if it was in a vice. He sat back down again and put his hand on my arm in a comforting gesture. 'This will have been coming on for a while. Big boys don't cry and all that. Big boys do cry! Big boys *should* cry!'

'He's ever so clever, *ever* so clever.' I don't know why I was telling him that. It was as if I wanted to let him know that your brilliant brain could withstand the onslaught of your heart not beating. I shook my head despairingly. 'He's only ever wanted to be happy though.'

'If he gets through this, he's going to need a lot of help.' A nurse rushed in, her face agitated. 'What's wrong?' he asked, jumping up.

'Doctor, you're needed.'

He put your chart down and dashed out. He was an immensely kind and deeply caring man who wanted to save your life and bring you back to me without even knowing how remarkable you were.

On my own in that pitiless room, I placed my hand on yours and dropped my head onto your bed. How long I would have to be there doing that, I had no idea, but I would until you opened your eyes. I would stay there until out of the darkness you would walk towards me and into the light.

'Amy,' you had said, 'I've forgotten how to live.'

'Don't be scared, Bear. I'll keep holding your hand. I won't let you go. You told me you were damaged and wounded. I'll heal you, don't worry. Little Wolf and me, we'll heal you. We'll take you to Ireland.'

Over the next few weeks, Patrick and I took it in turns to sit by you. You were never alone and watching you breathe, listening to those breaths and breathing them with you, I went through your life, charting its difficult and thorny path and wondering how it led to this. Your chest would move up and down, rising and falling and I would synchronise my breaths with yours for hours, willing my strength into your body. Your face was without expression and I would watch the machines, listening to every terrifying bleep and sleeping when I could.

You had me, Bear, you had *me*. Where did you go in those last few moments when you decided you no longer wanted to be here? It must have been somewhere pretty dark and lonely.

'Let's touch the stars, Amy Lee. Let's dance with the fairies and gaze at the moon. We can breathe in the magic and touch the wings of dragonflies, ride on unicorns across wide open beaches and watch the water sprites as they swim under the waterfall. Be still, watch them. Watch them all. We can be with the angels in Ireland.'

How can anyone who viewed the world like you did, find himself wading in such a deep, dark river of depression and pain? Where did *that* Bear go? How did we get *here*? What would have happened if I hadn't felt your despair in my chest? Perhaps that was the destiny awaiting us from the very first moment we set eyes on each other and maybe, just maybe, that was why we met.

Is that how it works? Was it all planned long ago and had fate waved its magical wand and weaved a spell around us both as we glanced at each other? Did that happen so I could save your treasured life?

'What's your name, boy?'

'I'm Bear Flynn, sir.'

'That's not your name, that's a nickname. What's your *real* name?'

'It *is* my real name, so it is, as my parents wrote it on the form when I applied here.'

When I had stated my name, you had looked across the room,

your hazel eyes like a curious cat and our fate was sealed. It brought us to the moment where I had climbed in your window, pounded on your chest and begged you to live because the angels know you have to. They know my life depends on it.

Are your unseen friends here with us? I hope they are because you really do need them now. Did they drag you back as you ran towards the darkness? They must have done surely, because you are such a gentle soul and they don't need you there, but I do.

When my mother had told Patrick you were in the hospital he had arrived, sweating and anxious with tears running down his face. He wiped them away continually but they just kept coming. He was inconsolable. We hung on to each other and he whispered in my ear, in his flat and unusual way.

'Amy, is he going to die?'

'No, he isn't,' I had replied firmly, my voice too loud for a hospital room, 'I promise you. I won't let him die. Do you believe me?'

He nodded but the tears continued to fall and he choked on some words he was trying to say, so he signed them to me. I couldn't understand them. How I longed to turn to you and ask what he meant. 'Patrick, I can't understand what you're saying, but I can guess. I don't want my life without Bear in it. Is that what you're trying to say?'

'Yes,' he gasped, 'yes.'

'He'll get better, I know it.' I took his face in my hands. 'I won't let him give up. You need to let your mammy know.' He shook his head sadly. 'You must, Patrick and his daddy. His daddy needs to know.'

Your brother's sorrowful eyes conveyed so much about your relationship with your mammy and he said you wouldn't want her there. I recalled how you had watched me one day in Ireland, Bear, when I had little Wolf comfortably asleep in my arms. You had said that Wolf was so secure against my chest and in my love and that you had never felt that with your mammy. There was a gaping hole where her love should have been.

'I'm damaged by her, Amy, damaged and betrayed because I can't feel her love.'

I watch as the medical staff come and go and they all know my name. I know their names too and although they were the angels in disguise who you prayed to I wished I didn't know them all so well. Little Wolf is fretting for me and asking why you haven't come to read to him at bedtime. When I'm at home, I explain that you are very unwell at the moment but all the clever doctors are making you better. He asks all the time if it will take long.

'Yes, Wolf, it will take a long time but we'll be so happy when Bear is home, won't we?'

One day he cried bitterly. 'Daddy teaches me numbers and letters and he said I'm very clever. He said I can drive a train if I want or be a farmer.'

'Did he, darling? Yes, well, he's right about that. You can do anything you want to.'

'Daddy said I must be happy.'

I had hugged his little frame and stemmed the flood of tears burning the back of my eyes. I knew why you had told him that and I wished so much that somebody had said that to you. If they had, just once, perhaps your life would have been different. Maybe, just maybe, we wouldn't be here now.

There were two doctors who cared for you and a team of nurses. The glamorous one is actually the senior doctor but we don't see her very often. One of the doctors smiles constantly while my heart is breaking into tiny pieces. He just can't seem to help it. It's just how his face is. I feel like saying to him, for God's sake, stop smiling so much! I.C.U. just isn't a place for smiles.

The other one, older and more experienced speaks in hushed tones and I can tell, over the course of his career, he has given so much bad news to relatives, he now speaks that way all the time; quiet, low and slightly cautious, realistic but compassionate. They study your charts, the machines and look in your closed eyes by lifting your lids while I hold my breath.

Annie and Max came one day and I cried bitter tears on their shoulders. They both held me up, sat with me, listened to me and the warmth of their affection sustained me for days. Annie had kissed your forehead lovingly when they left and said, 'Bear, you poor darling, you must have been suffering so much.'

Max had whispered kindly to me, 'Amy, this is going to be a long haul and it's going to be tough.'

'I don't care,' I had replied vehemently, 'you know I don't care. It can take forever and I'll still be waiting here.'

He had nodded and said sadly, 'I know you will and that's what worries me.'

Then one day you opened your eyes and blinked quickly a few times. I was sitting beside you and so was the young, smiley doctor. 'Ah,' he cried, 'there you are, my friend. I thought you'd be with us today. Your vital signs have been improving so much. You must come from strong, Irish stock.'

I gasped and stood up so I could get closer to you to be sure I really had seen your eyes move. I could hardly contain my excitement. 'Can I kiss him, doctor?'

'Yes, you can, very gently, *very* gently. Don't crowd him. He's still very fragile although his eyes are open and he's probably still locked in somewhat. He won't be aware of much yet, but do talk to him, he can hear you.'

I put one hand on the top of your head and kissed your cheek as softly as I could, my lips just brushing your skin. Your eyes were glazed and held no recognition of who I was.

'Oh, Bear, please, *please* don't you go without me.' I could say no more because my throat was closing. I simply held your hand, sat down heavily in the chair once more and laid my head on your bed. I was exhausted.

The young doctor placed his hand on my shoulder. 'Are you okay, Amy?'

All I could think to say was, 'I just want him back.'

He pulled another chair up beside me and that action and his body language told me he was going to talk with me seriously about your future. 'You'll get him back, but it'll probably be another version of the man you knew. This is going to be very hard on you, *very* hard and his rehabilitation will take months. Do you understand that? There are no short cuts with this.'

'I don't care how hard it is or how long. I'll look after him.'

He didn't answer straight away but when he did he shattered my heart once again. 'Amy, there may be no way back to the relationship you had before. This will alter him dramatically and many relationships don't ...'

'We'll be okay, doctor. I know it's going to take a long time, but we'll be fine. We have known each other for so long. There is no other life for either of us, except to be together. I don't care how long it takes. It can take years, I just don't care. He'll get back to being the Bear I know and love.' He gave me a sympathetic smile and I knew he doubted me. 'Don't you believe me?'

'I admire your spirit and your tenacity.'

'I'm very stubborn too!'

He laughed quietly. 'I bet you are.'

'Doctor, do you believe in anything? Do you?'

'Do I believe in anything?' He frowned and looked thoughtful. 'I don't know really. I suppose I believe in the wonders of medical science and the power of love. That's about it, I think.'

'Do you believe in fate and destiny, that kind of thing?'

'No, not really; I don't think like that. I'm a scientist after all.'

'Well, I do and so does he. I always knew I would save him one day. I had no idea what I would save him from and I never imagined this, but I believe we met for a reason and the reason *was* this. He's always called me his Guardian Angel.'

'Well, all I can say is, he's going to need you in the future.'

'And I'll be here.'

Ten days later, without any further improvement in your

condition, I was beginning to wonder if you would stay locked inside your body, inside your mind for good, without your brain functioning as it had. But I prayed hard, Bear, I prayed hard to your beloved Angel of Mercy, that your exceptional brain would not be affected. I prayed for that because I loved the person you were and are, not because I wanted anything else from you.

I spoke on the phone to your daddy regularly, almost every evening. He said your mammy couldn't talk to me because she couldn't stop herself from crying. He told me he was desperate to come over to see you but that Patrick had said to wait until you would know he was there. I agreed with that even though I knew it was very tough on him. But he was an unselfish man and said he would do whatever I thought was best for you.

It was a mellow day with late October sunshine streaming in the window and across your face. Weeks were passing, nature was changing gradually and you were missing it all. There were trees not far from your room and a gentle wind was blowing the last leaves towards the ground. I remembered my father, just days before he died saying, 'The leaves are falling now, Amy and winter will soon be here.'

'Dad,' I said out loud, 'Dad, help me bring him back to himself. You know how much I love him.' I leant over you and placed my hand on your head again. 'Say my name, Bear. *Please*, say my name.' Your dull eyes, so full of confusion in the past, flickered slightly. You frowned and I held my breath hoping to hear your voice, but you didn't utter a sound. 'I know you know me. I know you do. This is breaking my heart and it won't be put back together again unless you say my name.'

Still no sound came out but you mouthed at me. 'Amy Lee.'

## Chapter Fourteen

*There is nothing I want but your presence.*
*In friendship time dissolves.*
**Rumi**

Bear, now you are awake at last, I can stop talking to you constantly about our lives. I like to think that hearing our history and reminding you of the wonderful chapters in our story as well as the difficult ones, have slowly brought you out of your sleep of forgetting and despair. Now I've written it all in a journal and I'm reading through it. We will read it together to little Wolf in years to come when he can understand it all.

Time is passing without you here. You are here, but you aren't here. It is now

Spring again, can you believe it? The seasons are passing without you to find the beauty in them and I miss seeing them through your eyes so much. I try to remember how you would describe it all to me, but the words often escape me because I am focussing so much on your recovery.

Your daddy came over from Ireland once you had opened your eyes. He said he'd longed to come before and sit by your bed with me, but Patrick told him to wait, you would need him more in the future. Your mammy couldn't face it and would come when you were able to talk to her. I tried to understand her and her actions but I can't say with any honesty that I did. Your daddy made excuses for her but I could tell by the pain in his eyes when he told me that he couldn't understand it either. He sat by your bed for days, holding onto your hand and kissing your forehead. You would sometimes stare at him with unfocussed eyes as he told you repeatedly how much he loved you, but often you were asleep. His presence gave me a few days respite where I tried to spend all my time with little Wolf.

Patrick told me that when they had been there together and your daddy first saw you in that bed, with your vacant eyes and white face, he sobbed uncontrollably, his body shuddering, until he was exhausted. He had begged you to fight for a future together where you could get to know each other and make up for lost time. He had glanced across the bed at Patrick one day with despair written all over his face. Patrick told me what he said.

'I should have been there for him all his life. I wanted to be, so much, but it was his mammy's wish that I stay in the shadows. She was wrong, she was so wrong.'

When you were stable enough you were moved to a rehabilitation centre. It was actually a kind of nursing home too for people who had similar mental and physical problems to yours and for those with head and brain trauma. I never called it a nursing home. In my eyes you *were* rehabilitating, albeit it very slowly.

It was an extremely trying and heartbreaking time for me because you didn't want any visitors at all at first and I missed your presence as I would miss my heart beating in my chest. I longed to look at your beloved face, to kiss you and touch you but you wouldn't allow me in. I would gaze at your photo constantly, especially the group one taken of our class when we were much younger. It was a photo that showed your character perfectly. Your brilliance literally shone out at me. You were the sparkling star amongst a mass of forgotten faces and I was standing behind you smiling happily, inches away. Without you, Bear, I felt bereaved. It was bereavement with no end in sight.

I badgered the matron of the centre constantly to let me in and allow me to bring little Wolf in too. She was kind, but with a core of steel and slightly scary and she wasn't going to have any nonsense from the likes of me. Every time I approached her I saw her take a sharp intake of breath.

'Amy, you can't see him yet.'

'I can help him get better, Matron,' I had told her, my voice betraying my anguish. She was a big woman, built like a battleship, with a round, chubby face and steely eyes. 'I know him as well as I know myself.'

'I don't doubt it, my dear, but this is quite common when patients first come here. They don't want anyone seeing them like this, but he'll come round, I'm sure he will.'

'But our little boy is pining for him so much.'

She took my hand in hers. 'I know and I understand but he's adamant. He can't speak very well, but he made it perfectly clear, no visitors! I have to abide by that. Just be patient, things will improve slowly. He's probably a little ashamed too.'

'What do you mean?'

'People who try to take their own lives sometimes feel ashamed of all the heartache they've caused. He'll be feeling that about you and your little boy and he'll feel very guilty. That's probably why he can't face you because he's hurt the people he loves the most.'

Your room was on the ground floor overlooking a small but pleasant flower garden and the park just beyond. I walked there every day, on my own but sometimes with Patrick, who was a great comfort to me in those weeks. When your daddy had returned to Ireland, I missed his comforting presence greatly. He was one of those people you could lean on. He promised he would be back with your mammy. You had shown no recognition when he leant over you every day and stroked your face gently, but Patrick had told me, on the day of your daddy's departure, silent tears had fallen down your face. You were in there somewhere, Bear.

I had to give up my job at Annie's farm because I couldn't concentrate on anything but your recovery. I had gone months before to explain everything to both her and Max one November day when the slanting rain and thunderous skies mirrored my turbulent mood. Annie was extremely disappointed and upset, but understanding, as I knew she would be.

'Oh, Amy, I'll miss you so much, sweetheart,' she told me, trying her best not to cry. 'You and me, we got on right from the start, didn't we?'

'Yes, we did but that was mainly down to you being so easy going as a boss. Bear couldn't believe you put up with my shenanigans as he always called it. He didn't ever think any boss would be able to contain me. But you understood me.'

'Your eyes still light up when you mention his name.'

'Do they?' I asked, plaintively.

'You really do love him very much, don't you?'

I used your phrase, Bear. 'Yes, to the death and beyond.'

'Then go with my blessing and get him well again, but I'll always be here if you want to come back. I know we'll always be friends. I won't get another number two like you again.'

'Thank you, but when he's better we'll go and live on his granny's farm, if that's what he wants to do.'

'You do that then,' she urged me. 'If it's a beautiful place where he can find his peace of mind, do that.'

'He'll get his health back there, I know it. It's where the angels live.'

Annie told me I must bid farewell to Max and I wandered down the quiet lanes that led to the stables with some trepidation. Working there seemed a lifetime ago and it was. It was a lifetime where you had been in America and I had found some solace in

Annie's friendship and Max's willing arms. It was a lifetime before you had wanted your life to end. I found Max sweeping out the yard and he waved as I approached.

'Hello, Amy, how is he?' My face crumpled and I shook my head. 'Oh, Amy, you looked shattered.'

'I don't know how he is, Max. He won't see me now he's in the rehabilitation centre.'

I half stumbled, half fell into him and he threw his arms around me as I cried. I don't know why I cried more in his arms than in anyone else's, except perhaps because he was strong and steady and he represented stability at a time when there was none.

'Oh, Amy, you poor girl,' he said soothingly. 'What has he done to you making you love him so much? Do you ever long to be free of that love, to save you all this heartache?'

'Never, never, no I don't.'

'Then remember what I said to you. Stay by his side if you must, but be prepared to bleed.'

'I am bleeding now! I can't stop bleeding. I'm almost bled dry.'

'But it won't ever be as bad as this again. He's come through the worst of it.' He finally let go of me and we sat on the wall outside the stables in the pouring rain, neither of us caring how drenched we were. 'Imagine the terrible turmoil he must have gone through when he decided to end his life.'

'But he had *me*, Max and little Wolf.'

'Depression as bad as his is an awful place to live. It must be exhausting trying to fight it all the time. I had a bit of it when I was younger and it's the pits.'

I turned to him, bemused. 'You've had depression? Did I know that? I think Annie mentioned it once. I didn't think you were the type.'

'Why should you? And there isn't a type. I don't talk about it often. Us men never do and we must, we *must*. He will have convinced himself that you would be better off without him. He was probably trying to set you free. Or maybe he couldn't think clearly at all. He would have just wanted the pain to stop. Don't think he doesn't love you both because he obviously does, very much. It's not your fault, Amy, please remember that.'

'Do you get depressed now?'

'No, not much because I work out here in this wonderful place and I can always talk to her Ladyship. She's a great listener as you know and she pulls me up by my boot laces and comforts me in her own way. She once told me, I could tell her anything, *anything* and she'd support me. She does too. That's why she's so bloody wonderful. It's always slightly in the background though, waiting to pounce, if I'm not careful.'

'The black beast ...'

'What?'

'Bear calls it the black beast.'

'It's a great name for it.'

We chatted for about half an hour until I left him, with some sadness. 'I'm taking Bear to Ireland when he's better. Will you visit us, Max? Please say you will come, you and Annie.'

'We will,' he replied with a smile, 'now off with you before I get upset. I have lots of work to do.' I walked away reluctantly. I'll be honest, Bear, if I hadn't loved you my whole life, I would have stayed. 'And, Amy,' he called, 'take good care of *you*.'

I told the matron and your doctor and physiotherapists' and anyone else who would listen that I was fully prepared to care for you when you eventually came home. Every time I spoke of it, they would avert their eyes and inform me it would be a monumental task, physically and emotionally. They told me categorically that I would need help. I challenged everything they told me with a blind optimism borne out of my deep love and compassion for you. After a frustrating couple of weeks where I continually badgered the staff to allow me in, the tough, but compassionate matron called me into her office.

'Amy, sit down, please,' she said gravely and my heart skipped so many beats I felt breathless.

'What's wrong? Is Bear okay?'

'I think it's time he had people visiting now. We're losing him.'

'Losing him?' I gasped, 'what do you mean? He's not in danger, is he?'

'No, no, not physically, I meant mentally he isn't picking up and he needs to. He needs to try harder with his physiotherapy too. You are going to have to encourage him but you'll need to be tough on him too. Can you do that?'

'Yes, yes, of course, I just want to be with him. I know I can help him, I just know it.'

Her plump face with the saggy chin appeared touched by my words. 'Be aware that depression like his just doesn't disappear overnight. He now has the added turmoil of still being here when he didn't want to be. It's all very complex and I'd take a guess that Bear is a very complex person.'

I suddenly felt immense gratitude towards her for understanding you. 'He is, very much so.'

'Hopefully, in time he'll pick up. I must warn you, it's going to be a long haul though. There will be highs and lows and setbacks and then more highs and lows, so be prepared. I've seen this many times before and he probably doesn't want to be a burden. He was only trying to protect you.'

'He could never be a burden!'

'I know, *I* can see that but you'll need to impress that on him. I can tell you're a very determined young woman. You are going to need every ounce of that determination and compassion. Go on now, go and do your best for him.'

I rushed up the corridor that day and opened the door to your room. It was so stuffy. I opened the window immediately to let in some fresh air. It was the first day out of many that I sat with you while you stared blankly at the carpet. That first time, I was shocked by your appearance and had to swallow my tears. That room was soulless, dreary with cream walls and a single bed. There were two of those awful, dull, boring paintings you see in hospital corridors and another door leading to a small bathroom. I almost choked at the sight of the wheelchair in the corner and a wave of anger surged through me. It was an anger I couldn't quite quantify except to say that the room and the wheelchair felt like they were nothing to do with who you were. They couldn't possibly contain the Bear Flynn I knew at all.

You were sitting in an upright chair, looking down at your hands. I was horrified at how thin you were, how pale your skin and your hair was longer than I'd ever seen it. You reminded me of a tramp, a homeless person, a down and out and I knelt by your feet, trying hard to keep a check on my overwhelming emotions.

I took hold of your hands, one was warm and the other very cold and when I squeezed them gently there was no response from you. One side of your face appeared quite different as if it was frozen.

'Bear, it's me,' I whispered, 'it's me, Amy Lee. Oh my poor, lovely, Bear, what have you done to yourself? I didn't know it was that bad. I'm so, so sorry. I didn't abandon you, but they wouldn't let me in. Matron said you didn't want to see anyone. I've missed you so much and so has little Wolf.'

There was no reaction and your watchful, hazel eyes were like deep water with no ripples and no life, just a blank stare, but you were looking directly in my eyes and I took that as a positive sign. I knew I could get you to live again, so day after day I sat with you, talking about nothing and everything. At times you appeared to be listening but at other moments your eyes took on a faraway look and that look broke my heart. It broke my heart because I wondered if you still wished to be somewhere else. But it didn't break my spirit, nothing would do that except the loss of you and you were still with me, albeit a very different version.

I would massage your thin, wasted legs and I spoke about Ireland and the way you calmed the angry bull and how we had swum under the waterfall and listened to birdsong on the moor. I described the sunsets where the angles lived and although there was little reaction, I convinced myself you were dreaming of being back there on granny's farm. One day, when one of the kindly and dedicated nurses came in to check on you, I was momentarily clothed in a tight blanket of rare pessimism. It was almost smothering me and I could hardly breathe.

'Will he ever be Bear anymore?' I had asked her as she was about to leave. Her face was so young and with freckles like mine, Bear, and she showed such empathy with me, I almost burst into tears right there in front of her. 'Please just give me some hope.'

'Well, it's up to him. He needs to try harder with his exercises and work *with* the physiotherapists instead of against them. But he's still depressed and the apathy comes from that. We are trying him on another tablet, so fingers crossed, but encourage him as much as you can and don't give in to him. The doctor will speak to you one day and explain more.'

Each night, when I put Wolf to bed, he would ask when you could come home and read to him again. 'He can't come home yet, darling because he can't lift himself out of his chair and he'd be too heavy for me.'

'I can help you,' he said, his eyes alight and I had to turn away for a second. 'Can I come and see him?'

'Yes, Wolf, very soon, don't you worry.'

I complained to my mother about the way the nurses combed your hair. 'They comb it to the side, like you would for a primary school photograph. It's flattened against his head and he's got gorgeous hair, but it doesn't look like him.'

'That's not like you, Amy.' She was busying herself in the kitchen and leant on the serving hatch. She did that so often, I was surprised there weren't two grooves where her elbows had been. 'Did you hear me? I said, that's not like you.'

'Yes, I heard you, but I don't understand what you said. What isn't like me?'

'The old Amy would have gone in and messed it up or combed it like it used to be.' Her words hit home and I couldn't answer for a moment but Mum carried on anyway. 'Tomorrow, go in and do what you want to with it.'

'Mum, what do you mean, the old me?'

She appeared a little reflective for a moment. 'Amy, don't lose your own personality and character because Bear has lost *his* for a while. I know full well how much you love him, I've always known from day one, but you have to keep strong and keep being the Amy Lee he loves too. That's the only way you'll get him back.'

Her words, so calmly and kindly said, resonated deeply with me and I began to think of a plan to get you back to yourself. It coincided with your mammy and daddy arriving from Ireland. Patrick had warned me he had called them to tell them you were out of hospital. I had arrived at the centre to find your mammy outside your door, weeping quietly. She wiped her tears away quickly when I approached her, almost as if she was ashamed of them.

'He won't see me,' she told me, her voice choked with emotion. 'When we walked in just now and he saw me, he began crying and shaking his head and shouting at me. His words were unintelligible but they were plainly aimed at me. Wolf has just ushered me out.' I felt for her and put my hand on her arm in a gesture of support. She gritted her teeth. 'Amy, I warned everyone he was too fragile. I know my son, of course I do. Nobody would listen to me. He's my baby, so he is. But his daddy wouldn't believe it. He pestered me so much and I told him, if he comes to find you day after day, you *must* warn me, but he didn't. He didn't and now look at him! Look at him! Mother of God, my Baby Bear, what have you done to me?'

It wasn't lost on me that her final words were about how it was affecting *her* and not you and everyone else. I put my arm around her shoulders but she felt stiff and unyielding.

'He'll get better, I know he will and then you can rebuild your relationship from the start. But it won't be yet, he's not ready.'

I left her there, still weeping silently and opened your door with some trepidation, hoping your mammy's presence hadn't affected you too badly. You were sitting in the wheelchair and your daddy was standing in front of you, bending down and stroking your hair. He was attempting to put his arms around you. It was proving difficult with the arms of the wheelchair so high up. He was talking to you softly and you were looking intently into his face as a baby does when very young. When he saw me, he shook his head in despair.

H ran both his hands through his hair and almost groaned as if he was feeling a physical pain. His frustration at not being able to hold you then boiled over suddenly and he leant forward and picked you up in one swift movement. He was so strong and muscular it looked as if he was picking up a feather. You looked like a lost child as he held you in his arms with your feet only just touching the floor. He clung to you and cradled the back of your head in one hand and your face was against his.

'Bear, my wonderful boy, look at you. Where are you? Why did you do this when you are *so* loved by me and many others? Look at you, son, you must have been so desperate. What did we do to you? You must come back to us, you must! I've waited so long for you, my gorgeous boy, don't leave me now. If you aren't Bear anymore, I will die with the agony of not knowing you all your life.' I could hear you crying, Bear above your daddy's anguished words and it sounded like a hurt animal, wounded and alone in a dark forest. 'Don't you be crying now, my boy, everything will be grand, I give you my word. You can be whoever you want to be with me. You can do whatever you want to do. I will let you be whoever you are, no judgement.' He sobbed so deeply his whole body shook. 'This world will hold nothing for me if you aren't in it. I'll love you to my death and in the afterlife too. I hope you can feel my love. Look, Amy Lee is here, my boy, she loves you too. Bear, I can't let you go. I want to hold you like this forever, but if I let you go, you have to try and live. Oh my beloved son, just live and come home to me.'

I had never seen a grown man cry like that before and I was stunned at the depth of his suffering. It was such a moving and intimate moment between two people who should have been close for years. What would your life have been like if you *had* been close since your birth? Who would you be if this kind, loving and gently spoken man had lived with you instead of Zachary? I will never know the answer to that question and neither will you, but we could guess.

He put you gently back in your chair and tenderly ran his hands through your lank hair. Then he kissed the top of your head and told you he would be back later that day, on his own but he wanted you to fight from this moment on. He wanted you to fight with everything you had to get home to Ireland where he could come and see you every day to make up for all the lost time. He kissed your face repeatedly as if you were going to be parted forever and you looked up into his eyes, tormented by his suffering. Eventually he reluctantly pulled his body away from yours. I followed him out and closed your door, surprised to see your mammy was no longer standing there. His first words were for her though.

'Bear's mammy warned me he was too fragile, she did. She was frightened he wouldn't be able to cope with his emotions. She said he was too troubled in his mind. It looks like she was right.'

'But *you* aren't his problem, you are his solution.'

He ran one hand over his rugged face. 'I have longed for a relationship with him all his young life, but it was his mammy's call. As time went on I began to wonder if she didn't want to share him with me. I still don't know, Amy. But I love the woman she is. I love the bones of her so I have to push those thoughts to the back of my mind. Don't hate her, please.'

'That's what Bear said to me.'

'I can't blame it all on his mammy. My sister suffered like Bear and so did our father. I truly believe it *is* a genetic thing. My sister, my dear, lovely little sister, she took her own life. She was similar to Bear, gentle, complex and exceptionally bright, beautiful in every way, but she couldn't be saved. We tried, we really tried, but there was no helping her.'

'I'm sorry, Wolf, I really am. Thank God *he* was saved.'

He gave me a warm smile that creased his face and lit up his eyes. 'I remember you in the church that day, Amy. You were so bold, so fiercely protective of him, it shone out from you. Beside you, my Bear looked half there, like an abandoned child. My sister didn't have an Amy Lee in her life unfortunately. You'll bring him back to himself. I know you will. Everyone should have an Amy Lee.'

'I *will* bring him back, I promise you. I won't ever give up on him and if he thinks I will, he has another think coming!'

'I believe you, Amy.' He leant forward and kissed my cheek. 'I believe you.'

That day, after your daddy had been, you looked exhausted, but there was a flicker of something in your eyes that I hadn't seen before. I didn't know what that something was, but it was definitely there. I knelt down in front of you again and held your hands.

'I know you're in there somewhere, Bear. Your daddy loves you so much and he's loved you all your life. Think of the future and having the loving, close relationship with him you have always wanted. You are *so* like him. It's as if you have found your other self at last. If you think you'll be a burden to me, you are completely wrong. You'll never be that. Imagine a future with little Wolf. Think of watching him growing up, maybe in Ireland, if that's what you want. He needs a gentle, loving daddy, you know that. I want for him what you didn't have, don't you? Imagine us without you. I know you don't want to leave little Wolf. I know you, Bear. I just wish I'd seen the signs of your distress much earlier. I should have. Thinking back, it's now all so obvious. Your fate is forever linked with mine, to the death ...'

I paused for you to finish for me. There was that flicker again, a ghost of a fleeting feeling, some kind of emotion and your mouth moved for a split second, but it *was* only for a split second. Then you went back in your shell again and I dropped my head onto your lap in hopelessness and frustration. But then I felt your hand touch my hair very softly. It felt like a butterfly's wings brushing by me momentarily as it flew by. Feeling that touch again, however brief and however light after so long, opened the floodgates of my emotions. I sobbed into your body until it all came out. I looked up at you again.

'I know you're in there, Bear and I *will* find you. I will.'

I began to wonder if your heart stopping, however briefly, had wiped out your memories, your personality and your emotions. I gazed at the moon every night, while listening to Wolf's deep, steady breathing and ached to have you back in some small way. I was terrified that you mouthing my name in the hospital had been just a rare flashback in your brain, a blip that wouldn't happen again. I could hear your voice everywhere.

'You can smell the fresh, morning dew, you can feel the earth breathing under your bare feet and you can taste life at its rawest, at its newest and at its beginning. You can feel the vibrations under you, seeping into your body and reaching for life at its most spiritual. Here, in Ireland, I can feel *everything* in nature reaching for the light. In the silence of nature you can hear the truth of who you are. Do you ever feel we have everything wrong, Amy Lee?' I would stand and watch the dusk falling every night and think of sitting with you in your granny's back yard. 'Look, Amy, you can see the Milky Way so clearly here.'

'I quite fancy one of those right now.'

'You're funny, so you are.'

I would open my bedroom curtains slightly and look at your empty bedroom window, where you should have been signing to me. *The breeze at dawn has secrets to tell. Don't go back to sleep.*

There was just an empty space where you used to be and that space was growing and shaped like a gaping, black hole that would swallow me up. It was almost as if the you I *used* to know had died that day. I was trying to prepare myself for the fact that you could be someone entirely different in the future. But I found it impossible to think like that. I told myself that the brilliant, exceptional brain that everyone had spoken about was now going to save you in a way nobody had envisioned.

'Amy, you need to study for your exams and stop your shenanigans.'

'Bear, what use is Chaucer and what's Shakespeare on about most of the time?'

'It's beautiful, so it is. It eases my soul to hear the lyrical quality of Shakespeare's sonnets.'

'I don't understand any of it and why aren't they called poems if they *are* poems? I can't sit inside studying. I want to be outside on my bike.'

'I want to heal myself with the sun on my back. I want to look at the moonbeams and listen to the barn owls under the stars and I long to feel the keen Irish air through my hair.'

Remembering your words, I immediately felt grief stricken and a sharp pain in my chest stabbed at me and made me gasp out loud.

One day I met your daddy in reception at the rehabilitation centre. He had been with you and he appeared quite distraught. But he smiled when he saw me and looked somewhat relieved. 'Amy, he's having physiotherapy at the moment and they're being quite rough with him. I can't stand to hear him cry out, so will you be taking a walk with me for a short while, please?'

We sat in the park, opposite your room, as if we both felt closer to you by doing that. There were trees all around us and children on bikes and people walking their dogs without knowing the trauma going on within yards of them. Your daddy didn't speak for a while but he seemed to be enjoying the sun flickering on his face. He looked up at the sky and then closed his eyes, just as you used to.

'Amy,' he eventually said, 'I would love you to fill me in a little on Bear's life, the life I missed. He hasn't told me much of it for fear of hurting me. Part of me feels I know him intimately because he's flesh of my flesh and so like me, but part of me feels like he's a stranger. The love is there between us, I feel it constantly, even now, but I long to know his mind better.'

'I'm glad you feel the love, even now. That gives me such hope. Where can I start though?'

'Well, perhaps start from when and where you met at school, I suppose.'

I didn't need any more prompting to talk about you. It poured out of me like the waterfall near the farm. I spoke about how you stood out like a spotlight amongst an ocean of forgettable faces and how we walked home every day from school, with me climbing, running and jumping and you, gazing at the ever changing clouds and teaching me poetry.

I explained to him about us, our friendship and how we had loved each other from the very beginning. I told him how we did our homework together every day, ate together with my family and messed about in my bedroom all evening, laughing, dancing and simply chatting. I said you were the brightest boy in the school, but that you detested the pressure put on you by everyone.

'Bear always said that nobody had ever asked *him* what he wanted to do with his life. They all told him it would be a terrible waste not to go to Cambridge and use his brilliant brain. They urged him to set the world alight, but all he ever wanted was to be happy and at peace. Zachary especially put so much pressure on him, it was unbearable.'

He was listening intently, some of my words causing concern, some causing immense pain. I spoke of how, when you went to Cambridge, I was bereft and how tough those years were on both of us, especially for you striving for the first everyone expected.

The difficult part to describe was your time in America and how you had met someone, someone vicious and controlling who had chipped away at the Bear I knew and destroyed him. Your daddy had put his hands over his face and appeared unable to speak. I continued, telling him how unselfish you were at urging me to find a life without him. I explained how you wanted me to forget you. He gave me a warm smile then.

'There was no forgetting him though, was there, Amy?'

'The depth of my feelings is so profound there are no words for them. There is no light in this world for me if Bear isn't with me. There's no light and no love, just emptiness. I did my very best to forget, but it was hopeless and I was reckless. I came home pregnant with little Wolf. I thought and I *hoped* I would find some affection if I gave myself to another man, but it just compounded my loneliness because they weren't Bear. No other man comes anywhere near him. They aren't as kind as him or as unselfish. They aren't as compassionate or as understanding. They don't speak like him or see the world like him. They don't even smile like him. Bear is named on Wolf's birth certificate. I don't want any other father for my little boy. It can only ever be Bear.'

He had appeared deep in thought for a moment, scrutinising my answers and my descriptions of our lives and his next words were said very softly and apprehensively.

'Why did he want you to forget him?' I said nothing but concentrated on the tattoo on his arm where your name proudly sat and thought back to the first moment I had seen it in the little church. I knew what he was leading up to. 'Amy, I need to ask you a very personal question.'

I didn't want to be disloyal to you, Bear. 'Don't ask me, please. I might not be able to answer it. Please, don't ask me.'

He had appeared touched by my words. 'I understand completely how much you love him, believe me, and I was witness to that love the first time I saw you both standing side by side.' He had swallowed hard, as if he was having trouble forming the right words to say and not entirely sure he should be saying them. 'But there was something in the way you were with each other that made me think, especially how he was towards you.'

'I can't explain ...'

He put his finger to my lips very gently. 'All is grand, Amy, all is grand, please don't fret. Let me say what I have to say. It won't make any difference to my love for him, none at all. I have loved him since I first knew of his existence and I will love him until my last breath leaves my body. I have missed so much of his life, I won't mess it up now with any harsh looks or harsh words or any judgement. I promise you that. I don't have any harshness or judgement in me. Do you believe me?'

'Yes, I believe you.' I studied his rugged, compassionate face as he spoke, with his rough skin kissed by the sun and the winds of Ireland. 'Ask me then, if you want to. I'll be as honest as I can be.'

'I think Bear is a special boy, in every way possible. He isn't like other people, I can see that. My little sister was the same. He is gentle, he is kind, he is fragile and troubled and I will spend the rest of my life making sure he won't *ever* be as troubled again as he has been. I can feel in my heart that he has had conflicting emotions and feelings in his love for you. He doesn't look at you the way most young men would. You are a beautiful girl, a force of nature like you told me your mammy is. Young men would be beating a path to your door if you let them, with their raging hormones and passion.'

My heart was racing. 'I understand what you're saying. I don't want them beating a path to my door. I have only ever wanted Bear.'

'I know, Amy, I know. Let me finish, please. You are the only person I will say this to. That's how I wanted his mammy, with love but with passion too. It was an overwhelming passion that I couldn't control whenever I was within a few yards of her, even when she married somebody else. My Bear doesn't look at you like that. He looks at you with adoration, with devotion and almost with reverence. He worships you and cherishes you and I can feel the love he has for you, Amy. I can actually feel it as it flows from his body to yours, but his passion is not ...'

'I know what you're saying and I understand what you're referring to. I don't want to be disloyal. I could never be disloyal to him. I have defended him from the moment we met, from all corners.'

'You don't have to defend him to me. Just tell me if I'm wrong. My dear Bear is not like other boys, is he?'

'No, he isn't.' Your daddy squeezed my hand very gently. 'Do you mind? Please say you don't.'

He gave a deep, almost contented sigh. 'No, Amy, I don't mind. I will love him even more because of it. How he must have suffered when he knew and couldn't tell anyone. How difficult for him being brought up by a man as aggressive as Zachary when *he* is so gentle. Now I understand where some of his turmoil lies. I'm very, very sorry for you though.'

'Don't be, don't be. I just want him in my life and I'll take him in whatever form he'll give himself to me. I travelled hundreds of miles to find another Bear and there isn't one. It was difficult at first but now, *everything* is different and I just want him back to being Bear.'

'What if he doesn't ever get back to being the Bear you knew? What then?'

'Then I'll take him as he is now. I'll do it, I promise you.'

'I don't doubt it for a minute. And you love him that much to do it?'

'I couldn't live my life without Bear in it.'

'I understand. I feel that about his mammy.'

'And what of his mammy in the future, can you tell me? He has such a complex relationship with her. It's not easy for him.'

He had averted his eyes momentarily, but when he looked at me again, his expression was one of determination. 'Bear's mammy lives with me now so I hope very much my unselfish attitudes will rub off on her. Living with Zachary did her no favours at all. She does love him, Amy. She loves all her boys but she is intensely selfish and always has been. In the future, if she doesn't act towards him as he wants her to, I will leave her. My boy will come first. I don't want that to happen, but I *will* leave her. I have loved her all my life and I will never stop loving her, but Bear will come first.'

I rested my head on his shoulder. He was the kind of man you could depend on and feel safe with. He responded immediately by putting his arm around me and he felt so firm and so resilient. Looking at your daddy then was like looking at an older, more robust version of you, Bear. 'Thank you, Wolf.'

'You're a grand girl, Amy, a grand girl and you are the best thing in my boy's life. Everyone should have an Amy Lee in their life. He's so lucky to have you.'

'Thank you for saying that, but it's the other way round.'

We had sat there for an hour, an hour where he learnt more about your life and I had recalled my own by your side. The soft breeze was moving through the trees around us and I could hear your voice so clearly.

'Amy Lee, will you come down from that tree? You'll be falling, so you will.'

'You'll catch me, Bear. If I fall you'll catch me.'

'Amy, if you stand very still and listen, you'll hear my unseen friends talking to each other.'

'I can't hear them.'

'That's because you aren't ever still.'

'I don't think they're here really.'

'If the sun goes behind the clouds, you can't see it, can you? It's still there though, so it is. Just be still and listen. Watch carefully and you'll see the fairies and nature spirits dancing.'

'Why are they here?'

'They're here because they love you, Amy Lee, so they do.'

'They love you too, Bear.'

Your daddy left me by the front door of the rehabilitation centre and kissed my cheek with a tenderness that was very like you. I wanted him to stay by my side. I wanted him to stay by *our* side. We both needed him and we would in the future too. Being with him reminded me how much I missed my own father and his steadfast love.

'Goodbye, Amy and thank you.'

'He will get better, he *will*. I can hear him in here.' I pointed to my head. 'And I can feel it here.' I then pointed to my heart. 'I have a plan.'

'I hope it works.'

'It has to work. My life and little Wolf's life depends on it.'

'I'll let you into a secret, Amy, so does mine.'

Just before I opened the door to your room after being with your daddy, I met Marcus. At first, I had no idea he was a doctor because he had hair swept back off his face into a short ponytail and pierced ears. He had quite an intense look but compassion shone from him like a golden light and it settled on me as soon as he began to speak.

'Are you, Amy Lee?'

'Yes, I am,' I replied, hoping he wasn't going to impart any bad news.

'Bear's father said you were the best person to speak to.' He extended his hand towards me. 'I'm Marcus, his psychiatrist.' His words made me shiver. It sounded as if you were mad and you were always the sanest person I knew. 'Have you known Bear very long?'

'Yes, since we were eleven. We met at school. He's the father of my child.' Saying that always made me feel so contented and proud, Bear. 'Are you going to give me bad news, Marcus?'

'No, no, I'm so sorry, I didn't want to worry you. He won't or can't answer my questions at the moment, but I know he's aware of what I'm asking him. His case is confidential obviously, so I wouldn't be able to repeat anything he said to me anyway, but if he won't tell me about himself then I need to find out in other ways. I just want to know him a little better.'

'Ask away then.' It was obviously my day to describe you in detail, Bear. 'I'll tell you whatever you need to know.'

'I'd just like to know,' he started, but then he paused for a few moments as if he was trying to find the best way to frame his question, 'I'd like to know if there is a place where Bear feels safe and secure, where he feels at peace. Complex, bright, sensitive people like Bear are often trying to survive in a world they find quite toxic and demanding and it's a world in which they are often too delicate to survive in. It isn't their fault. Is there a place ..?'

'Ireland,' I said, interrupting him, without having to think about it. 'The countryside of Ireland is Bear's place. He needs to be in Ireland.'

'Good, that's a start.'

'Doctor, is he going to get better than this? This isn't Bear.'

'He is and physically he is actually getting stronger and can do more for himself, so I'm reliably informed by his lead physiotherapist. Mentally and emotionally is going to take a bit longer. He needs to work with me but I'm pretty sure there will be some improvement soon. We just need to find the right key to unlocking the prison he's in at the moment. You can't hurry him. He needs time to come to terms with the fact that he's still here when he had given up on his life. He needs to deal with the guilt too.'

'You have no idea how those words torment me. How could he give up when he's so loved? I didn't realise how bad he was. I assumed because he had me and our little boy that he wouldn't *ever ...*'

'I know, I know, it's very tough for you to hear that. But when someone is suicidal, they don't think rationally like everyone else. If you've never had clinical depression then it's extremely difficult to understand. How can I describe it? It's as if they go to another place just before the decision is made and it's a place of such severe pain, it's actually better to end their life.' I had closed my eyes, unable to take in what he was saying. 'I know how hard this is for you. You hope, at the last minute, that your love and support will pull them back from the brink of despair, but that's not how it works, I'm afraid. They just want the unbearable pain to stop. We've put him on a different anti-depressant so that should help. It can take a while sometimes to find the best one suited to the patient.'

I felt a little faint, as if the blood was from draining from my head slowly. It had been an emotional day. 'Thank you for being so honest.'

'Can I just ask a few more questions?'

'Of course you can; anything to help Bear.'

'Were his relationships with his parents quite difficult? Often these problems begin when we are very young. I *can* tell you, when I mention his mother he shakes his head and puts his hands over his face. Was his childhood stressful? Was his father ..?'

'Doctor, I could stand here for hours and explain the stress he was under and it wouldn't be long enough. He feels betrayed by his mother and lied to by her. The man he thought was his father and who brought him up, was aggressive and controlling and put so much pressure on Bear ever since he was very young. He bullied Bear constantly. He found out about his real father when he was sixteen.'

'Thank you for that.' He wrote some notes and appeared thoughtful. 'Has he suffered with depression for a long time?'

'Yes, I think so. He calls it the black beast. Bear is incredibly bright and complex and his life has been a web of secrets. He's so intelligent, he was expected to achieve so much, but it wasn't what *he* wanted. It was what everyone else wanted. Bear just wants to be happy and at peace.'

'Yes, I understand,' he said, his voice so soft and consoling, I could have shared our whole history with him right then and there. 'It's often the case that the person expected so much of, can't match up to those expectations because they can be wholly unrealistic. You need drive and ambition as well as brains and if you're not that way inclined then it sets up a war inside your head. Often, the brilliant person can feel they have disappointed everyone if they don't achieve. It's a very difficult place to be. Add depression and anxiety to the mix and you create the perfect storm.'

'Yes, the perfect storm inside his head.'

'Thank you for the information. I can work on his storm and hopefully calm it down,' he said, smiling reassuringly. 'One more thing, regarding his relationship with his mother, was it always difficult?'

I felt at a loss as how to describe your feelings about your mammy, Bear. I hope I said the right thing though when I remembered your words. 'He said he could never feel her love. It was as if there was this great, gaping hole in his chest where her love should have been. I think that says it all really.'

He raised his eyebrows. 'Yes, that's all I need to know. Thank you.'

'Before you go, there is something else, but it's so personal, I'm not sure I can tell you, even it helps you understand him more.'

He frowned slightly. 'Well, it's up to you.'

I felt at a loss as to how I could best explain your conflicting emotions about your sexuality. 'When we were growing up, Bear didn't always feel he was being true to himself.'

He was scrutinising my face and asked, 'Can you tell me in what way exactly?'

'I don't know how to put it We've always loved each other. That's not the issue really and never has been. But when we were younger, Bear felt he had to explore his other feelings. It caused him a lot of heartache.'

He wrote again on the papers he was holding and gave me another reassuring smile. 'Okay, I understand. Thank you for being so open.'

'I hope it helps you get Bear back for me.'

He nodded and went to walk away. I was about to open your door but he turned quickly, as if he had forgotten to tell me something important. 'Amy,' he said, 'this is going to take a while, but when he eventually comes home, my advice would be, take him to Ireland.'

## Chapter Fifteen

*Stop acting so small.
You are the universe in ecstatic motion.
Rumi*

TIME WAS PASSING BY US, BEAR. THAT DAY, AFTER speaking with your daddy and Marcus, I felt a little more hopeful momentarily but when I knelt in front of you, you seemed to be shrouded in mist like your beloved mountains.

You had always been a child of nature, affected greatly by the rains sweeping across the moor towards the farm and the thunder and lightning crackling in the darkening sky. You loved the warm sun on your back, the radiant summer flowers and coarse, mauve heather and the birds singing to us in the unearthly silence of an Irish morning. You were as deep as the ocean and as magical as a dense forest and you shone as brilliantly as the stars in the black universe, but the impossible twists and turns of your life had sucked all that brilliance out of you.

'Watch the wind catch the leaves, Amy Lee. Watch the sunlight chasing the shadows. Those trees there allow us to breathe, so they do. Put your hands here on their rough bark, feel it scratch your skin. The trees are speaking to you.'

'What are they saying then?'

'They're saying, you are an angel, Amy, an angel of the universe. There's so much unseen in this world, so much, but if you tune in with all your senses, you'll hear them, so you will.'

'Bear, I can't sit still long enough to hear them speak. I'd prefer to climb them.'

'I know that, so I'll listen for you. They are telling you that they'll look after you, so they are.'

'I want *you* to look after me!'

'I'm not sure I can do that, Amy.'

I spoke to you that day about my conversation with your daddy earlier. I explained how I had filled in all the blanks for him about our lives. You studied my face as I spoke and in your watchful eyes, I detected a tiny glimmer of a light instead of a dull space but the light seemed very far away.

'I told him about your life with Zachary and the pressure he put on you and about Cambridge and America. Bear, I know you can understand what I'm saying. I miss you *so* much. How can I convince you I'm not angry you tried to leave us? I'm just so sad I couldn't make you stay. I know that wasn't you. The *real* you has been fighting the black beast for so long, you had nothing left to fight with.'

You gave a deep sigh then, so deep it seemed to come from the depths of your mighty soul. Your eyes conveyed some sort of expression, I'm not sure what of, but it was there, a reaction of some sort. I carried on, speaking from my heart to yours.

'All the people around you who always wanted something from you, including me, should hang their heads in shame. I ask nothing from you now, nothing at all. I won't *ever* again as long as I live. Bear, I'm so ashamed I tried to turn you into someone you weren't. I'm sorry for all the times I made you cry with frustration because you knew you couldn't give me what I longed for. I don't want that now. It's all completely irrelevant. I know how it hurt you to send me away because you wanted me to find someone else. My God, it must have been agony. Forget all that! All I long for now is for you to be back to being the Bear *you* want to be, not who *I* want you to be.'

Tears fell down your face and I rejoiced silently that you were at least reacting to my words, even if they made you cry. Any reaction was remarkable. I took hold of your cold hands and kissed them both before placing them gently in your lap again.

'I know what I'm saying is upsetting you but you need to hear this, it has to be said because it'll help you in the end. My God, I didn't even ask you about putting your name on Wolf's birth certificate! What was I thinking? You were going to change your name from Bear Flynn to Bear Carroll, to rid yourself of Zachary. You didn't though because it said Bear Flynn on that certificate. Something as important and as permanent as that, I just did it without your consent. I'm just as guilty as Zachary and your mammy and Eddie and Dean. When I think back, I was so jealous of Eddie and I ruined that friendship for you. I can't believe I did that. My only defence is immaturity.'

Again, more flickers of recognition, more tears and you shook your head slowly. Did you mean I wasn't as guilty as them? I thought you did. I *hoped* you did. Thinking about our lives then, it all became as clear as the air when snow fell, how you always gave so much of yourself and asked so little in return.

I had loved you, from the first moment I saw you sitting at a desk near mine with your tie perfectly straight, your uniform pressed perfectly and your hair like shiny conkers. But had I tried to turn you into someone you weren't? If I had and I had contributed to your pain, I would spend the rest of our lives making up for that.

'I need to tell you something else and I hope it won't hurt you. Your daddy guessed your secret. I didn't tell him. I never would, but he's your daddy and he knew.' You closed your eyes for a moment, as if you didn't want to hear and didn't want to see. I grabbed your hands again. 'But he doesn't care. He loves you *so* much, he doesn't care. Please believe me. He says he will spend the rest of his life loving you exactly as you are. Did you hear that? That's the unconditional parental love you've always longed for. So there is nothing to worry about anymore. No more secrets in your life, no more! You can change your name to Bear Carroll if that's what you want.'

You opened your eyes and gazed out of the window. You looked as if you still longed to be free of it all. I hoped to God I was doing the right thing by you and not making it worse. I felt as if I was running through a thick fog with no idea of where I was headed and with no recognisable markers. You seemed exhausted and leant your head back on your chair, your eyes full of bewilderment. I had almost finished everything I wanted to say to you but telling you about the last part was going to be particularly tough for both of us. But I was fighting for your life, Bear. I was fighting for my life too and little Wolf's and everyone else who loved you and wanted you back. I drew a deep breath and started to speak again.

'Bear, look at me, *please* look at me. This is going to kill me but I'm not going to come in this room again until it's time to take you home. This pitiless room has nothing to do with you. It's stifling you and imprisoning your body and your mind, but it can't contain the Bear I know. You are somewhere else, in Ireland with the little people and the angels and water sprites. I'm going to coax you out, however long it takes.' You had dropped your head so I took hold of your chin and turned your face towards mine. 'Now listen, every morning at eleven thirty, after your physiotherapy, I want you to look out of this window. I'll ask your nurses to put your chair right here. Do you understand? I'll be out there whatever the weather, but I won't walk into this room again until I take you out of here and home to little Wolf.'

I kissed your forehead and cheek lovingly, your skin cool beneath my lips and looked into your eyes one last time. I went to leave, my stomach churning with distress and tears burning the back of my eyes, but you clutched one of my hands and mouthed, 'Amy.'

There was no sound, just your lips moving. Your grip was stronger though and it was as if all your sorrow, anguish and frustration flowed out in that desperate touch. To say it was a wrench to tear myself away at that moment is an understatement. I longed to stay and comfort you and tell you that I loved you and I would for the rest of my life, but I didn't. I couldn't, however desolate you looked.

I had a vision in my mind, a plan and I wouldn't stray from my path even though it appeared hopeless. I would hold that vision there. However tormented you looked, however heartbroken, I couldn't deviate. Your usual smell washed over me as I whispered in your ear.

'I love you so much, but I can't watch you slowly destroy yourself anymore because it's destroying me too and I can't let that happen to little Wolf. Watch out of the window every morning, eleven thirty, don't forget. It's up to you now, Bear. Don't let us down.'

How I left that joyless room that day I'll never know. It felt as if I was abandoning you forever to your fate. I ran down the corridor and through reception, blinded by a mass of tears and so distraught I have no idea how I ended up at home because I didn't remember getting there. My mother was out with Wolf luckily, not that I would have fooled her, but I had no intention of upsetting my little boy. I flung myself on my bed and howled like a wild animal caught in a trap. My cries came out in loud, pitiful, shuddering sobs, wracking my body with intense pain. How many times I screamed your name I have no idea. I cried until I heard Wolf and my mother arrive home and then I jumped off my bed and rushed into the bathroom, splashing cold water over my face. Wolf called out for me.

'Mama, where are you? Nana took me to the swings. I went very high.'

'Aren't you a lucky boy to have a nana like that?'

'We saw Patrick. He's coming for tea.' I ran downstairs and scooped him up in my arms. 'Patrick can read to me, can't he?'

'Yes, he can.'

'When is Bear coming to tea?' His eyes were large and questioning. 'Bear hasn't been for ages.'

'Bear will be coming for tea very soon,' I replied, with renewed optimism that I hoped wasn't misplaced as I carried him into the dining room. My mother was in her usual place, pottering about in the kitchen and calling through the hatch.

'Is he coming home then, Amy?' I kept my face turned from hers and when I didn't respond, she added, 'Are you okay, love?'

'He will be, Mum. He will be, if I have anything to do with it.'

'I asked if *you* were okay, darling.'

'Yes, I'm fine. I've got a plan. I'm so tired of seeing Bear in that place. I can't go in and look at him like that anymore.' I glanced over at my father's comfortable chair by the fireplace. The empty space wasn't getting any smaller although the intensity of my grief had lessened a little with time and now I was utterly consumed by you and your painfully slow recovery. 'I'm going to try something new, something rather risky and difficult. It will break me, but it might help him. It's a bit radical but I'm taking a chance. There's nothing to lose.'

'I wondered when you would get round to it.'

'I don't know what you mean.'

'Yes, you do. You are so absorbed by all this you are forgetting who *you* are. I told you that before. I'm your mother, I know you. Now, you get him out of there and then you can both start to live again.'

I managed to get Patrick on his own that evening despite

Isabelle trying to monopolise him completely. She would kiss his cheek repeatedly and put her arms around him, even at the tea table and my heart ached for you, Bear. At times, with certain facial expressions, Patrick resembled you and I had to look away. You had different fathers but many similar mannerisms and I found that hard. He was gentle and compassionate like you and although he obviously found Isabelle's displays of affection a little embarrassing, he didn't tell her so. He simply responded with a tender smile. He looked in my eyes deeply whenever I spoke too, just like you did. That intensity, that watchfulness was so reminiscent of you my mood would drop because you didn't do that anymore. Your eyes were empty, dull and vacant. When I explained my plan to Patrick, a look of delight spread across his face and he appeared energised and pleased by it.

'Perfect, Amy, just perfect,' he said, signing at the same time.

'Do you really think it's a good idea?'

He hugged me tightly and nodded enthusiastically. 'Mammy and Wolf are going home tomorrow so it's a good time to start. He will miss his daddy I'm sure, so your plan will take his mind off it.'

That night, with a cold moon hanging in the sky, I stared at the ceiling and decided on the details of my scheme. The following day I went across to your house and let myself in with the spare key Patrick had given me a few weeks before. Your daddy wasn't there, he had gone to visit you and Patrick was at work. Your mammy was sitting in the front room packing a bag. Her face was pale, her eyes quite sunken and her dark hair hanging loose and lank. She appeared a very different woman to the one I had seen kissing your daddy that day by the waterfall.

'Oh, Amy, have you come to say goodbye?' I hadn't but lied and told her I had. She smiled gratefully. 'That's very nice of you.'

'I hope you have a good journey home,' I replied, a little flustered. 'What time are you going?'

'We go when Wolf comes back from visiting Bear.' Neither of us knew what to say for a moment and there was an uncomfortable silence before she added, 'I didn't go with him in case it upset Bear. I hope he doesn't think I don't love him because I do, very much.'

'Of course you do,' I said, feeling for her.

'There's a lot of water gone under my bridge, so there is, and much of it has been stormy water, but I'm not a bad mother. I love all my boys, but my relationship with my Baby Bear is complicated.' She glanced at me to see my reaction and her eyes were so troubled it was disconcerting. 'You have a son now, so you'll learn that not everything in life is straightforward. We all make mistakes. But it's not *all* my fault, Amy. Bear has always been different, always troubled. He seems to need more love than the other three. They were easy compared to him, even Patrick with his hearing loss. It was always a mystery knowing what Bear was thinking and feeling. He's so deep, so complex, I couldn't reach him.'

'I'm sure you'll build a good relationship when he gets better, a *new* relationship.'

'Sweet Jesus, I hope so. I can't take much more guilt. It's the Catholic in me, so it is. His daddy doesn't want to leave but I told him we could be here for months waiting for Bear to recover fully. He has you and Patrick to watch over him. We have to go home at some point.'

I found it very difficult listening to her. I was trying to imagine leaving little Wolf if he was in your place and even the thought of it made me shudder. 'I just need to go upstairs and find a book for Bear, if that's okay with you.'

She didn't appear to care what I wanted or which book. She was too depleted by her own worries and emotions, so I left her there and ran upstairs to your bedroom. Being in there without your presence was soul destroying. I went to your desk and found the book of Rumi poetry immediately. It was a small cream book with a deep purple inside cover and gold lettering. I held it in my hands as you would with a newborn baby, caressing the front and hugging it to my chest.

'Rumi was a clever bastard,' I said out loud to the empty room where you had stood signing to me so often throughout our young lives. 'And now he's going to save you, Bear.'

Once back downstairs I said a quick farewell to your mammy, telling her I would see her in Ireland one day and she gave a wan smile and said she hoped so. I thought it a tragedy that she was often incapable of expressing her love for you or making you feel it.

That first day of my plan it was bright, sunny and warm with a fresh breeze blowing through my hair and cooling my burning face. It was burning because I was apprehensive and my stomach full of butterflies. When I reached the park, I was almost too frightened to look over at your window, but when I did my heart sunk to my knees. You weren't there.

I had an extremely large piece of card in my hands and I felt a little foolish just standing there with it. A few people gave me some odd glances but I ignored them and prayed to your angels that the staff would remember what I had asked of them. I didn't take my eyes off your window for one second until you eventually appeared ten minutes later. I waved frantically and caught your attention easily. I had written in large letters with a black Magic Marker pen on one side of the placard: 'Don't turn away, Bear. Read my messages every day, please.' I then turned it and I had written on the back my first Rumi quote: 'There is a path from me to you that I am constantly looking for.'

When I thought you'd had enough time to read and digest it, I waved at you and walked away quickly. I didn't look back. I couldn't. The following day, you were sitting there before me, your normally silky hair flattened as usual and your face pale. That day, the placard read: 'Words are a pretext. It's the inner bond that draws one person to another, not words.'

On day three, there was a cloudless sky and I could see you had one of your old, favourite T-shirts on. It was dark grey and had always suited you. You had worn it in Ireland and for some reason it made me feel hopeful. The placard read: 'What do I long for? Something felt in the night, but not seen in the day.'

On day four it was even warmer and I wore a summer dress you had always loved and commented on. You said it reminded you of the flowers in the hedgerows near the farm. The placard read: 'This is how I would die into the love I have for you, as pieces of cloud dissolve into sunlight.'

You had frowned and looked weary, but I waved cheerfully and left you there. It was one of the toughest things I have ever done, leaving you and not being able to give you any comfort. I wondered if it was the physiotherapy making you feel shattered or the emotion of seeing my signs with words that you loved.

Day five, the weather had changed and the wind had shifted to the north, bringing with it a squall of summer rain and it was much cooler. The nurses had dressed you in your dark blue sweater. I smiled to myself because your granny had said your blue sweater matched your eyes. When I remarked that your eyes were a hazel green, you had shrugged and told me, that was your granny and it was best not to argue. The placard that day read: 'Your heart knows the way. Run in that direction.'

When you read those words, I saw you take a deep sigh, as if something was stirring in you, but your expression continued to be quite blank. I had to do everything in my power to keep my spirits up.

On day six, a white sun was high in the sky and it was hot and rather humid. I wondered if a storm was brewing. I thought of the electric storms in Ireland, Bear and how they had made your eyes shine. There were children in the park playing football and people walking their dogs. A few gave me a smile and glanced at the large pieces of card before moving on. The words that day made you shake your head slightly. The placard read: 'You had better run from me, my words are fire.'

I had no idea if perhaps you were asking me *not* to run from you. If you did, there was no danger of that. I was bound to you for life, to the death and beyond. But that was the trouble, Bear. I had absolutely no clue about what you were thinking at that point. Was I even doing the right thing, standing out there every single day?

For day seven, I had chosen a quotation that I hoped would convince you I didn't care what happened in the future. I hoped it would tell you that you could burn as brightly and as fiercely as you pleased. I would burn with you. The placard read: 'If your beloved has a life of fire, step in and burn along.'

There had been no reaction to that but the following day I had sensed a change in you. It was as if you were anticipating the next words and perhaps trying to second guess them. You were staring hard at me, frowning in expectation. The placard read: 'Life is a balance between holding on and letting go.'

There was an imperceptible nod of your head. Were you holding on, Bear? Were you holding on as tightly as you could by your fingertips? Were you trying your best to let go of the past? If you were, my next words would need to encourage you to keep holding on and be who you wanted to be, without any expectation or pressure from anyone.

Day nine was difficult because after you had read the words, you covered your face with your hands. How I didn't just run towards you and climb in your window to hold you I have no idea. I gritted my teeth and swore under my breath, but I told myself sharply, at least it was a reaction. The placard read: 'These pains you feel are messengers, listen to them.'

On day ten, the rain was torrential and I was feeling cold and pretty miserable because time was passing and I had expected more improvement by then. I couldn't give up on you though. I was fighting for your life. I was fighting to get you back to being the Bear I knew and adored. You had never given up on me when I wouldn't study or behave at school. Your infinite patience, kindness and compassion made me want to be a better person. I *was* a better person because of you, Bear. Who would I be if I had never met you? The placard read: 'You have to keep breaking your heart until it opens.'

Another slight nod of your head and your face appeared a little more alert. You were wearing the blue sweater again and I longed to bury my face in it and take in your unique smell. I wondered what you were doing all day without me or your daddy to talk to you. Was I doing right by you? Was I igniting your sleeping brain and your emotions by quoting Rumi? Or were you missing the stimulation of my conversation? Was I really doing right by you?

Day eleven, the sun was out again but there was a fresher, clearer breeze. People were strolling by me, hand in hand and it hurt. The weather reminded me of being stretched out in the heather with you that day, without any clothes on. The soft, Irish summer wind had blown across my back and legs while we held each other. You had asked if it was enough for me. I was enjoying every precious, exquisite moment of feeling your skin against mine but I *had* secretly wanted more from you. But I told you it *was* enough. I would have given my soul to the devil for more but now I simply wanted you back as *you* instead of looking over at your pale face and flattened hair. The placard read: 'Outwardly I am silent. Inwardly you know I am screaming.'

That day, there was the first faint ghost of a smile. You realised, I'm sure, that I was trying to let you know I understood. I understood that the black beast had overcome you eventually and that you had been fighting him for as long as you could remember. Depression was a part of you, a part like any other.

Day twelve, it was raining hard again and it reminded me of how the wall of grey cloud and rain had swept across the fields and lashed against the windows of the farm as we lay on your bed with our foreheads touching. You had been telling me about Irish mythology and laughing when I said it was weird and terrifying. The placard read: 'The desire to know your own soul will end all other desires.'

That day, you had attempted to stand and pushed hard against your wheelchair. It was no use though and you slumped back down again. I had to turn and walk away quickly because I didn't want you to see me crying. I knew your soul. It was akin to mine, Bear. It had been since before we met, but we just didn't know it.

Day thirteen, warm sunshine again and the changeable weather was matching my moods. I wanted you to know I would be standing there, in that garden every day until the seasons changed and snow fell and beyond that too. The placard read: 'I will be waiting here for your silence to break, for your soul to shake, for your love to wake.'

Another faint smile and you appeared lighter in your mood. I felt, at last, that something was happening, but it wasn't happening quickly enough for me. I had always been impatient, stubborn and erratic.

Day fourteen said everything I felt about you. What more can I say? The placard read: 'There is nothing I want but your presence, in friendship time dissolves.'

You began to cry silently. I could see the tears clearly and mine matched yours. Bear, I longed for you then. All I wanted was to hold you and feel you holding me. But I couldn't give up. I waved at you and walked away again, my heart shattering into a million tiny pieces.

On day fifteen, hot sun flooded back and I wore the flowery dress again in an attempt to cheer myself up a little. I was still just as determined and my stubborn nature was helping me somewhat. The placard read: 'Stop acting so small, you are the universe in ecstatic motion.'

That was the worst day for me because you opened your mouth as if you were going to call out to me, but then turned your wheelchair and disappeared from view. I dropped the huge piece of card and sunk to my knees. A man passing by asked if I felt faint, but I shook my head and said I was fine. I wasn't fine, Bear. I was distraught, desperate and despairing. I just wanted you back.

After day fifteen, we were all sitting round the tea table and

Patrick had joined us again. Everyone knew my plan and what I was doing each day. As usual, I was only half there, the other half with you.

'Is anything working, Amy?' Ava asked and her normally cheerful and lively face was quite forlorn. She was missing you too, Bear. 'It should have by now, wouldn't you say?'

'I really don't know,' I said, succinctly because there was nothing else I *could* say at that point.

Patrick knocked the table twice, as he used to do to get your attention, signing and talking at the same time. 'Keep going, Amy, keep going. He *will* respond one day. You *must* keep going, for Bear.'

I tried to smile at him but my mouth froze because my heart was being trodden on by wild, stampeding horses.

Day sixteen came and I wanted to let you know exactly how I was feeling. I missed telling you how I felt. I missed hearing your voice. I looked through the book, searching for the right one. The placard that day read: 'My longing for you keeps me in this moment. My passion gives me courage.'

Nothing happened, no shake of the head, no nod and no smile. I almost gave up then, but your expression *was* ever so slightly different. There was more of a light in your dull eyes, more focus. That gave me hope at least.

Day seventeen, you had retreated into your shell again. It felt like one step forward and five back but my sensible mother reminded me that the staff had warned me it would be a long haul. The placard told you what you already knew: 'My heart and your heart are very old friends.'

By day eighteen I was beginning to feel quite distressed and agitated, but the quotation I chose was an attempt to let you know how wonderful you were and always had been. It read: 'It is your light that lights the worlds.'

The following morning little Wolf accompanied me to the park. We took the car that day because the placard was so large. He had been badgering me for days to take him along and on day nineteen he was holding on grimly to the other end of the cardboard. He struggled to hold up his end but he was determined to do it because I had told him it was very important for your recovery. It read: 'Why do you stay in prison when the door is so wide open?'

There was a ghost of a smile once more and you appeared to mouth his name. I took it as a sign that you wanted to see him so we folded up the placard, placing it in one of the bins and walked into the nursing home once more.

I had made a vow that I would not step in that room again until I wheeled you out of there. So I stood by your open door as Wolf ran in and immediately jumped on your lap all arms and legs and childhood joyfulness. There was no shyness, no holding back because he hadn't seen you for so long, just spontaneity and love. He had always been a demonstrative child and the affection between you had been instantaneous and deep.

He put his face near yours, his little hands in your hair. I could see in his eyes that he was finding you very changed. You stared hard at each other and neither of you spoke, but you appeared to be quietly thrilled at seeing him again. I don't know how I could tell that, except to say that I could read your body language so well, even if it was muted by your recent problems. You didn't smile but you did seem overwhelmed and it was almost as if you were both communicating without words. I wished I could join the conversation but I stayed by the door, determined not to go back on the stand I had made. Eventually Wolf spoke.

'Bear, when are you coming home? You have to read me stories.'

Seeing you together filled me with hope and despair in turn. The fleeting feeling of hope was that you would be home soon and be the daddy to Wolf I longed for. The despair was that you never would. A nurse brushed by me with your tablet and a glass of water.

'Here we go, Bear. Take this tablet for me. I'll help you.' She put the small white pill in your mouth and held up a glass of water to your lips. 'Come on now. You help me with this. I know you can use your right hand. Don't be lazy now.'

You did as she asked like an acquiescent child and your hand shook. Wolf was watching with his huge, inquiring eyes. I saw in his face his need to help you and it was almost too much for me to stand. I felt, at that moment, as if I would burst open and splatter my insides all over the walls.

'Daddy, your hand isn't well,' he said sweetly, 'I'll help you, shall I?'

I couldn't look at you both because an overpowering surge of love for you mixed with hopelessness stampeded through my body. I walked down the corridor for a few minutes and took deep breaths to stem my emotions. I returned to find you were stroking Wolf's hair with your strongest hand and he was chatting away to you, telling you that Patrick read to him sometimes and so did Isabelle and Ava, but he wanted you to come home and tuck him in at night.

'Will you come soon, Daddy?' he implored you and you leant forward slowly and kissed him. I beckoned to him to come out when he glanced at me briefly for reassurance.

He jumped off your lap and ran to me and I saw you move your weaker arm and reach out for him. Wolf was now holding my hand and out of your view so your head dropped onto your chest and I reluctantly closed the door. Wolf was so buoyed up by being with you; he was like a completely different child. If I had ever wondered how much influence being close to you was having in his young life, it was silenced then. That evening at teatime he told everyone at the table that you had spoken to him.

'I don't think he actually spoke, darling,' I told him gently, 'but he was pleased you were there, Wolf. I could see it in his eyes.'

'He did speak,' he said defiantly, pushing his bottom lip out a little.

'Good, that's good he spoke,' Patrick told him, patting his

head gently.

I didn't contradict him then but when I put him to bed and kissed him goodnight, he questioned me about you coming out of the nursing home.

'He can live with us and Nana, can't he? Is he coming home soon?'

'He can't come home until he can move a bit more, darling. I can't lift him if he falls, you see.'

'I can help you,' he replied, his eyes alight with excitement.

'Yes, you can, I know but he needs to stay just a bit longer, Wolf.' I was stroking his cheek and he appeared upset for a moment. 'Don't worry too much about him, he'll be fine.'

'Bear doesn't like it there, Mama.'

'How do you know he doesn't?'

'He told me that.'

'Wolf, I know you want him to speak to you, but he can't yet, not quite.'

'He can!'

'Alright, alright, what did he say to you?'

'He said, "home" and "Ireland." I heard him. He *did* say that, he did.'

My heart leapt. 'Did he *really* say those two words?'

'I promise,' he said, nodding emphatically, his eyes becoming heavy.

Happiness then surged through me. You *were* in there then, Bear.

I took Wolf with me the next day and we had an even bigger placard. You were there, waiting and watching for us and for the first time I saw expectation on your face *and* in your eyes. It was almost as if you were trying to guess which Rumi quote I would use next. The one I'd picked expressed perfectly what I felt about us and it was my favourite quotation of all of them. I was already crying as we held it up. The placard read: 'As soon as I heard my first love story I started looking for you, not knowing how blind that was. Lovers don't finally meet somewhere. They're in each other all along.'

It was very cumbersome for Wolf to hold up with his little arms. 'Can I drop it now, Mama? Has Bear seen it? Mama, I can't hold it.'

I had been so busy watching you, I hadn't answered straight away but I saw you smile and nod your head very slowly. It was the smile I had been waiting for, the smile that had always floored me. 'Yes, he's seen it. Put it down, darling and blow Bear some kisses like this.'

'How many kisses?'

'Do loads and loads and loads so he knows how much we love him and how much we want him to come home.' He did so willingly and I stared in disbelief as your hand moved towards your mouth and you attempted to put your lips together in a similar way to us. 'Keep going, Wolf, keep going.'

You didn't blow a kiss though, you signed something and I gasped. Frustration gripped me because I couldn't read it. 'What's he doing?' Wolf asked, as your hands made the same movements over and over again. It was done slowly, almost painfully, as if the messages from your brain weren't getting to your hands quickly enough.

'I don't know. It's sign language that Patrick does. Bear is the only one who does it with him.' I shouted over to you, 'I'll bring Patrick tomorrow. I can't understand it.'

When I explained to Patrick what had happened he appeared reluctant to go with me. 'It probably doesn't make sense, Amy. Don't get your hopes up.'

'It will make sense, it *will*. I know it will. I can see a change in his eyes. They are becoming more expressive, like the old Bear. They've been dull and lifeless for so long so I recognise the light coming back to them. He smiled properly too. You know the smile I mean. Nobody smiles like Bear. You will come, won't you, Patrick? Patrick, please.'

Your dear, compassionate brother took pity on me. 'Okay, I'll tell work I'll be late. Please don't be disappointed if it's just a few words that don't mean much.'

'It *will* mean something,' I said defiantly and that night I gazed on the crescent moon with less anguish and with less troubled eyes.

We were at the park, Patrick and I, dead on eleven thirty. The time had dragged so slowly until then. You weren't at your window and the feeling of ease that had settled on me the night before was diminishing and quickly vanished like the early morning mists around your granny's farm. You had never been that late before and anxiety was tugging at my guts. We waited patiently and at one point I must have looked so distraught, Patrick took my hand and squeezed it in a gesture of solidarity. Ten minutes passed, then fifteen and twenty and I told Patrick to leave for work if he so wished.

'No,' he declared, 'Bear is more important.'

Twenty-five minutes dragged by like a wet afternoon in November and I was just about to give in and run inside to demand where you were from the staff, when you suddenly appeared.

'Patrick, he's there.'

'Sweet Jesus,' he muttered and we both moved a little closer to your window.

I called to you, 'Bear, sign what you did yesterday, please. Show Patrick, can you?'

There was no hesitation this time although your hands were slow and shaky. Patrick was frowning and studying you closely. My heart was doing somersaults because I knew you were trying so hard, it must be important. My impatience was causing my head to feel as if it was being squeezed hard.

'What's he saying?'

'I can't quite make it out.'

'Keep watching, keep trying. What are you signing to him?'

'I'm telling him to take his time. He hasn't done this in so long and his brain has been injured. I'll get it eventually, Amy.'

'Come on, Bear. Come on!'

'Aha,' he cried suddenly. 'I have it, I think.'

'Tell me! Tell me!' Patrick appeared choked. 'Just say it as he signed it. It'll make sense to me, I know it will.' He turned towards me. 'Patrick, put me out of my misery.'

'"My heart is yours. Don't give myself back to me."'

All I could do was watch in wonder as you signed it repeatedly and I felt a wave of euphoria sweep over me. I just muttered, 'Bear, you're coming back.'

'There's something else,' Patrick was saying.

'What is it?'

'He's says, don't be afraid, Amy Lee.'

Everything just exploded around me. The fear, the frustration, the desperation, the agony and the terror all came rushing out, but as it boiled over to be felt and acknowledged, it turned into delight and joy and I felt ecstatic. How I stopped myself running in and covering you with kisses I have no idea but I still hadn't heard you speak so I told Patrick to wave farewell and we left you there. We walked away with our arms round each other. Patrick was in tears.

'He's slowly coming back to us, Amy.'

'Yes, Patrick, he's almost home.'

I had been warned by all the medical staff, one step forward wasn't a permanent recovery and the next day you seemed to be back in your own world again. I couldn't let that happen. I had this gnawing feeling inside me constantly and it was telling me that your recovery would stall if I didn't get you home.

As I walked towards the rehabilitation centre, I was recalling times we had spent together, where you had described every living creature to me and every flower and every cloud. I was remembering all our conversations when walking home from school. Well, *you* had been walking and I had been running, climbing and jumping. Did you think of our childhood often in those difficult days, Bear?

Did you think of the happy times in Ireland when we were lying side by side in a meadow, surrounded by long grass and sweet smelling flowers with our hands clasped together? I think of them all the time and how we swam under the surging wall of water, full of life and full of hope and so young.

'Can you see the water sprites and fairies, Amy? Can you see the angels above us?'

'No, I can't. Let's stay here forever, can we?'

'I have to go to Cambridge. I have to succeed and be grateful for my brain. I have to get a first and make everyone proud of me. What if I just want to be happy?'

'Just be happy then, Bear. Don't worry about all of that. Do what *you* want to and I'll do it with you.'

You would whisper to me, 'Amy Lee, you're my Guardian Angel, so you are.'

I sat on my bed that night listening to little Wolf's quiet but steady breathing and imagined you were standing under a tree watching me climb. 'Watch this, Bear,' I had called to you, 'I can swing on these branches like a monkey.'

'Come down now, Amy Lee, you'll be falling, so you will.'

'If I fall you'll catch me.'

'What if I'm not here to catch you?'

'Don't say that! If you weren't here to catch me, I won't climb anymore.'

I hadn't climbed in so long, I didn't know if I still could. But how could I climb without you? You were sitting in a wheelchair in a rehabilitation centre and you were learning how to walk again and how to speak. Why was I not being the Amy Lee you knew and loved? What had happened to the lively, energetic and fearless young girl who had always fought for you? The Bear I knew had been lost in the last year, but so had Amy Lee. My mother was right. Where was *that* Amy?

If there was a time to stand up and fight for you, it was now before living in that place began to demolish you even further.

They were medical experts, they were immensely kind and patient but they didn't know *you*. They saw you as someone whose depression had engulfed him and made him suicidal. I saw you as a child of Ireland, a child of nature and the universe who believed wholeheartedly in little people, fairies, water sprites and unicorns. I saw you as the unique and caring young boy who had waited patiently for me every afternoon and allowed me to be daft and scatty while you taught me poetry. I saw you as the teenager who was pulled apart by his secret because he loved me and the bright star whose teachers and parents pushed him to his knees.

You were my soul friend who was happier about my meagre success at school than his own glowing results and the boy who sent me away because he cared more for my happiness than his own. You were the Bear who had been forced to the edge by his fractured and complex family relationships and by a controlling and manipulative man who professed to love you. And you were my lovely, unforgettable Bear whose last thoughts before entering the next world were for me.

'Don't be afraid, Amy Lee.'

I had to free you from that prison where the Bear I knew was slowly suffocating because you needed to be outside in the fresh Irish air. The next day there was no placard and I waited under the tallest tree in the park with the thickest trunk until you appeared. You were late and appeared quite exhausted and I imagined them pulling your limbs about in physiotherapy and being kind but cruel to you.

I waved at you and pointed to the tree behind me. You knew immediately what I meant and your face fell and you shook your head. I looked up at the branches twisting and turning above me and reaching for the light. I could almost hear them whispering, 'Climb through us, climb high and breathe in our freshness. Climb us again, Amy Lee. Get back to yourself.'

I had a powerful desire to be young again and forget all the troubles in our lives. I longed to feel as if all things were possible, to feel limitless, optimistic and carefree. I looked over at you again and in your eyes I detected a kind of yearning for something just out of reach. I pointed to the top of the tree again. It was beckoning to me, holding out its arms and urging me to feel the rough bark beneath my fingers. I put my foot in a small hollow in its trunk and grabbed the lowest branches. It felt easy and right to be amongst its fresh leaves. The woody, earthy smell filled my senses and I climbed higher. I imagined you had called out: 'Be careful now, Amy Lee, you'll be falling, so you will.'

'You'll catch me, Bear,' I said out loud, my words floating upwards towards the sky. 'You'll always catch me.'

I glanced over at you and I thought you would be smiling at the memories but you had one hand over your eyes and you were shuddering with sobs. I continued to climb upwards intensely moved by your reaction. It wasn't the reaction I had wanted but at least it *was* a reaction instead of an impassive face and dull eyes.

I was near the top where the branches were thinner and not so tough, almost touching the clouds and as I put my weight on one of them, I heard a loud cracking sound and it snapped. Glancing over at you once again I could see you frowning so I moved my body onto another branch, holding on with the strongest grip I could manage. Sunlight trickled through on my upturned face and more of your words came into my head. I had complained about my freckles to you constantly.

'Amy, it means you've been kissed by the angels, so it does.'

There was another loud crack and I lost my foothold as another branch snapped and fell to the ground. I was hanging on with one hand and for a moment I imagined losing my grip and tumbling to the ground. I heard you shout out loudly and clearly.

'Amy Lee!'

I still hung on and managed to find another foothold. I pulled my body up and rested with my head against the trees solid, ancient and reliable trunk. Once I was safe, I looked over to your window to find you standing up, holding on grimly to the sides of your wheelchair. I saw plainly the anguish and frustration on your face but I was smiling triumphantly as you collapsed back down again into your chair. I came down very carefully and once my feet were on solid ground again, I blew you a kiss and walked slowly away.

'We're almost there, Bear. We're almost there,' I said repeatedly all the way home.

That evening, after telling Patrick and my family what I had done, my mother had looked across at me with a knowing smile. I asked her why she was smiling that way.

'That sounds a bit more like the Amy Lee young Bear knows. All you have to do now is mess up his hair!'

The following morning after breakfast, I was reading Wolf his favourite story. He was sitting on my lap and he was speaking to me but I hadn't heard one word. 'Mama,' he said, taking hold of my chin. 'You aren't listening to me.'

'I'm so sorry, darling. What did you say? I was thinking about something.'

'What were you thinking about?'

'I was thinking about Bear.' Something was igniting in the pit of my stomach, something intense and powerful and I could ignore it no longer. 'I was thinking about Bear, darling, that's all.'

'Bear wants to come home, Mama,' he said quite innocently. I placed him on the floor. 'We haven't finished my book.'

'Come on, Wolf.'

'Where are we going?'

'We're going to set Bear free.'

'Is he coming home then?' he asked, his eyes alight.

'Yes, he is, now let's make the last sign and this time we'll take the car.'

You were waiting that morning and I saw you strain forward in your chair as we held the placard up. Wolf was being very brave and held it up as high as he could even though it was enormous. There was a strong breeze that day and it was flapping about alarmingly.

'Is this high enough, Mama?'
'Yes, well done.'
'Can he see it?'
'Yes, I think so.'

The enormous placard read: 'Dancing in ecstasy you go, my soul of souls. Don't go without me. The two worlds are joyous because of you. Don't stay in this world without me. Don't go to the next world without me.'

You were nodding emphatically to me but Wolf and I were already running towards the front door. Matron was in reception talking to a man in a smart suit with a stethoscope hanging round his neck.

'We're taking Bear out for a walk, it's such a fresh day,' I said, in passing. She merely smiled and carried on with her conversation.

I opened the door to your room with such excitement mixed with apprehension I was shaking. Wolf stayed outside, to keep watch, he told me. That room was so stark, so humdrum and so soulless. You had never been in there, Bear. Someone had been in there, but it certainly wasn't you. You were somewhere else, in your imagination and your dreams. You were still by the open window and those dreams were of Ireland and mountains and open fields, no doubt.

Your skin was pale and your hair flattened. You turned your head, expecting me to be there and you tried to speak but at first your mouth wouldn't move. I put my hand in your hair and messed it up. If you were coming out into the outside world you couldn't look like a tramp and I had been longing to do it for so long. I then crouched down in front of you and held your hands.

'"Stop acting so small. You are the universe in ecstatic motion."' You shook your head and pulled them away. You pressed your lips together and you were whispering falteringly. 'Say it louder, Bear. I can't hear you.'

You slurred the words but I heard them clearly.

'I'm sorry, Amy Lee.'

'Oh, Bear, don't you dare say sorry to me for being who you are! Don't you dare! You are the sky, the trees, the sun and the moon. You are the ocean, the rain, the golden sunsets and every bright dawn. You are unique like every snowflake. You are silver frost, birdsong and the beauty in every flower. You are the stars. You are love. You are all of life. For me there will only ever be you. All my life I've worshipped you and I'll go on worshipping you to the death ...' I let you finish.

'And beyond ...'

'Now, where do you want to go?' You didn't understand so I repeated the question. 'Where do you want to go?'

You whispered, 'Ireland.'

I took my huge handbag and stuffed it with your few clothes and the photo of us on our last day of school together. It's the one where you are looking at the camera with troubled eyes and I am gazing up at you fearlessly. I then put your trainers on and turned your wheelchair towards the door.

'Right, we'll pretend we are going for a walk in the park. If anyone says anything just keep your mouth shut, alright?'

The irony wasn't lost on you and I saw your shoulders moving with laughter. You reached out to touch Wolf's hair and he clutched your hand. He was relishing every moment of our escape. One nurse called out to us to be careful and not to be long because lunch was at half twelve and the matron didn't like anyone being late. I leant forward and whispered in your ear. 'Bugger matron!' We were both shaking with suppressed laughter and Wolf was laughing too although he had no idea why. 'Keep quiet,' I told you both, 'we've almost escaped.'

How I managed to get you in the car I have no idea but with the little strength you had, you manoeuvred your backside onto the passenger seat from the wheelchair. I lifted your thin, wasted legs in with a little help from Wolf's tiny hands. I left the wheelchair at the side of the road. I never wanted to set eyes on it again. We would walk with you from now on.

When I jumped in next to you and started the engine, I put my hand on the gear stick and you immediately placed yours on mine. Tears streamed from your eyes and my heart burst open with joy. I felt more alive in that moment than I had in years. You tried to form some words but they wouldn't come.

'Are you happy at last? Please say you are.'

You whispered, 'Happy, Amy Lee.'

'Bear, "this is love. To fly towards a secret sky, to cause a hundred veils to fall each moment, first to let go of life, finally to take a step without feet."'

―――

A year later we are on the farm in Ireland sitting under the Milky Way. We don't have much money, but we don't care, we have enough. We have your granny's legacy. She left everything to you. She knew you were different. She knew you were troubled and that you would need it. Your daddy visits most days and his part in your rehabilitation cannot be understated. Knowing you have his unconditional love has changed you so much. Every day he walked with you round the back yard so patiently, holding onto your arm lovingly as you struggled to regain your strength, until you no longer needed him to. I would watch from the back door as you talked together and laughed constantly.

You are gradually rebuilding your fractured and complex relationship with your mammy, but it may take a while. I'm not sure it will ever be as you wish it to be but her selfish ways don't hurt you like they used to because the love from your daddy fills you up.

I had previously cursed the day we swam in the waterfall when we caught sight of your mammy kissing a silver-haired stranger. Now I believe it was another moment of fate touching your head lightly and leading you to the man who you should always have been close to.

My mother asks me what will happen in the future. I tell her I don't know, but nobody else does either. Loving you has been the easiest *and* toughest part of my life. You are no longer leading a life of quiet desperation and you won't take your song to the grave with you. I won't let you. You can sing it now. I just want you to be yourself, your authentic self, whatever that may be. All I know for sure is, we have to be together. There is no other way for either of us.

Wolf runs free in the keen Irish air and you teach him maths and the power of poetry. He even sounds like an Irish boy now. You needed your brilliant brain in the end, Bear, but not how anyone originally thought you would. Ultimately you needed it to fight the damage that had been done by your heart stopping. You still slur your words occasionally. Your voice makes me laugh because you sound slightly drunk. There are still days when you need a stick to help your balance because you drag one leg slightly, but they are becoming fewer as each week passes.

You have recovered at last and stepped into the light of who you truly are and always were to me. Tonight we were sitting in your granny's back yard under the stars and you began smiling. I asked you why you were. You replied by shrugging your shoulders and you reached for my hand.

'Dance with me, Amy Lee.'

We held on to each other, our foreheads touching as the moon fell asleep and the barn owl looked down at us. You could always dance. You still can and now you even dance without music because you are alive. You don't need to fight the black beast anymore. He has been slain with the help of medical science and being allowed to be the man you want to be without any pressure from anyone.

As we clung to each other, I said to you, 'We got here in the end, Bear.'

'Amy Lee,' you replied, 'Amy Lee, you're my Guardian Angel, so you are. "Close your eyes. Fall in love, stay there."'

And we will ...